"Captivating and rich, these tales will win your heart as surely as the heroes they portray."
Sherrilyn Kenyon, *New York Times* best-selling author of *Seize the Night*

"*The Journey Home* is a tender, triumphant collection of stories from some of the most talented authors writing today. . . . Each story . . . is celebration of hope, reminding us that no matter who wins or loses the battle, love will always be the greatest victor of all."
Teresa Medeiros, *New York Times* best-selling author of *Yours Until Dawn*

"Ten of today's most talented authors combine their skills to produce a truly poignant and emotional anthology. . . . This celebration of wounded warriors and those who love them is emotionally wrenching yet tremendously uplifting."
Jill Smith, *Romantic Times Bookclub Magazine*

"A stellar cast of authors . . . have combined their talents in a moving anthology all about the wounded hero. . . . What a wonderful concept, and what a worthy cause!"
Tanzey Cutter, *TheBestReviews.com*

About the Authors . . .

"[**Mary Jo Putney**] has few peers when it comes to creating emotionally satisfying romances. . . ."
  ~ *Library Journal*

"**Ms. Putney** gets better and better."
  ~ *Nora Roberts*

"**Rebecca York** delivers page-turning suspense."
  ~ *Nora Roberts*

". . . blistering romance and heart-in-your-mouth suspense."
  ~ *Romantic Times*

"Talented author **Lucy Grijalva** brings a special life and depth to her characters."
  ~ *Romantic Times*

"With each consecutive book, **Diane Chamberlain** confirms that she is one of today's most powerful and stirring authors of fiction. . . ."
  ~ *Romantic Times*

"**Ms. Mallory** is a gifted author [whose] talent . . . cannot be denied."
  ~ *Ayden Delacroix, Library Reviews*

"[**Catherine Asaro** is] Impressive . . . elegant . . . absolutely brilliant."
  ~ *Romantic Times*

"Magic, mischief, and sweet sensuality . . . **Linda Madl** weaves an irresistible spell!"
  ~ *Betina Krahn*

"Superb, superb, superb! [**Patricia Rice**] displays amazing depth of character [and] protagonists who really call to your heart. . . ."
  ~ *The Old Book Barn Gazette.*

The Journey Home

extraordinary tales of
courage, honor, and love

* * *

Mary Jo Putney
Patricia Rice
CB Scott
Linda Madl
Lucy Grijalva
Candice Kohl
Mallory Kane
Catherine Asaro
Diane Chamberlain
Ruth Glick writing as Rebecca York

compiled and edited by
Mary Kirk

ImaJinn Books

THE JOURNEY HOME
Published by ImaJinn Books, a division of ImaJinn

Copyright © 2005 by Mary I. Kilchenstein, Patricia Rice, Linda Madl, Ruth Glick, Rickey R. Mallory, Cynthia Klimback, Lucy Grijalva, Candice Kohl, Mary Jo Putney, Diane Chamberlain, and Catherine Asaro
"The Stargazer's Familiar" © 2001 Mary Jo Putney
Cover Design by Mary I. Kilchenstein and Rickey R. Mallory
Cover Photo by Keith L. Sanderson
Book design by Mary I. Kilchenstein

ISBN: 0-9759653-5-2

10 9 8 7 6 5 4 3 2 1

PUBLISHER'S NOTE:
This book is a work of fiction. Names, characters, places and incidents are products of the authors' imaginations or are used fictitiously. Any resemblance to actual events or locales or persons, living or dead, is entirely coincidental.

Books are available at quantity discounts when used to promote products or services. For information please write to: Marketing Division, ImaJinn Books, P.O. Box 545, Canon City, CO 81215-0545, or call toll free 1-988-625-3592.

ImaJinn Books, a division of ImaJinn
P.O. Box 545, Canon City, CO 81215-0545
Toll Free: 1-877-625-3592
http://www.imajinnbooks.com

Acknowledgments

We, the authors and editor, are sincerely grateful to Linda Kichline, Owner and Publisher of ImaJinn Books, for her generosity and support, and to Lightning Source, Inc., for their contribution in printing and distributing this book. We would also like to thank Elaine English, agent and literary attorney, for her dedication to and careful thinking about the project. And to Kathryn Falk, Founder and Owner of *Romantic Times BookClub Magazine*, and Co-Founder of Support Our Soldiers (SOS) America, Inc., we offer our thanks and our admiration for her dedication to helping others.

With gratitude and appreciation for the sacrifices made and hardships endured by American troops, the authors are honored to donate half of their royalties to Support Our Soldiers America, Inc., a non-profit organization dedicated to providing much needed support for our brave men and women in uniform.

Dedication

To all the men and women who, throughout history, have laid down their lives that others might live free.

Come, my friends.
'Tis not too late to seek a newer world. . . .

Ulysses, Alfred Lord Tennyson

Contents

Preface

What true-blue romance fan can resist a wounded hero?

None that I know. Through the pages of some of the genre's most memorable classics, we've cheered him on as he struggled with his demons, looking for peace or simply a home. He holds a special place in our hearts, and nothing gives us greater satisfaction than seeing that brave man find happiness—and (of course) the love of his life, as well.

The Journey Home is about the wounded hero. The man who does what he must. The soldier who risks his life for his beliefs, his family, his country. It's about the man who goes to war and discovers, when it's over, he's a different man—and maybe he isn't certain who or what he's become.

It's also about the woman who loves such a hero: the one who waits at home, worrying, wondering. When her man finally returns, will her love be enough to heal the invisible wounds of combat? Will she even recognize the stranger sleeping alongside her at night?

Whether victors or vanquished, all survivors of a conflict must face the aftermath. But where do battle-scarred warriors go to lick their wounds and heal? Will they—can they—return to hearth and home? Or are they destined to live in isolation, unable to find a woman brave enough to love a man whose heart has been shattered?

The award-winning, best-selling authors of *The Journey Home* have created a wonderfully romantic collection of tales about wounded heroes who find healing love in unexpected—even strangely uncanny—ways and places.

Patricia Rice captures the flavor of the tumultuous 1970s in **"Home Is Where the Heart Is."** Thomas returns from Vietnam missing part of his foot, bringing with him the ghost of his best friend—and hardly daring to hope that his antiwar high-school sweetheart will still love him.

In **"Heart Crossings," Linda Madl** takes us back to 1918, where Brian Mason must honor a promise he made to his twin sister, who died while he was fighting in The Great War. Thoroughly disbelieving, he asks psychic medium Amanda Sherman to contact his sister on "the other side." But Amanda knows it's Brian's own grieving, cynical soul that needs to be brought back to the land of the living.

For **Rebecca York's "A Hero's Welcome,"** we take a leap into the future, where rebel Ben-Linkman has won a hero's boon, helping his enslaved people take control of their Earth-colonized planet. But nobody except Kasi, daughter of his former master, can give him what he wants most: her heart.

Then it's back to the States for **Mallory Kane's "A Better Man."** Lying ill in a Union prison, Jared is rescued by his Confederate officer brother. Rob leads Jared home, charging him to take care of Christianne, Rob's wife, and leaving him on the doorstep, unconscious. But when Jared awakens, under Christianne's care, he doesn't know how he can honor his pledge to Rob when being with Christianne, whom he's loved in silence since childhood, breaks his heart.

In the fantasy world of **CB Scott's "The Sacrifice,"** Aedon McNair left his wife Kiara to fight for what he believed was a righteous cause. But after two years in an enemy prison, all he believes in is his love for Kiara—and he'll go to any lengths to return to her. But will she ever forgive him for what he's sacrificed to be with her again?

"The Dreamer" by **Diane Chamberlain** brings us back to the real present. Once, Brian Meyerson dreamed of being a doctor. But for fourteen years he's dreamed only of the day in Kuwait, during Desert Storm, when a mistake he made cost him his leg, his peace of mind, and the woman he loved. The woman, Cindy Gold, has returned, but how can he dare hope she might help him exorcise the nightmare that haunts him?

Medieval romance lovers will revel in **Lucy Grijalva's "Shadow of the Rose."** Sir Thomas Kelham doesn't *mean* to skewer Lady Cecily Bowen with his sword. He was trying to *save* her life, not take it. He keeps watch at the young widow's deathbed despite that it postpones his mission: to avenge King Richard III's death by killing the usurper Henry Tudor. During the long night, Thomas learns that Cecily has no intention of giving up—and she has a plan to save her home that's in opposition to his own quest. He also learns there's far more to the lady than meets the eye.

Catherine Asaro gives us a glimpse of the universe of her award-winning Skolian saga in **"The Shadowed Heart."** Squadron leader Jason Harrick should be dead. The only one of four empathically linked pilots to survive a space battle, as well as the crash of his Jagfighter, he doesn't know how to go on living. But when Rhose Canterhaven finds him haunting the ruins of a technology park, Harrick wonders if he's found a woman with the courage, the compassion . . . and the special gift he most needs . . . to heal his shattered soul.

Candice Kohl's "Another Man's Shoes" takes us to the British colony of Georgia, where we meet two wounded men with nothing in common but their first names. Rebel Nicholas Gans dies in Redcoat Nicholas Sutcliffe's arms, but in passing, Gans bestowes upon Sutcliffe a precious gift—if Sutcliffe can find the courage to claim the gift as his own.

Finally, in "The Stargazer's Familiar," **Mary Jo Putney** has created a hero who . . . well . . . actually, no, I don't think I'll tell you. I'll let you find out for yourself about the handsome and courageous Leo.

So grab a box of tissues and get comfortable. Be ready to cry for a few more wounded heroes. But, because romances are about happy endings, also be prepared to smile and cheer as these ten worthy men defeat their personal demons . . . and, in doing so, find the love and happiness they long for and deserve.

Mary Kirk
October 2004

"Home Is Where the Heart Is"
by
Patricia Rice

Anytown, USA, 1970

"Someone's sitting there," Thomas curtly informed the other bus passenger hovering indecisively between the seat next to him and the one across the aisle.

The middle-aged matron in her flowered dress looked at Thomas's unshaven jaw and crumpled army fatigues and hastily retreated to the seat across the aisle.

"Yeah, save this seat for a blonde with bosoms. I got a hankering for a fox on my lap."

"Shut up, Horace." Moodily, Thomas glared out the window of the city bus as the first streaks of early morning light crawled across the concrete sidewalks and potholed streets of his hometown. The Greyhound station, where he'd arrived a while ago, wasn't in the best of locations, so he hadn't bothered calling his parents to meet him. He wasn't sure he wanted to see them again, anyway. Maybe he would just take this local bus right past the house and back to the station again.

"Ain't neither of our faults I'm like this," Horace reminded him.

"Who else you want to blame it on?" Thomas asked. "Nixon? God? Charley?"

The woman in the flowered dress glanced nervously at the empty seat beside Thomas; then checking over her shoulder, she clutched her patent leather purse, got up, and took a seat farther back.

"You scared the lady, man."

Thomas shrugged and continued watching out the window as the bus rolled away from the curb. The old five-and-dime had closed while he was gone. They'd served the world's best ice cream sodas. He and Penny always indulged in them after the movies on Friday nights.

Penny. He shuttered his mind against that path.

"Bringing me home with you ain't such a hot idea, you know."

"You got a better place to go?" Thomas shoved his hands in his pockets and slumped deeper into his seat. That had been a particularly nasty remark, even for him. He couldn't go home like this. He'd bite everyone's heads off and skewer them afterward.

"Wel-l-l," Horace drew out the word thoughtfully. *"If the Bible says 'Thou shalt not kill,' I can guess the only other place I'd be welcome."*

"You were defending your country," Thomas replied with heavy irony. "I'm sure there's something in there somewhere about killing before you get killed."

Horace muttered a filthy expletive and followed it with several more colorful epithets they'd learned in the jungles of Vietnam.

"Very articulate. If that's all you've got to say, you can shut up before the driver throws me off the bus." Although, he supposed, if he thought about it, getting thrown off the bus wasn't a half bad idea. He still had the cash from his last paycheck in his pocket. How far could he get on it? He muttered a curse of his own.

"Your folks sure gonna be happy to see their foul-mouthed son. What they like?"

Thomas cast his thoughts back two years, when he'd last seen his parents. His mother was short, plump, and prone to plucking the few gray hairs that appeared occasionally in her fading brunette hair. She'd never bothered with fancy ratted-up hairstyles but wore the same permed curls she'd worn in her pictures just after he'd been born. She worried a lot and had a fine net of wrinkles around her eyes, probably many of them from some of his more reckless escapades. She could be a bit bird-witted at times. She'd bought his corsage a full week before the prom, and he couldn't count the times he'd had to find rides home after baseball practice because she'd forgotten to tell his dad to pick him up. Still, he figured she'd be happy to see him. Mothers always were. She was the main reason he was on this bus.

Tears sprang to his eyes, and he diverted them by remembering his father. He'd inherited his height from his old man; he hoped he hadn't also inherited his balding head or his damned narrow mind.

Curling his upper lip in a snarl, Thomas glared at the kinky black hair of the passenger in the seat in front of him. If his father could see Horace, he definitely wouldn't welcome him into his home. No one would ever call Bud Smith a flaming liberal. Thomas had listened to his father and his beer-drinking buddies down at the plant complain about Kennedy and King and all the left-wing communist whackos bringing this country to its knees. But even his father wouldn't be proud of how his son had killed his best friend, even if that friend was a Negro.

Penny would say it served him right; he never should have gone in the first place.

She'd be right.

Clenching his teeth and his fingers, Thomas determinedly blanked out all thought as the bus rolled past a new shopping center where there had once been a horse pasture. In two lousy years, the town had sprawled concrete across the countryside worse than crabgrass ate up a baseball diamond. Dry cleaners, drugstores . . . hell, they even had a McDonald's now. Would have made it a lot cheaper when he and Penny had been dating if he could've bought thirty-nine cent burgers instead of the expensive ones at Frisch's Big Boys.

He'd dreamed of those juicy burgers, and Jerry's strawberry pie. His first few months in Nam, he'd dreamed of going home, circling the drive-in with Penny by his side in the car, sipping cherry Cokes and chowing down on strawberry pie. That had been a stupid dream even then. Penny had left him the instant he'd made the decision to go to Nam.

"How much farther to your place?" Horace demanded, jerking him back from morose memories.

Thomas glanced out the window at a vaguely familiar church. "Few more miles. We're really out in the burbs. I don't think we'll see any yellow ribbons tied to the old oak tree, though, so don't go expecting any fancy reception."

"Gotta be better than anything I woulda got."

He and Horace had exchanged homesick tales often enough during long steamy jungle nights and drunken bouts at base to know each other's lives inside and out. Horace had it right. His homecoming would have gone nearly unnoticed. He had never known his father, and his mother had eight other kids to raise. He'd been pretty much on his own for years, working cotton fields, dealing a little on the side, doing what it took to make a living until he'd chosen to join the army rather than serve time for a drug possession charge. At the beginning, Horace had said, he had some stupid notion of making a career out of the army, had even earned his stripes. Towards the end, like everyone else, he had just prayed to get out alive.

He hadn't.

"It's a stinking world," Thomas agreed. "If there was any justice at all, you'd be the one coming home to a welcome reception with all the hugs and kisses and home-cooked meals, not me."

"Yeah, right," Horace replied sarcastically. *"The big bad honky don't deserve no homecomin' 'cause he let his buddy down and got his own foot blown off in the doin'. Whine some more, buddy. Maybe we can make a song of it."*

Scowling, Thomas adjusted his injured foot more comfortably now that he'd been reminded of it. The crutch didn't bother him. The maimed foot hurt, but it wasn't the reason he didn't want to go home.

He couldn't imagine life without Penny.

God, it had all been so simple back then. What the hell had happened?

He'd been a righteous, honor-bound, frigging asshole, that's what had happened.

So, the army had paid his way through college. That didn't mean he owed it his entire life, did it? Of course, at the time, he hadn't realized being in the army meant giving up his life. Or if he had, he'd thought of it in terms of dying for his country, not losing everything that made life worth living. Funny, how it was easy to think of the glory of dying but not the ignominy of existing without a future.

"If she married some other guy, she ain't worth your time," Horace intruded.

"Shut up." Imagining his Penny in some other guy's arms tore into his gut worse than any land mine. Imagining her married and having some other guy's kids ripped out his soul. Tears stung his eyes, which made him angry.

"You might be in time," Horace urged. *"Maybe you can stop her."*

"Oh right. Like she'd drop a rich lawyer for a crippled, unemployed soldier with no prospects. Did you grow up in Never-Never Land?"

"It always works like that on TV," Horace said sulkily. *"White people always get the girl and the car and the money."*

"Yeah, I guess with no bodies, ghosts got no brains," Thomas retorted. "I'm the bad guy in this movie, all right? I'm the one who left the girl and went out and killed innocent women and children for no damned good reason at all. Penny's smart. She knows a loser when she sees one."

"You are so full of shit. I shoulda haunted Captain Deere. I coulda whispered sweet nothins in his ear and drove him screaming into the jungle where Charley coulda cut his balls off. Now that woulda been some fun."

Thomas snickered. "Remember the time you put the hairy spider on his head when he was sleeping?"

"If anybody's to blame for us being out in that minefield, it was him. He probably figgered out who laced his water with laxatives."

"I should have killed him," Thomas muttered. "If I had to kill anyone, it should have been murderous bastards like him."

"You prefer getting sent to the firing squad? Don't be more of an ass than you have to be, Smithey. You got a chance. Don't blow it."

"Naw, they'd've just given me a Section Eight and sent me home. If it hadn't been for the foot, they'd have done it just because I talk to you." Dismissing the topic, Thomas glanced out the window and stiffened. The next stop was his.

The old neighborhood hadn't changed at all. Trees were a little taller. The Courtneys had built a stupid picket fence around their poor excuse for a front yard. Jocko still had a car jacked up on blocks on the curb, but it was a Monte Carlo instead of an Impala. His mother had told him Old Man Snider had died and a couple with kids had bought his house. He must be turning over in his grave. The lawn he'd practically manicured with scissors was littered with kids' riding toys, and a sandbox sat where his prized zinnias had once grown. Everything was all the same, yet different.

He gritted his teeth as the bus trundled past his house to the stop. No yellow ribbons. He hadn't told his parents when he'd be home, and they weren't the celebrating sort, anyway. The small brick house looked the same as it always had, maybe a little shabbier. He hadn't been there for his father to browbeat into painting the trim.

The catering truck parked at the curb in front of Penny's house smacked him in the face. It was Saturday morning. God, was Penny getting married *today*?

Gut clenching, Thomas fought an internal battle. He couldn't bear it. He'd stay on the bus, see where it went, go back to the station and catch another Greyhound to anywhere in the world but here.

"Is that your Mom?"

As the bus halted at the corner, Thomas glanced over his shoulder and out the rear window. His mother stood on the front stoop, the morning paper in her hand, looking sadly toward the bus. He choked on the need to hug her into smiling again.

"Come on, honky. Let's go get some of those fat pancakes dripping with maple syrup you said she cooks. I ain't never had maple syrup."

"She's probably already got breakfast cooking." Grabbing his duffle and crutch, Thomas limped down the bus aisle without looking back again. He wasn't even certain at what point he'd decided to get up.

By the time he'd maneuvered the bus steps, his mother had gone in and closed the door. She'd probably watched the bus for days, had maybe given up on him by now. He hadn't phoned her since he'd hit the States.

She just knew he'd been injured and discharged.

Staring up the street, Thomas hesitated. He could still turn back. He could cut across yards over to the shopping center and catch the bus on its return route.

"Come on! Whatcha waiting for? Christmas?"

"Go haunt yourself, prickhead." Gritting his teeth, Thomas hitched his way up the sidewalk toward the squat brick house where he'd grown up. It looked smaller than he remembered, but more solid than anything he'd seen in Nam. A house like that wouldn't incinerate instantly with the first blast of napalm.

"Wonder what that girlfriend of yours looks like now? Maybe she's fat and ugly."

Penny would never be fat and ugly. He'd once had a dream in which she'd been heavy with his child. She'd been so glowing with pride, her long tawny hair framing her smile with such happiness, he'd nearly cried in his sleep. She wasn't as tall as he was, but she had long bones that would disguise any extra weight. She liked wearing those slinky mini-dresses that draped her curves just enough to show what she had without being blatant. He'd been the only one who knew she wore no bra under them. It had driven him insane.

Blood shot straight to his groin at the thought, and he had to stop and wait for the arousal to go down before continuing on. God, the things they had done in the back seat of his car those months right before . . .

Hell, he had to stop thinking of those things. He'd be better off remembering how Penny had screamed at him and called him names the day he'd told her he was going to Nam.

With the crutch propped under his arm and the duffle over his other shoulder, he limped up concrete cracked by tree roots, gaze focused on the front door. He resisted the temptation to go to the back yard and peer over the shrubs, around the chain link fence, to investigate whatever was happening at Penny's. His mother hadn't said she was getting married at home. Maybe the caterer's truck belonged to her brother.

Thomas hesitated on the front step. He looked like hell. He hadn't shaved in a week. He'd worn the same clothes since getting off the plane in San Francisco days ago. He couldn't remember when he'd last had his hair cut. His father would pitch fits at the length. And then there was the damned crutch and foot . . . Maybe he should turn around and leave.

"I smell bacon. Does your mama do fried potatoes? With lots of pepper?"

"Ghosts don't have noses," Thomas answered with irritation, reaching for the doorknob. He hadn't eaten anything in days, either.

Before turning the knob, he glanced at the upstairs window of the house next door. Penny used to have the garret room. Was she home? Was she sleeping in her bed beneath that window? If he threw pebbles at it, like he used to do, would she open the window and smile at him? Just the memory of that sleepy, sexy, smile shook him down to his knees.

Penny wouldn't be there. She'd finished college while he was in Nam. His mother had written to say she'd gotten some fancy job downtown. She was probably sleeping with the jerk she was marrying.

Of course she was sleeping with the jerk she was marrying. She wasn't precisely the poster child for modesty and virtue. But he'd been her first—and only—until he'd left her.

Crushed beneath the weight of guilt, Thomas shoved open the door.

Just his luck, at that moment his father stumbled out of the back bedroom, his old-fashioned undershirt barely covering his beer belly as far as his bulky trousers. His hair was almost entirely gone now, and what remained was too gray and short to be seen. He stared bleary-eyed at Thomas for a couple of seconds before nodding curtly and ambling toward the dining room.

"The prodigal son doth return!" he shouted toward the kitchen.

"Cool," Horace whispered.

Thomas snorted, dropped his duffle, and shuffled across the living room. His mother burst through the archway to greet him before he crossed half way.

"Tommy! Oh, Tommy!" She burst into tears before she could say anything else, and flung herself into his arms, nearly knocking him on his ass.

Dropping his crutch, Thomas patted her awkwardly and looked over her shoulder for help. Apparently, his father, who had already taken his seat at the dining room table, in front of his breakfast, couldn't be disturbed.

"Mom, help me out here," he finally managed to say through the tears choking his throat. "I can't stand much longer, and I'm about to starve."

The word "starve" acted like a shot of adrenaline. His mother immediately straightened, brushed down her apron, looked him in the eye, and, unable to resist a pat on his scruffy cheek, smiled through her tears. "I've got plenty of eggs and bacon and those biscuits you like so much. Would you like some pancakes, too? It will only take me a minute."

Without missing a beat, she handed him his crutch and bustled off toward the kitchen.

"Wow!" Horace whispered in awe. *"Real food. This is some place you got here."*

More guilt filled his soul. Until he'd been drafted, Horace had never had a full belly in his short life. Even the army couldn't fill him.

"You don't go get those eggs, I will," Horace threatened. *"Get your butt in there."*

He couldn't pretend his father didn't exist any more than he could pretend Horace wasn't there. Hell, if he could face a jungle full of Cong, he could face his old man.

Limping down the hall to the bathroom, Thomas scrubbed at his face and hands, and grimaced at the dark rings around his eyes, which matched the grimy beard on his jaw and the unruly thatch of dark hair falling across his forehead. Borrowing a comb from the vanity, he tried to restore some order before taking those last few steps down the hall toward the dining room.

"You could have called us when you got in," his father greeted him from his chair at the head of the small maple table.

"I could have stayed in San Francisco," Thomas retorted without thinking. Wincing, he realized he'd already fallen back into the pattern set long ago, in his rebellious high school days.

His father dug into his eggs without looking up. "Your mother worried herself sick. It's time you thought about others besides yourself."

"Hey, yeah, think about me," Horace whispered. *"I'm a lot more fun."*

Thomas almost snickered aloud. Resisting, he smiled feebly for his mother as she brought him a glass of orange juice and a cup.

"Do you drink coffee now?" she asked anxiously. "Or could I fix you something else?"

"Coffee's fine, Mom. I drank it all through college, so my stomach's pretty well used to it." He hadn't come home much during college. He'd been a smug smartass back then and thought his parents too low class, too shallow, too beneath his dignity, to visit except out of duty. He'd intended to carve his path through the corporate world as a highly paid executive who never soiled his hands, as his father had every day for the past thirty years.

So much for fantasies.

"You're home for good?" his father asked, flipping the newspaper open to the comics.

"I'm out of the army," Thomas answered evasively. He had no plans, but the thought of living in his old bedroom, in his parents' house, didn't sit well. Even in a state of vegetation, he'd have difficulty surviving in this suffocating climate.

"The pancakes will be ready in just a minute." His mother laid a heaping platter in front of him and pushed the cream and sugar in his direction. "You just eat your fill, and I'll make some more."

His stomach rumbled as the aroma of bacon and freshly baked biscuits wafted up to him. Oh, God, he was home. . . . To hide the tears, Thomas scrubbed at his eyes as if they itched. He hadn't seen such food in so long, he didn't know what to do with it.

"Shove your face in and wolf it down, clown." Horace laughed. *"Oh, man, I feel good just looking at all that. This has got to be heaven."*

"Sit down and have your coffee, Mom. You don't have to wait on me." Recovering from his unexpected bout of emotion, Thomas gestured toward the chair between him and his father.

She kissed his hair. "Of course I have to wait on you. You're my son, and you're home safe and sound, and if I don't keep busy, I'll burst."

He couldn't do this. He couldn't sit here calmly and inhale light fluffy eggs as if he hadn't blown up women and children and watched his best friend and half his platoon be blown to smithereens in return. The two halves of him didn't jibe. He wasn't that teenaged Thomas his parents knew. He wasn't even the arrogant college kid. He didn't know who the hell he was; he only knew he didn't like himself at all.

He sipped his coffee black and tried to think of some escape.

"Oh, man, look at them flapjacks!"

"Don't drool on me," Thomas snapped.

His father's head shot up, and his mother stared at him as she set the pancake platter on the table.

Embarrassed, Thomas dug his fork into his eggs. "Sorry, thinking out loud."

Horace snickered. *"Yeah, like thinking is what you do best. When you gonna tell me to get lost?"* he taunted.

Never. The eggs could have been sawdust for all he knew. He gagged them down for his mother's sake.

"Did I tell you Penny is getting married today?" his mother said brightly, finally taking her seat at the table.

So it was true. Dammit.

"They had to move the date up. Her mother's taken pretty badly, and they were afraid she wouldn't be able to leave the house."

Drive a knife in his gut, why didn't she? Flinching, Thomas helped himself to the pancakes and poured a lake of syrup over them. The resultant mess, as the syrup bled into his eggs, tossed his stomach.

"What's wrong with her mother?" he asked gruffly.

"Cancer," his mother said softly, as if the word alone placed them in a hospital ward. "They don't expect her to live another month."

Oh, shit. Why couldn't Mrs. Brown have waited until next fall or next year—or never—to get sick? Why did it have to be *now*? He might have had time. . . .

Damn, he was a selfish bastard.

"That's too bad," he muttered, shoving pancakes into his mouth. He chewed slowly so he wouldn't gag.

"You should have written to Penny," his mother nagged. "She had to come over here all the time to see how you were doing."

Her words acted like lightning, electrifying every nerve he possessed. Penny had *wanted* to hear from him? She'd told him he could rot in hell before she'd ever speak to him again.

"She could have written, too." He shoveled more eggs into his mouth.

At a knock on the back door, his mother leapt to her feet without replying to his comment. "Oh, maybe that's her now! She'll be so excited to hear you're home. I told her I'd help with the flowers."

Oh, God, please, don't do this. Don't make him face Penny on her wedding day. Especially when he'd had no time to prepare for it. If he could clean up, make himself presentable, maybe . . . Maybe what? Hell, he couldn't go over there with anything less than an M-16 and the intention of kidnapping her.

"Dear, it's Penny," his mother said excitedly, racing back into the room, flapping her hands. "She says she doesn't have time to come in, but she'd like to say hi. You go. I don't want to intrude. She just came over to borrow some sugar. Hurry, dear, or she'll be gone."

God had a wickedly sharp sense of justice.

"Get up, goofball," Horace whispered. *"This is your chance to fix things. You go out there, Mr. Smooth, make her sorry for ever thinking she could find another you."*

Thomas snorted at this ludicrous assessment of his abilities, but he staggered to his feet and grabbed his crutch. He might as well get it over with, put The End to his life. Then maybe he'd just drink himself into the gutter.

"She wants to see you, man. There's still hope."

"Shut up, Horace," Thomas warned as he limped from the room. If his parents heard, he didn't care. His gaze focused on the closed door that led from the kitchen to the back yard. Penny hadn't come in. Habits died hard. They'd always waited in each other's back yards rather than face the interrogation of their parents.

Swiping at the hank of hair that had fallen onto his forehead, Thomas pried open the door, maneuvered his crutch onto the back porch, and caught his breath.

Penny stood on the bottom step looking up at him, her tawny gold hair cascading in a rumpled river over her shoulders, as if she'd just gotten out of bed and hadn't brushed it. She used to iron it to keep it straight.

Her face had thinned and matured into a striking contrast of sharp bones and silky skin, unadorned by even a hint of make-up. She used to wear that shiny pink lipstick because she hated the fullness of her lips, and she thought the near-white color disguised them. He could have told her the color only drew his attention more, made him want to lick it all off and taste deeper, but that had been one time he'd been smart enough to keep his mouth shut. Now, she wore nothing but her own rosy moist color, and he ached to feel her mouth against his again.

He didn't know how long they stared at each other, neither saying a word. Penny had never been much of a talker. She gazed at him through wide brown eyes framed with dark lashes that she knew how to use to great effect when she wanted to, but that, at the moment, were unblinking. He scarcely noticed her brief shorts and loose shirt. She could have been stark naked. He'd seen her that way once, in the moonlight, and he saw her that way now.

She was his. She'd always been his.

"Man, she's some looker," Horace said reverently from somewhere over his shoulder. *"You musta been crazy, boy, to let her go."*

Arrogant, maybe, but crazy, no. He just hadn't expected her ultimatum. He'd thought no matter what she said, how much she protested the war, that she'd always wait for him. He'd thought she would understand that he had to do his duty. With the arrogance of youth, he'd spoken nobly of honor and other stupidities, and she hadn't understood a single word. But he hadn't realized that then, not even when she'd pleaded with him to go to Canada with her. He'd taken her love for granted. And he'd destroyed it.

"Tom-ass," she finally spoke, using the name she'd invented to tell him he was being a jerk. They'd grown up together. She'd seen him in all his jerkiness.

"Penelobelly," he replied dryly. They were full grown adults resorting to childhood epithets. Somehow, it seemed fitting.

"You've lost weight." She eyed him critically.

"Ten pounds for each toe." He didn't look at the injured foot. The doctors had said he'd be able to walk without the toes. He just wouldn't have the balance to run. They'd rambled on about torn muscles and ligaments and whatnot, but he hadn't paid much attention. He'd been a cross-country runner in college. He never would be again. It simply didn't matter anymore.

"Tell her you love her, you geek," Horace taunted.

"Shut up, Horace," he said calmly.

Penny gave a puzzled frown. "Your mother said you had a friend named Horace. Apparently, the two of you had a habit of painting the town red."

"Horace is dead." Thomas stated the words flatly, although each one twisted the knife deeper.

"No, I ain't. I'm a ghost," Horace cackled with familiar humor.

"You'll be a dead ghost if you don't shut up."

Penny tilted her head, letting the river of hair fall further over her shoulder and breast. He towered over her from the top of the steps, but still she pinned him with her gaze.

"Horace is a ghost?" She zeroed in on the crux of the matter without the blink of an eyelash.

Thomas shrugged. "Don't you need to hurry home and primp for your wedding?"

She looked briefly startled. Then, narrowing her eyes, she shrugged. "I've got plenty of time." She dragged her fingers through her hair, shoving it behind her ear again. "Are you going to keep looming over me, or come down here and talk like a regular human being?"

"I'm not fit company."

"Damn right," Horace hissed. *"You a pig-headed jackass, and you don't deserve that pretty thing. Why don't you just slap her while you at it?"*

"Shut up, Horace," he repeated the familiar refrain without thinking.

Penelope tapped her toe. "Maybe you should listen to Horace more often." Swinging around, she stalked toward the gate nearly hidden in overgrown shrubbery.

She couldn't have heard Horace. He was a ghost, a figment of his imagination. Nobody heard Horace but him.

Thomas stumbled down the back steps and limped after her. "Penny, wait. I'm sorry." He cursed as the sod and the crutch came together at wrong angles and he nearly fell flat on his face. Let her go, he told himself viciously. Let it all go.

She hesitated at the gate. Thomas righted himself warily. Was she waiting for him? Did she really want to talk with him? On the day of her wedding? What could he say that would make a difference?

"You never wrote," he accused, then cursed himself.

"Neither did you."

She turned toward him, and as the sunlight caught her face, he could swear there were tear stains down her cheeks.

"You never wrote, and I hate you for that," she said. "I had to find out where you were from your mother and watch the television to see if you'd been blown up. You're lower than a toadstool, Tom-ass."

She *was* crying. Or had been. He couldn't tell which. Damn, he'd thought her stronger than that, strong enough to tell him to go to hell and mean it. He still didn't deserve her. She was far better off with someone who had it all together.

"I may be lower than a toadstool, but I'm still taller than you," he replied nonsensically, managing to get the crutch back under his arm and swing it without falling until he reached her. She wasn't wearing any perfume, but he could smell her shampoo. He'd always loved the lemon scent of her hair. She'd told him once that she rinsed it in lemon juice to make it look more gold than it was.

She glanced up at him critically. "Uglier, too," she retorted. "Beards are out these days."

He shrugged, more comfortable with her insults than her tears. "What did you want to talk about?" He asked it offhandedly, as if he wasn't hoping she'd say "us" or something equally ludicrous.

"You," she said decisively, chopping off hope at the knees. "Tell me about Horace."

"Horace is dead, and I ought to be. What more is there to say? It's your wedding day. Shouldn't you be getting ready?"

"Right, it's my wedding day. Don't you want to hear all about the big strong, sensible man I'm marrying?" she asked with dripping sarcasm.

"No, I want to break his neck." He thought he'd said it calmly enough, but Penny blanched and opened the gate.

"I don't know you anymore. I don't know if I *want* to know you anymore." Without looking back, she walked through and slammed the gate behind her, leaving him standing there, staring after her as she climbed the back steps to her house.

"Good job, kid. Knew there was a reason you got all that fancy education. Turns the women on big time."

"What was I supposed to say?" Thomas grumbled, turning away. "That I'm happy for her? Think lying would make it better?"

Horace remained silent on that one.

His mother leaned out the back door, waving a cup of something in her hand. "Thomas, Penny forgot the sugar. You'd better take it over to her. I don't think her mama's nurse has arrived yet, and she probably needs to stay with her."

Oh, right, he'd balance sugar and crutch and just hobble right over there. Maybe he would crawl, then he really could be lower than a toadstool.

"You been crawling on your belly for two years. Won't hurt to do it once more," Horace murmured philosophically.

Grudgingly shifting his weight to the crutch, Thomas took the heaping cup of sugar from his mother. "Sure, Mom. Anything else?"

"No, just wish Katy June my best. I'll come over in a little while and sit with her so you and Penny can have a few minutes to yourselves, if you like."

His mother still couldn't believe it was over between them. This was Penny's *wedding day,* for pity's sake. Did she think a magic fairy would come down from the clouds and wave her wand?

Carefully balancing the sugar in his free hand, watching for hidden holes and lumps of crabgrass in the unmown lawn, Thomas maneuvered his way across the yard. He had to set the sugar on the post to open the gate.

"Hero material," Horace taunted. *"Carrying the sugar for her wedding cake. That ought to earn you sainthood."*

"I figure the only reason you're still here is because the devil didn't want your bad mouth in hell," Thomas muttered.

"You think so? Think me and old Satan can go at it one-on-one?"

At one time, Thomas had figured all master sergeants were Satan, but he'd learned otherwise. Despite the difference in their ranks and upbringing, he and Horace had learned to respect each other and had ended up saving each other's asses more than once. As a ROTC grad and an officer, he wasn't supposed to fraternize with the non-coms, but after a few months of Nam, he hadn't been able to stomach the self-righteous bigots inhabiting the officers' ranks. Despite his college education, his blue-collar background had stood in the way.

"I think you're just too tough to die," Thomas retorted, swinging his crutch carefully over the uneven ground.

Penny met him at the screen door as if she'd been watching his progress. He burned with embarrassment at the thought as he shoved the cup toward the door. "You forgot this."

She hesitated long enough for him to wonder if he should turn around and leave. Then, figuring she wanted to hide the wedding activities inside, he grew stubborn. "Your groom arrived yet?" he taunted. "Are you going to introduce me?"

She nearly smacked the sugar from his hand as she swung open the door. "You're still a jerk, Tom-ass. You may have grown six inches and a beard, but you're still a jerk."

"Am I invited to the wedding?" he asked to irritate her as he maneuvered the steps and pushed his way inside. "These are the cleanest clothes I own. Think they'll bother the guests?"

"I can still shove you down the steps." She turned her back on him and grabbed the coffee percolator from the counter. "You still like it black?"

So she remembered. Neither of them had ever had any money while going to school, but they'd spent long hours in coffee houses, sipping coffee and deciding the fate of the world. He wanted those days back so badly, he could taste them.

"Yeah." He slapped the sugar cup onto the table and lowered his bulk to the chrome and vinyl kitchenette chair. His foot couldn't take his weight for one second longer.

He glanced around in curiosity. No caterers. He frowned and watched as Penny carefully set two cups of steaming coffee on the turquoise tabletop. She had always hated the cheap, garish table.

He'd never felt uneasy with her in the past, but he felt like a first-class dunce sitting there, groping for words. "How's your mother?" That seemed the polite thing to ask until he realized how stupid it really was. Her mother was dying.

"I'm hoping she's doing better." Penny brushed her hair away from suspiciously red eyes and sipped her coffee. "How's your foot?"

"It's been better." Damn, maybe the M-16 wasn't a bad idea. He couldn't carry her off without falling flat on his face, but he'd drag her if he had to. He wanted her out of here, wanted time to make her see they were meant to be together. He wanted to blow up the groom and the invisible caterers and the whole damned ceremony. "Look, Mom said she'd be over in a little while to look after your mom. Want to go for a drive? I can go get cleaned up."

She shook her head. "Robert will be over after a while. If you'd told me you were coming home . . ."

Gritting his teeth, Thomas used the crutch to haul himself from the chair. "You'd have done what? Waited for me? Right." He nearly broke his neck tripping over the chair leg, but he managed the few steps to the door like a pro.

"You're the one who walked out on me!" she shouted angrily. "What did you want me to do, spend the rest of my life crying my eyes out?"

He stopped at the door but didn't turn around. "I didn't walk out. I went to hell because it was my duty to go. I wanted you to *understand*. I thought you loved me enough to—" He cut himself off. Then, with a shrug, he opened the door. "Oh, to hell with it."

"Nice going, buddy. Always leave 'em crying, is what I say."

Thomas didn't bother answering. Lurching down the back stairs, he halted in the yard and stared vacantly at the overgrown grass. What the hell was he supposed to do now?

The rumble of a truck motor from the road prompted him to turn in that direction. A florist's paneled van slowed and halted just out of his sight, in front of Penny's house.

Without giving any thought to what he was doing, Thomas hauled his bum foot through the grass to the gravel driveway. The gravel was even worse than the grass, but he reached the front yard before anyone got out of the van.

By the time the driver climbed out carrying a bucket of loose flowers, Thomas had settled on the front porch step with a grim smile. Anyone wanting to reach Penny's front door would have to get through him.

The driver eyed him uncertainly. "This the Brown residence?"

"Nope. They moved last week."

The driver glanced at his address card. "This 324 Anglesey?"

"Yep, no Browns here." The absence of flowers wouldn't stop a wedding, Thomas knew, but he took some perverse pleasure in dismantling the enemy by whatever means available. What he really wanted was to get his hands on this guy Robert. He'd sit here the rest of the morning waiting for the bastard to show up.

"Guess I'd better check with the office," the driver said uncertainly, backing off.

Sitting on the concrete step, leaning his elbows back on the porch, probably looking like a bearded gargoyle, Thomas didn't acknowledge that decision with anything more than a grim stare. His life had spun out of control the day Penny had walked out on him. It was time to gain back some of what he had lost. If he couldn't, he might as well find a gun and put a bullet in his head.

As the van rumbled off, the front door opened behind him.

"What the devil are you doing out there?"

"Waiting to meet Robert," he replied evilly. He'd always known how to get Penny's goat.

"Was that the florist who just left?" she asked with suspicion, not stepping from behind the screen door.

"Yep. As soon as your invisible caterers show up, I'll send them looking for him."

"My invisible . . ." She apparently followed his gaze to the truck parked on the curb. "Right. Why don't you send your invisible friend with them?"

Thomas shrugged, still not turning to look at her. If he looked, those big brown eyes would melt him into warm Jell-O again, and he'd forget what he was doing. "Horace goes where he wants."

She opened the screen door, and he could sense her settling into the webbed lawn chair beside the morning glory vines. "Maybe it's time for Horace to leave, then."

"What the hell?" Horace shouted in his ear.

"Maybe you're hanging on to him like that crutch. Maybe if you let him go, he could find another life, a better one. He deserves it, doesn't he?"

"Quit playing psychiatrist." Churlishly, Thomas glared at the road, refusing to acknowledge a direct hit. Horace deserved a hell of a lot better than this.

Horace remained ominously silent.

"I like to believe God gives us second chances." Penny's bare foot slid across the porch, practically brushing his elbow. She'd painted her toenails pale pink. "The next time around, maybe Horace would have a better life, one where he finds a nice wife and raises good kids."

"Sure, like that's gonna happen," Horace muttered, but there was an element of doubt and a note of hope behind the cynicism.

"Yeah, and maybe next time around, he could have a life like mine, where his girl leaves him for a rich boy who buys himself out of war."

The florist's van roared back around the corner before Penny could answer. This time, when the driver got out, she intervened. "There's been a change of address," she shouted. "Take them to St. Anthony's, down on Main."

The van driver saluted her, shot Thomas a dirty look, and roared off again.

Guilt washed over him. She'd planned this wedding so her mother

could attend. He glanced over his shoulder, but Penny looked unper-
turbed. "Your mother feeling well enough to leave the house?" he asked.

"I took her to the hospital last night. She died this morning."

She stated it so flatly, with such a rigid expression, that he went cold
to the bone. Tears welled in his eyes, and he struggled to right himself.
"Penny, I'm sorry. I'm a bastard. Dammit all, get down here where I can
reach you. What did you mean by telling me she was doing better?"

But he knew. Her little spiel about "a better life" hadn't been for
Horace, it had been for her mother. She wanted to believe her mother
had gone on to a better place, one where she had a husband who provided for and loved her, so she didn't have to toil alone, twelve-hour
days, to support a young daughter.

Thomas grabbed Penny's hand and tugged her out of the chair to sit
beside him. Pulling her into his arms was as natural as breathing, and
when she burst into tears and sobbed against his shoulder, he knew just
how to stroke her hair. He didn't have to say anything. She knew what
he was thinking.

He only wished it worked the other way around, that he knew what
she was thinking, too. "Tell me what to do, Penny. I don't know anything anymore."

"Just hold me, don't let me go. I'll be all right." She choked on the
words and buried her face in his shoulder again.

He rubbed his hand up and down the delicate curve of her spine.
God, he loved her so much it hurt in every fiber of his body. He wanted
to take her pain inside him so she could smile again. He hated his help-
lessness in the face of death. He wanted to reach out and grab life and
squeeze it until he forced it to do as he wished. Like he was holding onto
Horace, he admitted wearily.

"I wish I could make it better," he whispered, holding her close.

"It is better," she insisted, rubbing at her eyes but not lifting her
face. "She isn't hurting anymore."

That was true. Horace was having the time of his short life now that
he was dead. No pain, no fear, no worries. That was the meaning of
heaven, Thomas figured.

"What about your brother? Where's he?"

"I called him this morning. He's flying in tonight. It'll be okay,
Tommy, honest. I've had lots of time to know this was coming."

She choked a little on the words, but wiped her eyes and tried to
push away. He wouldn't let her. He wanted to hold her forever, to make
the world go away for her, to keep her from suffering anything bad ever

again. If he could do just this one small thing . . .

An orange-red convertible Mustang squealed around the corner and slowed as it drew near the house. Thomas glared at the man behind the wheel. Penny half-heartedly attempted to free herself again. He didn't think she'd heard the car. He could kiss her now. He knew he could. She might even be expecting it. Despite everything, there was still so much between them, so many memories, so many things unresolved.

But this was her wedding day, and he figured that was her groom. She would have to live with Robert for the rest of her life, unless he found some way out of this mess.

Thomas satisfied himself with hugging her and waiting for the clown to climb out of his clownmobile.

Wearing shades and a wind-blown look, Robert climbed from the car, watching the tableau on the porch with uncertainty. "You must be Thomas," he acknowledged as he strolled up the sidewalk.

Penny's head jerked up and she pulled away, shoving her hair behind her ears. "Oh, my goodness, it's late. Let me get dressed." Without bothering with introductions, she jumped up and dashed inside.

"The campus dork. I remember you now." Thomas pulled himself up with new resolve. No way was he letting his feisty, funny, beautiful Penny get trapped by this shallow Kookie-character. She might not want him anymore, but she deserved better than this frat creep who got drunk every weekend and lied about the women he knew.

"Her mother just died. You might want to consider funeral homes instead of churches." With what he considered mature aplomb, Thomas swung his crutches in the direction of his parents' house, a new scheme rapidly forming in his head.

"Keep your hands off my girl!" the moron behind him called. "If you weren't on crutches, I'd take your head off!"

Now, there was a mature, intelligent reaction. Thomas halted to consider taking the guy down with one crutch tied behind his back.

"Don't be an idiot," Horace hissed. *"You'd look real good flat on your ass, even if sissypants gets a black eye out of it."*

True enough. Thomas gallantly left the idiocy to the other guy. "I'll stand here and let you throw the punches," he offered. "Penny detests fighting."

"Yeah, and she hates your guts." Figuring he had the last word, Robert strode up the stairs and into the house as if he owned it.

Fire churning his insides, Thomas returned to his slow progress across the lawn. How could she stomach a bastard like that? A man who wouldn't fight for what he believed wasn't any man at all.

A man who wouldn't fight for what he wanted didn't deserve to have it.

That thought propelled him into the house, to the kitchen where his mother was washing dishes. "Penny's mother died last night. Her brother isn't home yet. Someone needs to help her with the arrangements. She shouldn't have to do that on her wedding day."

His mother threw up soapy hands in dismay. "Oh, my, that poor thing! Call Reverend Honaker, Thomas. He'll know what to do. I'll go right over there. She shouldn't be left alone at a time like this." She hastily dried her hands on the towel over the sink.

"Her boyfriend is over there," Thomas warned, but he was gloating inside. Sending his mother to intervene was pretty close to a blessed event.

"Well, he shouldn't be," she answered tartly. "I'll send him on his way."

And she would. Pleased that the enemy had been so easily routed, Thomas flopped down in the chair beside the telephone, propped his injured foot on a chair, and began dialing.

"What do you know about burying somebody?" Horace asked suspiciously.

"Not much, or you wouldn't still be here," Thomas admitted, waiting for the reverend to answer. Horace snorted but didn't reply as Mrs. Honaker answered the ring.

Thomas endured the happy acknowledgment of his safe return, then explained the problem. Pen in hand, he jotted notes as, first, Mrs. Honaker, then the reverend, instructed him on what to do. Orders, he knew how to follow. Now, if only he could ask how to stop a wedding . . .

No, he'd have to figure that out for himself.

He called the funeral home. He called the hospital. He called the florist. His mother returned, weeping, to say Penelope had left with the creep for the church.

Alarmed, he caught her arm. "I thought the wedding was later."

Hiccupping, his mother nodded. "Tonight. She's just decorating it now. She's so brave."

Flapjacks turning in his stomach, Thomas grabbed the key she handed him and, leaving his mother to call the neighbors, returned to Penny's empty house. He knew where she and her mother kept everything. He'd been in and out of that house most of his life.

He retrieved the address book from the overflowing desk and, using

Penny's phone, started calling relatives. They all knew him, and Penny didn't need to listen to their shock and tears and condolences. This was a duty he could handle, a burden he could take off her shoulders. If he'd been her husband, he would have done this for her.

Oddly enough, not one aunt or uncle or cousin inquired about the wedding plans. They expressed surprise that he was home, but not that it was he, instead of Robert, calling them. Maybe Penny had kept the wedding quiet out of respect for her mother's illness.

The caterer's truck had disappeared along with Robert and his pretty-boy car. Maybe the truck belonged to one of the neighbors. Penny wouldn't want to hold the reception here, anyway. Not now. He'd had some brief hope that she'd call off the wedding, but she was nothing if not stubborn. If she'd put her mind to getting married, a hurricane wouldn't stop her. But *he* might, if he hurried.

"You ain't plannin' what I think you plannin', are you?" Horace demanded as Thomas checked the last phone call off his list and strode for the door.

"Damned right I am." He locked the door and lugged the crutch across the lawn. His arms ought to be aching with the effort by now, but he refused to notice. He had a purpose again. He could save Penny from making a huge mistake.

"Go to it, boy!" Horace whistled in gleeful approval.

He didn't need Horace's encouragement. Yelling at his mother that he'd finished the phone calls, Thomas limped down the hall to his old bedroom in search of some decent clothes that might still fit him.

He didn't have much. The jackets were too tight, the shirts too garish, the pants too short. He rummaged through his duffel, retrieved an armful of smelly relics, and hauled them to the laundry room. Chirping in dismay, his mother grabbed the lot and began sorting it.

He didn't try to stop her. Instead, he returned to the bathroom to shower and shave. He had to wrap bread wrappers around the bandage, and Horace hooted in derision at the spectacle, but Thomas didn't care. For the first time since the mine had blown off half his foot, he felt alive again. He couldn't get his revenge on Charley, didn't really want to anymore. He couldn't bring Horace back, but Horace didn't seem to mind. Maybe he couldn't even get Penny back, but he could save her from a disastrous mistake. If he could save just one person . . .

Terrified of blowing his chance at salvation, Thomas shaved carefully. He wished he had time to get his hair cut. At least, without the week-old beard, he looked less like a gargoyle. The man staring back at him from the bathroom mirror startled him somewhat. The last time he'd looked in that mirror, he'd seen a boy. Penny probably had every right to reject the tough looking bastard he'd become. That was okay. He just needed to keep her safe.

He pulled on a white shirt and black dress slacks still hot from the dryer. He hadn't bothered with jackets in Nam, so he had none to wear.

"Is Penny back yet?" he yelled as he stepped out of the steaming bathroom, his hair still damp and the civilian clothes feeling oddly tight and awkward.

"No, dear, I don't expect her back soon. I told her we'd take care of everything, so she's probably still at the church. She works much too hard." His mother stepped out of the kitchen to admire him, patting his newly shaven cheek in admiration. "My, you've grown up. I'm so glad to have you back."

A tight knot eased around his heart, and Thomas smiled for the first time that day. "It's okay, Mom. I won't take wing and fly. Dad in the den? I need the car."

He felt like a teenager asking for the keys, but he'd sold his own car before he'd left. There hadn't been much point in leaving it parked on the street. His father looked up from the television and grunted what almost might have been approval as he fished the keys from his pocket. "It needs gas," he warned.

Figuring that was as close to a "welcome home" as he'd get from his old man, Thomas nodded. "I'll fill it up."

Relieved that his father hadn't asked how he would handle the clutch with only one good foot, because he didn't have an answer, he swung out to the driveway.

"What you think you gonna do that you couldn't do this morning?" Horace wanted to know.

"Lure her into the car and not let her out, if I have to." He could do it. He couldn't let himself believe anything else.

Fingers tense on the steering wheel, Thomas edged the car out of the drive. He hadn't driven in two years. His bad foot, heel pressed against the clutch, hurt like the fires of hell.

"You ain't ready for stock cars yet," Horace taunted.

"Don't need stock cars. Don't need toes. Don't need anything but Penny." The car lurched into the traffic at the shopping center.

"Don't need me?"

"Go find that other life Penny believes in. Find her mama and tell her I'm home to look after her little girl." Anybody watching would think him crazy, talking to an empty car. He didn't care. Penny believed in Horace. Maybe she was right. Horace deserved a better resting place than the muddled maze of his mind.

"I'll think about it."

Thomas concentrated on traffic. He didn't want to embarrass Penny in front of everyone. He would just pull her aside, talk to her carefully, make her see that they needed time to work things out between them. And if that failed . . . well, somehow he was going to get her into the car and away from the church, away from Robert.

The parking lot at the church was full. What the hell was everyone doing here this early? He'd figured he had at least five more hours.

The sight of the red convertible churned his gut. He prayed he wasn't too late. Had Penny lied to him and his mother about the time? Were they in there now, standing before the preacher? He couldn't bear it.

It never occurred to him to turn and run, though. Barging in through the door of the reception hall, he scanned the crowd of startled ladies hanging silver and white ribbons and setting out tableware. Not seeing Penny, Thomas swung across the tiles toward the door that led into the church. A path opened before him as the ladies scattered.

The full force of an angelic choir belted him in the face the instant he opened the church door. Stepping inside, the soaring notes of "Amazing Grace" swept over and around him, carrying him deeper into the cool, dim interior. Sunlight glowed in multi-colored rainbows through the stained glass window above the altar. Elegant, tall, white lilies adorned the far railing. Thomas almost stumbled to his knees and prayed right there in the aisle. If it would have stopped the service, he would have.

Eyes adjusting to the dim interior, he clutched his crutch at the sight of Penny and Robert standing before the altar. In his blind fury, he saw nothing else.

"Penny, don't!" he shouted. The words echoed over and over inside the empty stone walls. "Don't . . . don't . . . don't!"

Running as he'd never run before, Thomas staggered down the aisle, almost tumbling over the carpet at Penny's feet. Figuring this humiliation was fitting punishment for his arrogance, he cried, "Don't, Penny. He's not the one."

Gasping, vaguely realizing something wasn't quite right, he ignored Robert and faced Penny's puzzled expression. "Maybe I'm not

the one either," he continued hurriedly, "but I can't let you marry
him. You deserve someone who will love you for who you are, not
some moron who wants a trophy to flaunt. Don't do this, Penny.
Call it off."

She blinked, then carefully set down the vase of flowers she held in
her hands. The vase of flowers. Brides didn't carry vases.

"Robert, if you'll carry in the cake . . ." She shot the other man a
speaking glance.

With a muffled oath, Robert sauntered off, toward the reception
hall.

Realizing he'd made a bigger fool of himself than even he had an-
ticipated, Thomas closed his eyes and fought back a wave of depression.
He'd meant well. He just didn't fit anywhere anymore. The damned
idiot who'd gone to Nam didn't belong in the peaceful society Penny
inhabited. Still, he couldn't let her do this.

"I know I'm not good enough for you," he said slowly, trying to
remember the words he'd practiced on the ride over here. "But neither is
he. Don't rush into marriage thinking you're all alone. You're not. I'm
here."

The choir's hymn grew quiet, voices fading to pianissimo.

He took a deep breath and, in a pause before the voices soared once
more around them, offered his only ammunition. "I love you, Penny.
I've never stopped loving you. I only want what's best for you. Will you
believe that much?"

The hymn burst over their heads, and he opened his eyes to see a tear
trickling through the faint sheen of powder on her cheek.

She smiled tremulously as she touched his newly shaven jaw. "You're
back, Tommy-O."

"I'm not a kid anymore," he said gruffly, longing to take her hand
and clasp it against his face. He didn't know what was happening here,
but he had too much to say to stop now. "I can clean up on the outside,
but the inside is permanently stained."

Her smile didn't waver. "Your insides are like old Levis; the stains
only add character. I heard you outside my house with Robert. You
could have flattened him with one fist, but you didn't."

He shrugged. "I've had enough violence for two lifetimes. If he's
what you really want, I'll try to understand. I don't want to lose my only
remaining best friend." He dared glance around: no minister, no audience. He'd interrupted . . . what?

"You didn't go upstairs, to my bedroom, did you?" she asked with seeming irrelevance. "I gave your mother the key to the house and hoped you would."

Lost, Thomas studied her warily. "No, I just used the desk in the living room to call your family. I made all the funeral arrangements, Penny. I left notes on the desk. If there's anything else I can do—"

"I tied a yellow ribbon to my bed post each night from the moment I heard you were wounded. I've got a bed covered in yellow ribbons, Thomas. Coming home is all I ever wanted you to do."

"But, I thought . . ." Bewildered, he didn't know how to take this abrupt about-face. Yellow ribbons? She wanted him home? But what about the wedding?

Without his asking, she explained. "Your mother has a selective memory. Remember the time I said I wouldn't go to the prom with you because you were a bully?"

"And she went out and bought your corsage and rented my tux anyway." Thomas managed a half-grin. "You thought I was crazy when I showed up and told you I had to either come in or sit in the car all night. You forgave me, and we danced until dawn."

Penny nodded. "I must have told her I had a wedding today." Gesturing toward the vase of flowers, she added, "That's what I do for a living now—cater and decorate weddings and special events. Months ago, I told her I was going to marry Robert, but I changed my mind. I couldn't go through with it until I saw for myself that you weren't the man I loved anymore. If she told you today was my wedding day, she apparently got things a little confused."

Thomas grabbed her hand. "You're not marrying Robert?" he asked, nearly crushing her fingers as he waited for her reply.

"No," she whispered, studying his face. "I never stopped loving you. I could hate you for leaving me, but I could never stop loving you."

The hymn reached a new crescendo, the soprano voices carrying it to the rafters. They might have been singing *"Hallelujah!"* for all Thomas knew. The weight of the world floated off his shoulders and disappeared high into the upper reaches of the church. As he felt the burden leave him, Thomas caught Penny in his arms and sought the lips he'd been dreaming about for two long years. She offered them willingly, sliding into his embrace without concern for their audience in the choir loft.

He was home—it was his only thought as he kissed her. He didn't even hear the voice floating above him.

"Guess I ain't needed here no more. Have a happy life, Tom-O."

The light streaming through the stained glass glowed golden as if the roof had opened to let in the sunshine, and for a brief instant, a heavenly chorus of hallelujahs echoed those filling the church.

"Heart Crossings"
by
Linda Madl

October 1918, Springfield, Illinois

The séance was over, the candle flame extinguished. Amanda sat alone in the darkened parlor, suffocating from the terror that clutched at her.

"Clear your mind," she whispered. Eyes closed, hands trembling, she fought to escape the horrific impressions that had nearly overwhelmed her during the session. Poor Johnny Ames's passing on the French frontline had been so recent, his panic so potent, that his emotions lingered, making her head pound.

Sucking in a breath, she summoned her power to weaken the sensations, forcing them to fade until they evaporated like a bad dream at dawn. *Be gone*, she commanded unsuccessfully.

In the front hall, Elvira was bidding farewell to the séance guests. Amanda had no need of her gift to envision her elder stepsister, tall and gaunt, standing beneath the Tiffany chandelier. A look of concern played across Elvira's face as she grasped each lady's gloved hand in turn. Sympathetic words fell from her thin lips. She acknowledged the lady's compliments on her stepsister's amazing talent as her fingers discreetly grasped a cash donation.

Séances always ended with Elvira receiving the money and she herself drained. Amanda understood the need for the donations. Neither her trust nor her stepsisters' inheritance covered their bills and other expenses. Still, accepting money for readings troubled her. Especially when she'd lied, as she had during today's session.

Behind her, the kitchen door swung open, and Opal, her younger stepsister, entered.

"Amanda, are you all right, dear?" Opal, a shorter, rounder, sweeter version of Elvira, set the tea tray on the table. "Wasn't that a good session? Mrs. Ames seemed especially pleased you were able to tell her that Johnny is at peace."

Amanda nodded. Unexpectedly, the sharp scent of chlorine gas assaulted her again; at least, Johnny's spirit thought it was chlorine gas. The phantom stench sucked the breath from her lungs, then vanished before a cough could rise in her throat. Her headache worsened.

"It was bad." Opal wrung her hands. "Tea will make it better, won't it?"

"Yes, tea would be nice." Amanda rubbed her temples with her fingertips.

Think of something positive, she willed. That usually helped. Her suitcase came to mind. Tucked under her bed, it was partially packed for the day when she worked up the courage to leave. She would travel light: a few changes of clothing, her mother's Bible, and the necessary documents to secure a job. Elvira and Opal knew nothing of her plan. One day soon, she would carry the packed suitcase downstairs, say farewell to her stepsisters, and walk out of the house into a future unknown even to her.

The front door slammed shut, jarring thoughts of freedom from her mind.

Elvira's steps rang against the wood floor. She entered the parlor counting the bills she'd collected. "Twenty, twenty-five—"

"I do hope it's enough to pay Maggie tomorrow," Opal said.

"It will do." Elvira frowned. "Mrs. Ames was generous and says she will be back. Mrs. Wilson, however, was disappointed."

Amanda groaned inwardly. She'd known this was coming.

"We need that lady's generosity and her good endorsement, Amanda. You must encourage her."

"If Colonel Wilson's spirit won't come through, maybe I can learn more about him at the next thespian meeting." Opal treasured her membership in the amateur theatrical group. "He was a member of the company, you know, and quite an actor."

Amanda frowned at the prospect of future lies. In truth, she knew plenty about Colonel Wilson, U.S. flying ace. And if Mrs. Wilson learned about her husband's infidelities abroad, her generosity would certainly dry up.

"Well, tea is ready." Opal gestured toward the tray.

They sat down to leftovers.

Séances began with fruit tarts, cookies, and petit fours. Maggie, their Irish maid, was a good cook even with their small ration of sugar, white flour, and butter; clients gobbled up her baking. After a little chitchat, when Elvira deemed the ladies receptive, they gathered around the parlor table. Amanda took that as her cue to begin bringing the guests messages from the other side.

Not a single fruit tart went to waste in Elvira's household, though. War rationing only justified her Scrooge-like stinginess. When the guests left, the remains became supper.

Elvira surveyed the food. "I see Mrs. Ames ate all the petit fours again. She really could do without seconds."

The selfish observation annoyed Amanda. "I can't begrudge the poor woman a few petit fours. She lost her only son to the war."

"Umm, we've all made our sacrifices," Elvira said. "The fact is, we need more income from our séances."

Opal piped up, "I've been thinking about that. What if we joined Mr. Barnum's circus, like the Fox sisters did? What do you think, Amanda? Center ring?"

"A circus?" Amanda stared at her. Was Opal serious?

"That was decades ago, and the Fox sisters confessed they were fakes." Elvira's eyes narrowed, as they did when she was plotting. "Amanda is the real thing. But her performance needs more drama."

"It's not a performance," Amanda said—but the whole business had definitely become a circus.

They'd treated her gift like a parlor trick since the day in grade school she'd taken pity on Arnold Tredwell, who was near tears because he'd lost his homework for the third time that week and was in danger of being paddled. Amanda told him where to find his schoolbag. When he did, Elvira—ever the opportunist—demanded a finder's fee.

Amanda wished she could have kept her gift a secret, but it wasn't possible. Over the years, her talent had expanded. She knew things about people and about the dead, and sometimes she simply couldn't keep them to herself. So when the war's casualty lists began appearing in the newspaper, Elvira had seized the moment.

"Of course, it's a performance," Elvira said. "However, we aspire to do better than the circus. We need wealthy clients like Mrs. Wilson, who will send us their rich friends and relatives. That means, Amanda, you need to be more like the society mediums. Mrs. Leonora Piper in Boston, for instance, or that British medium, Mrs. Coombe-Tennant, who does automatic writing."

"The messages don't come to me in words," Amanda said, exasperated.

"But a burning candle simply isn't dramatic enough."

Opal slapped her hand on the table. "I've got it! What about Amanda wearing a sheer middy blouse?" She leaned forward, whispering, "What was that medium's name who wore practically nothing under her clothes? I read she attracted a huge following of men."

Speechless, Amanda looked from one stepsister to the other. Should she laugh or cry? They were talking about costuming her as if she were a trained monkey.

Before she could reject the notion, Elvira waved a dismissal. "Nonsense. Amanda needs a spirit guide like Mrs. Lenora Piper has."

"A spirit guide?" Amanda repeated. Her efforts to make these two understand her gift had never worked. But then, she'd lived with it all her life, and *she* barely understood it. She did know that when she touched the other side, her experience was unfiltered. It was real and raw—and frightening. That's what made it so exhausting. She was on her own, unprotected.

Odd, she couldn't face the same experience in real life, couldn't find the courage to carry her suitcase out the door. She was safe with her sisters.

Or was she?

"Yes, a spirit guide is perfect!" Opal gasped.

"I don't need a spirit guide."

"A sheik, like Rudolph Valentino," Opal continued as if she hadn't heard. "Or, no, like Hiawatha, a handsome Indian chief with brown skin and a broad chest. He'll wear nothing but a loin cloth." Her face grew flushed. "The briefest loin cloth draped about his lean flanks. Oh, yes, a spirit guide would bring the ladies to our séance table."

"What do you think, Amanda?" Elvira asked.

"No spirit guide," Amanda groaned.

"But why not?" Opal pleaded.

"Because I have no guide, and I won't lie about it."

The doorbell rang, silencing all of them.

Elvira set down her teacup. "Who could that be?"

"Everyone knows Amanda won't read again until Friday," Opal said.

"I'll get it." Amanda rose, wondering who it might be. The neighbors never bothered them on séance days, and none of them was being courted—though Opal obviously needed a gentleman friend.

"No, I'll get it." Elvira jumped up before Amanda could get around the table. "It might be a bill collector."

That unpleasant possibility made Amanda hang back.

At the door Elvira paused, gathering herself, before opening it to face the caller. "Good afternoon, sir."

"A man!" whispered Opal, who'd moved to Amanda's side.

"I'd like to see the medium, Miss Amanda Sherman," a quiet baritone announced, its timbre full of confidence, with an underlying note Amanda knew well—skepticism. Yet its appeal was so strong she was drawn into the foyer.

"My name is Brian Mason. I understand Miss Sherman lives here."

"She does." Elvira closed the door partially, preventing Amanda from seeing or being seen. "Miss Sherman only reads three times a week, and she has already finished today's reading. If you'd be so kind as to call back at two o'clock on Friday, I'm sure she'd be glad to speak with you."

"I'm sorry," the man said, his voice full of patient resolve, though Amanda heard the underlying urgency in it. "Miss Sherman comes highly rated by the American Society of Psychical Research, as I'm sure you know. I've driven from Chicago today. I'd be much obliged if she'd see me. I'll gladly pay whatever fee she asks."

Tempted though she was, Amanda shook her head in silent refusal. She was drained.

"That's generous, sir, but as I said, Miss Sherman has read today." Elvira's eyes narrowed as she estimated the man's worth. "We only accept donations."

"Naturally, I would be most appreciative," he replied.

Elvira's eyes widened momentarily, and Amanda gave a silent snort. Her stepsister would never refuse money.

"Perhaps we can help you." Elvira stepped aside to allow him to enter.

A tall, square-shouldered soldier stepped into the foyer. He was dressed in the olive drab uniform and shiny leather gaiters of an infantryman. He was a captain, if Amanda knew her insignias. Funny he hadn't introduced himself as an officer. He'd tucked his billed cap under his arm and stood straight as an arrow, feet together and hands at his sides. His dark hair was close cropped, his face clean-shaven. He had dark, solemn eyes and a beautiful mouth set in the telltale grim line of the bereaved.

She knew that look only too well. It made her heart ache.

"I'm Amanda Sherman." She didn't offer her hand. Most physical contact brought her nothing, but occasionally the experience could be disagreeable.

"Miss Sherman." He nodded, his tone a mixture of relief and, again, skepticism.

Elvira hung his hat on the foyer rack.

"Of course, I'll be glad to do a reading for one of our troops," Amanda said, ashamed of her earlier reluctance. She summoned the courage to face another session and prayed she wouldn't have to lie to a soldier. "By the way," she added. "There's no obligation to make a donation."

When Brian's eyes adjusted to the shadowy foyer, he saw a young woman in white standing before him. Amanda Sherman was unlike the other two mediums he'd met. She was young and pretty in her simple full-skirted dress with its lace collar. No scarves, no hoop earrings, no bangles on her wrists. Just ebony curls with chestnut highlights framing her face, an intelligent brow, a luscious mouth, and a natural blush in her cheeks.

She gazed at him with somber brown eyes as she introduced her stepsisters.

"Ladies." Brian managed to pull his gaze from her long enough to nod toward the pudgy young woman, who stared at him goggle-eyed, and the dry husk of a female who'd answered the door. Then his gaze was back on the girl in white. Her engaging directness fascinated him. "I appreciate your seeing me, Miss Sherman."

"With gasoline still being rationed, Springfield is a long way to come from Chicago." She gestured toward a pleasant but shabby room off the foyer. "Let's go into the parlor. May we offer you refreshment, Captain?"

"No, thank you." As he followed her into the room, he noted the tray of food on the table. Though unrepentant about bribing himself into Miss Sherman's presence, he said, "I'm sorry to have interrupted your tea."

"That's quite all right." The older stepsister swooped down and snatched up the tray. "Opal and I will just go into the kitchen. You can leave your donation in the ginger jar by the door, Captain."

When the stepsisters left, Brian sat down at the table, which now bore only a candlestick.

"Pay no attention to Elvira and her donations," Miss Sherman said. "Tell me why you're here."

"I wish to make contact with a relative who has passed," he began, conscious of the irony that a medium would have to ask such a question. "But, in fairness, I must tell you that I'm a skeptic."

Without appearing the least offended she seated herself across from him. "Then why come to me?"

"I made a promise to placate another before I left for France. We agreed that if anything happened to either of us, we'd attempt to communicate—across the veil, I believe is the term." He stopped, suddenly bereft; there were no words for the emptiness and disbelief that flooded him when he thought of Bethany. Frowning, he forced himself to go on. "When I made the promise I never believed . . ."

"Of course not." She reached out to touch his arm, a sympathetic gesture, he thought at first.

Her touch was light, gentle, and he wouldn't have minded if her hand had lingered on his sleeve. But she withdrew it instantly and blinked at him.

"You're more than you seem." Confusion colored her voice.

"I beg your pardon?" He knew how mediums worked. If this was her way of probing for knowledge, she was going to find him a difficult subject.

"There is more of you." She shook her head, clearly puzzled, then studied him closely. "You're . . . do you have a twin?"

He schooled his features to reveal no surprise. "Yes."

Her brows came together. "It's your twin you wish to contact?"

Very good, he thought, wondering how he'd betrayed himself.

"Your twin is a sister." Miss Sherman closed her eyes. "Her name begins with a B. . . ."

He remained silent, determined not to let any subtle prying make him give up clues that led to the next "revelation."

Her eyes opened, and she smiled. "How silly of me. Of course, a B. You're Brian. She is . . . it's a soft sounding name. Sweet. Biblical."

Faced with her smile, his determination vanished. It seemed only natural to fill in the blank for her. "Bethany."

"Yes." Her engaging smile broadened.

A whisper of warning slid down his spine. How easily she'd made him answer. He'd driven to Springfield, where his family was unknown, to ensure that information about him would be unavailable. If, by some impossible chance, he made contact with Bethany, the experience must be genuine. He would not be fleeced by a fraud, however charming.

Yet how had she known he and Bethany were twins?

"Did you bring something of hers with you?" Miss Sherman asked.

"No, the other mediums didn't seem to need anything."

"It isn't necessary, but it can help," she said, ignoring his reference to her competitors. "Do you have anything she gave you?"

Warily, Brian pulled from his pocket a ceramic key chain fob shaped like a four-leaf clover and placed the beloved good luck piece on the table next to the candlestick. "She gave me this as a farewell gift."

"Perfect. Now, I need your understanding, too, Captain." She gazed frankly into his eyes. "It doesn't matter if you're a skeptic or a believer. I cannot promise that you'll find what you seek. Crossing the veil is seldom as straightforward or as satisfying as people want to believe it is."

He was intrigued. She was the first medium to doubt the outcome of her own reading. "I told you, I don't believe."

She assessed him for a long moment.

He wondered what she thought of him. Not that it mattered, but he knew that after nearly a year in the trenches in France, he wasn't the dapper young lawyer he'd been when he'd joined the army. He'd been a smooth-cheeked fool, bursting with confidence and righteously determined to defeat the damn Germans for making war on civilian ocean liners. He'd been certain he could save the world—and come home to find that Bethany's illness had improved, if not vanished.

But the war and the loss of Bethany had wrung the optimism from him. Now there were lines on his face, scars on his body—and a gaping emptiness in his soul.

Silently Amanda Sherman took the box of matches and lighted the candle between them. A bright flame sprang to life.

He knew she'd decided something—in his favor, he assumed.

"Everyone believes in something." She reached for his hands. "Let's see if we can reach your sister."

His hands were cool and strong as they clasped hers. In his eyes, Amanda glimpsed a sensitive side that his demeanor didn't reveal. Skeptic though he might be, he wanted desperately to reach his sister.

"Captain, I'm not like other mediums," she began.

"So I see," he said. "Call me Brian, please."

"Then, Brian, call me Amanda," she returned, glad to see him relax a bit. "There will be no floating lights or table rapping. I don't even do automatic writing."

"No alphabet board and planchette?"

"No, nor any crystal ball."

"That answers my next question." He grinned at her.

She liked his features: level brows, intent eyes, a straight nose, and a mouth that especially fascinated her. Supple, despite a hint of stubbornness.

Suddenly, unbidden, a vision came to her: Brian Mason taking her into his arms and kissing her, a long passionate kiss that made her lips tingle. His hands roamed over her back, her bottom, then cupped her breasts, teasing her nipples. . . .

Stifling a gasp, she bit her lip, and pain shattered the incredible sensation—a trick she'd learned to control visions. Good heavens, she was becoming as frustrated an old maid as Opal. Closing her eyes briefly, she opened them to glance guiltily at the man across the table.

"Your next question?" she prompted, struggling to hold the thread of the conversation.

"What's the keepsake for?" He was looking at her closely, a perplexed frown on his brow.

"Ah, guidance, for the spirit," she stammered. "We light the candle, place the keepsake between us, and take hands across the table. Then we'll see what comes. If what I say is correct, I would appreciate your corroboration. If I'm wrong, say so."

"Right." He glanced at the key chain, his grip still strong and steady.

Then he met her gaze once again above the candle flame. Uncertainty wavered in his eyes, yet she caught sight of the barest trace of hope in his grieving soul. At that moment, she knew that whatever the cost—whether or not Bethany appeared—she had to help him find peace.

"We begin." She clutched his hands tighter and looked into the flame. The essence of light mesmerized her senses. She closed her eyes and allowed the images to flow. They came in rapid succession, like water sluicing over and around her. Images too quick for her to attach words to them.

Cold. Ceaseless drumming of rain on canvas. Cries. Cordite stinging her nose. Trees naked against sky. Stink of rot. Barbed wire coiling through mud. Hunger. The flash and boom of an explosion. Numbness. A shredded uniform on a grinning skeleton.

She gasped. Her eyes snapped open.

The candle flame between them flickered.

"Are you okay?" Brian asked, his tone laconic.

Her heart pounded as she looked at him. The images she'd glimpsed were his, without doubt. Her heart ached for him, but his frown warned that sympathy would be unwelcome.

"I'm all right," she lied.

"Were you in a trance? Am I to expect the voice of a spirit guide?" Derision iced his tone.

She gave a dry laugh. "No. No spirit guide."

Closing her eyes again, she concentrated. His grip remained firm as she searched again for the message he sought.

"You and Bethany were close," she began, reaching beyond the immediate images, hoping to snag something besides the obvious. To her disappointment, only the vaguest notions drifted her way. "You lost your parents when you were young, so you became close. You studied a subject having to do with scales, a thing that is analytical, logical. . . . It requires decisiveness but is subject to manipulation." The next revelation brought a smile to her lips, and she opened her eyes to study his face. "You're strong-willed but fair and want to hear both sides before making up your mind about an issue. You despise manipulation. You're no politician."

"Never," he admitted with a reluctant smile. "I studied law."

She squeezed his hands, closed her eyes, and went back to searching. She could hardly expect to astound him merely by divining his profession. She waited for more impressions, essences. . . . Nothing . . . nothing . . . Then a small warmth tingled through her.

"Bethany is different from you, though you shared a womb. She is fair and less . . . robust. And you're dark." Amusement filled the warmth. "You even made a private joke of the difference. People thought she was the good twin and you, the bad. But the truth was the opposite."

"Yes," he drawled, as if the affirmation was being dragged from him. After a pause he added, "Is there a message?"

"Not exactly . . ." The visualization puzzled her. Flat. Many young women facing her. Colorless. White against darkness. "It's posed. A tableau, I think," she said without opening her eyes. "I see young women. A group. Grass at their feet. Such dignified smiles. White caps. Was your sister a nurse?"

He leaned back in his chair, his grasp loosening. "My sister hated hospitals."

"Strange." His response confused her. The image of nurses was becoming stronger. Happiness and contentment radiated from it. She was meant to see this, whatever it was. He was meant to know about it. "I'm getting the sense that she spent much time with an activity having to do with a hospital. The young ladies are wearing a uniform with white pinafores and caps. I'm not sure which is your sister. Oh, but she's proud to be there."

"I told you, Bethany hated hospitals." His baritone had grown flat, cold. She was aware of him withdrawing, sorry he'd asked for a reading. "What you're seeing can't have anything to do with my sister."

"Perhaps she volunteered for the war effort while you were away." Amanda wondered why he would reject an image of his twin that was, to her, incredibly strong and clear.

"No, she didn't." Abruptly he released her hands and stood up. His eyes glinted. "Bethany died of a reoccurrence of tuberculosis after years of remission. She loathed hospitals. She'd never have joined a volunteer medical group, nor would she have been allowed on a ward floor."

Amanda released the image reluctantly. The candle flame had been extinguished, leaving only a frayed thread of smoke drifting upward. She'd lost the image—and him. "There may be another explanation."

"Like what?" He snatched the key fob off the table and started for the foyer.

She followed him, keen to ease his disappointment, but Elvira and Opal appeared, blocking the doorway.

"How's it going?" Elvira asked with a fixed smile. "We could hear you in the kitchen. Are the spirits being uncooperative?"

"I've had enough of spirits." He glared at each of them in turn, then brushed past. "Good-bye, ladies. And don't worry—I'll send a *donation.*"

"And I'll return it," Amanda called after him.

Elvira's brittle smile vanished, and she caught at Amanda's arm. "Get the money now."

"No." Sick at heart, Amanda pulled free. "Brian, wait."

She caught up with him putting on his hat. He'd been a frowning skeptic when he came in the door, a man unwilling to believe in the world beyond. Somehow, she'd made him even less willing. She'd also made him disbelieve in her, and that, she was ashamed to admit, felt even worse. "I neglected to mention one more thing," she said to him.

"And that is?" His back was to her, his hand on the doorknob.

"Please, give what I described serious consideration," she said. "The connection may not be immediately clear. Ask others about it. Friends, relatives—they might know something you're unaware of."

He seemed to be listening but didn't answer.

"Oh, Brian, I wish I had all the answers for you," she said, daring to go on despite his evident disapproval. "But I don't. I'm sorry."

"So am I," he said, icy regret in his voice. "When you knew Bethany and I were twins, I'd hoped you were different. But you're not."

He opened the door and walked out into the fall twilight.

Sorrow and frustration swept over her as she watched him drive off. The curse of Cassandra had struck again. No one really wanted to hear the truth. She should have lied. She should have told him that Bethany was happy on the other side, that she was glad he'd returned safely from the war and wished him a long life. Even if he remained disbelieving, the fib would have consoled him; his heart he would have clung to the hope that his sister was happy. To do so was irresistible—it was human nature.

Elvira strode into the foyer. "Did you get the donation?"

"No." Amanda closed the door, turned, and marched up the stairs. "I don't want to do this anymore."

The decision came to her fully formed and absolute. The hall clock chimed six times as she reached the door to her room, reminding her that the next west-bound train left in six hours. She'd memorized the schedule. Tonight she would leave Springfield and séances and her stepsisters behind. And she would leave Brian Mason's disappointment behind, as well.

In her room, she pulled her suitcase from under the bed and packed the last of her things: her comb and brush, her favorite book of poems. Just to be safe, she counted her carefully saved money and double checked the envelope containing the character references and diploma she'd need to apply for a teaching job in Nebraska, where she'd heard teachers were desperately needed.

But where was her mother's Bible? She couldn't leave without it. She searched the room, looking for her most important keepsake. *Think.* She closed her eyes, fighting tears of frustration. *I can find things for other people. Why not for myself?*

Unexpectedly, a comforting warmth whispered over her, swirling around her like a summer breeze, though the windows were closed against the chilly fall air. Vaguely frightened by the unanticipated awareness, she held her breath, allowing it to overtake her. As alarming as her experiences sometimes seemed, none had ever truly hurt her. And this manifestation, though powerful, was both gently approving and apologetic.

Suddenly, she knew who it was.

"Bethany?" she whispered, her eyes still closed. She focused, waiting for images to take shape. Laughter came first, then the force of love—deep and selfless. And full of mischief. Amanda stood in awe, learning all at once how profound the bond was between twins. For there was no doubt, this was for Brian. "He was here for you."

Jubilant, the sensation eddied around her, fluttering the lace at her throat and stirring her skirt. As though disappointed, it cooled, becoming hesitant, then bewildered. Then, shrinking, it vanished.

The truth remained. Amanda opened her eyes and drew a deep breath, enlightened. Her Bible was under a magazine in the nightstand drawer. And the tableau of ladies she'd seen during Brian's reading was a photograph of Bethany with her friends. Amanda didn't know why that had been unclear before. Maybe because she'd been so tired.

Relieved, she finished packing. Now, to say good-bye to her sisters—promising to send money, naturally.

She also planned to make certain Brian knew that what she'd described was a photograph, apparently one he'd never seen. She couldn't prove she was different from other mediums, but she could show him that truth sometimes arrived in baby steps.

"Tableaus? Nurse's uniform?"

Sitting in a chair in the hotel lobby, Brian listened to his Aunt Olive's high-pitched voice, faint over the long-distance phone line. When he'd checked into the hotel an hour earlier, he'd been too annoyed by Amanda's vision to let it go. The idea of Bethany in a nurse's uniform was ridiculous. The mere mention of a hospital could bring her to tears. Nevertheless, he'd called their aunt in Chicago. Their father's sister, Aunt Olive had been mother and father to Bethany and him after their parents' death. She would know if there was any truth in what Amanda had seen.

"Oh, no," Aunt Olive said. "Bethany didn't have a nurse's uniform, but it's strange you should mention it. A couple of months before she passed, she was made an honorary member of the hospital auxiliary."

"What?" He straightened in the chair. "She never mentioned it in her letters."

"Well, after you were shipped overseas, she wanted to contribute to the war effort," Aunt Olive said. "I think it helped her feel closer to you. Besides, you know she could never tolerate you getting the best of her."

Brian closed his eyes, thinking about what a devil of a time he'd had staying ahead of Bethany. He'd lost his front teeth first, learned to ride a bike first. He'd won the most checker games, and, usually, the race downstairs to the tree on Christmas morning. Yet, Bethany had always won the class spelling bees and had surpassed him in art.

"She started painting china that sold well in the hospital gift shop," Aunt Olive continued. "The grateful auxiliary ladies decided to make her an honorary member. I put all the newspaper notices in her scrapbook. You must look at it when you return. Oh, how I miss her, Brian."

"Me, too," he said, realizing it was the first time he'd acknowledged aloud the invisible wound that was more painful than anything he'd suffered in battle. He longed for Bethany's death to be a nightmare from which he'd awaken—not this cold reality.

He said good-bye to Aunt Olive, hung up the telephone, then slumped in the chair, one elbow leaning on the telephone desk.

Why hadn't Bethany told him about the honorary membership? It was exactly the sort of thing she'd have bragged about to tease him. But then, he couldn't be sure he'd received all her letters. Mail delivery to the frontlines had been erratic. The few letters he'd received were so censored they'd been barely readable.

Regardless, he was forced to admit that Amanda Sherman had hit on a fact about Bethany unknown to him. Maybe she was closer to the real thing than he'd given her credit for.

He envisioned her face as he'd seen it bathed in candlelight: long lashes against rosy cheeks, brow furrowed, luscious mouth pursed in concentration, and dark curls that invited a man's touch. What would it be like to hold her? His body warmed at the thought of her softness pressed against him.

He sat forward in the chair, suddenly aware of liking Amanda very much and of wanting to see her again. Damn, he wished he hadn't been so hard on her. The thought of dealing with another fraud had angered him. But there'd been another reason for his impatience, too. He'd hated seeing her being taken advantage of by her old-maid stepsisters— whether or not she was a fraud. What right did they have to hang on her like parasites?

"Hell," he muttered. If he returned, she'd probably slam the door in his face.

A flurry of activity at the hotel entrance caught his attention. A woman carrying a small suitcase walked uncertainly into the lobby. Brian looked closer, then rose from the chair, hardly believing his good fortune. He was across the lobby in an instant.

She didn't smile at the sight of him.

"Amanda, what are you doing here?" he asked, realizing belatedly how unwelcoming the greeting sounded.

"I must talk to you before I leave."

"Leave? To go where?" he asked, astonished that her stepsisters had let her out alone, at night. He took her suitcase, led her into the lobby, and gently seated her on a sofa.

"I'm heading west." She settled primly on the cushion's edge, her trim ankles pressed together and her small clutch bag perched on her dainty knees. She wore a dark blue tailored jacket over the white dress she'd been wearing earlier. Her curls, mussed by the fall breeze, wreathed her face. The night air had deepened the blush in her cheeks. "Why are you smirking at me like that?"

"Am I smirking?" He was too distracted by her earthy sweetness to realize how he appeared. "Actually, I'm glad to see you."

"Really?" Her eyes widened with surprise. As he sat down beside her, she scooted over, making more room for him on the sofa than necessary. "That's not the impression I had when you left."

"I'm sorry about that." He glanced away in discomfort. He didn't want to discuss the scene he'd made in front of her stepsisters. "I was about to have dinner. Will you join me?"

"No, thank you." She clutched her bag tighter. "I have a train to catch."

"Take a later one." He stood and offered her a small bow he'd found effective with the ladies. At least, Bethany had told him it was effective. "Don't hold my bad behavior against me, please. If you refuse, you'll be consigning a soldier to a lonely meal."

She glanced at him in exasperation. But then, to his relief, her mouth curved into a small smile.

"All right." She rose from the sofa. "But I think you're being manipulative, Captain."

"Guilty." An easy admission to make once she'd agreed to dinner. "But in this case, I believe my action is justified."

Placing her hand on his arm, he instructed a bellhop to look after her luggage and escorted her into the restaurant. He asked for a quiet table, away from the businessmen huddled in the corner. He wanted her all to himself, away from busybody stepsisters and eavesdropping diners.

As he helped her remove her jacket, he studied the vulnerable line of her neck and the delicate set of her shoulders. He draped her jacket on her chair, aware of the desire to kiss her bare skin right above her collarbone. He satisfied the urge with resting his hand briefly on her shoulder. Her skin was warm and smooth beneath his fingers.

"Now, why are you here?" he asked, once he was seated and they had ordered.

"I wanted to remind you to talk to others about the reading." She spread her napkin in her lap without looking up.

"Actually, I just did," he said, summarizing his conversation with Aunt Olive. "So, you're right. Bethany had a connection to the hospital that I knew nothing about."

"Then you believe me?"

"To a degree. It could be just a coincidence."

"I don't think so," she said, frowning. "What I saw, the young women posed together, is a group photo of Bethany with friends."

"I know of no such photo." The absurdity of Bethany in a group of nurses struck him again. Annoyed, he shifted in his chair. "She was an artist. She wore paint smocks, not a nurse's apron."

Uneasily, she glanced away. "Here comes our food."

As the waiter served the meal, Amanda turned their conversation toward observations about the season and the hotel. He followed her lead. After a year in the trenches, it was good to dine on freshly prepared food, served on a cloth-covered table, across from a beautiful lady who conversed about nothing more important than the brilliant autumn leaves and the tangy fall apples. For the moment, life seemed wonderfully mundane, and for the first time in a long while, he was grateful for being alive to enjoy it.

When they'd finished, the waiter served them coffee in the lounge. Alone together in the dimly lit room, Amanda settled on the sofa with less concern this time about making space for him. He put his arm along the sofa back and allowed himself to feel possessive, though he had no right to. He listened contentedly to the intelligent woman beside him talk animatedly about, of all things, the sad state of the country's grade schools. The topic was obviously dear to her heart.

And she had an enormous heart. She wouldn't be here sitting with him if she didn't. Still, at her core was a strength that, earlier, he'd been too caught up in his quest to see. Generosity, strength, and patience. She'd been more patient with him than he would have been in her shoes.

"Do your clients often tell you that you've said things they didn't know about their loved ones?" he asked.

"Frequently." Her nonchalance indicated confidence in her abilities. "I don't know why spirits reveal secrets after they've passed. Perhaps it's their way of establishing credibility. Or perhaps there's a breakdown in communications that compels them to reach out to us in riddles."

"Riddles?" he repeated, thinking how different the world must seem to her. She dealt in dimensions he'd never contemplated. "If I accept that you saw something connected with my sister, then I have to accept that you have a link to the beyond—and that there *is* a beyond."

"Is it so difficult to accept?" She gazed at him over her cup rim.

"I saw too many bloated bodies and cracked heads and sightless eyes to believe in a hereafter."

"Yes, I know," she agreed. "I saw them, too."

He waited for her to go on. When she didn't, he realized with a start what she meant. "You . . . received images from me?"

"Yes." She set her cup down. "I don't tell that to most clients. Many of my impressions come directly from them. I smell things. Or feel past emotions, such as fear, surprise . . . loss. Other times, the images are visual. In your case, there was a skeleton in a shredded uniform."

He went still. He knew exactly the image she meant. He set his coffee cup down, lest he spill it.

"It was laid out as if for burial." She crossed her arms over her breasts, like a corpse in a casket. "Wearing a hat, but the uniform was in tatters. Is it a symbol?"

"No. A grave." He withdrew his arm from the sofa back and sat forward, pressing fingers to the bridge of his nose and squeezing his eyes closed. He longed to deny what she'd described but couldn't. He especially disliked the thought that he'd unwittingly exposed her to such horror.

"The first week in the trenches, a detail of us found a shallow grave washed out by the rains, and in it . . ." He drew a steadying breath. "In it was a soldier laid out as you describe, his bones already bleached white where his uniform had rotted away. The sight of him stopped us in our tracks. He grinned up at us from the mud. Here's what destiny holds for you, he taunted. I'll never be able to erase that image from my mind."

"Brian . . ." She touched his arm lightly. "The thing to remember is that you're here. Things are the way they're meant to be."

Anger swelled inside him. "Hollow words, Amanda."

She drew back from him. He was glad. He didn't want her pity.

"Comforting lies," he rasped. "I know. I've written them time and again to the families of men who died under my command. I lied to people about their sons and husbands and brothers never suffering— empty words of consolation, deceitful words about courage and patriotism and quick, *noble death*."

"You wrote what you knew the families could live with."

The uncompromising firmness in her voice surprised him. When he turned to look at her, her lips were pressed thin with resolve—not pity.

"I've told the same lies at every reading," she said, "to grieving wives, widows, sisters, and sweethearts."

"Then you understand why I don't believe in life beyond this one."

She shook her head. "Brian, I haven't lied to you. What I saw is true."

He studied her a moment. "I believe you. If you'd lied, you'd have invented a more credible story. But what if you just hit on a lucky guess?"

"Not lucky. Accurate," she said with quiet conviction. "Just as accurate as seeing the image of the skeleton soldier in your mind. In the photo, Bethany is the one with fair, wavy hair and a hint of mischief in her smile."

"That's Bethany." He sat back on the sofa. Her accuracy and confidence made disbelief impossible—almost. "But you're describing a photo I've never seen."

She nodded. "Yes, and I think if we had it, we might be able to contact Bethany."

A feeble glow of promise ignited, and he spoke as evenly as he was able. "You didn't say that before."

"It's only a possibility," she warned, obviously uneasy. "There are no—"

"No guarantees. I know. Doesn't matter." Mobilized by a renewed sense of urgency, he rose and pulled her with him. "You're coming to Chicago with me."

Amanda resisted Brian's tug on her arm. The invitation had been an order, not a request. Her attraction to him had grown over dinner, and she felt safe with him despite his avowed skepticism. Still, she wasn't sure she was ready to go haring off to Chicago with him.

"But my train—"

"Postpone your trip." He faced her. "You're not going to tell me there's a chance we can make contact, then refuse to help."

"But . . . tonight?" As she spoke, though, she remembered the pain she'd seen in him when he talked about writing letters to his men's families. She recalled, too, the passion and intensity she'd seen in his eyes over the séance table. He might be a skeptic, but he was dedicated to keeping a promise to his twin despite that it meant risking his beliefs. How could she refuse to help a man with that kind of fair-mindedness and courage?

"Tonight," he insisted, raising a hand to summon the bellhop. "I'll get your things and mine and check out." He started toward the registration desk, towing her along.

Amanda followed without further argument. After all, her future was her own. She could afford to spend part of it with him, if she chose.

Soon, she was huddled in the passenger seat of Brian's Stutz coupe.

She studied his profile in the light cast by the dashboard lights.

"Why are we going to Chicago?" she asked as the Illinois country-side slipped by in the darkness.

"To talk to people, as you suggested," he said, his gaze fixed on the road. "We'll look through Bethany's scrapbooks and find the photo. Sleep if you like. I'm not tired. We'll be there before you know it."

Resting her head against the seat, Amanda closed her eyes. She was weary from the long day. But she was also content. She'd taken charge of her life, delivering a farewell to Elvira and Opal, who'd been too surprised to marshal any arguments. And despite Brian's denials, she knew she'd brought him closer to being a believer than a skeptic. With a little cooperation from Bethany, she hoped she could bring him the rest of the way and, in doing so, erase at least some of the pain from his heart.

Afternoon sunlight poured through the lace curtains of Brian's comfortable childhood home. The apples in the crystal bowl on the dining table filled the room with a homey aroma.

Amanda breathed deeply with both contentment and longing for something she'd never had as she watched Aunt Olive place a stack of scrapbooks on the dining room table in front of her.

The gray-haired lady smiled at her. "That's all of them."

Amanda had liked Brian's aunt immediately. During the wee morning hours she'd taken them in without question or even much surprise at hearing her nephew's guest was a medium. Over breakfast, she'd listened eagerly as Amanda had related her vision of the photo, and she'd offered unstinting help in their search. They'd already looked everywhere Bethany might have stored a photo. The scrapbooks were the last hope.

Amanda glanced at Brian, who was leaning against the doorframe.

He gestured with a nod toward the scrapbooks. "Where did all these come from?"

"I put them together," Aunt Olive replied. "You know I was always a shutterbug. I took pictures as if your parents would show up one day and want to see what you'd been doing. Still"—she frowned—"I don't recall anything with Bethany in a nurse's uniform. Unless it's loose and stuck between the pages."

"Well, let's get started." Brian sat down across from Amanda. "I'll take this stack."

"I'll begin here." Amanda took a scrapbook, smiling at him, grateful that he was seeking the truth and not merely discounting her vision. She prayed that their search would bring him consolation.

When he smiled back at her, her heart clutched, and she dropped her gaze to the scrapbook in front of her.

Bethany's sweet elfin face soon became familiar to her. Brother and sister had been close, sharing life's passages with an intimacy that she'd never had with her stepsisters. Birthday party snapshots. One of the twins posed on a gray pony. Photos of them with Christmas trees and Easter baskets.

Brian laughed at one of Bethany with a baseball bat. "I taught her to bat. She taught me to dance."

Amanda lingered over a shot taken at what she guessed was Lake Superior in which the ten-year-old twins, in bathing costumes, were building a sandcastle. The boy was spindly, far from the broad-shouldered officer sitting across from her, but his face held the promise of the man's good looks.

"You've filled out," she observed, with more admiration in her voice than she'd intended. She glanced up in time to catch his surprised look, and she realized that, at any age, his face was becoming very dear to her.

Aunt Olive laughed. "Yes, indeed, he has filled out, hasn't he?"

A blush warmed Amanda's cheeks. Hastily, she returned to her search, but she could feel Brian scrutinizing her. She'd wanted to keep secret her growing affection for him; he didn't need a woman with a crush on him adding to his troubles. She hoped her blush had gone unnoticed, but another stolen glance told her that he was still watching. He grinned, and she quickly looked back at the scrapbook, her face burning.

By the time the sunlight had faded, they were forced to admit defeat.

"Nothing." Brian closed the last scrapbook.

"Nothing here, either," said Aunt Olive.

Amanda shook her head, embarrassment creeping over her. She'd enjoyed the glimpse into Brian's life, but had she led them on a wild goose chase? Had she misinterpreted Bethany's message?

"There must be something we've missed," Brian said.

Just as Aunt Olive began to shake her head, the doorbell rang.

Brian stood, reaching for a stack of scrapbooks. "I'll put these away, if you want to get the door, Aunt Olive."

Amanda picked up another stack and followed him into the living room. He knelt, placing the books on a low bookshelf, then reached for the ones she was carrying.

"I'm sorry we didn't find anything," she said.

Shrugging, he straightened the stack of books. "We'll find the truth eventually."

"You're very understanding," she said, discouraged and uncertain.

He stood and looked down at her intently. "No, I'm persistent. And, I think, just a little love-struck."

Love? Had he said the word *love*?

They stood close, hemmed in by the bookcase and an overstuffed chair. She remained frozen, barely breathing, looking at his broad chest, only inches away. Finally gathering her courage, she raised her gaze to his.

He was smiling. She stared, mesmerized, as he took her by the shoulders, pulled her against him, and lowered his mouth to hers.

He had a wonderful mouth. She'd known that from the moment she'd first seen him, but the reality of those lips on hers sent a fiery thrill through her. She put her arms around his waist and gave herself up to the kiss.

He explored her lips, then her mouth thoroughly, hungrily. She whimpered with pleasure and attempted to taste him in return, imitating his skillful performance. She drew her tongue along the inside of his lip and teased the corners of his mouth. He touched the roof of her mouth and prodded the tip of her tongue with his playfully. Then with sweet suction he let her know that he would draw her into himself if he could. She pressed her body closer, yielding to his seduction.

Finally, they parted, both gasping for breath. He rested his cheek against her forehead. She licked her lips, aware of a heaviness in her breasts and a warm throbbing in her belly.

"I was afraid you were sorry you missed your train to come with me," he whispered against her hair.

"I was afraid you were sorry you'd brought me," she whispered against his throat.

"Never." He kissed her brow.

"Brian?" Aunt Olive called from the hallway. "Come, see who's here."

"We'd better go." He led her toward the hallway.

She hung back, wondering how visible the changes were in her heart. What she said, though, was, "How do I look?"

His gaze caressed her face, then he gave a soft laugh. "Like you've been kissed."

Her heart melted. "Well, yes. But, honestly—"

"Here, sweetheart, let me." He smoothed her hair, saying, "Though I like these beautiful curls all mussed. Come on, now—you look fine."

They found Aunt Olive with a young woman.

"Brian, remember Bethany's friend, Flo Howard?" Aunt Olive said. "She was in Bethany's china painting class."

"Of course." Recognition lit Brian's face. "Good to see you, Flo."

He introduced Amanda as a family friend, which pleased her, though she was still self-conscious about her tingling lips.

"I'm sorry to impose, Miss Mason." Flo's gaze flitted to each of them, her manner flustered. She carried a manila envelope. "But I found something I thought you should have."

"Let me take your coat," Aunt Olive offered. "Come into the dining room."

There, Flo sat across from Amanda and opened the envelope. "I'm embarrassed to say, I just got around to opening some forgotten mail. In the process, I found this. I've had it for months."

She slipped what Amanda saw was a photo from the envelope and handed it to Brian. She watched, her heart pounding, as Brian studied the picture, but his expression was stoic and unrevealing.

"It's a photo of the china painting class," Flo explained. "We painted tea cups for the hospital auxiliary sale. Bethany's work was quite sought after."

Amanda's heart pounded even harder when Brian raised his gaze to hers and she saw the elation—and the pain—in the depths of his eyes. Without uttering a word he handed her the picture.

There they were. Eight smiling young women in snowy white caps and aprons. She searched the faces of the young women posed against the side of a clapboard house: seated front row, second from the right, with fair hair and an impish grin was Bethany.

"We all joked about being too squeamish to be nurses," Flo continued. "But, oh, how we admired the ladies in white. Saving lives while we dabbled with paintbrushes. So we painted our hearts out for the hospital auxiliary's benefit. We were all so proud of Bethany being recognized by the auxiliary. Then, one day, as a lark, we decided to dress up as nurses and have our picture taken. It was Bethany's idea, meant to be a private joke among us—a statement that we'd done our part. Afterward, I gave my address to the photographer. I was to deliver the pictures when they arrived. Then Bethany became ill and . . . well, we were so shocked and . . . heartbroken when she . . . she passed away that I forgot about the picture altogether. I'm sorry." Flo had tears trickling down her cheeks.

Aunt Olive reached across the table to pat the young woman's hand. "There, there, dear."

"It's all right, Flo," Brian said.

Amanda noted, as he turned his dark, questioning gaze to her, that all signs of stoicism were gone.

She nodded. "Yes, this is what Bethany showed me. I'm sure of it."

"Do you have a candle, Aunt Olive?" he asked.

"Why, yes," she said, clearly perplexed. "Behind you, on the breakfront. But why do we need a candle?"

"We're going to see if we can contact Bethany's spirit," Amanda said. "I'm a medium, Flo. Will you join us?"

"A medium?" Flo's jaw dropped open. "Oh, yes! Bethany was my dearest friend."

As soon as Brian lit the candle, Amanda laid the photo on the table, instructed them to take hands, close their eyes, and clear their minds.

She'd hardly begun to clear her own when the response came so forcefully that her body shuddered.

"Amanda?" Brian squeezed her hand gently, but she could feel the urgency in him, the desire to find his sister.

The candle flame flickered, then grew long, bright, and steady.

"I'm okay," she said, reeling from the mental impact. She took a deep breath and seized control of her consciousness again.

Familiar warmth and humor filled her, then coursed from her around the table. "Brian?" She opened her eyes to see that he'd closed his. A softness had settled over his features. "Listen to your feelings," she urged.

"She's here, isn't she?" he whispered, wonder in his voice.

"Yes," Amanda replied, relieved and grateful that he wasn't going to fight the experience.

"I feel her, too," Aunt Olive whispered. "The laughter. It's Bethany."

"Yes," Flo said, her eyes shut tight, but a smile on her lips.

"She's laughing because she's right." Brian's grasp tightened until it hurt, but Amanda made no effort to ease his grip. "She's able to come across. She's telling me, 'I told you so.'"

Amanda closed her eyes again to concentrate. "Talk to her," she told him.

"Bethany?" he began, his voice husky with emotion. "I kept my promise. I want you to know that I never believed anything would happen to you while I was gone. I thought if one of us . . . well, that it would be me, a war casualty. But if I'd known—" His voice broke slightly, but he recovered. "I know you wanted to talk about saying good-bye, but I couldn't do it. And now . . ."

Forgiveness surged through the room, the candle flame flaring taller, stronger.

"She doesn't want you to blame yourself for anything," Aunt Olive said.

"No," Flo echoed. "No blame."

Amanda remained silent, her eyes closed, astonished but pleased to have others taking her usual role of interpreter. The presence was so potent, so completely lucid, she was needed only as a conduit.

Suddenly the spirit waned a bit, as if distracted. The candle flame wavered. Then Amanda sensed more spirits lurking beyond Bethany's, shadows either unwilling or unable to come forward. They'd passed long ago but still were determined to make their presence known.

"My brother is there," Aunt Olive said, clearly shocked.

"Dad?" Brian's painful grasp on Amanda eased.

"Yes! Billy!" Aunt Olive laughed delightedly. "He's far away, but it's him. Smell his cigar smoke? Billy, I'm glad you're with Bethany."

"She's not alone." Flo sighed in relief. "The girls miss you, Bethany."

The tip of the candle flame quivered slightly, and Amanda sensed the beginning of the end.

"Brian, we don't have much longer," she said. The presence was on the move again, shimmering through beautiful images and impressions of love and sharing that flashed by too quickly for her to make sense of them.

"Bethany, I'll miss you." His voice was quiet and low, but without the earlier anguish and despair.

Suddenly, an image came to her, and she asked, "Do you see that?"

The candle flame began to flicker wildly.

"See what?" He leaned toward her. "What do you see?"

"Bethany is tapping her finger to her nose," Amanda said, eyes still closed, concentrating on the vision. "Does that signify something?"

"Yes." Brian's chair creaked as he leaned back.

A sudden breeze swirled upward, snuffing the candle and gently rocking the chandelier above. A white thread of smoke spiraled gracefully into the air. The chandelier's prisms tinkled. Then silence fell.

"She's gone." Amanda opened her eyes and released a sigh, exhaustion stealing over her. When she turned to Brian, he was staring at her as if seeing her for the first time.

"What's wrong?" she asked.

"Tell us what the gesture means," Aunt Olive prompted.

Still studying her as if she were a stranger, he replied to his aunt's question. "Bethany and I had a secret sign language. Tugging the right ear meant 'Don't believe a word this person is saying.' Tugging the left ear meant 'I get the first turn.' Tapping the forehead meant 'Rescue me from this person.'" Still holding her gaze, his voice raw, he finished, "And tapping the nose meant 'Everything is okay. See you later.'"

Darkness had fallen by the time Brian heard Amanda moving around in the guest room upstairs. She'd been pale and spent after the reading. When she'd asked to rest, he could hardly refuse her, though he'd wanted to. He wanted to talk with her, be with her, share all the amazing, new things he was feeling with her.

During the hour she'd been upstairs, Flo had left. As the night gathered, he built a fire and sat with Aunt Olive, discussing what had happened. She seemed as astounded and elated by the experience as he was.

"It was Billy." She smiled fondly. "I know it was. He never would give up those cigars, though your mother detested them."

"I remember," Brian said somewhat distractedly. It was as if his world had been turned upside down, and he was seeing everything from an entirely new perspective. The day before yesterday he would have called what had happened hogwash. Power of suggestion. A trick of mesmerism. But now the experience was as real to him as the rifle rounds that had whistled past his ears on the frontline. He would swear on a Bible that, for a moment, he'd been in his sister's presence. Bethany's farewell, her finger against her nose, didn't make him miss her less. But it made losing her tolerable.

And Amanda had made it possible.

His heart was lighter than it had been for months and so full of the need to be with her that the moment he heard her moving around, he bounded up the stairs and knocked on her door.

"Come in," she called.

When he entered, she was bending over her suitcase, open on the bed. His gut twisted.

"You're not leaving already, are you?" he asked in as jovial a tone as he could manage.

"Not tonight." She turned to him. "I'm looking for my train schedule."

"You're welcome here as long as you like." He was ashamed to think she might be worried about her circumstances. He'd been so caught up in his own needs, he'd almost forgotten that he'd virtually kidnapped her. "You know, you're our guest, Amanda. If there's anything you need, name it."

"I'm fine." She gave him a questioning smile. "I hope you and your aunt feel better, now, about Bethany?"

"Yes, thanks to you." Her loveliness captured him more powerfully each time he looked at her. She possessed a vitality and selflessness he admired, yet it was the magic about her that touched his heart. And she could kiss. In his arms, with her breasts pressed against his chest, her thighs brushing his, and her mouth open to his, she'd come damned close to making him forget that Aunt Olive had raised him to be a gentleman.

The realization that he'd fallen in love with her came in a sudden rush that took his breath away. Yet once it hit him, it seemed so natural, so completely right, he'd never been more certain of anything in his life. He needed her. And he knew instinctively that she needed him.

"Ah. Here's the schedule," she said. "Did I tell you, I'm a runaway?"

"Runaway?" he repeated, slightly dazed. How could she even consider going anywhere without him?

"I was leaving home when you swept me away." Laughing softly she tucked the schedule into her suitcase. "I'm going to teach school in Nebraska. No more séances for me."

"I sure understand why you'd want to give them up. I saw how exhausted you were awhile ago." Wondering how he was going to stop her, he added, "But you've made a believer out of me."

She smiled. "I'm glad. Will you take me to the train station tomorrow?"

"Uh . . . let's talk about that." He crossed the room and reached for her hands. "Is teaching what you see in your future?"

She frowned and shook her head. "It's what I *want* in my future. And I *don't* want to go on living with my stepsisters."

"I'm glad to hear it," he said, the perfect plan taking shape in his head. "Did I tell you that the law firm I worked for has offered to take me back?"

"That's wonderful," she said, a tiny frown flickering across her brow as she cast a quick look at their joined hands. "Congratulations."

"Did you know they need teachers in Chicago, too?" He had no idea if there was or wasn't a teacher shortage, but if there wasn't, he'd make one.

"Really?"

"So how about staying here—with me?" His heart in his throat, he watched a wild mix of emotions cross her features: puzzlement, surprise—and, he was sure, a flicker of hope.

"With you?" she said, her voice a bare whisper.

He nodded. "Aunt Olive is here, and she likes you very much—you must realize that. And you could still see your sisters, if you wanted. I've had my eye on this new housing development up north." He stopped for a quick breath. "Amanda, I'm asking you to marry me."

"Marry?" she stammered.

His gaze held hers steadily as he vowed, "I know we haven't known each other long, but I also know I love you. And unless I'm badly mistaken, I think you have similar feelings for me."

She blushed, her entire face and throat becoming as rosy as her cheeks. "Is it that obvious?"

"You bet." He drew her close and slipped his arms around her.

She didn't pull away, but she wouldn't look at him. "Brian, just because you're grateful, doesn't mean—"

"Sweetheart, I swear, this is *not* about gratitude." And plowing his fingers through her hair, he covered her mouth with his.

He sampled her lips lightly until she pressed her mouth to his. Then he lashed an arm around her waist, lifted her against him, and slid his tongue into her sweetness. Moaning, she instantly went weak in his arms. And he took full advantage.

Well, not quite. He wanted to lay her down on the bed, undress her slowly, and make love to her all night—and all day tomorrow and the day after and forever. Too bad Aunt Olive was downstairs. So he took what advantage he thought he could get away with—and made the most of it.

Amanda slipped her arms around Brian's neck and kissed him back with all her heart. *He loved her.* Was it possible? Heaven knows, she loved him. As their kiss deepened, she sensed that all the cold cynicism and loneliness she'd seen in him only yesterday had vanished. He was reaching out to her with his heart, loving and passionate.

He raised his head to gaze at her, drawing a finger down her cheek. "Lord, I've wasted so much time. Loving someone changes everything, doesn't it? In war or peace, we carry on with love, and it makes life possible. No, more than that—it makes it wonderful."

"Yes, it does," she said, breathlessly ecstatic that he understood. "That's the only belief any of us needs."

"I love you, Amanda. Say you'll marry me."

Happiness she'd never known flowed through her. "I'll marry you, Brian. But don't count on me to know what the future holds."

"I already know," he said, lowering his mouth to hers again. "Lots of loving."

"Hero's Welcome"
by
Rebecca York

Planet Thindar, four months after the Dorie-Farlian War

He was taking a risk. He could lose everything—the estate he'd
been given and all the severance pay he'd invested in it. There was no
guarantee he'd ever make a farmer. Still, Ben-Linkman felt a rush of
pleasure as he activated the breaker jets and eased the bulky air truck
downward fifty more meters for a better view of his property.

"Mine. The spoils of war." He said the words aloud, savoring them
as he swooped low over the small lake, winking in the greenish glow of
the late afternoon sun, then circled the sprawling house. Catching his
breath, he swung away from the landscaped grounds and roared over the
broad, flat fields where oil-rich rokam had once grown.

Coming here was a huge gamble. He was betting everything that he
could bring the land back to life. But could he? Did he have it in him?
What if he failed? What if he—

Determinedly, he cut off the thought and set the air truck down
behind the house. This was no time for second thoughts, and if he didn't
want to lose the place to an enterprising thief, he'd better activate the
security perimeter.

He rolled his shoulders, fatigued from flying the heavy government
surplus ship eight hundred klicks from Spenserville, formerly Halindish.
The city, which had been a Farlian provincial capital, had been recently—
triumphantly—renamed after a legendary Dorre war hero.

Reaching behind his seat, he picked up his weapons and checked
them: the small laser gun in the hip holster and the larger projectile rifle.
High command had told him that gangs of deserters might be hiding in
the hills. He wasn't about to let them catch him by surprise.

The hatch beside him swung open with a push, and he levered himself out of the opening, stifling a groan as cramped muscles stretched.
The real pain came when he touched ground. He forgot to lock his bad
knee, and it crumpled under him, sending a jolt of pain all the way down

to the nonexistent toes. Gritting his teeth against a scream, he stood with his hands balled into fists.

The pills they'd given him were in his backpack. He could take one. Just one.

"No." He said it aloud.

He'd seen what happened when men started relying on the medication. They ended up needing more and more of the stuff, until their brains were so fried, all they could do was sit and stare into space. The pills were a one-way ticket to Farlian hell. He wasn't going that route.

Teeth still clenched, he walked to the back door of the large, well-proportioned house and worked the key pad with the combination they'd given him.

Inside, he paused to absorb the silence of the wide corridor before switching on a power light. Then he made his way to the central living area, where he took a quick look at the woven rugs and the graceful furniture. Expensive, he thought, running his hand over the glossy, red-brown kardin wood.

Glancing toward the small window, he saw that the light was fading. If his people, the Dorre, had built the house, there would be skylights in the vaulted ceiling. The estate had been confiscated from Farlians, though, which meant it was constructed to allow in only minimal outside light—like the caves Farlians had occupied to escape predators on the planet where they'd first landed after leaving Earth. Hundreds of years of cave dwelling had changed their eyes so that Farlians saw better in the dark.

A neat trick, but it hadn't won them the war.

Turning right, he headed for the control center. His father had been the maintenance supervisor in a rich Farlian household, so the equipment was familiar. In minutes he'd brought up the main computer and checked the circuits. About half the estate's power units, including the security perimeter, were working. He'd fix the rest tomorrow, after a good night's sleep. Tonight, he'd just do a sensor check.

First he scanned the grounds and detected nothing bigger than a tree sneep. When he checked the house, though, his hand froze on the controls. Eyes narrowed, he went through the drill again, but the screen didn't change. There was a Farlian in the house.

A wave of anger and hatred surged through him. Farlian and Dorre might come from the same human stock and claim Earth as their common ancestral home, but the only thing they had in common anymore was the war they'd fought for the right to rule Thindar.

Six months ago, just before the armistice, one of the slat-eating bastards had caught him below the knee with an energy blast that injected tissue poison. Amputation from the wound down had saved his life, but it hadn't stopped the pain that continually invaded the rest of his leg. Nor had it lessened his rage at Farlians.

If it weren't for the oppressive bastards, the Dorre never would have been forced to go to war. After abandoning the inhospitable planet where they'd lived, the Farlians had migrated to Thindar and colonized it. When the Dorre had arrived a hundred years later, on a generation ship from Earth that was at the end of its resources, the Farlians had saved his people's lives with food and medicine.

Then, when the newcomers had begun to prosper, the Farlians, afraid of losing power, had passed laws that made it impossible for Dorre to enter good schools, hold office, or even own property. A caste system had developed; his people were forced into the underclass—while the Farlians had consolidated relations with other space-traveling races, creating off-world trading partnerships, all the while growing ever richer and more arrogant.

Until the Dorre had risen in rebellion.

From the console, Link silently switched on some lights. Then he moved quietly toward the storage compartment where the sensors indicated the intruder was hiding.

His hand on the pressure trigger of his gun, he yanked open the metal door, nearly killing the Farlian behind it before seeing it was a female. A mane of red hair hid her face.

Grabbing her by the sleeve, he wrenched her into the open and tossed her onto the floor. She lay curled away from him, her ivory skin blotched by fear, her slender legs trembling visibly below a short tunic. Yet it was with regal bearing that she sat up and swept the fall of hair away from her exotic green eyes.

The sight of her familiar features knocked the breath out of him. "Kasimanda!"

She'd been beautiful as a child, more so as an adolescent. But now . . . by Atherdan, she was stunning. The pale skin, the cat-like eyes, and the wild red hair created a vision that called to him with a familiar, forbidden longing. For an instant, he wondered if this was really her or some dream from his subconscious come to life.

Her gaze flicked from his face to the laser pistol in his hand. "Would you kill me, Link?" she asked in that musical voice he instantly discovered still had the power to stir his senses.

He pulled himself together. "Why shouldn't I? This is forbidden territory for a Farlian."

Doubt kindled in her eyes. "We were . . . friends."

"*Friends.*" He threw the word back at her. Dorre and Farlian could not be friends. Yet he and the highborn Kasimanda of Renfaral had played together as children. And when they had reached adolescence, he had longed for more than friendship.

His eyes must have given him away, because he saw her relax a fraction.

"How did you get here?" he demanded.

She pushed herself off the floor and stood facing him defiantly. "Bribes."

"I hope you didn't spend too much, because you're leaving. Now," he said, emphasizing the last word.

She shook her head. "No."

He made his voice flat and hard. "You can't stay."

Her shoulders slumped. "Then kill me now."

"I don't kill women."

"No?" She raised her chin. "A Dorre raiding party killed my mother and sister. Are you so different?"

Sickened, though not surprised, by the news, he asked, "And they spared you?"

He saw her stiffen, swallow. "My mother pushed me into the refuse chute as they were coming through the front door. They didn't find me."

He tried to imagine Kasimanda of Renfaral hiding among the household garbage. Unthinkable. Yet he could see from her eyes that it was true—that and maybe worse.

"Why did you come here?" he demanded.

"To work."

He gave a short, sharp laugh. "You? Work?"

"Yes. The place was a mess. I cleaned it. I can keep it for you. I can cook. And I can help you with the rokam."

"Let me see your hands."

She kept her eyes on him as she held up her hands for inspection. He remembered them being soft and white, the hallmarks of a pampered woman. Now they were red and chapped.

Before he could comment, she went on quickly. "I was studying botany at the Grand Institute when the war started. I know about rokam. It's temperamental. You could lose the whole crop if you plant at the wrong time or if the minerals in the soil are out of balance."

He gave a tight nod. He knew the risks.

"I—"

"How did you get inside the house?" he interrupted her.

"I visited this estate several times before the war. I knew the access codes." With a gesture toward the south-facing window, she added, "I sold the ring my father gave me on my Passage Day—and some other things from the estate. With the last of the credits, I paid for a ride as far as the river."

His eyes narrowed. It was thirty klicks to the Little Jodda and two hundred klicks to the nearest settlement. "Some damn fool flyer pilot left you in the middle of nowhere?" he asked, his anger rising.

She gave a little nod.

"This is dangerous territory. You could have died if a storm had caught you on the plains. Or you could have run into a gang of deserters," he ground out, imagining the worst. "They're desperate. Dangerous."

"I have a laser gun."

"Weapons are forbidden to Farlians."

She met his gaze with steady eyes. "Are you going to turn me in?"

He heaved a sigh. "No." When she let out a little breath, he fixed her with a quizzical look. "How did you find me?"

"A woman who worked for my father is in the office where they keep information on troopers, and after . . ." She stopped, started again. "After I'd been on my own for a couple of months, I went to her, and she looked up your record."

"Why me?"

Her gaze dropped to the floor. "My parents and my sister are dead. So is my brother. There isn't anyone else. And my options are very limited."

"You're well educated. A lot better than me," he said. "Surely you can find something to do."

"Not many people are hiring ex-Farlian nobility." A shudder went through her. "There are houses where young women of my station entertain Dorre men. I would rather starve."

He struggled to keep his expression impassive as she continued.

"I won't beg you to let me stay, Link, but . . . I've brought something for your leg."

The blood drained from his face. Farlian hell, she knew about that, too.

"I bought some salve Farlian soldiers use," she whispered. "It draws out the poison."

His eyes widened. "There's a *cure*? Give it to me!"

"It's . . ." She stopped, shook her head. "They were testing it. I don't know if . . ."

He turned away so she wouldn't see the crushing disappointment in his eyes. An experimental drug. Probably it didn't work.

His jaw rigid, he stomped out of the room—to the extent that his limp allowed for stomping. He'd come here to hide his ruined body—from others or from himself, he wasn't sure. He didn't know how to cope with either the sudden reminder of the man he'd once been or with the false hopes she offered.

He threw his pack onto the floor in the hall and sprawled on the steps leading upstairs. Cursing under his breath, he rummaged in the pack. When his fingers closed around the tube of dried brew malt, he made a grateful sound. Not quite as good as pain pills, but it would do. He set the tablet in a plastic cup, poured in water from the bottle he carried, and watched the brew sizzle. Before the head rose, he began to drink. It was cheap beer, laced with brandy extract. In minutes he was feeling almost calm.

Almost calm enough to face Kasimanda as she came down the hall, carrying a small plate.

"You should eat," she murmured.

He acknowledged the advice with a grunt as she set the plate beside him. His resolve to ignore her wavered when he smelled nester cakes. Her family's cook had made them, and Kasi used to sneak them to him.

"You made these?" he asked.

"Yes."

He took a bite, wondering when and how she'd learned to cook. The cake was crisp and meaty, the way he remembered.

Tipping his head to one side, he peered at her through a brew-induced haze. "These are good. My compliments to the chef." His words slightly slurred, he asked, "But what if cooking and cleaning and tending rokam isn't enough? What if the one-legged man wants you in his bed?"

Her face went white.

"I see. The rules have changed, but I'm still not good enough for you."

She knitted her hands together in front of her. "I . . . can't."

The way she said it made him shudder. "Kasi?"

He put out a hand toward her, but she was already darting out of his reach, fleeing down the hall. He stared after her long after she'd disappeared.

Finally, with a heavy sigh, he made another cup of the strong brew. A shame to waste good nester cakes, he decided, cramming another into his mouth and licking his fingers. Sometime later he found the strength to get up and stagger down the hall to a bed chamber. Fumbling clumsily, he unstrapped his holster and shoved his gun under the pillow.

There was a mirror on the wall, and his reflection took him by surprise: A tall, dark-haired man with broad shoulders, his face too young for the pain-etched grooves in his forehead. He couldn't remember the last time he'd looked at his own face. It was changed, and not for the better.

Turning quickly, he pulled off his trousers before easing off the prosthetic extension of his ruined leg. Freed of its constraint, the stump throbbed, and he bit back a groan as he flopped onto the bed.

He must have slept. The next thing he knew, he was awake and listening to stealthy feet moving in the darkness. His hand shot to the gun. The intruder was quicker, surer. He heard the weapon clank onto the stand beside the bed.

"It's all right," Kasimanda whispered.

Some of the tension went out of him. In the semi-darkness, he could see her only in outline. When he remembered she could see him a lot better, his stomach knotted. "What're you doing here?" he growled, trying to pull the bedding over the stump of his right leg.

Her hand covered his. "Lie still."

He felt the mattress shift as she came down beside him. "I'm going to take care of the wound."

"No." He tried to slide away, but one of her hands gripped his shoulder, stilling him. When the other hand touched his ruined flesh, he went rigid. "*Don't.*"

"It's all right," she answered, a quaver in her voice. "I understand."

He uttered a short, humorless laugh. "Yeah? And how in Atherdan's name could you understand? What have *you* lost?" The instant the words left his mouth, he regretted them. Consumed by pain and humiliation, he'd forgotten what she'd told him only a short time ago, that, indeed, she'd lost everything.

She didn't reply, only stared at him. He couldn't hold her gaze, had to look away.

For several more moments, silence hung in the darkness between them. Then her fingers flattened against his hot skin.

"Let me see if this salve works," she whispered. "I want it to work. I want to give you that. Maybe it's all I can give you."

The soft sound of her voice kept him pinned to the bed as her hand
glided over his leg, spreading some kind of cream. At first her touch
brought him pain, and he clenched his teeth to keep from wrenching
away. But in a few moments he felt something else: deep, comforting
warmth, radiating through his skin, penetrating all the way to the bone.

Still, as her hand moved lower, toward the place where the energy
burst had charred his flesh, he felt cold sweat break out on his forehead.

She kept talking to him in a low voice, words he couldn't quite catch.
Yet they held him. He wanted to close his eyes, to pretend that the
darkness hid his mangled body. At the same time, he wanted to turn on
a light, so he could see her delicate features. He settled for straining his
eyes, watching her bending over him, the long flow of her spectacular
Farlian hair, with its rippling waves, curtaining her face.

"Is it doing anything?" she asked, her voice giving away her tension.

"I . . . think so."

"Good." The word eased from her lips like a long, satisfied sigh.

He reached toward her, but before his hand could connect with her
flesh, she sprang away. For a moment she stood looking down at him,
then she turned and ran out of the room.

The next morning, he might have chalked the whole thing up to
fevered dreams, except that he could see the orange salve on his leg. He
also felt a difference in the wound. The pain was less gnawing.

He limped to the bathroom, using the folding crutch they'd given
him in the hospital, and took a quick shower, bracing his back against the
curved wall and standing on one leg. When he had carefully dried the
stump, he attached the prosthesis and braced for the hot pain that always
came when he first put his weight on the damned thing.

It wasn't quite so bad.

He started down the hall, then, on second thought, stopped and
went back. Standing in front of the mirror, he ran his hand over the dark
stubble that covered his cheeks. He had intended to leave it. Instead he
slathered hair-dissolving foam on the nascent beard and washed it away.
The foam left his cheeks smooth and undisguised, forcing him to acknowledge the weight he'd lost. He looked lean and hungry and, in his
own eyes, angry.

He tried to lighten his expression, to erase the frown, to make his
lips curve upward in a smile. When he realized his attempts to rearrange
his features only made things worse, he grimaced and turned away.

Kasimanda wasn't in the galley. But there was a plate of grain cakes
on a warming square. And real coffee. Maybe the residents of the house

had left it in long-term storage, he thought as he breathed in the wonderful aroma, then poured some into the delicate ceramic mug she'd set on the table for him.

Her grain cakes melted in his mouth, like the ones his mother had made, and he realized that she must have used a Dorre recipe. He wanted to tell her how good they were, but she didn't appear when he called her name.

"You don't have to leave," he said more loudly, hoping his voice conveyed a note of apology for his insensitivity of the night before. "You can stay here as long as you want."

No answer.

Half disappointed, half relieved, he went back to the power center and spent the morning on repairs. When the sun had reached its zenith and begun its slow fall toward the horizon, he headed outside to inspect the farm machinery. He wasn't going to look for her, he told himself as he limped his way to the large barn, where the equipment was kept.

After satisfying himself that the riding scour and harvester were in working order, he returned to the galley, where he found she'd put away most of the supplies he'd brought and prepared another Dorre-style meal. Like the fairy people in a children's story, he thought with a low laugh. An unseen helper.

Stomping down the hall, he began opening doors. In a wing off to the left, he found the small chamber where it appeared she had been sleeping. The bed was narrow, the storage bay small. Servant's quarters.

Why in the name of Far— He stopped himself, realizing suddenly how insulting the curse would be if he slipped and said it aloud in front of Kasi: his people defiling the name of hers.

He started over.

Why in the name of hell was she sleeping in here? She could have the master bed chamber for all he cared. He opened the storage bay. There were only a few tunics, all of them clean but made of cheap cloth. Wasn't there anything better in the house, he wondered as he fingered the coarse fabric, imagining it next to her soft skin. With a curse, he turned and stamped away.

He worked outside for the rest of the day. By evening, his leg was throbbing. Back in his room, as he pulled off his clothes and removed the prosthesis, he decided he could use some more of that orange stuff.

Would she come to him again? Or was one good look at his mangled leg enough, he wondered as he lay with his eyes half closed, too keyed up to sleep. An enormous sense of relief swept over him when the door finally glided open.

"Was your leg better today?" she asked softly as she tiptoed toward the bed.

"Yes."

"I'm so glad." In her voice was a hint of the music he'd always loved.

"I think more of that salve would help," he admitted in low, rough tones.

In one quick motion, she perched lightly beside him. He wanted to feel her touch. Still, he flinched when her fingers made contact with the leg. Teeth gritted, he ordered himself to relax as she began to soothe the magic salve over his poisoned flesh. Again there was warmth and sweet relief.

In the darkness, he began to talk, his tone flat and devoid of emotion. "I was on a mission to secure a farm house. There was a Farlian hiding inside. He burned my leg. I put a hole in his chest."

Her hand stilled, then started again.

"I killed a lot of your people."

"Are you bragging or asking for my forgiveness?" she asked, a little hitch in her voice.

He might have tossed out a cynical answer. Instead he gave her honesty. "Neither. I just . . . I just needed to say it. I'm not sure I'm fit company for anyone. I feel . . . uncivilized."

"The men you killed were uncivilized, too," she answered. "They would have killed you if you hadn't killed them first."

He made a low sound in his throat. "I started out as an idealistic boy fighting for my people's freedom. I didn't know what war was going to be like. I didn't know how it felt to look into a man's eyes and kill him."

"You did what you had to do. And your people *are* free."

"And yours?"

"We've paid the price for years of conceit and presumption."

Her answer shocked him. "That's what you believe?"

She sighed, a sad sound in the darkness. "When I think about it, I understand that when we raised the price of rokam oil too high, our buyers on Kodon Prime made a business decision to ally themselves with the Dorre and back them in a war against us." She sighed again. "But mostly I try not to think about it. I try just to survive, one day at a time."

She said it with such heart-wrenching simplicity that he struggled to draw a full breath. Her next words only added to the crushing feeling in his chest.

"Link, you're a man whose body and soul were injured by circumstances beyond your control. A man with the strength to heal the parts that can be healed."

"How do you know?" he asked in a hoarse whisper.

"Because you had the courage to tell me your doubts. Because you let me put my hands here." In the darkness, she lightly touched the stump of his leg. "There are things inside all of us that we find frightening. It's how we deal with the fear that counts."

When had she grown up, he wondered. Where had she gained this kind of wisdom?

"Doesn't it change the way you feel about me when I tell you I killed Farlian men?" he demanded.

"I never saw things in terms of Farlians verses Dorre. Our races evolved differently, because my ancestors came from Earth much longer ago than yours and adapted to a new environment that changed us. So my skin is very pale, and my eyes see better at night than yours. But those physical differences are superficial. Our hopes and needs and feelings are alike. We're all still people, and in all ways that matter, we're the same."

"Then why did you stop me that night, when you knew I was going to kiss you?" He blurted out the question, then immediately regretted it.

He thought she wasn't going to answer when she rose and took a step away from the bed. Then she began to speak in a low, rapid voice. "Because I knew my father was standing in the doorway, waiting for me to come in from the garden. And despite his liberal leanings, he would have killed you if you'd put your hand on his high-born daughter."

Before Link could respond, she turned and fled the room.

He lay for long hours in the darkness, remembering each word of the midnight encounter, each touch of her hands on his flesh. He especially remembered that she'd been motivated by a desire to protect him from her father, not revulsion for him, when she'd refused his kiss all those years ago.

Some time in the early hours of the morning, slumber finally took him.

Despite the short sleep, he woke feeling better than he had in months, as if a giant weight had been lifted off his body. He knew it was Kasimanda's doing. She was the first person he'd told how he felt—about the war, about his leg, about anything at all. Maybe it was because he'd known her longer than anyone still living. Maybe it was the gentle way she had about her. Whatever the reason, he felt he could talk to her, share himself with her. And with the talking and sharing had come a kind of freedom.

He wanted to tell her, but she had disappeared again. Anguish grabbed him when he considered that she might have fled the estate. Then he reminded himself that she'd said she had nowhere else to go.

He ate the food she had left for him, then headed outside. With the riding scour, he began to clear away rocks that had washed down from the nearby mountain with the season's rains. No one had tended the field since the war had started, and there was a lot of debris.

While he worked, he thought about Kasimanda. Kasi, he had called her when they were young. Things had changed abruptly when they'd grown into awkward adolescents. And more recently, changed again—in ways he was afraid to imagine. They both had been ground up and spit out by the war.

He sighed. On Laster of Renfarel's estate, where he and Kasi had grown up, Farlian and Dorre children had played together as near-equals—until they began to mature and were suddenly cautioned to remember their places in society.

Those places had changed, though. The Dorre, in waging war against their oppressors, had stood the world on its head, creating chaos in the process: cities renamed, rulers reduced to humiliation, civilians murdered. Families, like Kasi's, torn apart. Men, like him, maimed.

With a grimace, Link centered his mind on the task of clearing rocks. When the sun dipped low over the hills, he returned to the house and revived himself in a long cool shower. After eating the dinner Kasi had left him, he flopped into bed. But rather than lying down, he propped his back against a mound of pillows and left a small lamp burning in the corner of the room—as if he were expecting company. Then, as the silent minutes dragged by, his tension mounted along with the throbbing in his leg.

He had almost given up hope when the door slid open, and she stepped into the room. Stopping, she shielded her light-sensitive eyes, took a step back.

"Don't go."

"The light—"

"I need to see you."

He held his breath as she hesitated in the doorway, then felt the air trickle from his lungs as she crossed the space between them.

She was dressed in a short gown, not unlike her daytime tunics. As he watched, she opened a small medical kit and took out the salve. Easing gingerly onto the bed, she kept her eyes down as she began to work on his leg, the medicine and her touch bringing that same deep, healing comfort. This time, though, the sensation soon became more than mere comfort. With the absence of the pain, he was helpless to stop the response of his body to hers.

He sat there, feeling the heat gather in his loins as her hands worked their way down his leg and up again toward his thigh. And he knew the precise moment that she realized how her touch was affecting him.

Uttering a strangled cry, she scrambled off the bed.

"Kasi."

The name from their childhood stopped her. Still, she stood warily, poised to flee.

He gestured downward. "I'm not going to run after you. By the time I attached that pitiful excuse for a leg, you'd be gone—to wherever it is you hide during the day." He made a sound that was almost a laugh. "Or I could hop after you. I haven't tried that yet—don't know how fast I'd be at it." Nor had he joked about the leg, he thought with a kind of detached amazement.

Her features contorted.

"Kasi," he said again, very gently.

She held herself stiffly, as if she might break in two, and the question that had been gnawing at him for days worked its way to his lips and came out in a half-strangled growl. "The Dorre soldiers who came to Renfaral—did they find you?"

Her whole body jerked as if he'd slapped her, and he felt a sudden pain in his gut, like the twisting of a knife.

"Did they catch you?" he managed, praying he was wrong.

Her head gave the smallest of nods. When she spoke, her voice cracked. "In the woods. They didn't know I was Laster's daughter, so they didn't kill me."

The look on her face told him more than the words. He clenched his jaw to keep from roaring his outrage. He had heard soldiers bragging of catching Farlian women and teaching them a lesson in obedience to their new masters.

"I would never do anything to hurt you," he said, struggling to speak around the fist-sized obstruction in his throat.

"When I touched you, you got . . ." She stopped, gulped.

"Hard," he finished for her, then went on to admit, "I was aroused. Do you know what that means?"

"That you want to have sex with me."

The stark look on her face pierced though his chest to his heart. "That's only a small part of what I feel. When you touched me and talked to me, you made me feel things I didn't think I'd ever feel again. Good things. Things I thought had died inside me."

She stayed where she was, her gaze searching his face.

"Kasi, I would never hurt you," he repeated. "I swear that. On the altar of Atherdan."

Her head came up. "On Atherdan? The sacred place of your people."

"Yes."

Her small white teeth worried her lip.

"I can't get up. You have to come back here, so we can talk."

The breath froze in his lungs as he watched her stand unmoving. Then, in a rush she came to the bed and perched on the side, just out of reach, her face turned away from him.

"Can you tell me about it?" he asked.

"I haven't told anyone," she said in a ragged voice.

"Last night you made me face things I didn't want to face. And this morning I felt better."

"What happened to me was . . . bad."

"I know." He wanted to reach for her, take her in his arms. He kept his hands flat against the mattress.

"Four of them caught me," she choked out. "And they dragged me into the old tool shed."

She told him things, then, that he didn't want to hear, things that made bile rise in his throat, though he listened until she was finished, until she began to weep, until he wept with her. Finally, when he couldn't stand it any longer and reached for her, she slid away. When he called her name, she slipped out of the room.

And he was left alone on the bed with only his troubled thoughts for company. He had come to this place feeling sorry for himself, for what he had endured. But his wounds were of the flesh. Hers were of the soul.

Still, she had summoned the courage to tell him her secrets. He would do the same. If she was still there in the morning.

As tired as he was from his work in the fields, Link remained awake for a long while before sleep finally claimed him.

To his surprise and vast relief, he found Kasi the next morning, sitting at the table in the galley. Her eyes were red, as if she'd spent the whole night crying, and her hands were clenched tightly in front of her.

But she was there.

He propped his hips against the counter, meeting her gaze with a steadiness that belied the pounding of his heart.

"So what do you think of me now?" she asked. "Kasimanda of Renfaral. The woman who served four Dorre soldiers against her will."

The calmness of her voice frightened him. He sensed he could lose her with a single wrong word. "I think you're as brave as any war hero, Dorre or Farlian," he answered from the depths of his heart. "Brave enough to keep going after you lost your whole family. Brave enough to go through what must have been hell to get yourself here. Brave enough to face me and my anger, and to take care of my leg, when I know what you *wanted* to do was run away."

She stared at him as if she couldn't believe the appraisal.

He ran a shaky hand through his hair, and fear made his words come out stiffly. "Kasi, when I first saw you here, I couldn't face what I felt. That's why I acted angry. I was terrified that you were going to hurt me."

Her lips parted, and her huge, gorgeous eyes opened wide in astonishment. "Me? Hurt *you*?"

"Oh, yes. The way you did that night seven years ago when you ran away from me in the garden." He swallowed, tried to gather some courage of his own to match hers. "Kasi, I have loved you since I was ten. A crazy, hopeless love. But now—" He gave a little laugh. "Now I guess I'm willing to wait for you until I'm a hundred, if that's what it takes."

Wildly conflicting emotions chased across her features.

"No pressure," he said, relieved that he had finally confessed the truth. "No demands or requests. No real expectations." He was lying, of course. Through his teeth. He had expectations, all right, enough to last several lifetimes.

Turning so that she couldn't see his face, he poured himself a mug of coffee. Then, without another word or even a glance in her direction, he grabbed a grain cake and headed for the fields.

She was waiting for him when he came in for dinner. While they ate the food she had prepared, they talked quietly about growing rokam and about the supplies she needed for the house.

He made his first wordless request when they were reclining on wide loungers beside the empty swimming pool. Moving his leg, he gave a small groan.

Her head swung quickly toward him. "Is it bad?"

He shrugged elaborately.

"You need more of the salve."

"I think you're right." He considered his options—his bedroom where she would be nervous, or out here where he would feel defenseless without his prosthesis. He chose her comfort. "We could use the lounger."

"Yes," she answered on a rush of breath that told him he'd made the right choice.

Still, his gaze slid away from her as he pictured himself taking off the leg. He wasn't ready to do *that* in front of her. Standing, he steadied himself against the wall. "I'll be back in a minute."

The sun had set by the time he returned. Overhead, stars winked in the black velvet of the sky, and the smallest of the four moons cast a blue radiance on the fields beyond the house.

He looked around anxiously for Kasi, afraid that she might have changed her mind. Then she moved, a shadow detaching itself from the wall of the house, and he watched her silhouette glide toward him. She was tall like most Farlian women, almost his height. But the blue light gave her a fragile, indistinct look. Long ago she had told him how things appeared to her in the moonlight. To her radiation-sensitive eyes, the light was soft and pink, giving objects a warmth he couldn't see.

Wearing a pair of short pants, with the folding crutch replacing his prosthesis, he limped slowly toward the lounger. He was rather amazed with himself, that he'd let her see him this way. But then, he decided, maybe it gave him an advantage.

The twisted logic brought a low chuckle to his lips.

"What's funny?" she inquired.

"I was thinking—how frightened can you be of a cripple?"

"Link, I can't think of you as crippled."

He snorted, disbelieving.

"You're a war hero."

"I'm no hero," he denied.

"Do they give rich holdings like this one to all the troopers?"

"No. But they knew my father was training me to run an estate, so they figured I had a better chance at producing rokam for them than some store clerk."

"It was more than that. They knew you had the will to succeed."

There was no point in arguing, he thought as he eased onto the cushioned lounger. Neither of them spoke as she sat on the edge of it and began to rub the healing medicine into his injured flesh. It wasn't long before her innocent caresses once again made his body grow hard.

He felt her touch falter, heard her breath catch.

He lay very still with his eyes closed and his arms at his sides, his fists clenched. And when he made no move to reach for her, she kept up her ministration.

"Thank you," he whispered, when she had finished. "Kasi, you've changed my life with that salve—given me new hope. But I'm not good at speaking the things in my heart. Words aren't enough. I can't tell you how I feel unless I touch you."

He heard her breath catch and went on quickly. "I'll keep my hands flat on the cushions. I just . . . I just want to kiss you. On the cheek."

She didn't draw back as he pushed himself up and brushed a whisper-soft kiss against her tender flesh. When she stayed where she was, he stroked his way down to her jaw line, then back up to the corner of her eye. He felt a little shiver go through her.

He turned his head, moved his mouth gently against her lashes, feeling them flutter at the touch, feeling his own body tighten painfully in response.

He wanted more, but he was ready to deny himself further pleasure. "Thank you." He drew away from her, but she stayed where she was, her eyes closed.

"Would you . . . do it again?" she whispered, her voice shaky.

"Yes," he breathed. "Oh, yes." This time he nibbled gently at her neck, feeling her skin heat and her breath grow thready, and he had to grip the lounger beneath him to keep from reaching for her. Raising his head, he planted small kisses on her chin and cheeks. Her lips were moist and parted. He wanted to devour them. Instead he stroked the curve of one beautiful brow.

"Link." His name was a breathy sigh. For long moments she sat very quietly, then tipped her face toward him. "Do you know, no man has kissed me on the mouth," she whispered.

He felt something catch in his throat.

"If you kiss me the way men and women kiss, it will belong only to the two of us."

He couldn't speak, could only nod as she slid millimeters closer to him. He kept his hands at his sides, leaning forward until his mouth touched hers.

He felt the tension in her. Slowly he brushed his mouth back and forth against hers, increasing the pressure by slow degrees, until her lips were sealed to his.

Heat leaped inside him as he felt the yielding softness of her, heard the low, purring sound in her throat. Yet he kept his hands where they were, the only contact point his mouth on hers as he opened her lips and gently probed the warmth and softness beyond.

When he lifted his head, her breath was ragged, and her eyes were soft and pleading.

"I want . . ." she whispered, the sentence trailing off.

"Anything," he answered, offering her his soul.

"I'm afraid of what I want."

"You don't have to be afraid. Not with me."

"I know. At least, part of me knows. The other part is terrified that you'll grab me and . . ."

"I won't."

"How do I know?"

"Because a man doesn't get any more aroused than I am right now," he said. "But the part of me that frightens you doesn't control my actions. My brain does. And my brain knows that anything worth doing with you is worth waiting for."

Her gaze went to his face, searching. He kept his own gaze steady.

She laid her head against his shoulder, and they sat silently in the darkness.

When she began to speak, her voice was wispy. "Do you remember the day I put my pet palistan in a boat and it drifted out into the lake?"

"I found you standing on the shore crying," he answered thickly.

"And you jumped in and towed the boat back to me. Your father came along and found you all wet, and you got a whipping."

He nodded, remembering.

"That was the day I fell in love with you," she breathed.

He stared at her, wondering if he'd heard correctly. *She loved him?*

"Until then you were just the big boy who was the leader of all the young people on the estate. That day, I lost my heart to you."

He started to reach for her, and her lower lip trembled though her eyes were soft and warm. Then her expression suddenly changed to deep alarm.

"What? Did I frighten you?"

"No. I saw something."

He turned, looked in the same direction, detected nothing but the blue moonlight on the stark hills. "What?"

"A man."

"Are you sure?"

"Yes." Her gaze stayed trained on the rise of ground as she sucked in a little breath. "Two men. Three. Dorre. Crouching, using the rocks for cover."

"How do you know they're Dorre?"

"By the way they're moving. They can't see where to put their feet. But they have weapons. A lot of weapons."

He swore under his breath, snapping into combat mode, his training taking over. The intruders weren't walking up to the front door. They were approaching by stealth, at night. Probably they were deserters, desperate men who wouldn't take prisoners.

"I guess they aren't here to beg food rations," he said aloud.

"What are we going to do?" she asked, the question coming out in a thin gasp, and he knew she was remembering what the soldiers had done to her.

"Make them wish they'd sneaked up on someone else."

"What if you can't?"

His hand closed over her wrist, feeling the blood thundering in her veins. "I will *not* let them get anywhere near you," he swore.

She sat still as a statue. He watched her rigid features and knew her terror might swallow her whole.

"Kasi, trust me to keep you safe."

At first he wondered if she were capable even of hearing his words. Then her shoulders straightened, and she raised her face to his. He saw the effort she was making to push away the terror and knew she was doing it for him as much as for herself.

Turning, she looked toward the intruders, then spoke with a detached, steely calm. "They have night viewers. But they haven't spotted us."

"Good." He gave her hand a quick squeeze. "Kasi, you're going to have to get my leg. And the laser pistol on the bed stand. I'll meet you in the computer room."

She nodded, darted into the building. Grabbing the crutch, he followed as fast as he could.

In the nerve center of the house, he scanned the alarms. Nothing. The intruders were too far away. They might have been there for days, watching, planning their move. If he got Kasi and himself out of this alive, he'd have to booby trap the hills.

If.

Bringing his mind back to the crisis, he activated the long-range scanners. He was rewarded by three sensor readings on the view screen. Three Dorre men, as she'd said, and they were moving this way.

Kasi came in with the prosthesis. It hurt to put the damned thing on so soon after he'd taken it off, but he ignored the pain, grateful that he could walk almost normally.

He kept his eye on the scanner. The raiding party had stopped. They must know he'd armed a protective ring around the house and the fields. Did they have torpedo launchers?

"I need them closer," he muttered.

"I know how to do that," she said with the same quiet calm that she'd summoned on the patio.

His head jerked toward her. "No!"

Ignoring the protest, she went on. "I can go outside—pretend I'm trespassing on the property. They'll jump at the chance to get their hands on me."

He stared at her, astonished. "Don't even think about it!"

"Do you have a better idea?" she asked, her voice remarkably steady.

He tried to think of one. Spenserville might send help. But he couldn't count on that—or on reinforcements coming in time. He looked in the weapons locker again. He had his own portable torpedo launchers. Not the most desirable of weapons, particularly since he'd bought them when he was almost out of money. He'd settled for the older models that the high command had taken out of service. Too bad he hadn't had a chance to test them.

Cursing under his breath, he thought about the tricky procedure for setting them up. He'd have to do it outside where the explosive gases couldn't collect. If he used a light, the intruders would see what he was doing. If he tried to work in the dark, he could blow himself up.

He raised his gaze to Kasi's. "I can't risk a light. If I tell you what to do, could you set up a torpedo launcher?"

She managed a little nod.

He pulled out the heavy case, opened it, and showed her the parts that had to fit together. Then he closed the carrier again and hoisted it to his shoulder. Outside, he picked a patch of ground partly screened by bushes.

He didn't tell her the danger of an accidental explosion. Instead, he explained each step while she fitted the parts together, her white fingers moving in the moonlight as she fit the launcher into the tripod and went through the check sequence. Holding his breath, he lifted a missile from the case and helped her guide it into the tube. Then he attached the computer cable. With a silent prayer, he pressed the activation button.

For heartbeats, nothing happened, and he thought it had all been for nothing. Then the screen flickered to life. As he tuned the probe, the same three blips he'd seen earlier came into focus.

A hissing noise overhead was followed by an explosion to the right. The slat-eaters were using rockets. Less sophisticated than computer-guided torpedoes—but just as lethal when they hit their target.

Kasi screamed as dirt and plant debris flew through the air. Link pushed her to the ground and worked the controls, adjusting the targeting. There was no time for fine-tuning, he realized as another explosion took off the roof above his left shoulder. All he could do was press the launch button and watch as the torpedo streaked into the sky.

The explosion was a lot more powerful than the previous two. The ground shook, and the night itself seemed to explode. Then, suddenly, everything went silent. He raised his head and looked at the targeting screen. Where the three blips had been there was only a concave depression—a crater twenty meters across.

It was over. The intruders were dead, and he'd killed them. His own people. At least he'd been spared from having to look into their eyes.

Beside him, Kasi whimpered, and when she raised her head, he saw blood seeping from a long gash on her temple.

"Damn the bastards!" he exclaimed, quickly moving to assess the extent of her injury.

"I'm all right," she told him, then slumped against his shoulder in a dead faint.

He managed to lift her, managed to carry her into the house without the leg giving way. His bed was the closest place he could lay her. Turning on the light, he examined the wound. It looked as if she'd been hit by a flying chunk of the building. Quickly he soaked a towel in water and cleaned the blood away—and sighed in relief when he saw that the cut wasn't deep. While he was dabbing on an antibacterial, her eyelids flickered open. She seemed confused for a moment. Then her beautiful green eyes focused on him.

"Did we stop them?" she whispered.

He nodded, captured by her gaze. "Yes. I thought I was through with killing, but. . . ." He drew a ragged breath. "Kasi, I'll do whatever it takes to keep you safe."

"We did what we had to," she answered, her gaze steady as it met his.

He had thought he knew her strength, but he realized he'd only scratched the surface. "You have more courage then half the men in my patrol."

She gave a little shrug. "I wanted us to be the ones who survived."

His throat ached as he found her hand and clasped it. "Yes. Us."

Her fingers tightened on his. "Stay with me."

"Here? In my bed?"

She tried to nod and winced. "Yes."

"You're sure?"

"Yes." This time the answer was stronger.

He turned off all but the small light in the corner and unstrapped the plastic leg before easing onto the bed. He planned to stay awake in case she needed him, but he was too exhausted to manage it.

When his eyes opened again, he could see a faint glow in the western sky. Kasi was awake.

"How are you?" he asked softly.

"Better," she said, her gaze fixed on the wall across the room. When she offered no more, he lay beside her in the big bed, listening to the thumping of his heart.

After a long time, she began to speak in a barely audible voice. "At first, I was afraid to tell you what happened to me. I was afraid you wouldn't want me here, in your home, if you knew."

"I hope, by now, you've figured out you were wrong." He turned toward her, his urgent gaze catching hers, holding. "I want you. For my wife. If you'll have me."

Tears gathered in her eyes. "Your wife?"

He nodded, but when he spoke, he couldn't quite keep the anxiety out of his voice. "Will you? Would you marry a Dorre?"

"Link . . ." She smiled. "I would follow you to the end of the world." With a laugh, she added, "I *did* follow you to the end of the world. But what if . . . if I can't . . ."

The question went unfinished, but he knew what she was asking.

"I want to know you're mine," he assured her. "On any terms I can get you."

"Oh, Link."

"Say yes."

He saw her even white teeth clamp her bottom lip.

"Say yes," he urged again. "We'll worry about the rest later."

"I can't . . . not until . . ." She swallowed audibly. "I want to . . . to love you. Your body joined with mine."

The words might be halting, but the look in her eyes told him she would only surrender on her own terms.

"I need to do everything—give you everything," she continued. "And I want to do it now."

"We will. But we don't have to do it *all* today," he answered, wishing she didn't have to push herself—or him.

"What are you afraid of?" she suddenly asked, and he knew she had read the hesitation in his expression.

He managed a rough laugh. "Not much, except that I haven't been with a woman since . . . the leg. It could make things a little awkward."

"Oh," she answered in a breathy whisper, and he knew that his doubts gave her a measure of confidence. Good. Score another one for the damned stump.

He turned toward her, gently stroking his knuckle across her lips, looking into her trusting but anxious face. "You're sure you want to do this?"

"Don't you?"

"Only if you make me a promise—that you'll tell me if I do anything that frightens you."

"I promise."

He kissed her tenderly, then drew back and deliberately began to open the fasteners down the front of her tunic, watching her face, ready to call a halt.

She said nothing, but he saw the edge of panic in her eyes.

"Does it worry you when I reach for you, with my hands?"

"Yes."

"Then I'll show you how much pleasure I can give you with just my mouth."

Dipping his head, he kissed her neck, then the slender ridges of her collar bone, before edging toward the tops of her breasts.

Delicately he pushed the fabric of the tunic apart with his face, his kisses gliding over the soft warmth of her breasts until he captured one distended nipple between his lips.

She made a strangled sound, and her hands came up to cradle his head and hold him to her as he took his pleasure and gave it back to her in kind.

He kept the pace easy, demanding nothing of her. Between kisses, he talked to her quietly, ardently, as he stoked the fires of her arousal—first with his lips and then with only the lightest of fingertip strokes.

Her body was long and lithe and so beautiful. He could barely breathe as he watched arousal bring a warm flush to her pale skin.

Aroused or not, when his hand drifted over the soft curve of her abdomen, downward to the triangle of fiery hair that covered her mound, she stiffened.

"Okay?"

Her face was tense.

"It's all right. We can stop any time you want," he promised, his words denying the clamoring of his body.

"I'm scared, but I don't want to stop."

"Good. Because I'm just going to touch you," he murmured. "Just my hand, stroking you, making you feel good."

"Yes . . . I already feel . . ."

"How?"

"Like a kriver flying too close to the sun."

"I promise, I'm not going to let you get burned."

"I know." Still, the breath hissed out of her, and she squeezed her eyes shut as his fingers slid downward, parting her silky folds and stroking her soft, sensitive flesh.

She was hot and wet to his touch, and he made a low sound of appreciation as he dipped one finger into her, moving his hand to give her maximum pleasure.

"That's good. So good," she gasped.

"Yes, love. Yes."

She was panting, rocking against him, and he whispered low, encouraging words while he pushed her higher, closer to climax, until all at once he felt her body go tense and ripples of sensation beat against his hand as she cried out his name.

He cradled her against him, feeling the aftershocks flicker through her. Gently he tipped her head up so that he could brush his lips against hers, seeing the wonder in her eyes.

"I didn't think I could let you get that close to me," she whispered.

"But you did. And it was . . ."

"A trip to the center of the sun—and back."

He smiled down at her, glad that she had given him her trust. Yet it was impossible to completely hide the tension still gripping him.

She drew back, studying his face. Then, in a rush, she slid her hand down and found his erection. When she moved her palm against him, he couldn't hold back a shuddering gasp.

"We need to do something about this thing that's had me so worried," she whispered.

He gave a short laugh. "If you keep your hand there, it'll take care of itself."

She raised her head and searched his eyes. "Is that what you want?"

He thought about lying. Instead, he shook his head. "Not if I have a choice."

"Then what should I do?"

"Nothing complicated. Just let me kiss and touch you some more."

"But . . . I think I'm having most of the fun."

He chuckled. "I guess you don't know what a man in love considers fun." Leaning down, he nuzzled his lips against her breast. "The thing I want most," he breathed against her skin, "is to give you as much pleasure as I can, because my pleasure is tied to yours."

"Then we'll fly to the sun together," she whispered, her heartfelt tone making his throat ache.

Gently, he pulled the tunic off her shoulders, freed her arms from the sleeves.

"So beautiful," he breathed, as he looked down at her slender body before kissing her bare shoulders and working his way slowly down her body.

He kindled her need once more with his lips and hands. And when he knew he would die if he didn't feel her silky skin pressed to his, he dragged off his pants and eased her on top of him, his hands on her back, moving her against him as he rained kisses over her face. She was wet and slick for him again, and she made tiny noises in her throat as she moved against the swollen length of him.

"Raise your hips a little. Let me . . ."

A high sound escaped her throat as he eased himself halfway inside her. Going absolutely still, he watched her closely, steeling himself to stop. But she gave him a tremulous smile, and the smile turned to triumph as she tilted her hips and took him deep inside. For a trembling moment she looked overwhelmed. Then she began to move again, slowly at first, then driving in a frantic rhythm that captured him, sent him up and up toward the heavens, into the heat of the sun. His shout of satisfaction mingled with her cries as she followed him into the heart of the fire.

His arms went around her, clasping her tightly, holding her to him, knowing that he would never let her go.

When she raised her head, her eyes were shimmering. "Thank you. Not just for the pleasure. For the healing."

His throat was so tight that he could only answer with a nod.

She slipped down beside him, cuddled against him, and his arm came up to cradle her close.

"So now you can't back out on the marriage part," he said, more gruffly than he intended. "We can do it over the comm lines, with the records office in Spenserville."

"Rushing me into a signed contract?"

"Before you have time for second thoughts."

"You've already had my second thought—and third and fourth and countless others," she murmured. "I remember when my father sat me down and explained why I had to stop following you around. Until then, I didn't understand much about 'proper relations' between Farlians and Dorre. But my father made it very clear." She sighed. "Still, I couldn't stay away from you. That night when you found me in the garden, I ached to tell you to wait for me, so we could go off and be alone. I ached to be with you—to do all the things my father told me I could never do until I was married to a man of the proper rank—and race. But I understood that being with you would only make things impossible for both of us if anyone found out. So I walked away. Now I know what I was giving up."

"Oh, Kasi."

"After the soldiers—" Her voice hitched. "After the soldiers, I thought I could never let a man touch me again. But then, I started imagining someone holding me in his arms, comforting me, making me feel whole again—and the man was always you. Never anyone but you. So that's your answer. Yes, I want to marry you. I want to know you belong to me."

"Always," he breathed before kissing her, a long, sweet kiss of longing and wishes fulfilled.

When it was over, he looked down at her and vowed, "From now on, this place belongs to both of us. It's *our* home. And I'm going to keep you safe here." Then his face contorted. "But I've got to figure out where to get the money to buy more defenses."

She gave him an uncertain look. "Maybe we don't need more money. Maybe we just need more people."

His eyebrows drew together in a puzzled frown as he watched her eyes take on an excited glow.

"When I saw the estate," she said, "I started dreaming—about refugees living here. Orphans, Dorre and Farlians who've lost their homes. And good people who could make a community where all of us would be safe." She stopped, flushed as she anxiously studied his face. "Maybe it's a bad idea."

"No!" With the adrenaline of excitement flooding his veins and his mind suddenly alive with ideas, he said, "It's a wonderful idea! You're right—children will accept people for what they are. And maybe some of the men I met in the hospital will want to join us. Men who never want another war. I'll send for a few of them first so we'll have a defensive force."

She gave him a tremulous smile that touched him to the depths of his soul.

"The war was a horrible thing," he said thickly. "But it brought you to me."

Wordlessly, she nodded.

He pulled her close. "I came here not caring whether I lived or died. Now, I'm going to thank Atherdan for every day I have with you—and for every day we can make a difference, at least, in our little corner off this damned, screwed up planet."

She stroked his damp hair back from his forehead. "Oh, Link, I know why I fell in love with you. You've always had vision and courage. You were a leader even when you were a boy."

"I forgot who I was," he muttered. "But you've made me remember."

And he clasped her tightly, the most precious thing in a world that had turned, overnight, from dark to light.

"The Better Man"
by
Mallory Kane

Camp Douglas Union Prison, Chicago, June 1864

It was always the same. First came the pain. Old pain, new pain, sharp enough to suck his breath, dull and never-ending. Then the stink of vomit and the smell of death.

Prison. He was a prisoner in hell, more commonly known as a Union prison camp. His only respite was sleep. When he slept, he dreamed about home. About happy childhood times before the war. About Christianne. But then, all too soon he would awaken, and when he did, the pain was there. Pain in his shoulders, wrenched so many times he could hardly move them, and in his back, striped with scars from the lash. Pain in his gut, from the swill they fed him, when they remembered to feed him at all.

But mostly, pain in his heart. A pain far, far worse than the physical pain, because he didn't think even death would free him from the guilt and the grief.

"Jared?"

He cringed involuntarily, expecting a blow or a kick or a dousing of cold, filthy water. But none of the guards called him Jared. Something stirred inside him, something he didn't quite recognize.

"Jared." The voice cut the still, chilly air.

Careful of the new cuts on his back, he got his hands under him and struggled to his knees, still wary, still expecting the whoosh of fetid air and the crack that preceded the awful sting of the lash.

He pushed a hand through his matted hair and wiped his face, cursing God for letting him live another day.

"Jared?"

He froze. The first time, even the second, he'd believed he was dreaming the voice. But with its third repetition, his chest contracted in agony, his throat clogged with an emotion he couldn't name. He forced his cracked lips to form words. "Wh-who are you? Where—" His voice failed.

"Out here."

He squinted up at the tiny opening two feet above his head, then glanced toward the door to his cell. "Who . . ."

"Jared, it's me. You've got to listen."

"R-Robbie?" Jared squeezed his eyes shut. The thing in his throat was choking him, and he couldn't deny it any longer.

It was hope. He inhaled, and his breath caught at the top like a sob. "Robbie." His brother. "How'd you—"

"Find you?" the voice floated through the little opening on a laugh. "It wasn't easy."

Jared squeezed his temples between his hands, fighting to stay in control. A violent shudder shook him. God, he was about to cry like a kid. "Robbie," he whispered, "get away. They'll capture you."

"Nah, they won't. Trust me."

That was Robbie. If Jared could have remembered how, he'd have smiled. Robbie, his older brother. Always the same, sure of himself, on top of things. Always pulling his kid brother out of trouble.

"Jared? Listen to me, okay? We've got to get you out of there."

Jared stood, or tried to. His knees buckled, and darkness edged his vision. He put a hand out, steadying himself against the wall. "I can't, Robbie. Too . . . far gone."

"Hey, kid, what have I always told you?"

Jared nodded slightly. *There's no such word as can't.* "Not this time, Rob. Too late." God, he couldn't even find the strength to talk to his brother. He clenched his fist against the trembling. "Get on back home to Christianne. Tell her I love . . . tell everybody I love 'em."

"No way, kid. Come on. We've got a few hours before dawn. If you'll get a move on, we'll have you out of there before the guards come. Or are you enjoying the accommodations too much to leave?"

Jared made a noise. "No thanks," he croaked. Hope kept sucker-punching him. "I can't leave my men, Rob." He stood, clawing at the wall to remain on his feet.

"Jared, concentrate. Listen to me. Your men are all dead. Remember? Last week they killed Cade Thornton, right in front of you."

"Cade." The memories slammed into him, harder than the guard's boot in his ribs. "They're coming to get me this morning." He coughed, fighting for breath, and wiped sweat off his face.

"That's right, kid. Now, come on. Let's get you out. Do you see that chink in the lock, where someone tried to gouge the wood around it?"

Jared stumbled over to the door. Each step increased the dizziness and pounding in his head. He rubbed his eyes and tried to focus on the lock. "Yeah. Somebody spent a long time working at it. Wonder what they used?"

"Fingernails. See if you can get your fingers between the metal and the wood."

Jared propped one hand against the door and dug with the other. "Can't. Too narrow."

"Try harder."

Raw frustration blurred his eyes. "Damn it, Rob," he yelled, then clamped his jaw shut. "Just because *you* can do anything . . . Why don't you come in here and help me?"

"Why don't you quit grousing and get it done?"

Hot anger washed over him. What a pain in the butt Rob was. He growled and forced his fingers into a narrow crevice two times too small for them. He gritted his teeth, sweat pouring down his face. He strained his screaming shoulders, pushed and pulled with raw, bleeding fingers. And finally, with a huge groan, the metal gave way.

"All right, kid! That's it. Now work it, back and forth, until the metal breaks."

"What're you . . . doing out there . . . that you can't . . . help? Having . . . a party?" Jared punctuated his questions with grunts as he worked the twisted metal back and forth. Suddenly, it gave, and the door creaked open.

"I'll be damned. You were right." He stared at the opening, his legs shaky, his head spinning, his belly cramping with nausea.

"Told you."

"Shut up, Rob," he muttered. Slowly, both because of caution and dizziness, Jared stepped through the narrow opening. His feet touched wood, slightly cleaner than the straw-covered dirt of his cell, and he realized he was barefoot.

He looked down. His breeches hung on his hipbones. His shirt draped across his shoulders in bloody tatters.

"Well, Colonel Payton, you are not looking your best."

Jared wiped a sleeve across his forehead and leaned against the wall. "Give me a minute," he whispered.

A couple of deep breaths helped, but he knew he was sick. He was feverish, and something as heavy as an anvil sat on his chest. He stared at the door in front of him for several long moments before he could dredge up the strength to push it open.

Outside, in the cold, fresh, night air, Jared's resolve almost failed him. He sank to his knees and wiped his hands on clean, damp grass, then brought them to his face, cooling his skin. God, when had he last been outside? Hot tears mixed with cool dew on his cheeks.

"Jared!"

He looked up. Robbie was astride a chestnut gelding, with a white-stockinged bay beside him. He was pale as a specter in the moonlight. His eyes were sunken, his big frame gaunt.

"Rob, you look awful."

Robbie grinned. "Not as bad as you, I'd wager. You're a stick, your beard and hair look like a rat's nest, and you stink to high heaven. Now climb up. We don't have time to waste."

Jared sighed as he eyed the horse. "Hate to tell you this, big brother, but . . ." He took a long breath and coughed. "I'm not sure I can."

"I'm holding him, kid. Come on."

Jared pulled himself onto the horse's back. For a moment he slouched over the saddle horn, until his shoulders quit throbbing and the nausea abated. Several of the worst cuts on his back had opened up. The trickle of blood and sweat stung.

"All right. Let's ride."

"Rob, hold up. Not so fast. I'm . . . a little weak."

"Know what you mean, kid. I've not felt my best in quite a while. But we've got to make time while it's still dark. You just hang on."

And hang on Jared did, barely, as Robbie grabbed the bay's reins and spurred his horse. They raced through the trees and brush, over rocks and hills. Jared concentrated on staying in the saddle and let Rob lead them. The flying hooves seemed barely to touch ground.

A long time later, the horses changed pace, and Jared roused himself. He'd been less than half-conscious for most of the journey. Dreaming about home.

As the horses slowed, he unwrapped his cramped hands from the saddle horn and relaxed his thighs, only to regret it as the blood began to flow back into his lower legs. The horses settled into a rolling walk. The bay drew up alongside the chestnut gelding.

"How . . . long 'til light?" Jared asked.

Rob glanced up at the sky. "We've got a while yet."

"Thirsty . . ." Jared croaked.

His brother swung a canteen by the strap, and he caught it. He drank deeply, and poured water over his face, then held it out to Rob.

Rob shook his head, so he hung it on his own saddle. He coughed convulsively. He was so tired.

"Rob, remember the time you and me and Christianne got caught busting up watermelons? I haven't had a watermelon in so long."

"Rest, kid." Rob's voice echoed in his head, soothing him.

"Jared."

It was always the same. First came the pain. Old pain, new pain, sharp enough to suck his breath, dull and never-ending. The smell of cool, fresh air. Jared tensed, then opened his eyes. Robbie rode beside him, watching him with an odd intensity.

"Robbie," Jared breathed. "I thought I was dreaming. I've dreamed about you a lot, wondered how you were doing, whether you'd gotten home."

Rob nodded. "I know what you mean, kid. I've dreamed about you a lot too. So how're you feeling?"

Jared stretched gingerly. "Better. How long 'til dawn?"

Rob grinned, shaking off his strange mood. "We got plenty of time. In fact, I think we can stop for a while, over there." He guided the horses to the edge of a creek and dismounted.

Jared sank to his knees next to the water. "Don't suppose you have a razor?" he asked, eyeing his reflection.

"Nope. Wish I did, though. I'd like to see that face of yours again before . . ."

"Before what?"

But Rob just turned on his heel.

By the time Jared finished washing, Rob had a small fire going, and the smell of coffee filled the air.

Jared watched his older brother fill a tin cup. His movements were stiff, his concentration on his task intense. Jared had never seen him like that. Things always came easy for Rob.

"Need some help?" he asked softly.

Rob's head jerked negatively, but he never took his eyes off the cup. Jared reached out, but Rob ignored him and set the cup on the ground within easy reach. Jared picked it up, savoring the warmth that seeped into his fingers. The hot liquid soothed him.

"Damn, that's good. Do you know how long it's been since I had anything hot? Aren't you having any?"

"Already did," Rob said shortly, then looked up at the sky. "We should be off soon."

Jared glanced upward, but he couldn't see any difference in the heavens. "How far do you think we are from home?"

"Home." Rob stared into the tiny fire. "You're probably less than a hundred miles."

"That close." Jared shook his head. "Hard to believe. I can't wait." Sky blue eyes and wavy brown hair rose in his vision. "You heard from . . . anybody lately?" He took a last huge gulp of coffee and held out the cup.

"Nah." Rob carefully picked up the pot and poured. His face turned white with effort.

"You're injured," he said, suddenly realizing what Rob's strange actions meant.

Rob grunted. "I was. Better now."

"How did you know? Where to find me, I mean?"

Rob shrugged, his gaze on the fire. He held out one hand, as if reaching for the warmth. "People talk. Someone saw your last stand. It was worth a try."

Jared stretched cautiously, still careful of the wounds on his back. He felt a bit better, not so feverish. Maybe it was the coffee. "Well, thanks. I mean, here you are, rescuing me again."

Rob laughed. "It could be a full time job." His voice held a note of indulgence. "I'd do it every day."

Jared nodded. "I know. My big brother. Always the same. I always could depend on you."

A minute of silence passed.

"It'll be great to be home, won't it?" Jared said. "I mean, how much longer can the war go on, anyhow?"

Rob's lips compressed briefly, then he said, "It'll be over in April."

"April? What are you talking about? That's the best part of a year away. "Anything can happen between now and then."

"Yeah. Well, you just mark my words, kid."

"Want to place a wager?"

Rob smiled and shook his head. "No. You'd be making a sucker's bet. I don't want to take advantage of a kid."

"You polecat. You're just scared you'll lose." Jared grinned for the first time in months. It felt good to be here with his brother, just like when they were kids. He thought about those days, and his thoughts flowed over the years, over the death of their mother, over their growing up, and inevitably to Christianne.

Christianne laughing. Running across the yard. Sniffing the bouquet of flowers he'd picked for her. Tears shimmering in her pretty blue eyes as she gently told him she was going to marry his brother. He frowned.

"How do you think they are?" he said, sitting up. He flexed his sore shoulders gingerly and finished his coffee, tossing the dregs aside. "Rob?"

"Sorry, kid. What'd you say?"

"I said, how do you think they're doing at home?"

Rob shot him only a quick glance, but it was long enough for Jared to see the faintly horrified look in his eyes. "I, uh, I'm sure they're fine. I know they're worried about you."

"And you. . . . Robbie?"

"Yeah?"

"There's something I need to tell you. Something that's weighed on my mind for a long time."

"Nah, you save your strength for riding. Come on. We've still got a bit of darkness left." Rob stood and kicked dirt onto the fire. His movements were awkward and jerky.

"You sure you're okay?" Jared asked.

"Sure, I'm fine. Let's get a move on, kid."

Jared looked around, then up at the sky. "Feels like we've been here for hours. It must be nearly dawn."

Rob didn't respond, just mounted his horse.

Jared did the best he could, but he was slow; by the time he'd mounted, he was limp with fatigue. Rob nagged him to stay awake, though, until they were back on the road, making their way south and east, toward home.

The night was eerily quiet and clear, the silence broken only by their horse's hooves and the occasional screech of an owl. Jared realized that Rob was deliberately leading his horse at an easier pace than before, and he had less trouble staying on.

"What is this road? We haven't passed a soul."

Rob kept his eyes on the road ahead. "We've been lucky."

Something wasn't right. Jared knew he was sick and exhausted, but his sense of time wasn't that distorted, was it? They'd been riding for many hours, but the sky was still dark. They were on a well-traveled road, but they'd seen no one. "What's going on, Robbie? Where are we?"

"You're on your way home, kid. Now, pick up the pace. We've still got a ways to go."

Jared rode, his gaunt frame rolling in the saddle, matching the horse's pace. He felt his fever rise again, and he knew he couldn't stay awake. His head nodded.

Sometime later, he roused, realizing gradually that he must have blacked out. Rob had the bay's reins, leading him again.

"How long 'til dawn?" he asked, his voice little more than a croaky whisper.

His brother didn't look around. "A while yet."

Jared clamped his jaw on an angry retort. He should be grateful for the continued darkness, but he knew there was something mixed up about his sense of time. After a while, he spoke again. "I was serious before. I need to get something off my chest."

Rob coaxed the bay up even with his horse, and tossed him the reins. "Kid, if you're going to confess to breaking my knife when you were eleven, I already know. You lied about it to Pa."

Jared smiled, remembering. "And you beat the hell out of me." Then he sobered. "No, that's not it. It's about Christianne."

Rob's eyes went dull. He frowned and looked away. "What about her?"

Jared ran a hand over his face. He was still burning with fever. "I don't want to lie to you, but I don't want you to hate me. I swear, I never have and never will do anything about it."

"Hell, Jared. Never done anything about what? Get to the point, will you?"

Jared swiped again at the sweat pouring down his face. Damned fever. "I love her, Rob. I always have. Ever since we were kids. When we were ten, I asked her to marry me. But she always loved you. Makes sense if you think about it. But in case anything happens, I need you to know . . ." He stopped, exhausted. After a minute, he continued. "I kissed her, Rob. I kissed Chrissy."

Rob reached over and grabbed the reins of the bay, pulling both their horses to a halt, then turning in the saddle to look at him. Jared met his brother's gaze directly, feeling the intensity of it despite the darkness.

Despair and self-loathing overwhelmed him. "I'm sorry, Rob. It was a long time ago, before you two were engaged. Chrissy and I were eleven, and you were fourteen." He shook his head. "Don't worry. I think she loved you even then. She got the better man."

"But you love her? *Really* love her?"

Jared held up a hand. "Listen, I know you could beat me all to hell in a fight, even if I wasn't sick. I swear, I never did anything else. Just leave it be, okay? I'd never hurt you or her."

Rob closed his eyes for a moment.

Jared watched him, frowning. "Rob? You okay?"

"Yeah, I'm okay," he said.

But Jared watched in puzzled shock as Rob yanked the glove off his left hand with his teeth, then slid the wedding band off his finger.

"Here, kid," he said raggedly. "Hang on to this for me." He tossed the ring.

Jared caught it in mid-air. The metal felt icy cold against his palm.

"And promise me something."

"Sure, but—"

"Take care of her, okay?"

"But, Rob—"

Rob held up his bare hand. "Just promise me. She's going to need you. Keep her safe."

"I promise." Jared took a deep breath. "But, Rob—"

"Now, stop yammering. We've got a lot of miles to cover." Rob turned loose the bay's reins and urged his horse into a trot.

Jared opened his palm and looked at the wedding band. He slid it onto the middle finger of his right hand, smiling wryly. Rob had always been bigger than him, though they were nearly the same height. But as their father always used to say, he was wiry, and after starving in prison for months, he couldn't even be sure the ring would stay on. He tore a strip of cloth from his tattered shirt and wrapped the ring in it, then tore a thinner strip to secure the small bundle. He stuck it in the inner pocket of his pants.

They rode for hours without speaking. Jared slept fitfully, his body unconsciously adjusting to the horse's pace. His fever grew worse, and it became more and more difficult to stay in the saddle. But Rob urged him onward, promising him it was just a few more miles.

Finally, after what seemed like days, even though the night remained dark, the moon never moving, they came in sight of the Payton home. Relief sent blood pounding through Jared's head. He couldn't think, couldn't focus. The last of his strength was gone.

"Jared? Hey, kid."

"Robbie?" Jared muttered without lifting his head. "I'm done for. You go ahead. You've got Christianne. When you have a passel of . . . kids, name one of 'em Jared, okay?"

"You're home, little brother. Remember what I said. Take care of her."

"What? I can't . . ." His mouth wouldn't work any more. His body was soaked with sweat, and his head was too heavy and painful to hold up. His hands felt numb. "Robbie . . . wait."

He slid off the horse's back and crumpled to the ground.

* * *

"Jared?"

It was always the same. First came the pain. Old pain, new pain. The pain of loss. The pain of illness. His only respite was sleep, because when he woke, the pain was there. Pain in his back, hot and poisonous. Pain in his heart, far, far worse than the physical pain.

"Jared?"

The voice was as soothing as a spring shower. A hand touched his forehead; then a cool cloth drew some of the stinging from his eyes. He must still be dreaming. He didn't know how long he'd slept, but in his dreams Christianne had kissed him and cried over him and held his aching head.

"Jared?"

Her voice sounded so real.

"Jared. I can't bear it if you die. Please hang on."

He tried to say her name, tried to ask after Rob, but the anvil was back on his chest, and he couldn't pull in enough air to make a sound.

The cloth gently covered his eyes, and for a while, the pain slipped away.

"Rob?" he croaked.

A soft sob and a touch like the brush of an angel's wing against his cheek. Christianne was crying. He felt like crying too, because his big brother was going off to war.

"Don't . . . don't worry, Chrissy . . . he'll be back. You . . . you know Rob. Nothing can . . . beat him. He asked me to . . . to take care of you. And I will."

"Shh, Jared. You're dreaming. Rest."

Slowly, cautiously, Jared opened his eyes, and his gaze met a liquid blue one.

"Chrissy . . ."

"Oh, my God." She put a hand to her mouth. "Oh, Jared, we thought you weren't going to make it." She leaned over and kissed his forehead. "You gave us quite a scare."

He blinked, shook his head carefully, and looked again. It really was Christianne—but not the curvy, pink-cheeked girl who'd married his brother and unknowingly broken his heart. She was too thin, and her eyes shone too brightly in her heart-shaped face. Yet she was still the most beautiful girl he'd ever seen, still the woman he'd loved from the first time he saw her.

He licked his lips, and she held a glass of water for him to drink. The liquid eased his hot, dry throat enough so he could talk. "Where's . . . Robbie?"

Christianne's eyes filled with tears, and she looked away. He grabbed her hand. His grip was feeble, but it didn't matter; she held onto him.

"Chrissy? Where's my brother?"

She bit her lip and ducked her head, then sighed. She grasped his hand in both of hers and held it to her cheek. "Jared, you're so weak. Why don't you sleep for a while?"

"Chrissy . . ." He was having trouble thinking clearly. "Rob's sick too, isn't he? I knew he was hurt. Why are you here? Go . . . take care of him." A fit of coughing stopped his outburst.

Christianne touched his forehead and smiled sadly. "You're always the same, aren't you. I've never known anyone who loved his brother as much as you loved Rob."

Jared relaxed back against the pillows. "He's twice the man I'll ever be. You know. You chose him."

Christianne turned away for an instant, then a cool, wet cloth covered his aching eyes.

"You're just as brave, just as strong," she said. "You made it all the way back here by yourself." She patted his hand, and he felt the soft touch of her lips against his fingers. "Now, sleep. You need lots of sleep, sweet Jared."

"Not by myself," Jared whispered. He clenched his fists, and realized there was something clutched in his right hand. His thoughts rippled and broke up, like the reflection on a disturbed pond. But then he remembered. Rob's ring.

With a huge effort, he raised his hand.

"Do you finally want me to take that wad of cloth?" Christianne asked. "As weak as you were, no one could pry it out of your hand."

The anvil was pressing on his chest again. He shook his head. "Chrissy, where's Rob? I need to see him."

She put her cool palm against his hot cheek and turned his head toward her. Tears streamed down her delicate, too-thin cheeks. "Sweet Jared, listen to me." She closed her eyes for an instant, as a sob shivered through her body. Then her gaze met his directly. "You have to be brave, now. As brave as I know you can be. I am so sorry, but Robbie is dead."

"Dead? No. When? He was . . . fine, better than me." Jared stopped at the look of horror in Christianne's eyes.

"Oh, Jared, I'm so sorry." She squeezed his hand gently. "I should have waited."

"No! Tell me." His head pounded in rhythm with his heart.

She swallowed and wiped tears from her cheeks. "They brought him home last fall. He'd been shot in the stomach."

Jared couldn't get his breath. Christianne's words echoed in his head, loudly at first, then fading.

"He lingered for a couple of months, but then he passed away right before Christmas, eight months ago."

"Passed . . . no! That's impossible." Jared's eyes burned, his voice stuck in his throat. Robbie dead? "He rescued me! He saved my . . . life!"

Tears ran unheeded down her cheeks. Her lower lip trembled. "You need to rest. I shouldn't have told you. You're too weak, too confused. I'm sorry, Jared."

He shook his head. "No. No." He grabbed her hand. "He was here. He rode in on the chestnut. Didn't anyone . . ." He stopped because he could see he was scaring her. Of course, her words had scared him, too. He looked down at her hand, her left hand—and noticed that her wedding ring was gone.

"Wh-where is your ring, Chrissy?"

Her blue eyes widened at his question, then filled with tears again. "I put it on his hand, on the little finger, next to his. I buried our wedding rings with him."

Jared let his head fall back onto the pillow. He closed his eyes and let go of her hand. His brain wasn't working right. That had to be true because no other explanation made sense. "Tired," he whispered.

"I know, sweetie. You rest. I'll have some broth for you later." She touched his cheek. "You're going to be all right."

Jared couldn't let it go. He knew he wasn't crazy. Knew he had to tell her . . .

"Chrissy, he was here."

She gave him a watery smile. "Rob will always be here." She put her hand over her heart, then over his. "And here."

Jared covered her small hand with his. "Are you all right?"

She nodded. "I miss him. I always will. But he made it home, and

I was with him when he died." Her voice caught. "There are so many who just wait. For them it's never over. But I'm better, now that you're home."

She kissed him quickly, softly. His heart pounded at the touch of her lips against his. She stared into his eyes for a brief moment, her face so close to his he could have kissed her again, if he'd had the strength to lift his head. A mixture of confusion and surprise crossed her features.

Then a puzzled frown flickered across her brow, and she straightened. Looking down at her lap, she said, "You know . . . you've been talking pretty strangely. Talking to Rob. Dreaming about happy times when we were kids. And you asked me to marry you." She smiled. "That's twice, now, in fifteen years. If you keep asking, one of these days I might say yes."

He clenched his jaw against the stinging in his eyes and tried to smile. "Well, he did make me promise to take care of you."

She turned her palm up and clasped his hand, looking thoughtful. "You're not the only one who's had odd dreams. I dreamed about him several nights ago. It was strange. I don't usually remember dreams, but I remember every bit of this one. It was dark, and he was on his horse. He called out to me." She swallowed and blinked away tears. "He told me he loved me, and . . . and he said 'you and Jared take care of each other.' Then his horse reared and he . . . he turned it and rode away."

Jared squeezed her hand. "Chrissy, I'm sorry."

"Don't be." Her eyes glittered with tears. "Now, I've got to tell your mama you're awake, and you need to rest." She rose and started toward the door.

"Wait, Chrissy." He raised his head, and the room started to spin. "I need to show you something. To tell you something." He collapsed back against the pillows, and patted the bed beside him. "Come, sit for a minute."

She sat down beside him again. She straightened the covers and brushed a fallen strand of hair back from his forehead.

Watching her, he shivered with doubt. What if he'd dreamed it all? For an instant, when she'd told him about her dream, he'd felt a connection, a shared knowledge. But then, he'd always felt that with Chrissy.

Shaky, unbelievably weak, Jared lifted his hand and looked at the bundle he'd fashioned from his ruined shirt. Groaning as his cramped fingers protested, he opened his fist and unwrapped it.

"What is that? Do you need me to help you?"

He shook his head. "Chrissy, I know anybody else would think I'm out of my head. But you and me, we've always been able to talk, right?"

"Of course we have. Ever since we were children."

"I know why you married Rob. He was so . . . well, so big, so strong. He was the best. It was natural you fell in love with him."

Her tear-filled eyes sparkled. "Remember how we used to tag along everywhere he went?"

"I remember." Jared's throat clogged. "Chrissy . . . how did I get home?"

"I don't exactly know. The stable boy said there was a second set of hoof prints. Don't you remember? Did another soldier help you?"

"Yeah." He untied the bundle with shaky fingers. "Rob saved me."

"But—"

"He was there, at that damned prison. He called out to me, told me how to escape. He was pale and strange, and he wouldn't let me touch him. And, Chrissy . . . the night—it went on forever. We rode for hours, and the moon stayed straight overhead the whole time."

Tears were streaming down her face as she whispered, "Jared, that's . . . it's just crazy."

"Maybe." With an effort, Jared pushed himself up to a sitting position. "But you've got to admit, it's always been the same with Rob. He was always pulling me out of one scrape or another."

He folded back the last little flap of material, and there it was. The gold band Robbie had tossed to him.

Christianne gasped, staring at the ring. Then she reached out a trembling hand to take it. Jared knew what she was looking for. Engraved inside the ring were the letters R and C, and 1862.

Clasping it in her fist, Christianne raised her clear blue gaze to his. Despite his determination, his breath caught in a sob.

"Oh, my God . . . oh, my God, Jared, how . . ."

He smiled sadly. "You know how, Chrissy. Rob told you that night, in your dream. He wanted to be sure we took care of each other. He made sure I got home, for you."

She opened her fist and looked at the ring. With fingers he saw tremble, she picked it up delicately and kissed it. Then she handed it back to him. When she looked at him, Jared saw a change in her. She wasn't as pale anymore, wasn't as bowed with grief.

"You hang onto that ring, Jared Payton," she said, her voice growing stronger, "and you eat and rest and get better until you can wear it without it falling off." She brushed his stubbled cheek with her fingers, then kissed his lips lightly and pressed her cheek against his.

"And then," she whispered, "you ask me again to marry you."

Jared turned his head to press a kiss against her hair. "I just might do that."

"The Sacrifice"
by
CB Scott

Kiara McNair worked her garden with a fervor that frightened the villagers. Her hair slipped loose from the dark knot atop her head; the wild ends dripped with sweat as she tugged at weed after weed, throwing them down into her basket in both disdain and despair. She no longer cared that the villagers watched her with careful eyes, as though at any moment she might knock over her basket and flee into the woods, screeching like a madwoman.

Her muscles ached as she kept bent to her work. She snorted her breath through her nose, forcing away the too-sweet fragrance of her renowned rosebay willowherb. Nor did she let her gaze rest upon her yellow pimpernel, radiating so brightly beneath the sun that the star-shaped petals hurt her eyes. But mostly she kept her back to the tall, craggy mountain of Minerva.

She refused to give in to the temptation the witch whispered in the wind, as had so many other young wives, nearly out of their minds with waiting and wondering, finally making the sacrifice to bring their young men home from war.

The young wives did not discuss their sacrifices. No one spoke of anything at all, afraid to curse their husbands' returns.

Skin grimy with sweat and mud from the seasonal rains, she tugged at a stubborn little weed that would not budge. Gritting her teeth, she gripped it and gave the unwanted beast a harsh tug. As it came free, its roots quivered, outlined in the sunlight. Something cut at her heart as, for the first time, her eyes traced thin, spiny veins, freshly yanked from the ground. It reminded her of the delicate lines of a baby's spine.

Suddenly, her throat was choked with unshed tears. In the time Aedon had been gone to war, she could have carried two babes and be heavy with a third. Instead she carried her thin body on heavy feet, from bed to window in their empty dwelling, from weed to weed in their lonely garden. Tending, tending, tending . . .

Her lower lip trembled as she looked at the dying weed in her hand. Her Cylanian husband was considered a weed in the neighboring kingdom of Benonite, where he'd led his warriors to protect their sister lands from an oppressive ruler. But the Benonitians were exhausted from years of starvation and violence, and they no longer wanted to fight. They wanted the Cylanians gone. By any means. They seemed to have forgotten that, to help them, the Cylanian warriors had left their homes, plucked from their own families and lives by the roots.

She wanted to throw the weed as far as she could, not wanting to look at its vulnerable roots, sure to shrink up and die its slow death beneath the relentless sun. But she imagined her husband sprawled, lifeless and limp, tossed away as though he were naught, and she could not do it.

Her beloved since childhood, Aedon had told her that if he were killed, she would feel a snap, as though something inside her had fractured, broken beyond repair. He had promised her that she would know, as he'd kissed her hand and basked in her eyes—"as seductive and violet as the Cylanian moon," he called them. Then he had made *her* promise never to lose faith, no matter what she heard, until she felt the snap. Only the snap.

She had made the vow, and she'd clung to her faith; but as she looked at the weed in her hand, she realized how foolish a notion it was that she would feel anything at all if he should die. She had plucked the weed from the ground by its very roots, yet the world had not fallen away. It was no different for a man. Nay, naught bowed at the death of one small life.

Anger bubbled in her blood, along with desperation, as she looked around her magnificent garden, suddenly hating its beauty, its life, its indifference to the weed and to her torment. She wanted to hack the haughty, robust blooms from their stalks. She wanted to slip the little, uprooted weed into her pocket, protect it, make amends.

She stood on shaky legs, a sharp tool near at hand. She knew she was nearing the edge of her sanity . . . not much to send her over . . . not much more than a silly, little weed. . . .

She did not hack her garden. She simply stood and cried. Vaguely, she was aware of the passing villagers looking at her anxiously. She turned her back on them and looked up at the mountain.

"Soon," she said. "Soon."

* * *

King Rogan was pacing his sparse, utilitarian chamber. Strewn across his great table lay maps, swords, candles, and his untouched morning meal. As she approached, Kiara noted the haggard circles beneath the king's sharp eyes—the toll of directing a distant war of dubious outcome.

Then the man with the king drew her attention, and she sucked in a sharp breath. His black and violet tunic—her husband's colors—was bloodied and torn, and his leg was bound in a makeshift, wooden splint.

"Brennus," she whispered. Her husband's second in command.

His tired eyes darkened with pain and pity before he looked away from her. The meaning of his averted gaze was unmistakable.

She stopped, as though she'd walked into a wall. "But I . . . I did not feel . . . there was no snap," she said, disbelieving, clinging desperately to the faith that had carried her through so many lonely days and nights.

The king moved forward, grasped her elbows. "He is gone, Kiara. Brennus saw it himself."

She could barely breathe. Her body felt cold, dead, despite the blood rushing in her ears with the pounding of her heart. "But . . . what of his body?" she managed, the words sounding unreal to her.

Brennus spoke, his voice low and cracked. "We were unable to recover him."

"So you do not know . . ."

"No one could survive that cut down. I saw the blood, the bone . . ." He winced and, again, turned from her. "I am sorry, Kiara."

"Nay!" she said, trying to pull away from the king. "You do not know! You do not!"

The king gripped her arms. "Kiara you have been growing more fragile by the day. I hear the tales and can see for myself that they are true. You will stay here, in the castle, until . . ."

She glared King Rogan into silence. "I will never again be well."

Hesitating only a moment, he continued. "Someone must look after you. Brennus has offered—"

"Nay! I am bound to Aedon by the blood of the Cylanian gods. There is no higher sacrament. No—"

"Kiara, wait." Brennus leaned on his crude cane to hobble closer, his red-rimmed eyes no longer bright with the promise of war. "Aedon is dead."

"Nay!"

King Rogan spoke through gritted teeth. "I will allow you a full moon cycle for grief, Kiara, but you *will* marry Brennus. Left alone, you will mourn yourself into the grave."

Left alone, she thought as she yanked her arms from the king's grasp, she would go to Minerva. She would make the sacrifice.

Kiara did not run screeching into the woods like a madwoman. She walked steadily and with purpose, carrying a large basket filled with every bloom from her garden. The villagers had witnessed the massacre—the slashing, the shocked, beheaded stalks—and moved away from her scratched and bloodied face and hands as she passed. Behind her back, she knew they made the sign to the Cylanian gods that would ward off madness.

For endless moon cycles, she'd watched the horizon, waiting for Aedon. One after another, she had seen the warriors come home to hold their wives in their strong, tired arms. With each one's return, it had grown more difficult to ignore Minvera's vow that, for a sacrifice, she could bring home a warrior.

The witch's offer taunted Kiara as she recalled the promise she'd made to Aedon: that she would hold to the belief that he was alive as long as she felt no snap. She had held to it, for it was all she'd had of him to hold. A loud, pitiful cry escaped her throat. What a fool she'd been to believe her will alone would keep him alive.

Stumbling, she hitched up her skirts as she climbed the rocky trail to Minerva's cave; higher and higher, she went, until she could see the land below stretched all the way to the clouds that hovered on the distant horizon, where lay the cursed land of Benonite. She squinted, her gaze searching for lone figures walking the long road home, but she saw none. No sign of her Aedon.

She focused once more on the trail ahead of her.

She knew what her sacrifice would be. For if Minerva's spell proved false, she never again wanted to set eyes upon that tortuous, empty horizon.

The burning orange sun lowered in the sky, the violet Cylanian moon rising to take its place, before Kiara reached the end of the path. Here, the treeless mountain peak jutted with gray rocks, and the ground was barren and bleak.

She found the old witch outside her cave, scattering stones and muttering oaths. When Kiara's slippers scraped the gravel, the witch straightened, her back cracking like a hundred knuckles.

Kiara set the basket of blooms on the ground between them. "I've come to—"

"Eyes the color of the moon are rare indeed," Minerva said in her scratchy voice, shuffling closer. "So reflective of the fear within."

The old woman had only one eye herself, gray as a heavy winter sky; the other eye was sealed shut and framed in wrinkles. Kiara shrank back for a moment, as though the witch might cut out her eyes with her long, brown fingernails. Instead, with a wave of the gnarled fingers, the witch motioned her into the cave.

Humidity clung to the stone walls draped in ancient tapestries. Beeswax candles burned, and black pots boiled steam over small open fires.

"I am not a conjurer of the dead," the witch said. "Your offerings will not change what has already been done. But if he is alive, he will come home."

Kiara stood strong. "I am ready."

The witch sniffed and stirred a pot. "Then let us get on with it."

Kiara woke to darkness, her throat dry. The cold floor permeated the thin pallet, yet she felt the warmth of a nearby fire. For a moment she forgot that her eyes were gone. Then fear shot through her like ice.

She raised a trembling hand to find her eyes still in their sockets. She blinked again and again, knew her eyes to be open, but still she saw no licking flames of a fire.

The old witch had taken her sight but not her eyes. She felt a rush of anger. Was this some sort of trickery?

"The color is gone, my dear. Your eyes are as black as the night. I left the eyes themselves so your lids would not sink into your skull. As you wished, no man will want you. Not even Brennus."

Kiara closed her eyes—forever, she vowed—and knew she could not return to the village with her sacrifice so blatant and frightening. Many had made sacrifices to Minerva, but she knew of none that were as immediately observable as her own. No one would want to see the darkness and desperation that her sightless black eyes symbolized. Especially not when that symbol lived on the face of Kiara McNair, wife of the fiercest warrior in the land. If she had lost herself to such despair, they would wonder, what would their own fates be? She might inspire a panic—and her own murder.

Kiara climbed to her feet, her body stiff. With her palm against the cave wall for guidance, she made her way to the mouth of the cave. She felt the kiss of the sun on her skin, the whisper of the southerly breeze. Yet she saw naught but darkness. Not the glaring sun nor the lush green valley fermenting with new life, nor the mavehawk that screeched high in the sky above her. She would have sank down and wept, but despite the tingle of what used to prelude tears, her eyes seemed unable to cry.

Just as well, she thought as she gritted her teeth against the fear. She had done far too much crying. And as long as Aedon came home, naught else mattered.

Behind her, she heard Minerva come out of the cave. A moment later, the witch's gnarled fingers grasped hers and wrapped them around what Kiara realized was a walking stick.

"I am not so bad," the old woman said. "You will see. You will see."

See? Nay, she would not.

Angered by the taunt, Kiara sought to leave quickly. She began stumbling down the hill, the stick her only guide. Horror at what she had done filled her, yet she felt a spark of hope. Mayhap she had made a difference. Mayhap, now, Aedon would come home to her. She refused to consider Brennus's claim to have witnessed her beloved's death.

Kiara soon learned that as long as she remained calm, she was able to map her way down the mountain in her mind. She had always had a keen sense of direction, and it served her well. It took her a mere two sun cycles—discerned only by the differences in temperature and animal cries, for the days were as dark as the nights—to make her way through the forest and to find the cottage. A few times, she fell, screaming in frustration. And more than once, she crawled on her hands and knees, muttering prayers to the gods as terror of losing her way consumed her.

But then she would think of Aedon, dead or at the mercy of some other ungodly fate, and she would muster the courage to go on. She had done what she could to save him. Now she must wait . . . wait still, a little longer . . . to learn if her sacrifice had served its purpose.

She wondered if Brennus had given up the search for her. No doubt, the king had dispatched a band of warriors, with Brennus, broken and bruised, leading them. The gruff warrior believed it was his duty to care for his fallen friend's wife, and the best protection would be to marry her. But with the blackness of death staring out of her face, what man would want her? Minerva had claimed none would, and she was certain that was true. She hoped Brennus would not find her. She hoped she would be spared his pity and horror.

Finally, although she was scratched and battered from her blind journey, Kiara reached her goal—the cottage tucked deep in the woods that was Aedon's and her secret place.

Upon their wedding night, he had given her his sly smile, his dark eyes glittering with heat and love. He'd pulled her up onto his war horse, seated her on his lap, and whispered into her ear the things he had planned for her. Her skin had heated beneath his breath and his words, and he'd coaxed her into a blindfold, promising a sweet surprise.

After a short ride, he'd handed her down, then carried her in his strong arms toward the scent of sweet, fresh-cut wood. He'd removed her blindfold and swept her over the threshold of the cottage he'd built with his own two hands. A love retreat, he'd called it, and proceeded to kiss her and, for the first time, make love to her, claiming her as his own.

Kiara swallowed the hard lump that rose in her throat as she stood on the threshold of their trysting place. She was as blind as she had been that night, wearing Aedon's scarf tied around her head. But she was not nearly the same woman.

When she stepped into the cottage, she noted its musty, neglected smell. In the long days since Aedon's departure, she had avoided coming here alone. Now she had nowhere else to go.

In the following weeks, Kiara spent her days sweeping away cobwebs, gathering wood, and collecting berries and other wild fruit and vegetables. With her mind on survival—and gradually becoming attuned to the world through her senses of smell, hearing, and touch—she cleared the brush and fledgling trees from behind the cottage and prepared a garden. A vegetable garden. As she crept into the village by night to steal a plant or two at a time from her neighbors' patches, she wondered what she had ever seen in the frivolity of a flower garden, wondered that she could ever have lived in such peaceful oblivion.

The heat of the Cylanian summer invaded her scrap of woods, but Brennus never came looking for her. She guessed that, witnessing her murdered garden, hearing the tales of her scratched face, and knowing her desperation, the king had decreed her as lost as he believed Aedon to be. Mayhap they all looked upon her disappearance as a blessing. For surely she was a sore reminder of the warrior they had abandoned on enemy ground.

At night, lying on a pallet placed near the cold hearth, she was tortured by bittersweet dreams of her husband. She never went near the bed, tried not even to look at it, sitting in the corner, with its rose-carved headboard. She tried, too, not to think of the nights she and Aedon had spent in that bed—times of wine and nakedness and laughter.

Times such as she would never know again.

* * *

The women of the village glared at him. The men averted their eyes.

Plodding beneath him, his pilfered swayback mount drooled in quivering strings after the long, grueling journey.

Aedon McNair was home. Only he was not the same man. Nor was the village the place he remembered.

He half expected the women to grab pitchforks and torches and run him back to Benonite, to where their husbands and sons had spilled their hot life's blood on the green grasses. To where he himself would have glimpsed his last of the smoke-smeared sky but for the rough hands that had dragged him away. But the villagers spoke not a word to him as he passed.

His hands gripped the reins, slick with sweat. He had led his warriors from their homes amidst cheers for their nobility and bravery and cries for liberation. Now the parents and wives and children watched him as though he were delivering the plague. Surely, he felt as though his unwashed body reeked of death.

Mayhap, once he bathed and shaved and met with the king, he'd find his voice and the courage to walk in the village and speak to those in mourning. To seek out those who'd lost a husband, a son, a brother, and relay the tales of valor . . . and of the quick, painless ends. Mayhap, he would speak, too, to those who had returned from the battlefield, their scars deeper than blood and skin . . . wounds, he feared, that would never heal.

His back ached to sag in the saddle, but he forced it to remain straight and rigid. Just as he'd forced his eyelids to remain open through what seemed an endless cycle of moon and sun on his relentless mission to return to the woman who'd kept him alive.

His Kiara. He had vowed to die only while drowning in her violet eyes, where he had always found solace and reason and love. . . .

Exhausted as he was, his body tingled with life at the thought of her nearness. His gaze skimmed the clutter of rooftops, traced the familiar lines, until he found the crooked stone chimney and thatched roof. His blood warmed, remembering their last night together, the urgent lovemaking . . . her soft, naked breasts against his chest as she'd rubbed him and whispered her love.

The next morning, hair tousled and lips swollen, she had swallowed tears and walked him to the village gates. As the men had ridden out, he had seen her wrap an arm around the shoulders of a weeping woman, offering comfort despite her own fear. And when she'd raised her gaze to meet his for the final time, her sweet lips had silently mouthed, "Come home."

His heart twisted as he wished back their innocence, their flawless love, their utter conviction that only death, if even that, could tear them apart. He wished back that moment at the gate when naught but circumstance blighted the pure emotion between them.

"Come home." The plea had kept him alive—and had made him perform deeds of which he could never speak.

Aye, he had come home. But he was vacant, numb, defeated. He had lost some essential part of himself in the dark dungeons of Benonite. Truly, he was no longer sure who he was.

As he drew closer to his cottage and saw no hearth smoke curling into the sky, Aedon's anxiety mounted. Mayhap Kiara was visiting a friend or, more likely, tending her precious garden. No matter. He would find her. He would sink into her violet gaze and warm himself beneath her love. And if the gods were merciful, he would never have to tell her what he had done. . . .

Despite his uncertainty and his inner shame, he knew he could not deny himself her touch or the feel of her silken skin against his. As he approached his home, his mind drifted through memories of hot, passionate nights . . . Kiara sitting in front of the fire, brushing her long black hair that shimmered like a curtain of magical obsidian . . . and later, as she lay above him, those silken strands brushing his skin as she cried out in pleasure. . . .

The fantasy faded abruptly as he reined his nag to a halt at the path leading to his front door. 'Twas the height of the summertide, yet the garden was withered, boasting not a single blush of color. The tall, brittle stalks bowed beneath the sun as though in anguished prayer.

Aedon felt a chill race down his spine. Kiara had not been home in some time.

Heart in his throat, he dismounted. He wanted to run to the threshold, roaring at the villagers for not warning him. But he could not blame them for what he himself had wrought. He had left her alone for nearly three full turns of the seasons. How long had he expected her to wait, not knowing when or even if he would return? Doubtless, with every message sent from the battlefield bearing a list of the dead, her certainty that he was dead would have grown. Expecting no more than he deserved, he followed the slate garden path toward the front door, one sluggish boot at a time, as though moving toward his doom.

A strong hand clamped onto his shoulder, stopping him.

"Hell's teeth, Aedon! I saw you cut down!"

"Brennus!" Shocked to hear the familiar voice, he turned to meet his friend's embrace, grateful beyond words that Brennus had been spared.

Then, glancing once more at the grim, weed-infested garden, he grasped Brennus's arms and met his gaze. "Kiara . . . ?"

The warrior's eyes were darker than Aedon remembered ever seeing them. Without speaking, Brennus let his gaze slide toward the tall, craggy mountain that loomed over the village.

Aedon swallowed. "You told her I was dead."

Brennus closed his eyes briefly and nodded. Then, waving a hand at the ruined garden, he said, "She slit the throat of every bloom, Aedon, then disappeared into the woods. The village women say that she went seeking Minerva and took the flowers as an offering. They say she had been watching the mountain for weeks, talking to it, but we searched the cave and found only the old woman."

Aedon gave his head a quick shake. "Kiara does not believe in witches."

"She is not as you remember her, my friend. She grew . . . desperate with your absence. So frail in mind and body, that King Rogan ordered her to . . ."

"What?" Aedon barked. "What did he order?"

Brennus drew a deep breath. "He ordered her to marry me. He believed it best, and I wanted . . ." The warrior hesitated, seeming nearly to choke on the words as he continued. "I failed you on the field. I left you to die. I wanted to atone by saving what you loved most."

Aedon laid a hand on Brennus's shoulder. He was finding it difficult to breathe, but he managed to rasp, "'Twas a gesture born of loyalty and friendship." *As was Kiara's,* he added silently.

He imagined her ignoring Rogan's decree, hacking away at her garden, crying all the while. And he saw her carrying the flowers up the mountainside, to the cave of the old hag who was rumored to be a witch. He could hear her voice, offering the hag anything if it would bring him home.

Aedon's blood chilled with fear. What had she done? What had she sacrificed?

"How long has she been gone?" he asked.

"Months."

"By the gods!"

"I searched, Aedon," Brennus hurried to add. "I swear to you, ten of us searched for half a moon cycle but found no trace of her. I fear she is—"

"Nay. I felt no snap."

Brennus stilled. "She said the same of you."

"Aye, she would." Marching back up the slate path, he grabbed the reins of his friend's horse. "May I? Mine is spent."

"Of course, but . . ." Brennus looked to the lathered nag standing next to his own, a startled expression crossing his features, as if he had only just realized the import of their conversation. "By the gods, Aedon! What happened? Where have you been?"

"Coming home. To Kiara."

As Aedon rode hard through the woods, leaves whipping his cheeks and blue crows screeching from the treetops above him, the uncertainty of Kiara's fate drove him nearly mad. He hated every sick, gut-wrenching hoof beat as he tracked the notches in the mighty knot trees. No path lead to their tiny cottage, only the illegible marks he'd cut into the soft bark of the twisting trunks.

He had taught her how to follow the notches. He had not told her that his purpose in building the cottage hadn't been simply to have a place for their passionate trysts; he'd intended it to serve as a sanctuary to which she could run if he was not in the village—or alive—to protect her. He could only hope that she had understood without his speaking the words.

Charging through the maze of knot trees, his heart pounding, he considered that she, too, might have lost herself in this damnable war. That she, like he, might be a different person than the one he had left behind. Had she suffered as he had small deaths each and every day until she no longer knew if she was alive?

Was she alive?

He prayed to the Cylanian gods that he would find her so.

She was standing in a burgeoning vegetable garden, her back to him, a plump red jubai-fruit in one hand and a walking stick in the other. He could tell by the stiff tension in her shoulders that she'd heard his approach.

He jumped from the horse's back before it came to a full halt and strode toward her. "Kiara!"

She didn't move, like an animal stunned into stillness. He understood her fear. What if he were only her imagination? Another cruel hoax.

He slowed as he saw her clench the fruit in her hand, the ripe, red juice running between her fingers. "Kiara. Turn to me."

"Nay."

Breathing heavily, he drew closer, but when he touched her shoulder, she shrank away and cried out. Frightened, he grabbed her hand and spun her around.

Like a feral creature, she appeared, a being raised in the woodlands, knowing only the laws of scent and touch and instinct. Her soft, white skin was an ancestral memory beneath rough, browned hide. Her pearly, half-moon fingernails were cracked and discolored, and her long, lustrous hair was a tangled mass.

"Open your eyes," he demanded, trying to curb his panic.

She gave her head a near-violent shake.

"Look at me, Kiara!"

She moaned, cringing a little, but, slowly, she did as he had bidden.

He felt the shock roll through him, then settle like a stone in the pit of his belly. Her once-violet eyes stared at him, black haunted windows to her soul.

"Kiara! Gods have mercy! *What have you done?*"

With a cry, she tore from him and ran toward the cottage. Too stunned to move, he watched as she slammed the door. The sound of the bar falling into place, locking him out, jolted him out of his paralysis.

He charged after her, pounding his fist on the thick, solid wood. "Kiara! Open this door!"

Tears clogging his throat, he peered through the windows, but she'd blocked them with the shutters that he'd hung inside for privacy. For protection.

His sword useless, he stalked around the cottage to the towering wood pile, where he found an axe. Teeth clenched, he returned to the front door, lifted the axe, and began to chop his way inside.

Kiara scrambled onto the bed. For the first time since the sacrifice, she felt the slide of soft sheets against her skin, and it cut her to the bone. Of what use was her marriage bed? Of what use was *she*, no longer the woman he loved but a husk with an empty soul and a face hollowed by black, hellish eyes? He would look upon her and see only his own failings, then blame himself for hers. Aye, she could keep her eyes closed, but he would know. He would never forget. Or forgive himself.

She heard him grunt as he chopped at the door. She imagined his strong, handsome features set in determination.

He was alive.

Alive!

And she had brought him home.

All the desperate, tormented years of the war washed away like a riptide into the ocean. What rushed forward to take its place, though, was equally appalling: the shame, the dread.

When she'd heard the horse's hoof beats approaching the cottage, she'd somehow known it was Aedon. Yet, despite her certainty, her first thought had not been of his safety but of what he would think of her. He had survived war only to return home to a new torment . . . his broken bride. She ached to touch him, but she did not dare; she would not be able to bear it when he pulled away.

The thick wooden door cracked, and an instant later, she heard the axe thud heavily onto the floor. His heavy bootsteps followed.

She let out a sob, reaching to grab a pillow and cover her face.

"Kiara, what madness is this?"

"I *am* mad," she cried. "Stay away!"

"I will not!" He crossed the room, then sat on the bed, the mattress sinking with his weight.

He tried to take the pillow, but she clutched it tightly. He tugged harder and yanked it away, and she threw herself facedown into the bedding.

His hand cupped her chin, and he tried to lift her head. "Kiara, look at me. Did Minerva do this to you?"

"*I* did this."

She struggled against that achingly familiar touch—that strong, callused hand against her face—but he was too strong for her. She recalled with anguish how safe she'd always felt wrapped in his arms as she allowed him to turn her face toward him.

He did not pull her to him, though, but held her at arm's length. "Why?" he asked. "Why did you do this?"

"I had to," she said, the rawness of the words scraping her throat.

"By the gods, she took *your eyes!*"

"I gave them to her."

"Nay!"

"Aye! For your safe return." She tried to twist away from him, but he gripped her securely.

"Kiara . . . my love, I am here." He stroked her cheek. "I am here."

She could feel his hot, labored breath on her cheek, the rise and fall of his chest. Her heart split open as she recalled running her hands over his naked flesh in pure, sweet abandon. "Oh, Aedon . . . where have you been," she whispered.

"Surviving. As you have."

"I have not survived. I am ruined."

He uttered a low, violent oath and growled, "I'll be damned if you are." Then he pushed off the bed, grabbed her hand, and hauled her after him.

She knew where he was dragging her. "Aedon, no!" she cried desperately. "Do not threaten her! You will bring down a curse upon us!" Stumbling after him, she pleaded, "Stay here, with me. I will feed you, clothe you, give you whatever you need. Even if you do not desire me, I . . . I will lie with you if . . . if you can bear to look at me."

With no word of response nor any hesitation, he mounted his horse and pulled her up in front of him. She gasped as her feet left the ground, clinging to his arms, feeling his muscles tighten beneath her fingers. Still, he did not speak but wrapped one arm tightly about her waist, then spurred his horse forward.

Her teeth rattled, and every bone in her body jarred at the furious pace he set through the woods. He slowed only slightly when they started to climb the path up the mountain—the path leading to Minerva's cave. She didn't try again to change his mind or even to speak to him.

In truth, she'd never before encountered the hard, silent man whose arm around her waist was like a manacle made of iron. She'd never heard his harsh and angry voice. His body against hers was rigid and unyielding, not at all like the warm, resilient body she'd recalled nightly in her dreams. And, of course, she could not look at his face, into his eyes, to know whether or not her much-loved husband now looked upon her in disgust.

A cold chill prickled her skin as the thought stuck her—he was as unfamiliar to her as she must be to him. They had become strangers to each other. She had sacrificed her sight to bring him home. But she now had to wonder if both of them would live only to regret it.

"Old woman!" Aedon felt the horse dance nervously beneath him at his harsh shout, and he tightened his hold on Kiara.

A moment later, Minerva hobbled out of the cave. "See, Kiara, I told you he would return."

"She cannot *see*, witch!" He swung to the ground, then grasped Kiara around her waist and lifted her down. When she tried to cling to him, he left her standing as he stomped toward the old hag. He itched to wring the crone's scrawny neck, but he satisfied himself with roaring, "How *dare* you fool my wife with your trickery? If you can take her eyes with your magic, you can put them back!"

The witch shook her grizzled head. "A bargain is a bargain, Aedon McNair. You have come home."

Her statement made him hesitate for the first time since he'd begun the headlong rush up the mountain. Aye, a bargain was a bargain, and keeping it was a matter of honor. He might have lost his own honor, but he could not force Kiara to renege on the promise she had made and, thus, give up her honor, as well.

He needed another solution, and it came to him immediately. "Take my eyes in her stead," he said gruffly.

"Nay!" Kiara cried, stumbling across the clearing toward him. "Nay! This is my doing, not yours."

He caught her before she fell and, giving her shoulders a gentle squeeze, he said, "Aye, I know you did it out of love for me, Kiara. Everyone in the world can see how great your love is—everyone but you. Now I want everyone to see how much I love you."

He slid his dagger from its scabbard and extended the hilt to Minerva, saying, "I wish to negotiate a different bargain with you. I wish to replace in kind that which you took from my wife."

Beside him, Kiara let out a sob—a sound of despair that twisted in his gut. He ignored it as he waited for the old hag's answer.

Minerva sniffed, ignoring the dagger. "You are a warrior. A man ready to give life and limb for his kingdom. Losing your sight would hardly be a sacrifice."

"But if it means never looking into her lovely violet eyes again, I—"

"As violet as the Cylanian moon? Nay, 'tis done. Your eyes are no match for hers."

Again ignoring the tiny sounds of distress coming from Kiara, Aedon shoved his dagger back into its scabbard. "Tell me what you want," he demanded. "I will give you anything that's within my power to give, if you restore Kiara's sight."

"Aedon, please . . ." Kiara whispered.

"Hush," he said. "As you made your bargain, without my interference or agreement, I will make mine without yours."

"Hmm . . ." As the witch moved closer, Aedon caught the earthy scent of herbs wafting from her, and he wondered what wicked potion she had been brewing. He wondered what she had done with his wife's eyes. "Hmm," she hummed again. "Mayhap you do have something precious to offer me."

His voice held a note of wariness as he replied. "Speak it."

"Oh, I think you know what it is, Aedon McNair. That precious thing you intend to hold close to your breast, unseen by anyone, forevermore."

His heart skipped a beat, and for the second time that day, he felt suddenly dizzy. "What do you mean?"

"I speak no riddle."

The old woman's one gray eye reflected no condemnation, no judgment. Only a depth and stillness that spoke of ancient ways and understanding. She knew things, saw things. And somehow, she knew what he had done.

Realizing what the witch wanted from him, what she wanted him to do, Aedon thought for an instant that he might be ill. If he agreed, not only would he lose Kiara—a notion that nearly brought him to his knees—he would hurt her deeply.

"Surely, this is unnecessary," he growled. "Has she not suffered enough?"

"Haven't you both?" the old woman said, and she tossed a handful of stones he hadn't known she'd been holding across the dirt. "Do not listen to me. Listen to your heart. Hear what it tells you—then tell me that I am wrong to make this demand of you."

He could not tell her that, for he knew it wasn't so.

Kiara touched his shoulder, whispering his name in puzzled query, and he whirled away from her, his boots scraping gravel as he paced to the far side of the clearing. There, he wrapped his arms around his ribs and stared at the distant horizon.

The witch was right. He could not lie to Kiara. Indeed, he didn't know how he had ever believed he could. How could he look at her and even dream of carrying this dreadful secret, like a bag of river stones, for the rest of his life?

He saw himself lying awake in the silence of nights to come, his mind twisted with the images of his betrayal, while Kiara lay, sightless, beside him. He imagined her as he had found her at the cottage, filled with feelings of unworthiness, and she would be grateful and beholden that he had not left her. . . .

Nay, he could not allow that. He would have to tell her the truth, no matter how much it hurt her.

No matter that, in telling her, he surely would lose her.

"Aedon . . ."

Her voice, uncertain and filled with pain, made him turn around. Slowly, he crossed the hard-packed ground to take her hands in his. "My love . . . I know you believe yourself unworthy of me, yet 'tis I who do not deserve you."

"Aedon, I was foolish. I—"

"Nay, Kiara, I understand the not knowing—how it makes one go mad. When Brennus told me that everyone believed you were dead . . ." He trailed off, shuddering. Then, drawing a ragged breath, he gathered his courage and spoke hoarsely. "Kiara, our sacrament . . . our sacrament by the gods and by the blood of our hearts . . ."

A frown of confusion flickered across her brow. Then, as he saw comprehension begin to dawn on her features, heard her suck in a quick, sharp breath, his heart broke.

"Say it, Aedon," she said. "If we are to survive . . . if we are ever to know one another again . . . you must."

Aye, he must.

Dropping to his knees before her, still clutching her hands, he touched his forehead to the backs of her fingers. "Kiara, I have long-since surrendered the man you knew. I have done . . . My love, to escape my enemy, I seduced and made love to his daughter."

Eyes closed, he waited what seemed an eternity for her response.

Finally, the question came—a breathless whisper. "You gave yourself to another woman?"

"Aye," he muttered. "To survive . . . to win my freedom, I used the only weapon left to me—my body—and I used it in a way I swore to use it only for you. Kiara, I love you with every shred of my being. The only reason I did not die—or let myself die—in that dank dungeon was so I could return to you. But to do it, I sacrificed our vows and . . . and that which I know you valued most about me—my honor."

She pulled her hands from his and placed them on his head. He looked up into her beloved face, and it was a blade to the gut to see it pinched as though she were crying. Except, he realized, she could not cry, for no tears leaked out from beneath the lids that covered her death-black eyes.

It amazed him when her lips curved into a small, sad smile. "There is no honor lost, my love," she said. "What man is more noble than the one who fights for justice and for peace? You did what you must to save innocent lives. Your own life is no less important, and it matters not to me what means you used to save it. It matters only that you have come home to me, and I will be forever grateful."

He scarcely could believe his own hearing—hardly dared believe the meaning of her words. She knew the truth, knew he had lain with another woman, and . . . and she forgave him. As the realization sank in, he felt an enormous weight fall away from him.

Kiara let out a little sob. "It is I who am no noble warrior. I fought no great battle, only my own demons and weakness, yet I succumbed to them. I could not wait for the snap. I promised you I would, but I could not do it. I lost faith and, in doing so, gave away that which you loved most. My eyes—and mayhap my soul, too. Oh, Aedon, how can you love a woman so hideous, so disgraced . . . so weak?"

He rose quickly to his feet, leaning over to kiss her on each closed eyelid. "How could you think I would not love you? And how could you think that you lost faith? You believed strongly enough to sacrifice your eyes to ensure my return. And here I am, safely home, mayhap only because you had such faith—and because the love you carry in your heart is powerful enough to perform miracles."

He wrapped his arms around her and clutched her to him. He had never loved her more than he did at that moment.

"Never leave me again," she said.

"Never."

Suddenly he felt tears against his cheek. His heart leapt as he pulled back and met his wife's wet *violet* gaze, the tiny black pupils staring at him in wonder. The light of the world made her squint and blink several times before she was able to hold his gaze. Then, as the truth of what had happened took hold of her, he watched her be reborn.

Both of them were reborn.

Aedon felt his own eyes burn, felt the tears spilling down his cheeks. He knew that he and Kiara were no longer the innocents they had been, nor was their love the flawless, unblemished thing it once had been—the perfect state he'd once thought the epitome of what a man and woman could hope to achieve. Tested by time and doubt and circumstance, it now bore the scars of battle. Yet, still, it remained pure and strong and more true than his sword, long since lost upon the battlefield.

Raising a trembling hand, Kiara touched his face. "Pale. Worn. So different, and yet the same."

His hold on her tightened. And as he lowered his head to bring his lips to hers, he was vaguely aware of Minerva shuffling back into her cave.

"I told you," the old witch said with a chuckle. "I told you, you would see."

"The Dreamer"
by
Diane Chamberlain

Saudi Arabia, fourteen years ago

Brian Meyerson ran from his tent toward the chopper, adrenaline pumping. Heat rose from the Saudi Arabian desert, and he was sweating even before he pulled on his helmet.

The *whomp, whomp, whomp* of the chopper's rotor was deafening by the time he reached the Huey. Standing outside its gaping door, he buckled the helmet beneath his chin.

"What is it?" he shouted into the microphone attached to his helmet.

Crazy Eddie, the Huey's pilot, shouted back to him. "Road kill! In Kuwait."

Brian looked toward the mess tent, where Jason McSweet stood idly near the entrance, his usual dazed expression on his face.

"Hold on, Eddie." Brian took a few steps away from the roar of the chopper, cupped his hands around his mouth and shouted. "Hey, McSweet!" When he had the boy's attention, he waved him over. "Into the Huey!"

Panic flashed across McSweet's face, followed quickly by a look that said "You don't mean *me*, do you?"

"Yes, *you*, Private," Brian ordered, then pointed to his helmet. "Put your Kevlar on."

McSweet stumbled toward the chopper, climbing aboard like a kid walking into a dentist's office.

Brian followed him in, the whirring of the helicopter thundering in his ears. Only then did he realize Cindy Gold was the other medic on the flight.

She grabbed his arm and shook her head, shouting, "He shouldn't come with us. He's too green."

"He'll be fine," Brian shouted back.

Taking a seat across from Cindy and McSweet, he snapped on his safety belt. Brian watched Cindy chew her lower lip as she eyed the pale young Private beside her, and he caught her eye, mouthing again *He'll be fine.* Cindy gave a one-shouldered shrug of acceptance.

Then, as the speed of the rotor increased above their heads and the helicopter lifted into the air, her expression softened, and she smiled at him. He grinned back, holding her gaze. The night before, they had made love for the first time. That secret hour hovered in the air between them.

When Cindy shifted her gaze to the window, he turned to see what had caught her attention. In the distance, thick black smoke filled the air.

"Hey, Eddie," he yelled into his microphone. "Are we headed near the fires?"

"Not too close," Eddie called in reply.

Brian relaxed. The choking clouds of smoke from the oil fields could cause his MedEvac crew to miss injured soldiers lying on the sand. It had happened before. He didn't want it to happen today, especially with rookie McSweet as part of the team.

Eddie turned from his seat at the controls to glance at McSweet. "Kid's looking a little green around the gills," he said into his microphone.

McSweet's head rested against the wall of the chopper, bouncing a little from the vibration. His eyes were closed, and there was a deep crease between his eyebrows.

"Should we give him a thrill?" Eddie asked.

Brian knew the pilot—his best friend in this god-awful place—was itching to put the Huey through its paces, but this was not the time. "Chill, Eddie," he said.

Cindy looked out the open side of the chopper. "You sure this is the right road, Eddie?" she called into her microphone.

Brian glanced through the window next to him, his gaze following the narrow road that dissected the desert in a straight line toward the horizon. Far to the west, rock formations rose from the earth, and to the east, oil fires filled the sky with smoke.

"Honey, I have supernatural powers," Eddie called back to Cindy, "Don't you know that? I could find the guys we're looking for without a map, and I— *Whoa.*" Eddie's sudden exclamation blasted through Brian's earphones. "Looks like the shit hit the fan down there."

Brian peered again through the window, this time looking directly at the road a few hundred feet below them. He sucked in his breath at the scene of utter devastation. Four vehicles—two army trucks, one of them an eighteen wheeler, and two civilian sedans—lay overturned in the sand. Smoke rose from the smaller truck, and the cars were charred to a crisp. From this high up, it was hard to tell the human beings from the supplies. He'd picked the wrong first mission for Jason McSweet.

"Shit," he said under his breath, then louder, "We're going to need backup."

"I'm calling it in now," Eddie said.

The Huey bucked a little as it started its descent. Cindy was already reaching for one of the aid bags. McSweet's eyes were open, but the back of his helmet remained glued to the chopper wall.

"You okay?" Brian asked him.

The young private didn't look at him, but he managed a nod.

Eddie landed the chopper with a soft *thud.* Cindy sprang out, one arm protecting her face from blowing sand. Brian grabbed a backboard and followed her.

"C'mon, McSweet," he called over his shoulder. He didn't wait to see if the boy was following as he ran toward the accident site.

"Over here!" someone called from behind one of the trucks.

"No, help me first, please!" another voice begged.

Words in Arabic mixed with pleas in English, and Brian felt pulled in a dozen directions, surrounded by broken bodies and groans of pain. He did the best he could, running from one injured man to another, determining who needed help most.

He quickly lost count of how many injured there were. Ten soldiers, maybe? Eight Kuwaiti civilians? He couldn't say. He smelled the charred remains of someone who had not escaped a burning vehicle in time, and the odor made his head spin. Perspiration ran down his face, stinging his eyes, making him want to rip off his heavy uniform. It was too goddamned hot!

He spotted Cindy kneeling next to a Kuwaiti man, a circle of blood staining the sand around the victim's head.

"Gold!" he hollered. "You need help?"

Without looking up from her patient, she called back, "Yeah, I do!. I'm losing this guy. But someone's hurt behind that burned-out car, and I haven't had a chance to get over there."

"I'll check," Brian said.

He ran around the side of the sedan and found a Saudi woman clad in a black *abaya* and *burka.* She was sitting on the ground, her body rising from the sand like a small dark mountain. Only her eyes were visible as she raised her arm toward him, pleading for help. She said something in Arabic, her voice raspy, and he noticed the swaddled bundle she was holding in her other arm: a baby.

"Brian!" Cindy called. "Please hurry!"

Torn between helping the Saudi woman and returning to Cindy, he suddenly remembered McSweet. He looked over his shoulder to see the kid standing at the side of the road, helmet off, the sun beating down on his short, pale hair. He looked as shell-shocked as the survivors of the accident, clearly in no shape to deal with the worst of the injuries.

In a split-second, Brian assessed the options and made a decision.

"McSweet!" he barked. "Take care of her." He nodded toward the Muslim woman, who didn't appear to be badly hurt. If the baby was in worse shape, McSweet would just have to deal.

The boy didn't move. "I don't think I can, sir," he mumbled, his face ashen.

"Get going, soldier!" Brian ordered.

Still, McSweet didn't budge.

Fed up, Brian stormed over to him, grabbed his arm, and began dragging him across the sand. "*You're* healthy," he said. "These people aren't, and it's your job to help them."

He let go of McSweet's arm, and the boy continued walking toward the woman. Brian waited to be sure he actually reached her, and he watched as the young private bent low to examine the bundled baby. He was about to return to Cindy when he noticed a sudden change in the woman's dark eyes.

Her expression sharpened with a look that said *Aha! Victory!* At the same time, she reached toward the infant with a hand that was decidedly masculine. The swaddling fell away, and from the layers of fabric, the "woman" drew a gun.

"Shit!" Brian yanked his own pistol from its holster, but he was too late. The man—an Iraqi soldier—barely took time to aim. A shot cracked the still desert air, and McSweet flew backward, landing in a lifeless heap in the sand.

Enraged, Brian took aim at the disguised Iraqi soldier, but he didn't have a chance to pull the trigger before the man tossed a grenade in his direction. In the next instant, searing pain—a thousand machetes—cut through his back and his leg, and the entire world went dark.

Brian woke up with a scream caught in his throat. Flinging off his covers, he sat up so quickly the bedroom spun around him, and he had to fight to catch his breath.

Damn it. He pounded his fist against the wall next to his bed. He was sick of this. Sick of having the same horrible dream night after night. Sick and tired of reliving the worst day of his life.

He looked at the clock on his night table. Three in the morning. Pressing his hands to his temples, he shut his eyes and wondered if he dared go back to sleep. He had to be at work by nine. A meeting with the boss at ten. An appointment with his social worker, Leslie Shipman, all the way over at the VA hospital, in the afternoon. He'd be wiped out by the time he got home if he didn't get some more sleep.

But he couldn't face the dream again.

Leaning over, he unlocked his wheelchair and pulled it toward him. He would get up. He'd read or watch TV or do some work on the computer. The truth was, he was more afraid of the dream than he was of being exhausted. He was more afraid of it than he was of dying.

* * *

That afternoon, Brian wheeled his chair through the halls of the VA hospital on his way to Leslie Shipman's office. He'd spent more time in this place than he cared to remember. Fourteen years ago, it had been his home. In one of these rooms, they'd taken off what remained of his left leg. In another room, a doctor told him he'd never be able to walk again.

And in yet another room, he'd told Cindy Gold to get out of his life forever.

If he hadn't known he loved her before that moment, he knew it then. The last thing he'd wanted was for her to be saddled with a paraplegic amputee for the rest of her life. They'd only been involved for a few months, he'd told himself. It wasn't as if they were married or even committed to one another, although he'd known they were heading in that direction. Ending it had been his gift to her.

She'd fought him, writing him letters, calling him. He'd sent the letters back and hadn't return the calls, and she'd finally given up. Still, whenever he came to the hospital, it wasn't the phantom pain of his missing leg he remembered or the months of grueling physical therapy. It was the expression on Cindy's face when he'd told her to move on with her life and forget about him. The tears in her huge blue eyes—tears of pity, he'd thought—were his last memory of her.

Yet he saw her every night in his nightmare. Crazy Eddie Carlucci was a little blurry in the dream, and McSweet was just a skinny pale-haired kid in a too-big uniform. But Cindy was there in detail. Her blond hair was so short, he couldn't even see it beneath her helmet. How many women could wear their hair that short and still look feminine? There was a calm self-confidence in her eyes as she sat across from him on the Huey. She was a good medic, and she knew it.

That was what initially had drawn him to her, and she'd told him she admired him for the same reason. They'd shared a common goal: they'd both planned to go to medical school and eventually work in a trauma unit. He often wondered if she'd succeeded. He hoped so.

Brian found Leslie Shipman's office door open. The social worker was sitting at her desk, engrossed in something she was writing, and he watched her for a moment before knocking.

Odd, her asking him to come in. He was usually the one to call for an appointment. Leslie had been his sounding board for a decade. When the dreams got so bad he didn't think he could stand one more night of them, he'd come in to talk to her. Sometimes, talking about his time in the Persian Gulf would make the nightmare go away for a day or two. But it always came back. Over the years, Leslie had sent him to a couple of psychiatrists, who tried fighting the dream with a variety of drugs, but no sleep seemed beyond the reach of the nightmare.

He knocked on the door jamb. "You ready for me?" he asked.

The social worker looked up and smiled.

"Hi Brian," she said, putting down her pen and sitting back in her chair. "Come in." She was a nice looking woman. He'd known her long enough to watch her hair go from brown to gray. She wore it short with deep bangs that, despite the gray, made her look very young.

He wheeled into the room and parked in front of her desk. "How's it going?"

"Great," she said. "How about you?"

"All right." It was true—he was as all right as a one-legged man paralyzed from the waist down could expect to be.

Her phone rang, but she just rolled her eyes and ignored it. "This place is a circus."

He laughed. "What else is new?"

"How's work?"

"Good." He worked for the Veterans Administration maintaining their website. He could have gotten disability and stayed home feeling sorry for himself, but that had never been his style. He liked the technical work he was doing, although it was a far cry from his once-upon-a-time ambition of being a physician. For two or three years after the attack in Kuwait, he'd been deeply depressed about the loss of that dream. Gradually, he learned to accept his limitations—owing in no small part to the woman sitting across the desk from him. "So, why did you want to see me?"

Leslie tapped the thick folder on the desk in front of her, and he recognized it as his medical chart. "Dr. Welch asked me to talk to you about something," she said. "She has an idea and wants me to see if you're psychologically ready for it. I've already told her, 'hell, yes,' but she insists I talk to you about it face to face."

He was perplexed, but Leslie's demeanor made him smile. "What's the idea?" he asked.

"There's a study going on at Middleton Memorial in Wisconsin," Leslie said. "They have a new intravenous drug that's showing some promise in reversing nerve damage in cases of paralysis. It's no cure, but the results so far have been encouraging. You're a perfect candidate, so she wanted to see if you'd like to participate."

"Hell, yes," Brian said.

Leslie laughed. "See how well I know you?" she said, then sobered. "The thing is, you'd have to be there about three months. I know it will screw up your work sched—"

"I'll manage." He'd manage anything, rearrange his whole life, for the chance she was offering him: a potentially miraculous treatment that might allow him to walk again—with a prosthesis for his missing leg, of course.

"I can help you get temporary disability," Leslie said, then went on to explain the particulars. He would spend a few days a week in the hospital and live in military housing the rest of the time while participating in the study.

When he questioned her about the science behind the new drug, she shook her head. "You'll have to talk to Dr. Welch about that end of it." Then she smiled. "You're still a medic at heart, aren't you?"

"You've got it," he said. He was a hungry sponge when it came to medical information. Always had been and probably always would be.

He started to wheel himself toward the door, and Leslie stood up.

"I'm glad you're going to do this," she said, folding her arms and leaning against her desk.

"Well, if it doesn't help me, maybe it'll help the next guy," he said, but in his heart, he knew he was hoping the drug would be his miracle. With his hand on the doorknob, he said, "Now we just need a drug that will put an end to nightmares."

Leslie grimaced. "I'm sorry we've failed on that one. When you get back, we'll try again."

Brian left her office and wheeled his chair down the corridor, the excitement he'd felt only moments ago overshadowed by his never-ending anxiety over the nightmare. Even now, when he was wide awake, images of that day ran through his mind.

He'd made poor choices. He'd made decisions that had cost Jason McSweet and many others their lives. McSweet had been in the Persian Gulf only two days, and he'd had a long way to go before becoming a man, much less a soldier and a medic. His baby face and skinny physique earned him the nickname "Sweety" within twenty-four hours of his arrival. He had been so panicked by the threat of attack that he was pretty well useless. The road kill mission—an accident, rather than a combat situation—had seemed like a good way to give the boy some experience without his having to wear the bulky chemical suits and masks that seemed to freak him out.

Brian still saw McSweet's frightened face as he'd forced him toward the masked Iraqi. His own miscalculation—and his need to turn "Sweety" into a real soldier—had killed not only McSweet, but thirteen other soldiers and civilians, as well. They'd died either from injuries suffered in the grenade attack or because they hadn't been evacuated in time. The explosion had sent the chopper's co-pilot, Jim Dabrowski, flying through the air, and Brian could still hear the sickening thud as the man's body crashed on top of one of the burned-out sedans.

The dream was vivid, full of pale sand and a blue sky, marred by the smoky oil fires in the distance. Over and over again, he saw the black figure of the "woman" cradling her faceless baby. He should have known that a Saudi woman would not be on that road in Kuwait, but being stationed in Saudi Arabia, he'd grown accustomed to seeing *abaya*-clad women. That, combined with the confusion and adrenaline rush of the moment, had sapped his judgment.

He couldn't forgive himself for his mistake. And his conscience made him relive it every single night.

Thank God, Cindy and Crazy Eddie had survived the attack.

Fun-loving and good-natured Eddie Carlucci had been the most popular guy in their encampment. He'd wanted to be a test pilot and had been in the Army's test pilot training program before being sent to the Gulf. He'd hated any routine mission behind the controls of the Huey. Brian knew Eddie would only be happy doing something that involved both flying and risking life and limb.

Smiling to himself, Brian remembered Eddie talking ad nauseam about having supernatural powers. He had sworn he could bend spoons with his mind, although he refused to do it in the mess tent because, he said, it took too much out of him, and a pilot should never do something that might reduce his concentration. He swore he could read minds, too, and talk to the dead and be in two places at once. But the only so-called supernatural powers Brian could remember seeing Eddie display involved reading Tarot Cards. At night, when there was little else to do except wait anxiously for a possible scud attack, he'd pull out his deck, and the other soldiers would gather around him.

"Your girlfriend will cheat on you if you don't answer her letters," Eddie would tell one soldier as he studied the cards. "You should invest your savings wisely or a friend might take advantage of your generosity," he'd tell another. He'd sounded like the insert in a fortune cookie to Brian. It had been a harmless enough pastime, though, and they certainly had needed the diversion.

For the first few years after the incident, Brian had received a letter from Eddie every now and then. His old friend would reassure him that he was fine and send good wishes for his recovery, but he never visited despite numerous invitations. Gradually, their correspondence had faded away. Brian had made plenty of new friends over the years, especially among his fellow veterans, but he still missed the camaraderie he once had shared with the irrepressible pilot.

As for women, there had been only a few since Cindy. He worried that a woman might agree to date him out of pity. Not many women could truly understand what he'd been through, nor were many willing to face the challenge of intimacy with a man who was paralyzed from the waist down. The few who had tried to make a go of it with him had been frightened off by his violent dreams, and he didn't blame them.

He wished the study he was about to enter *was* designed to get rid of nightmares. A man could get by without a leg. He could even live a fairly decent life without any feeling below the waist. But how was he supposed to keep going when, every time he closed his eyes, he was forced to relive the most horrific hour of his life?

* * *

It took a month to get enrolled in the study and another couple of weeks before Brian flew to Wisconsin and checked into Middleton Memorial. The hospital room where he would spend four days out of every week had two beds in it, but he had it to himself when he arrived.

They gave him a hospital gown to change into, but he persuaded the cute young nurse to let him wear his one-legged jeans and T-shirt. He'd spent too much time in hospital gowns, and he could see no reason to wear one for this treatment. She agreed with him, and once he'd settled into the bed nearest the door, she started his IV.

"The only side effect of this drug that we're aware of so far is drowsiness," she told him.

Great, he thought. Just what he needed was more sleep. More chances for the nightmare to course through his brain. But once she'd left the room and he'd raised the head of his bed and settled back against the pillows, he felt pretty good. He'd brought a stack of books with him—novels he'd had no time to read over the past couple of years—and there was a nice-sized TV hanging from the ceiling near the foot of his bed. This was going to be a vacation. He even dared to wonder if the change of scenery and being away from the stress of work might make a difference in his sleep patterns. Had the nightmare followed him to Wisconsin?

That afternoon, he had a book open in his lap, a glass of iced tea in his hand, and the television tuned to Dr. Phil when he heard a knock on the door.

"Come in," he said.

A woman stepped into the room. She was dressed in dark pants and a white lab coat over a red blouse. Her blond hair was loose around her shoulders, and she wore black, narrow-rimmed glasses. Her smile was familiar, but he couldn't quite place her.

"Hey, Sarge," she said softly. She took a step closer, and he could see the blue of her eyes behind her glasses.

"Cindy?"

"That's right." She walked to his bed and leaned over to give him a hug. Although the embrace was awkward and her body stiff, he felt momentarily lost in the scent of her hair; she pulled away, though, before he'd breathed in enough of it.

"I was so surprised to see your name on the patient admission list this afternoon," she said.

Oh, she looked beautiful. He liked the longer hair. He liked the glasses. He even liked the tiny lines at the corners of her mouth. He wanted to reach out and touch one of them.

Get a grip, he told himself.

"You look great," he said.

"You, too."

"A little worse for wear," he admitted.

She shook her head. "I would have recognized you anywhere," she said, the words coming out in a rush. "You have those"—she raised her hands to her cheeks—"those high cheekbones that make you look like there's a little Native American blood in you. And those thick eyelashes. And you still have those beautiful dark eyes, and—" She opened her mouth as if she had more to say, then clamped down on the words. "I'd recognize you anywhere," she repeated. She suddenly shifted her gaze to the television as though the commercial for toothpaste was something she desperately wanted to see.

Brian saw patches of red forming on her neck. She was uncomfortable with her outburst.

Wanting to put her at ease, he lifted his arm to display the IV. "I'm here for the new nerve drug. Think this stuff will do anything?"

"Well, I understand it's a step in the right direction." She walked around the bed to read the information on the plastic bag hanging from the IV pole above him. "I think it's great you're participating in a study," she added.

Her glasses were cute, and they certainly altered her appearance, but in his eyes, she was still the girl he had made love to in her tent in Saudi Arabia. The young woman he'd spent so many hours with. They'd talked endlessly about their plans for medical school, their love of old movies, their favorite books—anything they could think of to pass the time in the desert. He remembered observing her during her first MedEvac mission. She'd been in the Gulf all of one day, yet she'd handled the grisliest injuries with a composure and skill. He'd started loving her right then.

He wished he could touch her now. He dared to reach out and smooth his fingers over the hem of her white lab coat. "You became a doctor," he said. "Just like you wanted."

She nodded.

"I knew you could do it," he said. "Emergency Room?"

"Yes," she replied as she walked around the end of the bed again. "I was lucky. Everything fell into place for me."

"Pull up a chair and stay a while." He motioned toward the green vinyl-upholstered chair in the corner of the room.

She hesitated for just a moment before walking over to the chair and dragging it back to his bedside. "I only have a minute before I have to go to the ER," she said, sitting down. She was in control of herself again, a serious, professional demeanor replacing the girlish exuberance of a few minutes earlier.

"How are you doing, Brian?" she asked, leaning forward. "How are you doing *really*?"

"I'm okay." He nodded toward his one leg. "I mean, after all this time, I've adjusted to it."

She looked down at her hands. Her fingers were laced tightly together in her lap, and for the first time, he noticed the simple gold band on her left ring finger. His chest tightened with disappointment. He knew he was being ridiculous. They'd had a few months together, followed by fourteen years of no contact. He'd told her to get out of his life. What the hell had he expected—that she'd still be waiting for him to come to his senses?

"I thought about not stopping in," she said. "Last time we spoke, you were pretty clear that you didn't want to see me again."

"I just wanted you to be able to . . ." It was his turn to feel awkward. "I wanted you to have a normal life, Cindy. Let's face it. You wouldn't have had one with me. Besides, that was a long time ago, and now I'm very glad you decided to come."

"Where are you living?" she asked.

"San Diego." He took a sip of his iced tea and felt a tremor in his hand as he gripped the glass. She was not the only one anxious about this visit. "I have a house near the beach. And I'm a techie. I work on the VA website."

"Ah," she said, smiling. "You found a niche for yourself. I bet you're really good at computers and the internet and all that stuff that baffles me. You were so smart."

He started to tell her a little about his job when his gaze fell to the embroidered letters above the pocket of her lab coat. *Cynthia Carlucci, MD.*

"You married a *Carlucci*?" he exclaimed.

Her hand flew to the embroidery as if she'd forgotten it was there, and the flush returned to her neck, spreading upward to her cheeks. Hesitating for a moment or two, she said, "I married *the* Carlucci."

"Holy . . ." His voice trailed off, his chest aching again. "Well, congratulations," he said, but the smile he gave her was forced.

"Thank you," Cindy said. "We've been married ten years."

"I can't believe it. How did it happen?"

She let out a sigh. "I think . . . you know . . . what Eddie and I went through just pulled us together. The grenade attack and all." She looked apologetic for bringing it up. "We really were just friends for a long time. Then we became best friends." Her tone was flat, as if she'd given the same explanation many times before. "Then we decided friendship was a pretty good foundation for a marriage, so. . . ." She ended with a shrug.

Brian frowned, searching for the real meaning behind her words. "What about . . . passion? Fireworks?" *Like what we had.*

"That's personal, Brian." She gave him a smile that told him to shut up. "Eddie's a great guy."

He guessed he'd insulted her. At the very least, he'd put her on the defensive. "I know that," he said. "He was my best friend at one time, too. But I didn't *marry* him."

She laughed.

"Do you have kids?" he asked.

"No. We would have liked to, but . . ." She shrugged again. "Too much going on."

"You and Crazy Eddie." Brian shook his head, still struggling with the idea of the woman he'd loved marrying a man he'd once considered his closest friend. He had no right at all to be jealous. "I've always been glad you two came through that mess unscathed," he said. "It was a miracle, don't you think?"

Cindy looked down at her hands again, where she was twirling her wedding ring on her finger. "We were lucky," she said.

Brian shifted a little on the bed, getting more comfortable. "So how is Crazy Eddie doing? Did he become a test pilot like he wanted?"

She laughed. "You're not going to believe it. He's a psychologist."

"No way!" Brian laughed. "Crazy Eddie's a *shrink*?"

Cindy smiled again. "I know it doesn't quite fit the man you knew," she said.

"It sure doesn't." Brian raised an eyebrow at her. "That guy was born to fly. *Recklessly.*"

"People change," Cindy said, "and he's actually very good at what he does. He works here, at the hospital."

"You're kidding! Call him up right now, and get him over here."

She gave her head a quick shake. "He's incredibly busy."

"Well, I'm not going anyplace," Brian said. "I'll be here four days a week. Tell him I want to see him. I need my Tarot cards read. Does he still mouth off about his supernatural powers?"

"No," she replied. "He's quieter about them now."

"Remember how he told everyone he could bend spoons with his mind?"

"That's the least of what he can do." Abruptly, Cindy stood up and pushed the chair back into the corner. "I'll tell him you're here. Maybe he can give you a call some day soon."

Brian frowned. "I'm going to be here for three months, and the best
he can do is give me a call? Is he mad at me or something? Is it . . . you
know, because you and I had something going before—"

"No, don't be silly," she said quickly. "It's nothing at all." She looked
at her watch. "I've got to run, Brian, but I'll tell Eddie you're here the
first chance I get, okay?"

"Does he blame me for what happened?" Brian asked. "Do *you*
blame me?"

Her lips parted in a look of surprise. "Of course I don't blame you,
and neither does Eddie. Any one of us could have made the same mistake."

"You didn't want me to bring McSweet on that mission."

"I didn't?" she said. "I don't even remember. It's ancient history,
Brian."

He watched her walk to the door, the lab coat clinging lightly to her
hips.

"Wait a sec, Cin," he said, and she turned to look at him. "Do you
have nightmares?" he asked.

She looked confused, but only for a second. "You mean . . . about
that day?"

He nodded, wondering if she could see the guilt that rested heavily
on his shoulders. Wondering, too, if that day still haunted her as it did
him.

She slipped her hands into the pockets of her lab coat. "I did at
first," she admitted. "I'd see . . . blood . . . blood everywhere . . . and the
explosion and . . . things flying around. It faded over time, though."
Her brow drew together in a concerned frown. "You don't still have
them, do you?"

"Every night," he said. "Every time I go to sleep. I relive the whole
thing, from start to finish."

"Oh, Brian," she said. "How terrible for you. Have you talked to
anyone about it? A therapist or someone?"

"Dozens," he said.

She folded her arms across her chest again, her brow still furrowed
as she studied him. "Your life is really a challenge, isn't it."

He had never cried over all he'd lost, so the sudden threat of tears
took him by surprise, and he had to swallow hard to speak. "It has been.
Sometimes. But I'm okay."

The look on her face let him know she wasn't fooled.

"I'll see you later," she said. Then, with a quick smile, she turned and left.

He fought sleep all afternoon. At first, it was easy because his mind was on Cindy. She looked fantastic. She'd found the career she always wanted and undoubtedly excelled at. But her marriage to Eddie sounded . . . what? Empty? Maybe she'd made it sound that way to keep from hurting him.

What would have happened, Brian allowed himself to wonder, if he hadn't pushed her away? Surely, the past decade would have been much better for him—and far worse for her. She might never have been able to fulfill her own dreams.

No, he had done the right thing letting her go. His life *was* challenging. She would be trapped with a man whose physical and psychological handicaps created daily hurdles. A man who could not satisfy her sexually—at least not in the way he once had. He groaned with the memory of their one night of love making, when the future stretched out before them, a field of limitless opportunities.

Even thoughts of Cindy couldn't fend off sleep for long. Before he knew what was happening, he was in the Kuwaiti desert, pushing Jason McSweet toward the woman in the *abaya*. He watched the swaddling fall away from the infant in her arms and saw the black mouth of the pistol emerge from the fabric.

"McSweet!" he shouted.

"Brian!" Cindy called from somewhere nearby.

The blast exploded from the gun, and McSweet flew backward onto the sand.

"McSweet!" Brian shouted again. He tried to run toward the young private, but someone grasped his arms, holding him back. He thrashed furiously at his assailant.

"Brian, it's me!"

Cindy.

He opened his eyes. She was sitting on his bed, her hands on his shoulders as if she had been trying to hold him down. He tried vainly to move his legs—often the only way he knew the dream had been just that, a dream. "Where am I?" He struggled to sit up. "I don't—"

"Shh." Cindy ran her palms up and down his arms. "You're safe, Brian. It's 2004. It's early Tuesday morning. Do you hear me? You're okay. You're at Middleton. You're not in the Gulf."

"Oh, God." He raised a tremulous hand to cover his face. How long had she been in his room? What had he said in his sleep?

Cindy leaned forward and wrapped her arms around him. "You're okay now, Bri."

"Damn," he said, embarrassed. "I must look like an idiot."

"No." She pressed her cheek against his, and he raised one arm, cautiously returning the embrace. "I'm so sorry you're still struggling with this," she said. "I'm so, so sorry."

He shook his head, reluctantly extracting himself from her arms to offer her a weak smile. "I'm okay," he assured her. "Once I wake up, it's fine. It's no big deal."

"Don't make light of it," she said. "Tell me the truth. Is this what it's always like? Are the dreams always this bad?"

He started to deny it, to offer her some bull about it being worse when he wasn't at home. But he couldn't do it. He couldn't lie to her.

Sighing, he nodded. "It's like I'm there. Like it's happening all over again."

Cindy gnawed on her lower lip as she looked hard into his eyes. "You need to talk to Eddie," she said suddenly, firmly. "He's really good at helping people with . . . well . . . guilt or whatever it is that's making you have that dream every night."

Brian scowled. "From what you said before, I got the feeling he wouldn't be all that interested in seeing me. And I *don't* want to see him as a shrink."

"I called him, and he's very excited about your being here," she said. "That's why I stopped in. I wanted to let you know that he wants to see you. But there's something else I have to tell you."

Her expression was so serious that he was afraid to hear what she had to say. "What?" he asked, wary.

She lifted his hand and held it in both of hers. "I know he told you that he wasn't injured in the attack in Kuwait."

"Right," Brian said. "You and Eddie were the only two who weren't. I was so glad of that."

"But Eddie *was* injured," she said. "He didn't want you to know. That's why he never came to see you. He knew you already felt guilty enough and didn't want to—"

"Injured how?" Brian interrupted her.

"It's not too bad," she said quickly. "It's his eyes. No one was sure what happened. Pieces of flying metal or something. So he has scars around his eyes, and I just wanted to warn you so you didn't . . . so you knew."

"What about his vision?" Brian asked.

"It's . . . well, it's not twenty-twenty, but you can talk to him about it when he sees you."

She was hedging. There was more—more that he wasn't going to like. Brian was sure of it.

But she waved off any further question he might have asked. "Eddie can explain it better than I can." She smiled and gave his arm a little punch. "He's still the same old Eddie. You don't need that long face."

"I wish he'd told me," Brian muttered.

"You had way too much to deal with without worrying about him, too." She let go of his hand and stood up, and the bed felt suddenly very empty. "Let's turn on your TV and get your mind focused on something other than that dream." She picked up the remote and clicked the power button. An advertisement for a cell phone company popped onto the screen.

Brian leaned back against his pillow. "This stuff"—he looked up at the bag of liquid hanging above him—"makes me so tired. Would you ask someone to bring me a cup of coffee, please?"

"Okay." She leaned over to examine the IV in his arm, the touch of her fingers warm against his skin. "They'll probably give you a sleeping pill tonight," she said. "Will that keep you from dreaming?"

"It hasn't in the past."

"Then listen to me." She sat down on his bed again and gripped his hand. "I want you to stay awake tonight, okay? Don't sleep."

Brian laughed. "What kind of medical advice is that?"

"Eddie can't get in to see you today, but he can come tomorrow morning," she said. "I don't want you to go to sleep until he's had a chance to talk to you."

"Cindy . . ." He leveled a look at her. "Please, don't kid yourself. Talking with a shrink for ten minutes isn't going to fix fourteen years worth of nightmares."

"Promise me." She pressed his hand between hers. "Promise me, you'll at least try to stay awake."

"All right," he said, persuaded by her ardor. "I promise."

He refused the sleeping pill he was offered that evening, and he watched the late show and half of an old movie before he dozed off. The nightmare came and went, and he woke up at five a.m. with a shout that brought two nurses running. He apologized for disturbing them and asked for more coffee.

He'd had three cups by eight o'clock, when Cindy appeared in his doorway, her hand on the arm of a man wearing jeans and a navy blue cotton sweater. The man's tinted glasses were rimless, his hair silver, and the upper half of his face was crisscrossed with scars.

"Hey, dude!" The man broke into a grin as he crossed the room. Leaning over, he pulled Brian into a bear hug.

Brian's breath caught in his throat. "Eddie," he whispered.

Eddie let go and straightened. "I can't believe you're really here!"

Brian noticed instantly that Eddie's gaze did not quite meet his— and that his vision was a far cry from twenty-twenty.

"You should have told me, Eddie," he said.

"Told you what? You mean about stealing your girl?" Eddie held one arm out to his side, and Cindy slipped into the curve of his elbow, her own arm going around her husband's waist. "I figured you'd want me to look out for her."

"You should have told me about your *injuries*," Brian said. "How bad is it? How much can you see?"

"It's very manageable," Eddie said.

"How *bad*?" Brian pressed him.

"I know there's a bed in front of me, and I know you're sitting in it," Eddie said. "I see shadows."

"He's had seventeen surgeries," Cindy interjected.

Brian pictured their life together: Eddie being wheeled seventeen times into an operating room. Cindy waiting outside, praying for results that would leave her husband better off than he was before.

"That's why he couldn't fly," she added.

"Shh, Cin," Eddie said.

Brian felt the guilt pressing down on him. "I'm so sorry, man," he said.

"Cindy"—Eddie squeezed his wife's shoulder—"how about you give Meyerson and me some time to catch up?"

Cindy didn't move. Instead, she pressed closer to him, her forehead against his chin, and Eddie touched her cheek. The gesture was tender, loving. Brian felt like a voyeur.

"Are you okay?" Eddie asked her softly.

She hesitated a moment, then nodded.

"Are you sure about . . . ?" his voice trailed off.

She nodded again, her eyes on her husband and a small smile on her face. "Very," she said. "You?"

Eddie bent down to kiss her. "You know it, honey," he said.

"Will we . . . remember?"

"Don't know for sure," Eddie said, "but I think we might. Would that be okay with you?"

"Yes," she said. "I think I'd like it that way."

"What's going on with you two?" Brian asked, but they didn't seem to hear him.

Cindy walked toward the door. "Love you," she called over her shoulder to Eddie. Then she waved. "See you later, Bri."

The two men watched her leave the room, the door closing quietly behind her.

Then Eddie asked, "Is there a chair in here?"

"In the corner," Brian said. "To your right."

Eddie found the chair and dragged it to the bedside.

"Do you have your Tarot cards with you?" Brian joked, trying to ease the tension that had crept into the room.

Eddie smiled his old smile, one side of his mouth higher than the other, and Brian felt relieved to see that at least one thing had not changed about Crazy Eddie Carlucci.

"I haven't used my Tarot cards since the war," Eddie said, sitting down. "I don't even know where they are."

Brian reached toward the rolling tray table at the side of his bed, where the plate and utensils from his breakfast still sat. He picked up a spoon and held it toward Eddie.

"Here's a spoon for you to bend," he said.

Eddie didn't seem to see it. "I *could* bend it, you know," he said, "but I'm saving my strength for something bigger right now."

Brian laughed. "You always were a bullshitter." He put the spoon back on the tray.

Eddie leaned forward in the chair, his hands clasped together in front of him. "You know," he said, "sometimes when something crappy happens to you, you can look back on it and see that it helped you in some way. That you grew from the experience or that it changed you in a good way."

Brian winced at his friend's transparent attempt to counsel him. "Don't play shrink with me, Carlucci," he said.

"I'm not," Eddie insisted. "This is a conversation between old friends. I mean . . . I lost a lot of my sight and"—he chuckled—"even more of my looks." The smile faded from his face, though, as he added, "I also lost the ability to fly, and you know better than anyone how big a loss that was for me. Flying was everything to me."

The shroud of guilt tightened around Brian's shoulders. "I'm sorry,

Eddie."

"I've never blamed you, all right?" Eddie said. "Let's get that clear. Never blamed you. The reason Cindy and I never looked you up in all these years was not because we thought it might bother you to see us together, but because we didn't want you to know how bad it was for me. We didn't want to add to your problems. But now you're here, and it's time you knew everything."

"What do you mean by 'everything?'" Brain asked, not at all sure he wanted to hear the answer.

"I wanted to fly more than anything in the universe," Eddie said.

"I know that. I'm as sorry as I can be that you can't. I know what it's like to—"

"I loved flying more than I love Cindy."

Brian recoiled. "Shit, Eddie, I do *not* want to hear this! What's with you, anyway? I think the shrink needs a shrink."

"Cindy knows. She understands me. And I . . . well, let's face, it, Meyerson—from the moment she and I started dating, I understood that I was her second choice. I knew it was you she really wanted."

Shifting uncomfortably on the bed, Brian growled, "I don't see how this conversation is helping either of us."

"I think you will later," Eddie said.

"I doubt it."

"Tell me about the nightmares."

"No, thanks."

"Cindy says they're pretty bad," Eddie persisted. "What are they like?"

"I don't need another therapist," Brian said. "Besides, you were there. You know *exactly* what it was like."

"Is there anything good that's come out of what happened to you?" Eddie probed again. "I mean, are you grateful for what happened in some way? The way it's changed you or—"

"Are you out of your mind?" Brian cut him off. "If you mean do I appreciate being alive, being able to make a living, etcetera, etcetera, then sure. I have a different sort of appreciation for life and a different perspective on things. But if you mean, am I *glad* it happened, then, hell no, I'm not. I'd be crazy to think that losing a leg and my chance at a medical career was a *good* thing."

Eddie nodded thoughtfully. "Yeah, I guess you're right." Then, suddenly, he pointed to the IV bag hanging from the post above the bed. "Is that an IV bag up there?"

Blinking a little at the abrupt shift in Eddie's attention, Brian looked up at the bulging plastic bag. "Uh-huh."

Eddie started to laugh. "You know what that reminds me of?"

"What?"

"That time we sneaked vodka into our encampment in the IV bags."

Still confused by the sudden change in topic, Brian had to think a moment. Then, remembering the incident, he smiled. "I'd forgotten that."

"Remember that Saudi restaurant with the camel vomit?" Eddie asked.

"Oh, man." Brian shook his head with a laugh. "That stuff was good, though." They'd spread the pasty green dip on pita bread. It was a lot better than the food in the mess tent.

He and Eddie reminisced for a while, and Brian nearly forgot his discomfort over the previous conversation. It felt good to talk with his old friend, good to recall the few pleasant memories from their time together in Kuwait. He'd had no one else to share them with. When a man showed up at a shrink's office paralyzed from the waist down, he wasn't likely to be asked about the positive aspects of being in a war— the funny things that had happened, the camaraderie that had gotten him through the fear and the boredom.

After awhile, though, Eddie lifted the crystal on his wrist watch and ran his fingertips over the face. "I've got an appointment," he said, getting to his feet, then pushing the chair back into the corner.

"Thanks for stopping in," Brian said.

"Glad to do it." Eddie approached his bed again. "You know," he said, "There's one thing about me that hasn't changed."

He held out his hand, and Brian reached to shake it, asking, "What's that?"

"I still really love taking risks."

Eddie's fingers wrapped around his like a vice, and Brian nearly yelped with the bone-crushing pain. Eddie's eyes were closed, his mouth open a little, and Brian thought he might be having some sort of attack.

"Eddie . . ." he said, alarmed. "Eddie! Are you all right?" He tried to pull his hand away, but the other man held it fast. *"Hey! Eddie!"* Shit, was he having a seizure or something?

Fumbling with his free hand for the call button, Brian was stopped short, his breath catching in his throat, as a sudden jolt of electricity raced up his arm. His hand burned with pins and needles. *"Eddie!"* he shouted again.

Just as suddenly as it had begun, the incident ended. Eddie let go of his hand and opened his eyes. His cockeyed smile was back as though nothing the least bit odd had transpired.

"It was good to see you, Meyerson," he said. "I'm sure it won't be the last time."

Brian cradled his tingling hand in his lap as he watched Eddie leave the room. He stared at the closed door for a good five minutes, trying to calm his breathing and clear his head. He thought of calling Cindy in the ER to tell her he was worried about Eddie, and he might have done so if he hadn't suddenly been consumed by exhaustion. Exhaustion like nothing he could remember, sweeping over him like a tidal wave.

He managed to find the button on the side rail to lower the head of his bed. As his upper body drifted downward, he felt as if he were falling miles rather than inches, and he was asleep before he'd even closed his eyes.

Whomp, whomp, whomp.

The Huey bucked a little as it started its descent. He saw Cindy reach for one of the aid bags. McSweet opened his eyes. He looked sick.

"You okay, McSweet?" he asked.

The chopper hit the sand with a soft *thud.* Cindy sprang out of the Huey, and Brian grabbed a backboard and followed her. Sand blew into his face, and for just a moment, he couldn't see.

"Over here!" someone shouted.

"Help me!" someone else begged.

It was so hot! The smell of fire and death seared his nostrils, and sweat ran into his eyes as he ran from one injured soldier to another.

"Someone's hurt behind that burned-out car!" Cindy shouted to him.

"I'll check," he replied.

He ran around the side of the sedan and found a Saudi woman clad in a black *abaya* and *burka.* Her body rose from the sand like a small dark mountain. She raised her hand toward him, and he saw that she cradled a swaddled infant in her other arm.

Catching sight of McSweet standing at the side of the road, he barked, "McSweet! Take care of this woman!"

"I don't think I can, sir," McSweet mumbled.

"Get going, soldier!" Brian stormed over, grabbed the kid's arm, and forced him in the woman's direction.

After a few yards, he let go but waited to make sure McSweet continued walking. He watched as the kid reached the woman, then bent over to take the bundled baby. Brian was about to leave the scene when he noticed a swift change in the woman's dark eyes. *Victory!* her expression said as she reached inside the baby's swaddling. The skin of her hand was very dark, her fingers thick and masculine.

A wave of dizziness washed over him. The woman tugged at the swaddling in slow motion, the layers of fabric floating in the air in front of her, forming a black pile on the sand. Vertigo forced Brian to his knees, his vision clouding over.

"Sergeant?" McSweet asked. "What's wrong?"

What was a Saudi woman doing on this road in Kuwait?

Something dark and metallic lay hidden in the unfurling fabric. Brian knew without a doubt what it was.

Leaping to his feet, he pulled McSweet behind him with one hand and drew his Beretta with the other, aiming it at the woman.

"What are you *doing*?" McSweet asked him.

"Get back!" Brian shouted. His vision seemed clearer than it had ever been, and when the masquerading Iraqi man pulled a gun from the remaining yards of swaddling, he fired his pistol before the man had a chance to shoot.

The shot cracked the still desert air, the bullet cutting cleanly through the black fabric above the imposter's heart. A look of surprise filled the man's dark eyes as he fell backward onto the sand.

Brian turned to see McSweet, Eddie, Dabrowski, and Cindy standing nearby, all staring at the body of the Iraqi, their mouths open in stunned silence.

"Let's get to work," he said as he walked past them, his hand rock steady as he replaced the Beretta in its holster.

* * *

Brian awakened in the darkness, a small headache pressing against his temples. He could hear doctors being paged over the hospital loudspeaker and the sound of an ambulance siren in the distance. A door opened and closed near his head, and in another moment, someone shook him by the shoulder.

"Time to get up," a woman said. "Didn't you hear your page? Motorcycle accident coming in. ETA two minutes."

"What?" Brian asked, his voice muffled by sleep and confusion. The pain in his head receded as he propped himself up on his elbows.

"Nap time's over, Doc." The woman walked away, and the bright light of a hallway poured into the room as she slipped out the door.

He blinked his eyes, frowning.

"Paging Dr. Meyerson." The voice came from somewhere behind

him. "ER. ETA one minute."

Shit, what was going on? He sat up on the bed, swinging his feet to the floor. . . .

His *feet.*

He ran his hands over his thighs—*thighs, plural*—and pinched one of them, instantly wincing at the pain. *He had two legs. And he could feel both of them.*

He stood up, his legs holding him with ease, and realized he was in blue scrubs rather than the pajamas he'd been wearing. He walked into the brightly lit hallway, his gait sure and steady. He was not even limping.

A nurse rushed past him. "Your wife's already in with the patient," she said.

He nodded. His feet knew the way to the treatment room, even if his brain had not quite caught up with his body. He swung open the door to see Cindy helping the paramedics transfer a teenaged boy to the examining table. Vague images sped through his memory: a wedding, Cindy at his side. A house with a yard filled with trees. The birth of twin daughters.

The boy on the examining table groaned.

Above the patient, Brian faced his wife. "What's his status?" he asked her.

"Head injury," she said. "Never lost consciousness. We need to evaluate him for internal injuries and get a scan."

The nurse at Brian's side attached EKG leads to the boy's chest while he palpated his belly. It was hard to concentrate on what he was doing, though, because his eyes were tearing up. Glancing across the table at Cindy, he saw that she was battling tears, as well. But she also wore a smile.

Catching her gaze, he asked quietly, "What the hell just happened?"

The nurse heard him. "What?" she asked, glancing at the monitor against the wall. "Aren't the leads attached right?"

"They're fine," Cindy told her. Then to him, she whispered, "Later."

He couldn't wait. There were too many questions streaming through his head.

"Where's Eddie?" he asked.

"In Florida," she said. "He has perfect vision, and he's married to a saintly woman who puts up with him. He has three amazing kids." She gave him a devilish grin. "And he's an astronaut."

Brian let out a laugh so loud the nurse stopped her task of spreading instruments on a tray and looked at him.

"How about the co-pilot?" Brian asked. "Dabrowski?"

"Back in the Middle East," she said. "He's General Dabrowski now."

"And McSweet?"

"I don't know. We'll have to look him up and see."

"*What* are you two talking about?" the nurse asked them.

Her name was Sandra, he remembered suddenly. He could name every person who worked in the ER. His mind was growing sharper by the second.

"We're just talking about old friends," Cindy said to her.

"Well, maybe we should be talking about the *patient*," Sandra snapped. She could be a real bitch.

"You're right," he said. "We can play catch-up later."

"Catch-up?" Sandra looked both baffled and annoyed. "You two live *and* work together. What can you possibly have to catch up about?"

"You have no idea," Cindy said.

Two hours and ten patients later, he and Cindy were able to take a break at the same time. In the hallway, he caught her hand and pulled her with him into the physician's sleeping room, where he'd awakened a new man that morning. The light was off, and he didn't bother turning it on as he locked the door behind him.

He leaned down to kiss her.

"You look so sexy in these scrubs," he said.

"You always say that," she replied, laughing.

"Do I?" He smiled at her.

He turned on the little reading lamp at the head of the bed, swiveling it toward the wall so that the room filled with a soft, filtered light. Then he undressed his wife. She held very still, seeming at ease with her nudity, letting the pale light wash over her as though she knew he needed to look at every inch of her.

Sitting down on the narrow bed, he studied her as if examining a painting in a museum. Her breasts were small and round and beautiful. He reached up to run a finger across one taut nipple and heard her breath catch in her throat. He was perplexed by the scar across her belly until he remembered she'd had a C-section. He ran his fingertips over the thin line. The babies had been placed, one at a time, into his waiting arms.

"I want to see my daughters," he said, his voice thick. "They're eight, right?"

"Yes," Cindy replied. "Joanna and Molly."

"After our mothers," he said. "And they're identical. Except Joanna's hair is shorter."

"Right, baby," she said. She pressed his head to her belly, leaning over to kiss his hair.

Brian shut his eyes. "It was the handshake, wasn't it?" he asked.

"Yes." She chuckled. "He told me he was afraid he might have broken some bones."

Brian flexed his fingers. They were fine. "Why now?" he asked. "Why didn't he fix his vision before?"

"He wasn't sure he could," she said. "He . . . Brian, Eddie's powers were just beginning back when we knew him in Saudi. They increased over the years, and lately he's been talking about trying to . . . you know . . . make things right. I think he was afraid of what would happen, though. That it might go haywire—that his life would take a very different course, and I'd be left alone. But then you showed up here, and . . . well, he knew it was time."

"Unreal," Brian whispered. He looked up at her. "Thank you," he said. "For everything."

Cindy knelt on the floor in front of him and loosened the ties of his pants. He helped her tug them off, and in a moment, he was undressed, as well. He lowered her to the bed, lay down next to her, and kissed her, taking pleasure in the familiar scent of her, the familiar taste of her tongue. She was an impatient lover, though. She stroked his chest only briefly before sliding her hand down his belly. Finding his erection, she circled it with her fingers.

The sensations were so strong they were nearly unbearable. It was already difficult for him to remember what it had been like to feel nothing down there. More difficult still with every exquisite stroke of her fingers. When he entered her, it seemed like both the first and the millionth time. She wrapped her legs around him, rocking with him, gripping his shoulders with her hands. He struggled to hold back. It had been so long . . . so long . . . She cried out when she came, her body shuddering beneath his, and he allowed his own orgasm to explode, letting out a shout that surprised even him.

They giggled together afterward, whispering, wondering if they might have been heard in the hallway. He didn't really care, and he doubted that Cindy did either. There was too much joy in them to care what anyone else thought.

Brian wrapped his arms gently around her. Lifting her hand to his lips, he kissed her palm. He felt a contentment that had eluded him for more than a decade. Soon, someone would come looking for them, or they would hear one of their names paged over the intercom. For now, though, he would just hold his wife and revel in the feeling of life in her body and in his.

It was more than he'd ever dared to dream.

"Shadow of the Rose"
by
Lucy Grijalva

England, late August, in the Year of Our Lord 1485

"I will find that bastard Henry Tudor, and I will kill him."

The muttered words were all that kept Sir Thomas Kelham going. They had first exploded inside his head as he had staggered from the battlefield near the village of Bosworth, leading his horse. Both of them had been—and still were—filthy, exhausted, and bleeding from a dozen small wounds. God willing, both would survive long enough to hunt down the murderous usurper and put a dagger deep into his heart.

Thomas knew but did not care what happened after that. His death would be either instantaneous or slow and horrible. It mattered not. All that mattered was avenging the traitorous murder on bloody Bosworth field of his friend, his mentor, Richard of Gloucester, King Richard III, known also to his people as Dickon.

Thomas rode slowly down a deserted path between thickets of trees, intent on making his way to London as stealthily as possible. It had been several days since he had escaped the cursed turncoats and foreigners who began hunting the remnants of Dickon's loyal coterie as the battle wound down. He moved slowly; the countryside was crawling with Henry Tudor's men. He knew he was somewhere south of Leicester but did not know where precisely. Soon he must reach London.

When his horse shuffled and whickered, Thomas straightened in the saddle, ignoring the pain in his head, his back, his leg. He dismounted quietly and listened for distant hoofbeats. He did not intend to be caught.

He heard nothing. Even the birds were silent. Indeed, that fact, added to his faith in the horse's instincts, made him grab the reins and dive into an opening in the heavy woods beside the path. They moved quickly back into the cool, dark arms of the forest. Thomas prayed they hadn't left a trail of broken shrubs behind them.

Turning to look behind him, he took a backward step—and tripped on a root.

"Ouch!" whispered the root.

"God's Blood!" Whirling around, he reached for the sword that no longer hung at his side. Lost on the battlefield like so much else.

Of course, it was not a root. It was a pixie.

She was half-hidden in the foliage, sitting stiffly on a log and rubbing her ankle as she gazed up at him with wary eyes.

Thomas stood speechless for a moment. Then he blinked and realized she was not a pixie, but a woman. A small, young, terrified one at that, wearing a dirty blue gown. Her heart-shaped cap was crooked, nearly falling off, and her dark hair floated around her head as she whipped her face away and wrapped her arms about herself.

He controlled his first reaction, which would have involved a lot of shouting, and relaxed a little. She was not a likely threat. Unless she ran screaming from the forest and brought the Tudor's men down upon his head . . .

"Forgive me, madam," he said gravely. "I did not see you sitting there, else I would have stepped around you."

She glanced at him quickly, and some color crept into her cheeks. "You are King Richard's man!"

"Aye. Is it so plain?" He would have to be careful. No telling what loyalties might bind her.

She smiled, and suddenly the dirt and the wild hair didn't matter anymore. She was very pretty. He was not looking for a woman, but neither was he dead—yet.

"If you are hiding from the new king's men, sir, I suggest you find a different tunic. One that doesn't bear white roses."

He looked down at himself in dismay. To make travel easier, he had discarded his armor. But the shirt he had worn so proudly under it as he had gone into battle had been embroidered by his wife with the symbol of the house of York.

Anne had been heavy with their third child at the time. The tunic had turned out to be her final gift to him. Neither she nor the babe had survived the birth.

Now the shirt was torn and bloodied—and an immediate signal to any Tudor ruffian who crossed his path. He must have been blind and stupid not to have thought of it himself.

He looked at the wench. "Thank you. I will see what I can do to remedy such, ah, risky clothing." He cleared his throat. "You are also . . . um . . . ?"

"Hiding? Aye." She shivered. "They will kill me—or worse—if

they find me."

He frowned. "For what crime?"

"For my hall. My home." Her expression crumpled, and he saw the tears start to flow just before she hid her face against her knees. Her shoulders shook as she sobbed.

Thomas looked around uneasily. They were deep enough in the woods, safe, he hoped, from bloodthirsty knights traveling the roads in search of men like him—and women like her.

He need not embrace her troubles as his own. He had a duty to perform that was more important than one frightened wench. He could leave her here and move on. Southward, toward London.

But . . .

He lowered himself to the ground, pain flaring in several limbs. "They will not find us here. Please . . ." He reached out awkwardly to pat her back, then thought better of it. He was not in the habit of worrying about a woman's feelings.

She raised her head and swiped her hand across her face. "They will. They are in the woods. I saw one of them."

Thomas would not have thought he could move so quickly in his condition. He jumped to his feet and grabbed the horse's reins. "Why did you not say so sooner? We need to move on."

She smiled through her tears. "We?"

"Come," he said roughly. "I will take care of you." He wondered whether he could even take care of himself but shoved the thought aside.

She perched on his horse as he led the tired animal deeper into the woods, away from the lane and the cluster of cottages that were set at the foot of the gently rolling hills he had passed shortly before reaching the forest. The cottages stood in the shadow of a large manor house. He did not know what the village was called, knew only that it was on the way to London, in the roundabout route he was traveling.

When he felt it was safe to talk, he said, "Why do they want your house?"

"They think King Henry will award it to them if they already hold it." She was silent for a moment. "Fah! They are fools."

"And . . . they thought you . . . ?"

"They think I come with the house."

"The manor we I passed a short while ago?"

"Aye."

"Who are you?" he asked baldly.

"Lady Cecily Bowen. This is Midhampton. It is *my* home. And I will take it back."

Startled, Thomas stopped walking and turned to look at her. "Bowen? Wife to Sir John Bowen?"

"Aye."

He crossed himself. So she had been widowed for nigh on two years, her husband slain fighting Buckingham's rebellion. "I knew him but slightly, but he was a good man. He went down with his sword in his hand."

"That is how he would have wanted it," she said, and a shadow crossed her face.

He thought of the aging knight Sir John Bowen, loyal to Dickon till the end. He must have been a score of years older than his pixie-like lady. Thomas wondered how long they had been wed. She seemed a mere babe. Then he wondered if she had been grateful for her release . . . and slammed the door on such thoughts, surprised and ashamed of himself. He was not in the habit of worrying about what a woman thought.

"Tell me, sir, your own name."

He started. They had reached a little clearing in the woods, and he looked around them carefully before stopping to introduce himself. "Thomas Kelham, knight." He inclined his head. "Lately in the service of our king Dickon but . . ."

"Hush!" She twisted in the saddle, looking all around them, though there was nothing but trees and tangled undergrowth to see. She looked undecided for a moment, then said crossly, "Oh, I must trust you. I have no choice, have I?"

"Lady, there is no time for games. What is it you wish to say?"

"Quickly—do you see the little path up ahead? Between the great oak tree and the two smaller ones?"

"Aye, perhaps . . ." He scratched his head. It was not truly a path, merely a bit of an opening in the undergrowth. Then, at the same time he heard her sudden intake of breath, his head came up sharply. They had both heard it this time. Muffled voices in the woods to their right.

"Take the path," she hissed. "There is a deserted hut, a woodcutter's cottage—he is long dead, and we can bide there till they are gone."

It was too late. Into the clearing boldly rode two knights. The first one, wearing a scruffy red beard, was saying in French, "She cannot have gone far, a woman alone—" He stopped at the sight of the fugitives on the other side of the clearing and pulled hard on the reins, twisting his horse's head.

The other knight nearly ran into its backside before he, too, came to an abrupt halt. The first one recovered quickly and raced toward them with a furious roar. His sword waved in the air above his head.

Thomas reacted quickly, slapping his horse's rump in hopes it would take the lady out of harm's way. He may have had no sword, but he was not utterly defenseless. He pulled his dagger from its scabbard, dodged out of the way of the oncoming warhorse, then edged back into the cover of the trees. As he wiped sweat from his brow, out of the corner of his eye, he saw the other man, darker and slighter than the first one, wheel his mount and go after Lady Bowen.

"Come, sweeting, we mean you no harm . . ." the liar crooned as he charged after her.

The red-beard's horse swerved and came to a skidding stop, prancing in place for a moment. Thomas knew the rider was trying to decide what to do; he would be at a disadvantage trying to chase a man on foot through the dense woods. The man wore no helmet—who would think he needed one in this conquered country?—but otherwise was well plated.

He peered into the trees, looking for his quarry, and Thomas remained very still. Finally the knight snarled and slid slowly, clumsily off the horse, hampered by his heavy armor. Breathing hard, he started to tramp into the forest. But it was too late.

Before he could take two steps, Thomas closed the distance between them and pressed the knife to the knight's unprotected neck. No coward, the man struggled awkwardly, but this time he was on the losing side.

"For Dickon," Thomas growled. He slashed the red-beard's throat and threw him aside, leaving him face down in the vine-covered soil, twitching and gasping for air with wet, sucking noises.

If Thomas had to fight with all odds against him, at least he could thank the Blessed Lord for sending him the village idiot as an opponent. He took the idiot's sword and began searching for the others.

There was no sign of his own or the dead knight's horse anywhere, but it was an easy task to find the other knight. He was thrashing around in the undergrowth and saplings trying to hold onto his horse's reins and the struggling wench at the same time. Lady Bowen put up a good fight. She had already left several deep, running scratches on the knight's face. And . . . was that a bite mark on his ear?

When Thomas approached, sword in hand, the knight sneered and pushed the woman away. Thomas slowed, assessing the situation. The two of them were equally armed but not equally armored. That had been to his advantage in the last clash but would work against him in the coming one. Still, he had no choice. He raised the sword and charged his opponent.

The other man swung his own gleaming weapon, ready for battle. But then, suddenly, he dropped to the ground—the back of his head caved in and Lady Bowen standing over him gripping a large, bloody stone.

Thomas saw what was coming but, though he tried, could not check his momentum in time. With a helpless cry, he watched his sword slice into the lady's side before he yanked it back.

She looked at him for a moment, shocked. Then her eyes rolled back in her head, and she collapsed on top of the dead French knight.

The horses long gone, Thomas carried her to the woodcutter's hut. He had tarried in the clearing only long enough to pull the two bodies into an overgrown patch of shrubs, hoping no one would easily stumble onto them.

He wanted to undo the last hour. He wanted to bury the sword in his own midsection. He deserved to die a slow and painful death. But no, he had a mission to perform first; he must live a little while longer. He thought he must have sinned mightily to have earned such punishment.

Lady Bowen was still alive. She murmured something he could not hear. He bent his head close to her mouth, but she did not repeat it. Still, her lips moved silently, and he prayed she would survive till he found a safe haven for her.

The cottage was tumbling down and the forest growing back around it, but inside he found a few supplies. She must have been staying there already. A jug, a bundle of drying bread and cheese, and a few candles. There was a rickety stool and a pallet in one corner, the pallet full of rotting straw but covered with a homespun woolen cloak.

He laid her gently upon it and tore open her blood-covered gown with awkward fingers. He left as much of her chemise over her as he could, absurdly trying to preserve her modesty. Somewhere along the way she had lost her pretty little cap.

The wound was just below her ribcage, a bit left of center. He could not tell how deep it went, but at least it had missed her heart and her belly. The bleeding had slowed, and she was half-conscious. But she seemed to be having trouble getting air into her lungs; each breath came harder than the last. He could hear her chest rattle with the effort, and he doubted she had long to live.

What was he to do? Alone, he could escape these Godforsaken woods and be back on the road by nightfall. Granted, he would move more slowly on foot, but he would be better able to hear danger approaching. And, possibly, he would run across one of the horses.

Killing the Tudor usurper was—had been—all that mattered to him, and honor drove him to fulfill the mission. Yet it also forbade him to leave a dying woman. Lady Bowen—Cecily, she had said her name was—had risked her life to try to save his. And now she was like to die—by his own hand.

"Lady Bowen? Can you hear me?"

No response. He ran his fingers over her face. God's Blood, was a fever coming on already? Never had he felt so helpless. He had been away from home, as he so often was, when Anne had gone to her agonizing end . . . and here was yet another woman's death to add to his tally.

In truth, more than honor kept him by Lady Bowen's side. Rusty feelings tugged at his heart. She was so young, so lovely, so spirited . . . and he was so very guilty. He wanted to stay and protect her from evil, to try to atone for the evil he himself had caused. He could not keep her alive, but he owed it to her not to let her die alone.

If only there were gunpowder . . . He would be able to bind her wound with gunpowder, drown it in wine, and perhaps she would recover. But of course he had no gunpowder. Gunpowder was for cannons, and he was a knight.

All he could do was wad a piece of her torn gown and press it against the hole in her side. Her breathing grew more tortured. He knew nothing, really, of doctoring, having always left it to the wisewomen and surgeons. He should go now. His mission called. And she was going to die, whether or not he stayed. . . .

She moaned, tossing her head. Her fingers scrabbled at the bedding. He was afraid she would choke, so he bunched up a bit of the cloak she lay on and created a makeshift pillow for her.

"Please . . ." she whispered.

Her lips were dry and cracked. He opened the jug she had left and sniffed it. Mead wine. He allowed a little to trickle onto his forefinger and rubbed it across her lips. Her tongue followed the movement of his fingers. He gave her a little more.

She opened her eyes and gazed into his. "Thank you," she murmured. "You saved my life."

He had saved her life? God's Blood, she had saved *his*. And in return, he had taken hers. In that moment, Thomas knew that he could not leave her. He would stay till she recovered . . . or died.

Besides, Henry Tudor was likely in Leicester still. Giving him another day to get to London would do no harm.

The fever came on quickly. By late afternoon, Lady Bowen's skin was clammy and hot by turns. She murmured a few words occasionally, but Thomas could not make them out.

At sunset, he feared he was losing her. She had stopped tossing and lay quiet, except for occasional hitching breaths. Her fever was rising, and the blood-soaked cloth he was still holding to her side was useless. Yet he knew naught else to do.

He knelt beside the pallet, holding her hand tightly, and bowed his head in sorrow. There was no priest to shrive her, but he prayed for her immortal soul.

And then something wondrous happened. She spoke to him—no feverish ramblings, but her own sweet, clear voice, and it was full of urgency.

"Sir Thomas. Sir Thomas! You must leave off weeping and follow my instructions."

He looked up quickly, smiling through the tears he hadn't realized he was shedding, but she lay motionless, eyes closed.

"My Lady Bowen . . ." He laid a hand on her cheek. Still on fire, and the sweat beaded on her forehead. He brushed it away gently. "Tell me your desire."

"You must gather . . ."

But Thomas did not listen to her words as she continued. His heart nearly stopped as he watched her lying there near death, lips unmoving . . . and yet she was speaking. He could hear her clearly.

But she was *not* speaking.

He looked around the hut quickly. It was nigh dark inside, but he knew no one else was there. Still, perhaps from fear, he roared, "Who goes there?" His hand fumbled for the knife at his waist.

All was silent for a moment. Then Cecily spoke again.

"Sir Thomas. Please," she beseeched him, her tone almost impatient.

He swiveled back to her. He had been right when he first stumbled on her and thought her a forest pixie. Nay, worse—she was a witch. Or perhaps the woods were haunted. Perhaps they were both dead.

"Sir Thomas, do not fail me!"

Then again, perhaps he had been struck in the head and lost his wits. Or else his eyes were failing. He could hear her clearly, not like the faraway voices in a dream.

He summoned his courage, which had never failed him against any foe and which he prayed would hold even against witchcraft, if this be such. "My lady?"

"Please, you must do as I ask. We haven't much time."

"What is your wish, madam?"

"You must gather some cobwebs and bring them to me."

"Cobwebs?" he said stupidly. What kind of witchery was that? But . . . Aye! He remembered now. As a boy he had once seen the wisewoman in his village pack a gaping wound from a dog bite with cobwebs. The man had recovered and still lived to this day, as far as Thomas knew.

"Cobwebs," he said again. "I understand."

"Good. Then you must go to the clearing. Bring back the leaves of the milfoil flower. It grows wild there."

He felt himself blanching. What if he brought the wrong herb? "How will I know it?"

"It is everywhere this time of year. Look for white flowers and feathery leaves. Oh! Then follow the path behind the cottage. Take a cloth and rinse it in the stream. A candle—you will need a candle . . ." She broke off with a groan. Then she whispered, "Please, hurry."

"Aye, lady. I am off." He tore another piece from her crumbling gown. Striking the flint, he lit a candle, filling the small space with the acrid smell of burning tallow. He turned to her once more, indecisive, then patted her pale cheek and set out quickly to do her bidding.

As he headed through the forest, he scanned the trees surrounding him, wary of other magical beings who might be lurking. But his gaze could not penetrate the blackness of the night. Nor had he any time for fear.

Quickly he made his way to the clearing, averting his face and crossing himself as he passed the spot where he had hidden the French knights' bodies. Perhaps later he would bury them.

Lady Bowen had been right. He had not noticed before, but wherever the candle lit the night, he saw feathery white flowers and leaves. Yanking them carelessly from the ground, he gathered as many as he could hold in one hand, then headed back toward the cottage.

On the dark path behind the hut, he stumbled a few times, but he found the stream and rinsed the cloth. Then he cupped his hands and drank. The cool water revived him, and he splashed some onto his face, too. Quickly, quickly . . .

Hastening up the path, he arrived at the cottage to find Lady Bowen still breathing—but just barely.

Still, her voice was sharp and clear. "Cobwebs?"

He set the candle on the rickety stool. "Do not fear, my lady, they are everywhere in these ruins."

"Aye, of course." He could hear the smile in her voice. "Now, you must clean the wound and pack it with cobwebs."

He drew back, slightly horrified at the idea despite having known what to expect.

"Sir Thomas?" she admonished. "Do not fail me now."

Swallowing his repugnance, he assured her, "I will not, my lady."

Even as she directed his actions, her body remained eerily lifeless. At her command, he carefully peeled away the makeshift bandage he had pressed on her earlier. It dripped dark red in the candlelight, but it did appear that the wound had stopped bleeding. He saw no sign of infection as yet; nevertheless, her fever was a bad omen.

He dabbed the clean, wet cloth as gently as he could manage around the open wound. Then, biting hard on the inside of his cheeks, he patted the cobwebs gathered from the dark corners of the hut into place directly on the wound. She moaned, and he knew his actions were only exacerbating her pain. He felt that pain like stabbing deep in his own chest.

"What next, my lady? The flowers. . . ? Lady Bowen?" For one heart-stopping moment, he feared she was gone.

But then, she took a shallow, labored breath. And again, amazingly, when she spoke, her voice was strong. "Cover it with the milfoil leaves. Then bandage it once more."

"The leaves? Should I steep them first? I know not the wisewoman's ways."

"There is no time. Crush them with your fingers, and get on with it."

Thomas did as he was told. He was not in the habit of taking orders from women, but she surely had earned the right this day to issue them. Finally, he tore away the bottom of her chemise to make a bandage and wrapped more strips of linen around her middle to hold it in place.

"I thank you, Sir Thomas. That is much better." The smile was back in her voice.

He put out the candle. The glow might attract undue attention if anyone were about, unlikely as that was. It was far more likely that he felt better not being able to see her clearly. He didn't like to admit even to himself that he was frightened of her witchery. But oddly, he was becoming accustomed to her magical means of speaking.

Groping in the dark, he found the jug of mead and the bread and cheese he had seen earlier, then lowered himself beside her on the pallet. As before, he fed her a few drops of wine from his fingertips, then a little more. Perhaps it would help dull her pain.

Thomas recognized in a distant sort of way that he was nigh starving. He hadn't eaten since early that morn, when a peasant woman had found him asleep in her haystack and taken pity on him. The bread was stale and the cheese dried out, but they tasted like a royal banquet.

Cecily—he had started thinking of her by her given name sometime during the night—was no more than a shadow. He felt for her hand and warmed it in his. He would not let her be alone in the dark this night.

She said suddenly, "Sir Thomas! Did you not leave any supper for me?" and behind his eyes he could see her pixie smile. But her hand lay cold and motionless in his, except for a faint pulse.

He hadn't saved any food for her because he did not believe she would survive the night. Her voice might sound confident, but her body was weak. He thought perhaps he should keep that thought to himself.

"I am resourceful, my lady, and when you are ready, I will find something better to feed you. The woods are full of game."

He didn't admit, even to himself, that alone, on foot, armed only with a knife and a sword suited more to battle, hunting might prove difficult.

She smiled again, but her voice sounded weary. "You are a brave knight, Sir Thomas. Even when everything is against you. But I fear God has deserted us."

"Never, my lady. I have faith there is a reason behind our suffering." He thought of Dickon, and his eyes squeezed shut in pain. Perhaps God had his reasons, but Thomas knew he would never be able to discern them.

"And ours is not to ask why," she added. "Still, 'tis best we do what we can to help ourselves, as well." Then, as if she regretted her blasphemy and sought to make amends, she asked urgently, "Oh, where are my prayer beads? Where is my belt?"

In his mind he could almost feel her groping around, but her hand in his remained still. "Wait—I will find them."

He had tossed aside her belt when he had ripped off her clothing. He found it near the foot of the pallet and carefully freed her rosary beads. He knew not how she could talk to him in her unconscious state, nor how she could know whether or not she was holding a rosary—any more than she could have known when he had cleaned and dressed her wound. But as he placed the beads in her hand and wrapped her fingers firmly around them, he heard a distinct sigh of relief.

"Ah, there they are. Thank you. You are very kind."

He almost laughed, despite the underlying misery plaguing him. "That is not an accusation I have often heard made against me."

She smiled, too. He could almost see it . . . almost.

"I'm sure you are a very cruel, hardhearted knight," she said. "Doubtless you beat your horse every day, whether or nay he deserves it."

"Madam! Perhaps my children. Never my horse."

"Your children? Oh, tell me of them."

"They are boys, both of them. Edward and Richard. They are too young yet to be fostered—the elder is but four years—but I left them in the care of my sister." As he spoke, a sudden, unaccustomed pain gripped his heart. His two small boys . . . they would be alone, orphans, after his death. But it could not be helped.

"Your wife?"

"Gone," he said abruptly. "In childbirth, last year. The babe died, too. Another boy."

She made a comforting sound deep in her throat. "So much sorrow in the world. I grieve for your loss."

He accepted her words with a nod. "As I do yours. We have seen too many battles in this land. So many fine men lost . . . I have prayed for peace, to no avail. And now, all is lost."

"Perhaps not. Perhaps now we shall finally have some peace."

His head whipped around. "What is that you say? How can we have peace with a murderous usurper on the throne?"

"Henry Tudor has sworn to wed Dickon's niece, Elizabeth of York. Do you not think the two sides can reach harmony when they are joined at last?"

Anger made red spots in front of his eyes. He would have slain a man who spoke such treason. The Yorkist and Lancastrian lines, both descended from old King Edward III, had been fighting over the English throne for nigh onto a century. York had held it for most of the past five-and-twenty years. It was unthinkable that the upstart Henry Tudor, spawn of the bastard branch of the Lancasters, should marry his way into a legal claim to the throne.

Restraining his impulse to draw his sword—he had already skewered the poor woman with it once and was not about to do so again—Thomas muttered under his breath, "The Tudor will not live to wed the girl."

"Forgive me, I could not hear you."

"I will not allow him to rule," he said aloud.

There was a moment of stunned silence. "You will not allow Henry Tudor to rule? Has he not already been proclaimed king?"

"I am for London. He will arrive there soon, hoping to take the city easily. But I will not allow it to happen. I will kill him first."

A brief pause ensued. Then came her voice again, sounding faint in his head.

"How do you propose to accomplish such a feat? He will be surrounded by his men, and every remaining lord in the land will be kissing his . . . well, never mind that. He will be heavily guarded. You will do this alone?"

She had hit upon the weakest link in his plans. "I know not as yet how I will do it, but I am determined. Perhaps I will approach him to swear allegiance, then—"

"An honorable means of committing murder," she murmured.

He felt his face flush in the dark. "Then I will find another way. And it is not murder. It is war."

"And afterward? His men will tear you to pieces on the spot . . . if you are lucky. If not . . ."

She shivered. He felt it, but not with his hands or body.

He knew what frightened her. If he were caught alive, he could expect to hang, then be cut down alive and disemboweled. Finally, his head would hang on a pike from London Bridge. The thought frightened him, too.

"I will not be caught alive." He swallowed. And if he managed to kill himself first, he would burn in hellfire for all eternity. It was a price he was willing to pay. He owed it to Dickon.

"Sir Thomas," she said urgently. "I beg of you to reconsider. For the sake of your immortal soul."

"My immortal soul is no concern of yours."

"Then for the sake of your children. Would you leave them alone, to fend for themselves on this earth, tainted by a father who has murdered a king?"

"Silence, woman!"

She made a disgusted sound but subsided. They both lay quiet for a few minutes. Instead of disregarding her entirely as he wished to do and relax into sleep, Thomas could not stop Cecily's words from swirling around in his head. The sons he had barely had time to get to know, the little babes who already lacked a mother . . .

"Are you wakeful?" she asked.

"Aye."

"Do you think about your children?"

"Aye." He turned away from her on the scratchy pallet and tried to settle into a comfortable position for sleeping. He did not care to discuss the subject further.

"I, too, have children. Their fate worries me this night."

He turned back to face her. "You jest! You are barely old enough to be wed, let alone the mother of a passel of brats."

"There, I knew you were a kindly soul!" She laughed happily.

He almost smiled. Then his face fell. He might be under a magical spell—or merely insane, feverish, or dead—but conversing with a dying, unconscious woman was no doubt a brief stop on the road to perdition. Perhaps he should lie back and close his eyes. Then he could imagine he was speaking to a person who was alive and awake, and who was responding in kind . . . not merely inside his head.

"It is no jest," she continued. "I am past four-and-twenty. Well enough grown to be wed, a mother . . . even a widow."

"And your children? Boys?"

"Nay, they are girls. A disappointment to their father, but a great joy to me."

"No sons? You are fortunate to still hold your husband's estate."

"It was my own property. I was born on this land. Still, the king would have found me another husband—"

Thomas's brow darkened. "Aye. If he had had time."

"Now the new king will have to do so."

His breath caught. "Are you deliberately trying my temper, woman, or have you no sense at all?"

She paused to consider her words. "You are not the only one on the road to London, Sir Thomas. I, too, plan to seek out Henry Tudor, the *new king*. I will petition him to find a husband for me who will hold this land for him . . . and I expect the king to be alive when I find him!"

After Thomas stopped shouting—a feat accomplished only because Cecily refused to respond—he fell into a sulk. She left him to it for a time, for which he had to give her credit, but then she began speaking again—to his astonishment, as if he had not been spitting furious with her but a short while ago. Also to his great surprise, he gradually calmed down and, before long, began once again to enjoy the strange experience of conversing with a woman who was not quite *there*.

She told him something of her life. Sir John had treated her kindly, and she had been fond of him. As a knight in service to King Richard, he had frequently been gone from home, but no one questioned his ultimate authority.

After his death, it had become ever more difficult to run the estate. When the retainers knew the lord would return, they had obeyed orders given by the lady of the manor; Sir John's death had lessened her authority, but with Dickon on the throne, providing her with a vague sense of protection, she still had managed. Now that he, too, was gone . . . well, she was determined to hold the land but knew that, unless she acted swiftly, it was only a matter of time before she lost all that she held most dear.

"You saw it yourself," she said. "We are vulnerable to attack, and there is no one to protect us. The two knights we met yesterday are gone, but more will come in their place."

She shuddered, and Thomas experienced it within his soul.

Then she went on. "I hid my children and ran. But here in the woods, I had time to think. And it came to me that there is a solution. King Henry can—"

"Do not call him that."

She sighed. "*Henry Tudor* can find a husband for me."

"God's Blood!" Thomas exploded. "You would take a hanger-on from a usurper only to save your land? They are naught but filthy murderers."

"They are men," she said calmly. "I would sooner have a husband, and protection for my children, than have my property stolen and nowhere to take the babes. Think you not that Henry Tudor would give my land to one of his men as a reward?"

"Aye, he will. And that is why we should fight him."

"I am not a warrior. I am just a woman. I want my girls kept safe, and I want my home. So I will go to King Henry—nay, do not say it again!—and I will beg him for a suitable husband."

Thomas growled his frustration. "Then I have nothing more to say to you."

"As you wish."

They lay in silence for a few moments before he began to feel foolish. He reached over and placed a hand against her cheek. Still feverish. And her breathing sounded difficult and painful. He took her hand in his. She did not react. "Lady Bowen? Do you sleep?"

"I am awake."

He hesitated a moment, then asked, "Where are your children now?"

"In the village with their nurse. Her son has a cottage, and no one will bother them there. They can pass for village children until I return."

"What are their names?"

"Mary and Catherine." He heard the smile in her voice. "Twins. They are little ladies already. At Yuletide they will be seven years old."

"And what is the nurse called?"

"Edith."

She did not seem concerned by his questions. But he feared that, come morn, he might be called upon to search out the nurse and give her sorrowful news. He clutched Cecily's hand a little more tightly in his own.

"Sir Thomas . . . my children are most important to me. Even more important than my land and my house."

"Aye, I understand."

"Do you? Do you truly understand?"

"I . . . believe so."

"Because I think you cannot, unless your children are equally important to you."

"What nonsense is this? I love my children."

"You do not love your children enough."

Understanding her direction, he felt his blood heat in anger once again. "I *love* my children," he insisted. "And I could not face them again if I turned my back on my allegiance to my king."

"So you will turn your back on them instead. They are mere babes. And you would leave them orphaned and attainted."

He gave a disgusted snort. "You must have been a nagging wife. I hope your husband beat you."

"There was no need. I would never nag my husband," she said in a voice brimming with virtue.

For the first time in that long, dark night, Thomas laughed. It felt as though a knot were loosening in his belly, and it left a smile on his face. And for the first time, he dared to hope that perhaps . . . perhaps she would live after all.

She was not finished with him yet. "Think you that they will understand when they are grown?"

His smile faded. "I hope it will be so. There is much I wished to teach them."

"I am certain you have taught them much already."

"I fear I was often away in recent years and saw but little of my family."

"You saw enough of them to start three boys in as many years," she said tartly.

He knew no suitable reply and acknowledged the aptness of her statement with his silence.

"Fah! I *am* a nag. Please forgive such an unkind remark."

"Nay, it is but the truth. I have badly neglected my family."

"Dickon needed you, too."

"That he did. But now he is gone . . . Anne is gone . . . and neither am I like to see my boys again."

She murmured something soft, and he inched closer to her on the pallet. Not to better hear her—he had learned it would make no difference—but because he needed to feel her nearness.

She, too, had known the pain of loss, of being alone. Perhaps that was why he found himself speaking so freely to her. He was not in the habit of holding personal discussions with a woman. Most of the time, their heads were too full of . . . of women's matters to be able to conduct an intelligent conversation.

He shifted position a bit, unable to get comfortable again. But he didn't want to move away from her warmth. Instead, he wrapped her hand in his and held it to his chest as a great, throbbing, unhealable wound grew inside him.

"What grieves you, sweeting?"

The kindness and concern in her voice only added to his pain. "It's naught to concern you, my lady."

He hadn't intended to reply so roughly, but his loyalty to Dickon was a man's affair. She had made it clear that she did not accept it, would never accept it. Her world was made up of smaller things: home, children, family.

In truth, her world was something he had given up . . . and would sorely miss. He barely knew his children. The blood lust he had felt ringing in his ears after seeing Dickon cut down in battle . . . was it fading? But honor demanded . . .

"I have but one more thing to say to you this night, and then I will be silent," she said softly, and without waiting for him to reply, rushed on, "You spoke of your allegiance to your king. And it is right that you should be loyal to him and to his memory. But we have a new king. If you truly love your family and this kingdom—if you love life—then your allegiance will lie with the king, *whoever he may be.*"

She paused, seeming to search for the right words. "I do not believe Dickon would think it honorable for you to give your life needlessly in his name. I believe he would consider it a great waste."

To his horror, tears threatened. And then the second miracle of the night occurred. He felt her fingers flutter in his hand and stroke his palm. The movement, barely perceptible, stole his last shreds of control, and his shoulders heaved as he sobbed. The losses, the pain, the grief . . .

"Nay, sweeting, it will all come right," she crooned. "There now . . ."

When he was quiet again, he became aware of the night's third miracle. When it had begun, he would never know. But he could no longer hear her tortured attempts to take air into her lungs. Instead, she was breathing peacefully.

She slept. And, finally, so did he.

* * *

Consciousness creaked slowly into his brain. He lay still, because Cecily—Lady Bowen—was stretched along the length of his body, her head tucked into the crook of his neck. His arm was thrown across her shoulder, his fingers tangled in her hair. And, bless all the angels in heaven, she breathed still. With her forehead pressed against his bristly cheek, he could tell her fever had fallen.

Sunlight filtered through the unshuttered window, warming them. In truth, Thomas was in no hurry to move and break the spell. When had he last felt such peace and contentment?

Finally, though, he eased himself away and knelt beside the pallet to look down at her. Her eyelids fluttered.

"Nay, sleep, little pixie," he said, and brushed a stray hair back from her brow.

He rose stiffly and went outside to relieve himself. When he returned, he uncorked the jug of mead, swept the previous night's candle off the stool, and sat. A good swig of wine helped clear his throat and his head. He had been like to think he was losing his mind, but now in the clear light of day—

"Sir Thomas," Cecily said in a rusty voice.

He put down the jug and wiped his mouth. "My lady . . ." Suddenly, his head jerked up and his spine straightened as he realized he was hearing her not inside his head but with his ears. Twisting on the stool, he turned to look at her.

She lay on the pallet, eyes half-open, looking his way.

"You live! It is truly a miracle from God," he breathed as he crossed himself. Then he moved to the pallet and hunkered down beside her. "Does it not pain you to breathe?"

She shook her head slowly.

"Then let me change your bandage."

He lifted away the soiled dressing and checked her wound. It was not suppurating as he had feared. In truth, it looked very clean, though her skin was stained green from the milfoil. He tossed away the leaves and the bandage and wiped the injured area clean with a scrap of linen moistened in wine, gritting his teeth to continue when she flinched. He used the last of the linen to fashion a new bandage.

When he had finished, he laid a hand against her side and his fingers gently brushed her bare flesh, sending an unexpected shiver through him. Mere inches from his thumb, the immodest curve of her breast, barely covered in once-fine linen, distracted him.

God's Blood! Flushing, he glanced at her face, but she had turned away. Her teeth caught at her lower lip.

"Does it pain you much?"

"Aye," she croaked. "As do you. You need not stare."

"Forgive me, madam." But he could not bring himself to take his hand away. Not yet. His thumb stroked a light, gentle rhythm against her side.

He told himself there was nothing carnal in his need to touch her. It was merely his role as surgeon and nursemaid that kept him there. He felt like a large, clumsy oaf compared to her small, perfect form. But some unearthly connection between them made him loath to give her up.

This time it was she who shivered. She turned her face to him. "Sir Thomas . . ."

He looked up guiltily. But her expression was not of pain or fear or anger; rather, her eyes looked soft, and her lips were parted. He knew that look on a woman's face.

His hand left her midsection and slid into her fly-about hair. Then he leaned over her and, with agonizing gentleness, lowered his head. Her chin rose to meet him.

Thomas willed it to be merely a light kiss. *Nursemaid!* he reminded himself. But the tip of her tongue stole between the seam of his lips and pulled him into her magic spell, brimming with promise and hope. She awakened in him a dormant fire. He groaned and struggled to hold his body away from hers, knowing the pain he would cause her if he touched her the way he wished to.

Reason caught hold, and he said against her mouth, "Nay, that is enough!"

He tumbled away from her. But she lifted a hand toward him, and he took it, holding it tightly in his own, not wanting to let her go. Her cheeks were pink, and he knew without a doubt that this fever was of his making.

From the moment he had dashed into this enchanted forest, nothing had happened as he had planned. Thank God. For as he had slept, a new plan had arisen in his mind, and it held far more interesting possbilities than the old one.

He rocked back on his heels. "Let me see you speak."

She looked confused. "*See* me? Do not you mean hear me?"

"See you. Hear you. Do you not recall what happened during the night?"

"I know not . . . did aught happen?" Her cheeks reddened. "I was ill. You brought me here, I suppose—I do not remember that part. We talked a bit. But more than that, I cannot say."

"*Did* we talk a bit?"

"Aye! We spoke much . . . did we not?"

"You directed me to the milfoil plant."

"Aye."

"You spoke to me of your children and your home."

"Aye."

"You offered much unasked-for advice."

"Oh, *aye*." Mystified, she shook her head. "What more?"

"Lady Bow— Cecily . . . last night I witnessed a miracle. Either that, or you are a witch."

She paled instantly. "Do not say such a thing! I am no witch! You must be mad." Her mouth snapped shut, and she turned her face away.

"In truth, I considered that likelihood. But were I a madman, then perhaps I would not have been so disbelieving."

Slowly, she turned back to him. "Disbelieving of what?"

He took pity on her and cupped the side of her face with one large hand. In contrast, she seemed so small, so defenseless—and so completely terrified, more frightened than she had been throughout the long hours of the night. "You lay near death from sunset till near dawn. You were feverish, unaware, unconscious. You could not speak. Not a word."

"But . . . I remember . . . you said . . ."

"My lady, you spoke not with words but inside my head. Your lips did not move, but I heard your voice. I cannot explain it better than that."

"Nay, it is not so!" Her face crumpled.

"It is. And I do not believe you are a witch. God sent us a miracle, and you should be grateful and stop mewling like a babe."

"You understand naught." She opened her eyes and met his gaze. One hand came up and grasped his arm. Her voice was scratchy but steady as she said, "You must not speak of this to anyone. Promise me! Swear it on your honor."

"What do I not understand?"

"My granddam was a witch. She hanged for it. I will not go that road."

Nonplussed, Thomas stared at her for several long moments before finding his voice. "A witch?" he said hoarsely.

"She heard voices. I do not hear voices. I will never hear voices. And neither did you hear voices. Do you understand?"

He did understand and looked at her with new respect.

He nodded once, slowly. "In truth, it was a miracle sent by God. Perhaps a miracle best kept to ourselves."

"Aye, a miracle. Between us alone." She gave him a little smile, and her voice dropped nigh to a whisper. "Do you know, Sir Thomas, I believe death *would* have taken me, had you not been here to talk, to argue—nay, to keep my very soul alive."

Her words left him speechless once more. He wished to kiss her again but quashed the impulse. Indecisive, he let his gaze slide from hers. Then he thought he heard her breath hitch as it had during the night, and his gaze shot back to her in alarm. Her mouth turned downwards.

"Oh, it is useless . . ." She shook her head and lifted her hands in supplication. No nonsense, no hitching breath. "Now, please, sir, help me to rise. I cannot lie about all day."

With misgivings, he slid an arm around her shoulders and raised her to a sitting position. She tensed with pain and pressed her hands to her bandaged midsection.

"This is too painful for you. You must rest."

"Nay." She was very pale. "I believe you should move on. It is not safe to stay here long."

"We will bide another day or two, until you are well enough to travel."

"You are kind, but you've done enough. If you will stop by the village and notify Edith's family, they will come for me."

"We will go together to London."

"Do not tarry. Go to London without me."

"Now, it is you who are mad. Think you that I went to such trouble to save your life only to desert you when the sun rises?"

She raised her gaze to his. "And think you that I wish to watch you die? Nay, I will wait at Midhampton and see which way the wind blows."

Thomas scowled. "The wind blows cold and cruel. Still . . ." His scowl softened to a frown. "As I left the battlefield, I heard . . ."

"What?"

"That Henry Tudor will pardon any of Dickon's soldiers who swear allegiance to him." He searched her features, then locked his gaze with hers as he said, "Perhaps he will apply the same generosity to Dickon's knights."

Cecily's mouth fell open and remained so for an instant or two. But she was never long at a loss for words. "His hold on the crown is fragile. I believe that he would welcome a knight whose loyalty to the kingdom and the crown is above dispute."

Thomas was beginning to believe it, too. Still holding her gaze, he continued, speaking with deliberation and care. "The countryside is in chaos. It will need a strong hand to bring it under control again."

"The king cannot leave a manor like Midhampton untended for long," she said with studied care equal to his own. "He must place a trustworthy knight in charge of it. One who will care for its inhabitants as well."

"Aye."

"And likely, if that knight were not one of the king's close retainers, he would need not spend so much of his time away on the king's business."

"Aye. But it is a dangerous venture to go about," he warned her. "There is no guarantee the king would welcome an errant knight into the fold."

"Still, it is a venture worth pursuing, with a great reward possible for such a brave knight."

The words they were speaking were but a small part of the discourse passing between them; her eyes told Thomas all the things she was not saying, and he was certain his gaze, still holding fast to hers, was doing the same. He intended that it be so. He intended to tell her more about his sentiments than he had ever told any woman.

His fingers stroked her shoulder lightly. "It would be best if the lady of the manor were willing."

"But you would take her, willing or nay?"

"Aye."

"Aye," she echoed. "Perhaps you should kiss her again and make certain it is your heart's true desire."

"Perhaps. When the time seems . . ."

"*Now*, sir."

Sir Thomas Kelham was not in the habit of taking orders from women. When called upon, he was a fearless warrior. But he had learned it was in his own best interest to stay on the good side of pixies, witches, and others of their ilk.

"The Shadowed Heart"
by
Catherine Asaro

The colony Daretown on the planet Thrice Named, in the year 2276

Night protected him. He ventured out only after the sun had set. Then he sifted through the ruins, searching for pieces of himself. Surely the parts of his soul he had lost were buried in this debris. A technology park had stood here before the Radiance War, but all that remained were shards of dichromesh glass, melted Luminex, and mounds of casecrete.

Once he had been a Jagernaut, a starfighter pilot. Harrick, they had called him. He and Blackwing, his Jag fighter, had been one mind. Together, they blended with the rest of his squadron. Four pilots and four ships; they were a team without equal, able to deal with space combat in a way normal humans could never manage. That was why Jagernauts were empaths: they linked minds during battle. The difficult decision to send empaths into combat came from the desperate need of his people to counter the stronger forces of their enemies, the Traders. Nothing could match the versatility of a Jag squadron. They lived, breathed, and fought together.

And when they died, they died together.

Except Harrick had survived. His ship had crashed, and he had crawled out of the wreckage into these ruins. He had stayed here ever since, looking for the pieces of his lost soul.

Rhose had wandered too far in her search. She had promised her family that she would bring back a supply of "remnants," energy sources from vehicles or spacecraft that had crashed during the war. When scavenged, they could provide heat and light for a house. The remnants near their home had all been taken, so she had ventured farther than usual, out here to what had once been a thriving technology park but now stretched into a smashed, desolate landscape.

As the sun set behind the broken towers, she sought refuge in a building with no roof. Most of the walls had fallen into rubble, but in one corner they reached above her head. The batteries in her lamp had failed, and like so much else in Daretown, her spares hadn't worked, either. With the sky overcast, she didn't have starlight. She doubted she could walk the twenty kilometers back in the dark, and after dark, gangs roved the outskirts of Daretown. Law hadn't broken down in the town, but at night certain areas were best avoided. Although she had a stun gun to protect herself, it would probably be safer to stay here for now and walk back to Daretown in the morning.

Rhose wished she had a comm to let her family know she was all right. Their old one had broken a month ago, and no one in town had new ones. Nor did her family have access to a vehicle. She couldn't even get equipment for her school. Daretown had never been affluent and now its people were barely surviving. It wasn't unheard of for a colonist to be out for the entire night, but she knew her family would fear the worst, that she had been kidnapped or murdered. Rhose shivered as she settled into the corner amid the hard chunks of casecrete. At least the gangs never came to these ruins, which were far from the city and sup- posedly haunted with cybernetic monstrosities.

Night fell gradually and left her in an oppressive darkness. When she held up her hands, she could make out their shape but little else. Cold seeped past her layers of sweaters and leggings. She folded her arms around her body and wedged herself farther back among the bro- ken casecrete. Night lasted thirty hours at this time of year, which meant it was going to get a lot colder. She could sleep, wake, and sleep again before dawn lightened the world. She rummaged in a pocket of her outermost sweater. Good. Her meat roll and water tube were there. Although she would have to ration her food and she would be ravenous by morning, she wouldn't starve.

A cry echoed through the ruins.

"Saints," Rhose muttered. The wail sounded like an animal, but she couldn't be certain. She breathed in deeply. She had a curious sensation, as if she was aware of a disturbance in the air, yet she didn't hear, smell, or feel anything. She told herself that she had no need to worry about military assaults or land mines; the defending and invading ships had all destroyed each other in space. The enemy strikes against Daretown had come from orbit, a spiteful assault on a colony of civilians no one had any reason to attack.

Debris clinked across the room.

Rhose froze. She strained to hear, but the night had gone quiet. Too quiet. She hadn't realized how many whirs and clicks saturated the air until the tiny creatures that populated the ruins stopped their serenade.

"Who's there?" she asked.

No answer.

It's nothing, she told herself. Machine monsters didn't stalk this bleak place. Those were stories to frighten children.

Metal clinked.

She closed her fist around a chunk of casecrete and peered into the darkness. She couldn't see anything. With her other hand, she drew the taser from one of her sweater pockets. Bracing her arms on a boulder, she rose to her feet.

A scrape.

The noise seemed about twenty paces away, but she had no idea if it was friend or foe, alive or machine, big or small. If only she could see. An army of biomech creatures could be hulking out here, unnaturally silent in their mechanized lives. For all she knew, she was about to die.

A deep voice rumbled. "Who are you?"

So. It was a man. He spoke Skolian Flag, a common language taught many places and designed so that the disparate peoples of their far-flung settlements could communicate.

She switched into Flag. "I'm Rhose."

A light appeared—and revealed a stranger. He was huge, over two heads taller than she and at least twice her weight. His arms strained the ragged cloth of his body-shirt. His face was hard to see with his hand partly covering his sphere-lamp, and also because of his dark, tangled hair. His clothes were black: a tattered shirt, form-fitting trousers, and heavy boots. A huge gun was holstered at his hip. He stood with his legs braced apart, a giant defending his territory.

Rhose spoke under her breath. "Gods almighty."

His heavy accent gave his words a harsh quality. "You aren't welcome. Leave."

Rhose wished she could leave, and fast. He was blocking the ragged opening she had used to climb in here. With the wall at her back and no light, she had only one option to get out: squeeze past him.

"I don't mean any trouble." Rhose inched along the wall, then stopped when she hit a pile of rubble. "I won't bother you."

Incredibly, he jerked as if she had threatened him just by moving forward. He lifted his glowing sphere, and light leaked around his large hand. He had long fingers, gnarled and slashed with either scars or recently healed wounds. She thought she saw injuries on his forearms, too, through the rips of his shirt.

"You're hurt," she said. "Did one of the gangs catch you?" She had thought they never came out this far.

He answered tightly. "If only."

If only? She couldn't imagine why he would say such a thing. Something was wrong here, something worse than marauding gangs.

"Do you need medical help?" she asked. Given the limited resources in the city, she often ended up treating children in the school.

"No." Gruffly, he added, "Your voice is shaking."

"It's cold. And it's too dark for me to go anywhere." *And I'm afraid of you.*

"Come over here." He sounded oddly reluctant. "Let me get a look at you."

Rhose edged forward, still holding the rock and taser, picking her way through the rubble. He watched intently, his hand clenched on the glowing sphere. She *felt* his troubled spirit. Although she couldn't tell what bothered him, it disquieted her that she could pick up so much. Granted, she had always been good at reading people, but her awareness of him went beyond her usual sensitivity.

As she drew nearer, she noticed he was clean shaven. That he removed his beard despite living here suggested he wasn't normally a derelict.

She stopped in front of him. "Better?"

"Yes."

"Do you want me look at your injuries?"

"No."

"You've nothing to fear from me." Then she realized how bizarre that sounded, that a man of his size and obvious strength could possibly fear such a wisp of a woman.

"What do you want here?" he asked.

"Shelter," she said.

He didn't answer, but his silence had a different quality now, more thoughtful. She had always been a good judge of people's character and emotions, and her sense of his moods was even stronger than usual. It seemed tangible.

"Night here lasts a long time," he said.

Rhose blinked. The night was the night. It never varied much, only a few hours longer in winter than in summer.

"I guess," she said.

"You shouldn't have to freeze or starve because of that."

Rhose doubted she would do either. She didn't understand him.

Nor did she know what to make of his monstrous gun. She wasn't even certain it was real. But it told her a great deal about him that his first concern, even when he didn't want her here, was for her well-being.

"I'll be all right." She kept her voice soothing, the way she might talk to a spooked cat. Humans had brought felines to this terraformed world, but since the war many had become homeless and gone wild—perhaps like this man.

In a low voice, he muttered, "Can't turn away someone in need."

Some of her tension eased. "What is your name?" she asked.

He watched her like a wild animal ready to bolt. "Harrick."

"My greetings, Harrick." She started to lift her hand, then realized she still held the rock. Although she stopped, it wasn't soon enough, and she accidentally brushed his frayed sleeve. He jerked away, but not before she saw the network of recent scars, puckered and red, that covered his arm, as if shattered glass had scored his skin.

"Saints," she murmured. "Who attacked you?"

"Don't ask." He regarded her with eyes as black as everything else about him, including his mood. Then he closed his hand around her hand, his large palm enveloping her fist with the rock. "Unless you plan to do so?"

"No." She kept the taser in her other hand down by her side. She had little doubt he knew she held the stun gun.

"Have you come to bedevil me?" he asked. "To make me think angels of redemption exist?" His words were ragged, but beneath their edge, his voice had a cultured, well-educated quality.

Rhose was acutely aware of his hand on hers. "If I'm an angel, I'm a terribly behaved one. I sleep late and I hate cleaning up." She knew she was talking too fast. "And I'm absent-minded."

He lowered his arm, still holding her hand. Then he abruptly let go of her, as if he had just realized what he was doing. Rhose dropped the rock, and it clattered on the ground at her feet.

"Are you cold?" he asked.

She pulled her sweaters tighter. "More so by the minute."

"Ah, hell," he said. "All right. You can stay with me. But you must leave in the morning."

Rhose waited for the fear to come, her anxiety about staying with someone who looked so dangerous. Instead she felt comforted to know she would be in his protection for the night. How she knew he meant her no harm, she had no idea. Was it something in his voice? His gestures and posture? His expressions? She couldn't say. It was as if she were picking it straight from his mind. But surely that couldn't be possible.

"Are you sure you don't mind if I stay?" she asked.

"If you promise not to shoot me with that gun of yours."

Startled, she smiled. "Fair enough."

"Well." His flush was visible even in the dim light. He stepped aside, making room for her to pass.

Harrick lived in another toppled skyscraper. He had built a lean-to from scraps of metal and crammed it into a corner. His home had almost nothing inside, just water tubes, vending-robot food, and a blanket. The slanted ceiling was so low, Rhose could barely stand up straight. Harrick squeezed in behind her, bending over, and used up what little space remained.

"It is small in here." He sounded embarrassed.

"Yes." Rhose was aware of his closeness. She noticed his well-built physique and the way his muscles strained his clothes. It was hard to make out his face in the dim light, but what she saw of his rugged features appealed to her.

"I can stay outside," he offered.

Although she appreciated the offer, she knew he could freeze without shelter. Her fingers had gone numb from the cold already. "Don't do that," she said. "With us crowded in here, it will be warmer." A nervous tickle started in her throat. Maybe she was naïve to think she was safe.

"I won't hurt you," he said.

How did he know she was worried? Probably because it was the obvious conclusion. Oddly enough, though, he seemed more in danger from her than the reverse, though she wasn't sure why. She wondered if he was experiencing her moods, too. He reached her in some way she didn't understand.

"I need to sleep," he added. "I didn't during the day."

"You stayed awake for thirty-two hours?"

His face was lit with dim orange light from the lamp. "Yes."

"But why?"

"I can't— When I sleep, it all—it comes back."

"It?" She felt as if she were floundering.

"Nothing." He sat down and stretched out on the cracked floor. "You can have the blanket."

Self-conscious, Rhose knelt next to him. "Harrick, are you all right?"

Normally in a circumstance like this, she would have been too scared even to ask much, but she already felt as if she knew him well. On impulse, she laid her hand on his arm. "Can I help?"

His voice roughened. "I'm fine." He pulled away his arm.

Rhose understood his unspoken message: *Don't push.* With constrained motions, she lay on the blanket. Although it cushioned the hard floor, it was still uncomfortable. No wonder he hadn't slept.

Only a few hand-spans separated them. She was so sensitized to his presence, his tension seemed palpable. She felt too wound up to sleep, too nervous about the situation.

After a while his breathing settled into the deeper rhythms of sleep. Her mind synchronized with his, drifting, drowsy. . . .

A cry yanked her awake. Someone was looming over her and panic filled the night. She couldn't see—she raised her hands to shield herself—they hit someone's chest—

"Harrick?" she asked with a quaver. "Is that you?"

His voice wrenched out of the dark. "Who?"

"It's Rhose." She sat up slowly, careful not to bump him. "Remember?"

A pause. "I remember."

"Did you have a bad dream?"

He answered softly. "Oh, yes."

She felt him hurting as if his pain were a physical presence. Reaching out, she brushed his sleeve. He jerked, but then he curled his hand around hers. A shiver went through her. She felt wary, on edge, yet she also felt a connection with him, somehow, as if they had sat together this way on many other nights. Her first response with a stranger would have been to pull away, but she felt his need for comfort too much to deny it.

He smelled of soap-bots, another reason she didn't think he was a vagrant. It couldn't have been easy to find such cleansers in these ruins. She shifted position so she was sitting against the wall with him. "If company helps, I'm here."

He bent his head and pressed his lips against her hair. "Thank you," he whispered. The intimacy of his gesture should have felt strange, but that, too, was somehow right. He soon dozed off, sitting next to her. He stirred often, but if she stroked his hand or his forehead, he calmed.

Eventually she slept as well.

His muscles hurt.

It was Harrick's first waking thought. The darkness felt close, but for once it wasn't oppressive. He figured out why his body ached; he had slept sitting up. According to the atomic clock of his internal biomech web, he had been out for seven hours, the longest unbroken sleep he had managed since his crash here twenty-six long days ago.

A woven sweater scraped his arm. What? He had no such clothes.

It all came back then, the girl in the ruins, a waif with large eyes and gold hair wisping around her cheeks. He hadn't wanted to bring her here, but now he was glad she had come. Her presence comforted him.

He put his arm around her shoulders and leaned his cheek against the top of her head. She sighed without waking up, her body settling against his. The sweetness of her presence touched him. He marveled that she gave him this trust, because he sure as hell hadn't earned it.

Holding Rhose, he became aware of her shapely form through her sweaters. For the first time since the crash, his body reacted to the thought of a woman. He knew he should send her away. Hell, he could walk her back to town. He wasn't certain they could find the place at night, though, even with his lamp. Or maybe he just wanted to stay here, with her. She smelled good, like flowers and cinnamon.

Harrick knew about Daretown from conversations he had overheard among the people who foraged in these ruins. The looters only came in daylight. He did nothing to discourage the tales about monsters that frequented this place at night, stories that may have started when people had glimpsed him wandering around. The more they feared the ruins, the greater his privacy.

Every time he thought of going back, of contacting ISC, of letting anyone know he had survived, a protective darkness came over his thoughts. His squad had died. Their ships had died. His own ship had died. He had no right to live. A numb shell encased him, like a glass prison he could see through but never escape.

Except Rhose had come inside the glass. She didn't even seem all that frightened of him. He slouched down, bracing his boot heels against the opposite wall, and held her in his arms. Before he even realized what he was doing, he had pressed his lips against her forehead.

Rhose stirred in her sleep. He ought to wake her, find out more about her. If she kept unsettling him this way, his emotional defenses would weaken. When he turned his head, he misjudged her position and his lips brushed her nose.

"Harrick?" she asked, drowsy.

"Eh?"

"How are you feeling?" she murmured, her eyes still closed.

"In a glass shell." He hadn't thought the words strange until he heard himself say them.

"A shell?" Her face was only about two handspans from his own, but he could just barely make out the shape in the dark. She touched his cheek. "You feel trapped in a dark place where your life is suspended."

A flush spread through him. "How do you know that?"

"I feel as if you are . . . part of me."

Part of him. They were linking as empaths. Once he had shared a link with three other people—until their violent deaths burned out his spirit. Tonight, Rhose had joined her mind with his, never realizing the miracle she brought him. She was a salve on his torment, or water filling the scorched emotional void where he used to be part of a four-way link.

He had found a piece of his soul.

Harrick knew he shouldn't push. But even as he warned himself to stop, to pull back, to wait, he was lowering his head. He found her lips, full and warm, and kissed her with a gentle hunger he hadn't believed he would ever feel again.

Rhose braced her palms against his chest. He immediately started to let her go, angry at himself for taking advantage of someone who had sought his protection.

Then, incredibly, her lips softened under his. His loneliness poured in then, released by the simple act of touching another human being. Not just anyone, but this lovely girl who affected him so deeply. His pulse surged and he laid her on the ground, on her back.

Rhose turned her head to the side. "Please, slow down."

He silently swore, though he didn't know if his oath was directed at himself, for mauling this vulnerable girl, or at her, for breaching his emotional defenses.

He pushed up on one elbow. "Why aren't you afraid of me?" he growled. If she feared him, it would be easier to keep his distance. Then he would be less vulnerable to her. "You should be, you know. I have enhanced speed, strength, and reflexes, a microfusion reactor in my body for energy, and a node in my spine full of combat libraries. I'm a killing machine. I could crack you in two just like that." He snapped his fingers.

"Goodness." She didn't sound the least terrified.

Harrick wanted to growl more, but he couldn't when faced with her good nature and bravery. It was also difficult when he was so aware of her body. Their empathic link was also strengthening. She thought he was looped, eccentric, but she liked him. She savored the strength of his arms. She didn't understand what was happening to the two of them and made no attempt to hide her emotions.

Harrick let their link fade. He couldn't maintain an empathic connection that strong for more than a few moments.

Rhose cupped her palm around his cheek. "I wish I could see you better."

"I also, with you." It was an understatement. He lifted her sweater and found more sweaters underneath. "Are you cold?"

"Actually, I'm hot."

He tugged her sweater. "If you take this off," he said helpfully, "you won't be hot."

She laughed, a sparkling sound, and Harrick flushed. She knew perfectly well that he was trying to undress her. Yet she wasn't put off. Nervous, yes, because he was a stranger. Except they were no longer strange to each other. People could live together for decades and never blend their minds as much as he and Rhose were already doing.

"You've a beautiful laugh." He lay down and kissed her some more on her mouth, her cheeks, her nose. When she put her arms around him and pressed against his body, he groaned. Finally he found the bottom layer of her multitude of sweaters and slid his hand under them, across her bare skin.

"Ah . . ." Her breathing quickened.

Encouraged, Harrick explored further. He found her breasts, and they more than filled his hands. Her nipples hardened as he played with them. He pulled her sweaters up to her shoulders, leaving her torso bare. Saints, she felt good.

Rhose sighed and slid her palm down his chest, as if she wasn't sure where to put her hand. But she didn't tell him to stop. His pulse surged, and he fumbled with the tie at her waist until it came loose. She tensed as he pulled on her leggings, tugging the heavy cloth over her thighs, knees, ankles, and then all the way off. He slid his hand up her body. So curved and soft—

"Wait." Rhose caught his hand. "This is too much. Too fast."

Harrick felt as if he had hit a brick wall. Darkness shifted and flowed inside of him. "Do you want me to stop?"

"Y-yes. Please."

It took a great effort of will to still his hands, but he managed, one of his palms on her breast, the other on her thigh. She was so inviting, he thought he might expire of frustration. But damn it, he wasn't going to ravish her.

"Why?" he asked. "Why must we stop now?" The haunted feeling that had weighted his emotions since the crash crept back.

Her voice shook. "I guess I am scared, after all."

Well, hell. He knew that—or he should have. As an empath, he could pick up a vague sense of moods, though without the amplification provided by his ship, he had to be close to a person for it to happen. Even then, he couldn't maintain a link for long, and he couldn't manage that much unless he lowered his mental barriers, which he rarely did, both to protect himself and to respect the privacy of others. Since the crash he had hunkered behind his mental shields, locked away from all emotions.

Until Rhose invaded his sanctuary.

Harrick instinctively lowered his defenses during intimacy, which was one reason he rarely sought company. He was vulnerable to his lover's mood. If she found him lacking, he would know. What he picked up from Rhose was strong. Disconcerting. But *good*. She liked him, though she wasn't sure why. He understood better: as empaths, they produced pheromones targeted for each other, creating a strong physical attraction. It was one reason empaths managed to reproduce despite their rarity. Nor was it only chemical; if they started with any natural mental compatibility, their brain waves could resonate and intensify the effect, often almost immediately after they met. Poets called it "love at first sight," which sounded far more romantic than "a resonance of neural wavefunctions."

Then again, maybe he was just making arcane excuses for going at her like a rutting bull.

"I won't do anything you don't want," he said.

"I just—I need to take it slower."

Slower. That was a definite improvement over *stop*. He slid down her body so his weight didn't crush her. Then he took her breast into his mouth and suckled while he stroked her curves. Lovely curves. She wasn't such a waif after all. Her haze of arousal intensified, and she played with his hair. Her caresses made him warm in places she wasn't touching. He took his time, exploring, touching, kissing her everywhere.

After a while, he came back up and spoke near her ear. "Let me. You're ready. And so am I." *Saints*, but he was ready.

She spoke in a low voice, out of breath. "Yes. Now."

It was all he needed. He tugged at her sweaters, and she raised her arms so he could pull them off the rest of the way. He thought of undressing himself, but it made him feel open to attack. The last thing he wanted was for his spinal node to jack him into a combat mode and endanger her life. Knowing she wouldn't harm him didn't help; his need to protect himself went deeper than any physical threat.

Harrick opened his trousers and settled his hips between her thighs. She drew in a sharp breath as he guided himself into her. She felt so warm, so ready—*what?* He had hit a barrier.

"Oh," Harrick said. No wonder she wanted him to slow down. It astonished him that she trusted him enough to let him be her first lover. Perhaps it was the magic of this odd, surreal night and their unexpected affinity for each other, but he wanted to believe that he, and only he, was the reason.

"It is only you," she whispered.

He kissed her ear. "You're beautiful, Rhose."

She hung on to him and he felt her heartbeat. Her apprehension was there, yes, and bewildered surprise at her own desire, with a blur of sensuality that overlaid her thoughts. He pushed into her as gently as he could manage, though his control was slipping. When her barrier gave away, she moaned, but if it caused her pain, she gave no sign, either in her mood or body.

He tried to move with care, but it had been too long. When the shadows in his mind shifted and tried to darken his thoughts, the sheer, driving pleasure of their love-making obliterated the ghosts that haunted him. He lost control and thrust hard against her, his hands clenched in the blanket under them. The sensations exploded over him and his awareness of the world vanished.

Harrick began to think again. He was lying on top of her, sated and content. "Rhose?"

She let out a breath. "That was nice."

Nice was far more genteel than the words he would have used, but he agreed. "Are you all right?"

"Yes." She shifted beneath him. "You're heavy, though."

He rolled off her, onto his side, and felt around for his soap-bot cloths. He handed her one. "You can clean up with this, if you'd like."

Rhose took the cloth. "Thanks." She sounded half-asleep.

Harrick touched the soft skin of her breast and thought perhaps he was having a delusion. He stretched out against her side and closed his eyes. "Are you a phantasm?" he murmured. Maybe he truly had gone insane.

But such sweet insanity . . .

* * *

The cold awoke Rhose. She couldn't understand why one side of her body was freezing and the other side warm. And why had she fallen asleep on the floor?

It came back in a rush. Her face heated as she thought of what she had done, making love to Harrick and with such passion. She should be appalled at herself, but instead she felt . . . satisfied. This was so unexpected, so unreal, and such a sensually pleasing introduction to the ways of love. He was asleep against her side. The warm side. She pulled the blanket out from under her body and drew it over them both.

Harrick stirred. "Good morning," he said drowsily.

"Not for a while." She thought the night was probably about half over. "Maybe fifteen more hours."

He yawned and blew into her ear, making her tingle. "We'll just keep each other warm for a while longer, eh?"

"I would like that." She tugged at his body-shirt, trying to pull it over his head. "You don't need this."

He put his hand over hers as if to push her away. She could hardly see him in the dark, but his apprehension felt like a fog of sand against her face. Then he took an audible breath and said, "All right." He pulled off the shirt and dropped it behind her.

Rhose wondered at his hesitation. She stroked his chest, surprised and intrigued by its sculpted planes. Lying next to him, she moved into his arms as he pulled her close. It saddened her to think that when the sun rose, she would have to go home, leaving Harrick.

"Would you come to town with me tomorrow?" she asked.

His arms went rigid around her. "No."

"You might like—"

"No!" Then he said, "Stay here."

"I wish I could." She couldn't imagine it, though. Her family was poor, yes, their house small and rough, but it was home. She couldn't leave them or her students. "I can't, though. I have too many responsibilities."

After a moment, he said, "Responsibilities."

"You also?"

"I don't remember." In an oddly strangled voice, he added, "Can't remember."

She wasn't certain, but she thought he meant he couldn't allow himself to remember. "Does it hurt?"

His voice was low and subdued. "I used to go to a tavern with them.

We would laugh and drink Urbanali beer."

"With who, Harrick?"

His voice caught. "They are gone."

She felt his grief. "I'm sorry."

"We still—we still have tonight."

She held him close. "Yes. We do."

This time when they made love, it was with bare skin against bare skin. Their minds blended—only vague impressions, no definite thoughts—but she sensed that in the simple act of undressing, he had fought a battle with himself and won.

In the early morning light, outside Harrick's lean-to, Rhose had a good look at the man who had turned her night into such a wonder. They had slept, made love, slept, and loved again. Now that she could see him better, her breath caught. He had strong features, rugged and bold, with dark eyes.

She stood with him in the watery light of an overcast sky, surrounded by the fallen tech-tower, with coils of wire and shattered Luminex piled on the ground. Chill wind tugged at her sweaters. So many dreams had ended with the destruction of this tech park. Its people had evacuated in time, but their livelihoods had been shattered.

Harrick was watching her intently. "You're even prettier in the light."

Her lips curved. "So are you."

"I most certainly am not pretty." His face flushed.

"Handsome, then. Big. Strong." She wanted to say *sexy*, but she was too shy. She felt his mood, though. She affected him the same way he affected her. "Are you sure you won't come with me?"

"I can't."

"Is it the gangs?" She had felt the scars on his body; now she could see the fine lines through rips in his body-shirt. "Harrick, what happened to you?"

He said only, "Will you come back?"

She let it go. "Yes. I will." She pushed back the hair around her face. Her mother called it a "riotous mop," and Rhose had been trying to tame it lately. She hadn't had much success, but she wanted to put on a good appearance for Harrick.

"I like your hair," he said.

Rhose froze. "How do you know what I'm thinking?"

"Can't you feel it?" He took her hands in his. "You're an empath, like me."

"Oh." She reddened. "Sure."

"I'm not crazy."

If he wanted to believe such things, it was all right with her. For all his strangeness, and the shadows lurking around the edges of his mind, she trusted him.

"I will see you soon," she said. "I promise."

"It's hard to believe." Darkness seemed to fall over him, though nothing had changed in the murky light. "You're an angel that drifted into my life. Perhaps a malicious god sent you as punishment, so my life would be even more wretched after you left."

Rhose stared at him. "Punishment? Whatever for?"

"For surviving." His voice was hollow.

"Harrick—"

"No." He pulled her into a hug and kissed her, silencing her questions.

Rhose didn't want to ruin their last moments by insisting on answers. She leaned into him, savoring the warmth of his lips and his embrace. He had boasted last night of arcane abilities, enhanced strength and speed, and a "microfusion reactor," whatever that meant. He had probably made it up, but that wouldn't put her off so much as make her wonder at his eccentricities. What drove a man like Harrick to hide out here?

When they finally separated, her body was flushed. She spoke softly. "Good-bye."

His voice rumbled. "Good-bye."

Rhose walked a few steps and turned. He started toward her, then bit his lip and stayed put.

She wanted to go back to him. But she had to get home as soon as possible. Her parents would be worried and her students upset. The children were already dealing with the aftermath of the colony's destruction. Most of the colonists had survived because Daretown had received warning in time to evacuate to the shelters, but many suffered from post traumatic stress. It would destroy her family if they thought they had lost her, and she didn't want to add to the anxieties of her students.

Reluctant, she made her way through the debris. As she climbed a mound of broken casecrete, she looked back and saw Harrick watching. She lifted her hand and he waved.

The next time she looked, he was gone.

* * *

By the time Rhose reached Daretown, the town had cycled through most of its first waking period, and people were sitting down to first-dinner. She was exhausted, empty-handed, and missing Harrick. Last night already seemed like a lost dream.

She trudged along the road. It was dirt and dust today, no mud. The day was already heating up despite the overcast, and they were only a third of the way through the thirty-two hours of sunlight.

The destruction here had been less than in the tech-park, and huts had sprung up on either side of the road, as people tried to rebuild their lives. Most of the important infrastructure of the colony had been salvaged, but it grieved her to see how few of their hard-fought gains had survived the beam strikes. Every crushed house symbolized a family with broken dreams. They worried about hazardous chemicals or gases leaking, huge capacitors that discharged with killing arcs of energy, and broken water mains that had undercut several streets and caused their collapse. Even the homes that still stood had mostly gone dark, their inhabitants gone, their solar tiles stolen. Gangs had looted many of them.

Up ahead, three children ran out of a huge white pipe that had fallen on its side. Their laughter reminded her that people recovered even after a disaster.

Rhose soon reached a familiar turn-off. She left the road and walked among broken furniture and the skeletal remains of an office lobby until she reached a plaza. Her family's house stood there, with a vegetable patch in front and lantern light behind the curtains. They had lost their old house and belongings, but they had rebuilt here from the remains of another fallen building that had been in better shape. As much as Rhose missed her home, she was immensely grateful her family was alive. Buildings could be replaced, but not people.

Inside the house, she stood unnoticed in the doorway of the kitchen and fondly watched her family. They were gathered around the big table: her parents, grandmother, sister, and younger brother. She had another brother two years her junior; he had married last year after he finished high school and moved to his own house. Usually there was a great deal of laughter and talking at meals, but today everyone was quiet.

"My greetings," she said.

Her parents twisted around, and her mother's face suffused with welcome. "Rhose!"

Her siblings knocked over their chairs as they jumped to their feet. Within moments they surrounded her. Her brother put his arms around her waist and her sister reached around him to hug Rhose, while her father put his hand on her shoulder, and her grandmother squeezed her hand. Her mother cried as she tried to embrace Rhose around everyone else.

"Goodness," Rhose said, laughing, though her voice caught.

Her mother drew back and wiped her eyes. "We thought you were kidnapped! Or—or worse."

"I couldn't find any supplies," Rhose said. "I went too far and stayed in the tech-park last night." She wasn't ready to tell them about Harrick. She wasn't even sure yet how she felt about the encounter. "I'm sorry I didn't have any luck."

"No apologies!" her grandmother admonished. "We're just glad you're safe."

Rhose indicated a lantern hanging from the rafters. "You got more oil."

"I found a barrel outside town," her father said. "Closer to the port."

"We went to see the ships!" her sister exclaimed. She barely came up to Rhose's elbow and had a mop of curls very much like Rhose and their father. "We found out visitors are coming."

Offworld visitors? Rhose regarded her parents uneasily. "Is anything wrong?"

"It's good news," her mother said. "The Relief Allocation Service is bringing supplies, and Imperial Space Command is sending a delegation."

"ISC? Why? We have no military presence." Rhose heard the bitter edge in her voice. Daretown was an inconsequential colony that should never have been exposed to combat. It had been a fluke that a skirmish had been fought in orbit here, so far from the main engagements.

"Apparently none of the combatants survived," her father said. "ISC is sending people to investigate."

Rhose wished reinforcements had come *before* the fighting. An ISC squadron had been ambushed while traveling through this star system. She would always be grateful that they had managed to warn Daretown in time. Her people had made it to shelters before the invaders stabbed the populated areas of the planet. Shocked and bewildered, the colonists had struggled to recover since then. It wasn't until many days later that they heard the news: ISC had won the star-spanning war—just barely.

Rhose tried to smile. "Well, it is good if they can help with the rebuilding, eh?" She squeezed her brother and sisters. "I hope you all left me some food."

Her grandmother clucked. "Come on, Rhosallina. Sit yourself down."

With relief, Rhose joined her family. She tried not to think about Harrick—or her inescapable sense that he was in danger.

He walked.

Harrick had never ventured beyond the tech-park, but he had an idea how to reach Daretown, having overheard foragers in the ruins talk about their home. The colonists seemed resilient, able to pick themselves up and start over regardless of the hardships they faced. Some had even searched the remains of his Jag fighter. They found almost nothing to scavenge.

He shouldn't have survived, either. The ship had registered him as dead in the instant his squad's four-way link shattered. It had notified ISC of their loss. Harrick wasn't even convinced it had made a mistake in his case. He felt as if he were a wretched ghost. The living would have first priority with ISC, but eventually the military would come here to investigate the loss of his squad. He would float over them, a specter, dead and dark.

He shuddered and shook his head, trying to clear his thoughts. Before last night, he hadn't realized how bizarre his mental processes had become. Perhaps for Rhose, their love-making had been an exciting interlude, a time of sensuality to ease a difficult life, with the added spice of danger; for him, it had shaken his entire constrained life here. He thought she had felt more, too, but he couldn't be sure. He hadn't realized until last night that his mind was too injured to pick up emotions consistently. Only when the balm of Rhose's mind soothed his own did he realize how much he hurt.

His spinal node was making maps of the area as he followed the road. He had spent the day telling himself to stay in his refuge. But images of Rhose weakened his resolve. He wanted her. She endangered the shell of numbness that protected him. She was making him feel human again—and it hurt like hell.

He had suppressed his memories to keep his sanity, but now they were returning. Blackwing Squadron had been far more than four pilots and four ships. They had fought as one mind. It gave them a versatility, survival capability, and deadly accuracy beyond individual ships or pilots.

Mandi Jakes had flown with him for years. She had risen fast in the

J-Force, commissioned as a Jagernaut Quaternary, promoted to Tertiary, and then to Secondary, a rank higher than most Jagernauts ever achieved. Usually they retired first. Mandi had stayed on, the Goldwing of his squad—until she died. His Greenwing, Benz Zannisteria, had been a Tertiary. And Sal. His Redwing. She had been a Quaternary, only one year out of the Academy, bright and fresh, proud to fly with Blackwing Squadron. They had been four parts of a whole. And he had failed them all.

He had no right to live, to walk to town, to seek out Rhose. But he couldn't stop himself. He had been injured on a deeper level than the physical wounds that scarred his body, but he was only now beginning to realize just how much he needed help.

When Harrick reached the outskirts of town, it occurred to him that he might look strange, with his tangled hair and torn clothes. ISC regulations required that its officers either crop their hair close to their heads or wear it pulled back in a warrior's queue. His was wild around his face and shoulders. Rhose's family might be put off, too, if he came to see their daughter with a Jumbler on his hip.

He stashed his weapon in an underground vault that had escaped destruction. The gun was keyed to his brain, so no one could use it except him, and he also hid it with care. Then he tried to neaten his hair. When he was more presentable, he resumed his trek.

The road was hardly more than a rut, but it seemed to be the main thoroughfare in Daretown. He thought about his home in Vyan City on the world Parthonia, a place where droop-willows hung over placid lakes and marble columns lined boulevards. Huddling in the ruins, he had forgotten he had a history, that he was a man as well as a biomechanical warrior.

He met no one. At first he thought they might all be inside, sleeping. But according to his internal clock, the midday sleep should be over and the town into its second waking cycle.

His skin prickled. They were watching him. Maybe he was paranoid, but he felt certain that gazes followed him everywhere. Had his biomech systems been operating properly he could have sensed the presence of watchers more accurately by picking up their vital signs, but he couldn't manage that now.

Harrick jerked his head several times, then realized he was acting strangely and made himself stop. His fingers twitched and he wished he were back in the tech-park. After another few minutes, he rounded a curve—and saw five men approaching him. One had an EM pulse gun, another carried a laser carbine, and two had clubs. Heavy muscles corded their forearms. They wore coarse shirts and trousers, though their clothes were in better shape than his uniform. All were young, probably in their twenties, measured in standard years. Although Harrick had an apparent age in his thirties, he was almost sixty. Nanomeds in his body repaired his cells and delayed his aging, but it seemed unlikely the colonists could afford such treatments.

Harrick slowed down. The men watched with hard faces as they surrounded him, forcing him to stop.

A thought came from his spinal node: Combat mode ready.

Stand by, Harrick thought, with extra focus. Bioelectrodes in his neurons translated his thoughts into input for his node, and the reverse process changed the node's output into neural firings he interpreted as thoughts.

Waiting, it answered.

The tallest of the five men had blond hair razed close to his head. He stood in front of Harrick and idly swung his club, slapping it against his other open palm.

"You must have walked a long way," the club man said.

"From the tech-park," Harrick said.

"You weren't invited here." Club smacked his bat into his palm. "You got no sway. What I say, goes." Smack. "And I say, you don't belong."

"I don't want any sway," Harrick said, irritated. He didn't even know if he would stay. It depended on Rhose.

In his side vision, he glimpsed the other man with a bat. His node analyzed the man's posture, and his arm snapped up with enhanced reflexes. In the same instant, the man swung his club. Harrick easily caught the bat and wrenched it out of the man's hand, then cracked it in two over his leg and threw the pieces so hard, they sailed over the ruins. The entire scuffle lasted only seconds.

As one of the other men lunged at Harrick, Club drew his pulse gun, which would shoot serrated projectiles at accelerated speeds. Just one could tear a man apart and turn his insides into jelly. Using enhanced speed, Harrick dove to the side and rolled, coming up against a pile of broken mesh panels. The projectiles missed him and rammed deep into the road.

The man with the laser carbine unslung it from his shoulder.

Combat mode on, his node thought.

Harrick's mind accelerated.

He rolled to his feet just before the man fired his laser. Blinding light flared and the shot seared the ground, slagging rocks and dirt.

Harrick knew his body couldn't take the strain of accelerated movement for long, but he wouldn't survive this encounter without it. He sprinted into the ruins and ducked behind a huge white pipe. Pulse projectiles slammed the casecrete. He kept going, dodging in a zigzag pattern, driven by adrenalin. He couldn't have stopped now even if his attackers had disappeared.

Within seconds, he reached a thicket of barriers that had been hallways in a building and were now open to the sky. He darted among them until his node advised him to halt at a cracked wall. Looking through the crack, he saw his assailants stalking the ruins. They had attacked. He would defend. In combat mode, the world vanished. He felt nothing. He became pure Jagernaut, a human weapon.

The man with the laser was approaching the other side of the barrier. Harrick's node analyzed the cracks on the wall for weak points, then accessed his brain and created a translucent display he saw overlaid on the barrier. Several target areas glowed red. He waited until the man was on the other side of one target. Then he jerked back his arm and rammed the heel of his hand into the red area.

The wall shattered outward, showering the man with debris. Harrick sprang through the breach and tackled his enemy. It took only seconds to knock him out. He could have easily made the kill, but he let his assailant live. With his feet planted on either side of the man's body, Harrick reached down and took the carbine. It was an older model, army issue, probably stolen.

Scanning the area with augmented optics, he spied Club half a kilometer away, rummaging through another wrecked building. Harrick crept nearer to Club's location until he reached part of a building that still stood. Crumbling stairs took him to a hallway on the second floor. The hall ended abruptly, where the building had collapsed, and he crouched in the shadows there, hidden.

He waited.

It took thirty minutes for Club to work his way to the area below Harrick's perch. Then Harrick aimed his gun. That slight motion was the final one needed to upset the balance of the broken hall, however, and the floor collapsed under him. He dropped in a shower of debris and landed on Club, the two of them falling to the ground in a tangle of limbs. Harrick easily absorbed the impact in his augmented body and jumped to his feet. Club recovered almost as fast—and fired his pulse gun. With no time to aim, he missed, but the tip of a projectile serration sliced Harrick's shirt.

You must have immediate medical attention, his node thought.

Pumped into combat mode, Harrick felt nothing. In his accelerated state, everything else slowed down. His swing arced toward Club, who was slowly ducking. Harrick's fist slammed into Club's head and a crack reverberated through the air. Club toppled in slow motion.

Harrick's time sense suddenly jumped to normal. He heaved in a breath, then dropped next to Club and felt for a pulse.

He found none.

Harrick felt as if he were caught in a loop that wouldn't stop. Couldn't stop. Couldn't stop. Standing, he looked around for his other would-be killers. Either they had spread their search so wide he could no longer see them or else they had fled.

I need my Jumbler, he thought.

You need a hospital, his node answered.

Can't stop.

Shall I take you out of combat mode?

No! Harrick set off jogging through the rubble. He couldn't settle his thoughts.

He knew only that he had to stay alive and destroy his enemies.

Rhose walked with her students to the community center. The West End was the only area of town with a sizeable number of intact buildings, including the center. Its main wing now hosted offices for the mayor and his staff. She used the south wing for a school, where she taught about twenty-five students, depending on who showed up. Attendance had dropped since the attack.

Today the children chattered and giggled, ranging from tots barely the height of her waist to teens on the verge of adulthood. They sounded so normal. But a day rarely passed without one or more of them breaking down in tears. Lately, though, it happened less often.

At the center, they entered a lobby with consoles and desks everywhere, all of the city offices crammed together. Rhose's assistant Dhanni was waiting, and the children waved as Rhose handed them off to the younger teacher.

Rhose crossed the lobby. Ten men and women were gathered in the mayor's "office," which consisted of a desk between two columns. The only person Rhose recognized was the mayor, Berni Ivers, a rotund man with a ruddy face and graying hair. The others all wore crisp green uniforms with the gold insignia of the Pharaoh's Army.

Rhose hung back, uncertain if she should interrupt. Berni was deep in discussion with one of the army men. From Berni's deferential behavior, she gathered this visitor ranked high in the ISC hierarchy. Seeing Berni scrape and simper gave her a certain satisfaction. Although Rhose considered him a good mayor, he wanted her to fawn all over him, which just wasn't her nature.

She hadn't thought anyone knew she was there, but when he and the army VIP finished, Berni beckoned her forward. Self-conscious in front of so many strangers, Rhose walked over to him. The army fellow was busy setting up a schedule with his assistant.

"Morning," Berni said.

"And to you," Rhose said. "I wondered if any new houses were available."

Curiosity sparked in his eyes. "You planning to move?"

"Not for me. For the school." She didn't mention Harrick. She had no idea if he would ever come out of the ruins. If he did, he would need a place to live, and if not, the school genuinely needed more space. "I've been getting more students lately."

"You'll probably have even more soon," he confided. "ISC is going to help us with the rebuilding."

It was good news. Rhose started to answer, but a commotion burst out across the lobby. She looked to see two boys running through the lobby, both of the youths about ten in standard years. They slowed when they saw the ISC contingent, but then they came on again, undeterred even by the presence of offworlders.

Berni frowned as they skidded to a stop in front of him. "You shouldn't be dashing around here like that."

"It's Blaster and his men!" one boy cried, out of breath.

"We're scrubbing out those gangs," Berni said firmly. "Put Blaster and his punks in the clink." Although he spoke to the boy, Rhose thought he was talking for the army VIP. Perhaps ISC could help. Gangs had preyed on Daretown since the post-war exodus had left the town with less protection. Most of the thugs only looted, but the worst of them had kidnapped, raped, and even committed murder.

"You c-can't scrub him," the second boy said. "He's dead!"

"Dead?" For a moment Berni looked as if he were going to rejoice. Then he caught himself and presented a more somber expression. "How?"

"Another gang-fanger pounded him," the first boy said.

"A new guy," the second boy added. "Tall. Even m-more muscles than Blaster. A mean fu—" He stopped, blushing as Rhose glared at him, then amended, "A mean guy."

"Ah, hell." Berni's face turned red, even his bulbous nose. "We've got another one now?"

"It was self-defense," the first boy said.

"No, he was a m-monster," the second boy said darkly. "Black clothes, r-ripped up, and black hair all crazy. Big black boots."

Rhose blinked. "That sounds like Harrick."

Berni refocused his ire on her. "You hanging around gangs now, Rhosie girl?"

She hated it when he called her that. "Of course not."

"Harrick?" a deep voice asked. "Is that what you said?"

Rhose turned with a start. The army VIP had come back to them. A holo-badge on his chest read Colonel W. Coalson.

Rhose spoke self-consciously. "Yes. He's someone I met."

"Jason Harrick?" Coalson asked.

Rhose twisted the hem of her sweater. "He just said Harrick."

"Can you give me more description?"

Coalson's intense concentration unsettled Rhose. "Just like the boy said. And Harrick has a lot of new scars."

"Any other features?" Coalson asked. "Insignia? Tattoos?"

Rhose's face heated. Harrick had a birthmark on his inner thigh, but she didn't want to speak about something so personal to a stranger. "I-I don't think so."

Coalson studied her. "I hope you aren't withholding information."

Mercifully, she remembered something else useful she could give him. "He had a gun. He called it a Jumbler."

"Saints almighty," one of Coalson's people said, a woman with a badge that read Major Kames. "Could he have *survived?*"

Berni crossed his arms and scowled. "You know this fanger? If I've another killer loose, I need everything you have on him."

For the first time Coalson showed an emotion. Incredulity. He spoke in an even voice. "Jason Harrick is a Jagernaut Primary. He is one of the most decorated heroes in any branch of ISC. He led the squadron that defended this planet, and he's the one who transmitted the evacuation warning to your people. If not for him, you would all be dead."

Berni's mouth dropped open. "A *Primary?* Good gods. Why would he come to town and kill people?" Then he added, "Not that he would be the first to want Blaster dead."

"I don't know," Coalson said. "We thought he had died."

Rhose recalled Harrick's words. "That's why he said the gods were punishing him for surviving."

"He told you that?" Coalson asked.

Rhose nodded. "He said a lot of things. I—well, I'm afraid I thought he was a little crazy."

Major Kames stepped forward. When Coalson nodded to her, she said, "If Harrick survived the violent death of his squadron, he could very well have gone insane."

"Just how dangerous is he?" Berni asked.

"We can't know until we find him." Coalson turned to the first boy who had told them about Blaster. "What is your name, son?"

The wide-eyed boy stood up straighter. "Jessie, sir."

"Jessie, did you see where this stranger went?"

"He took the laser carbine and ran out of town. East."

Coalson glanced at Kames. "Have the cruiser see if they can get a fix on his location." As Kames activated her gauntlet comm, Coalson turned his intent focus back to Rhose. "Did Harrick tell you anything else?"

She described their meeting, though she left out their love-making. "He didn't seem violent. Sad. Eccentric, maybe. But I never feared he would harm me."

Kames looked up. "Sir, I have a report from Tracking up in orbit."

"Go ahead," Coalson said.

"They've located the signature of what may be a Jumbler," Kames said. "It's buried in the noise of all the scavenged energy sources people are using here. If we hadn't advised them where to look, they probably wouldn't have found it. They can't identify its owner, but they have a location. It's just outside town."

"Good work," Coalson said. "Let's go."

"I'd like to go with you," Rhose said.

"I also," Berni said.

Coalson frowned at them. "Only if you stay back, out of the way. Let our people deal with him."

Rhose's pulse jumped. "You won't hurt him, will you?"

Berni spoke harshly. "He committed murder, Rhosie."

Jessie started to speak, then hesitated.

"Go ahead," Coalson told the boy.

"He was defending himself, sir. Blaster and them roughed him up.

They almost killed him. He was bleeding awful! He could have killed all of them, but he only did Blaster, because Blaster was shooting at him."

Coalson went very still. "Harrick is injured?"

"Real bad," the boy said.

"He's probably in survival mode," Major Kames said.

"What does that mean?" Berni asked. "Survival how?"

Coalson spoke grimly. "If he's off-balance, he'll attack anyone who approaches him. Right now, mayor, you may have one of the most consummate killers ever created loose in your city."

"No," Rhose said. "He wouldn't hurt people. You heard Jessie. It was self-defense."

Coalson considered her. "What exactly happened with you and Primary Harrick?"

Rhose's face flamed. "We, uh, were . . . together." She was almost stuttering. "Intimate."

Kames swore under her breath. "If he's fixated on you, ma'am, it could make him even more dangerous."

Rhose wished she had taken Harrick more seriously last night. Yet even now, she didn't believe he would hurt her. He had called the bond between them—the sense of knowing how the other felt—empathy. She had never believed psions existed, but it would explain so much. "Please tell me you won't hurt him," she said.

"We would like to bring him in alive." Coalson regarded her steadily. "But if he is out of control and threatening the lives of civilians, we may have to kill him."

Harrick was on the second floor of a gutted tower when he heard noise outside. He sidled up to a jagged hole and looked down at the road.

Enemies.

They were walking along the road from Daretown. According to his internal sensors, some carried nodes in their bodies similar to his, though apparently less extensive. He couldn't tell for certain with his damaged components.

I can identify the signatures of their nodes, his own node thought. They are ISC. Not enemy.

Enemy, Harrick answered. They had tried to kill him.

Not enemy, his node persisted.

Silence!

It subsided. A node could never override the mind of the person who carried it. That security feature prevented opposing forces from hacking high-tech warriors and turning them against their own forces. His node obeyed only him. He had to protect himself. Protect Rhose. She lived here. He couldn't let his enemies hurt her.

Six invaders were on the road, which led to toward the plaza that separated this tower from the ruins of other buildings. It had to be a trick. They wouldn't leave themselves open. Sighting ahead of them, Harrick fired the laser. A brilliant flare of light burst out of his weapon and his optics filtered his vision. When it cleared, he studied the scene. The invaders had stopped. Although he had slagged a section of the road, the portion directly before them was untouched.

What protects them? he asked.

A reflector field, his node thought. Effective against electromagnetic radiation.

Harrick touched his Jumbler. *It can't reflect antimatter.* The gun was a miniature particle accelerator. It shot a stream of abitons, the antiparticle of the biton, a low energy sub-electronic particle. When abitons annihilated bitons, they produced harmless orange light. But bitons were part of electrons—and all matter contained electrons. A Jumbler beam annihilated anything it touched.

The invaders had deliberately drawn his fire to make him reveal his hiding place. He slung the carbine over his shoulder and sped down the stairs, then vacated the building, staying low behind broken casecrete walls. No one attacked the tower, though, which suggested his enemies were savvy to his strategy. He could no longer see them on the road. No matter. He was gone.

"Harrick!" The shout came from the ruins across the plaza. "We don't want to hurt you. Surrender and we won't shoot."

He peered through a crack in the wall. *Can you locate the source of that voice?*

A sensor shroud hides the source, his node answered.

What is its most likely location?

His node superimposed a display on the plaza, highlighting a jagged monolith that had once been a sculpture. Harrick concentrated on his Jumbler and felt a mental *click* as if a switch had flipped in his mind. Only his brain waves could activate the gun. He drew the weapon—and fired.

A beam of orange sparks appeared in the air. When it struck the monolith, the slab flared a brilliant orange and vanished, turned into photons created by low energy particle-antiparticle annihilations. When the light faded, the sculpture was gone.

Harrick ran behind the wall, crouching down. *Did I get them?*

I don't know, his node said. **However—**

Suddenly the wall ahead exploded. Harrick froze and protected his head with his arms as rubble showered over him. Shards of casecrete cut his arms and shoulders.

Harrick, his node thought. **You are forcing your own people to seek your death.**

Enemies.

Friends!

I will hear no more. He raised his Jumbler and prepared to kill his enemies.

"No!" Rhose cried the word as the explosion tore apart the wall. But the blast hadn't killed Harrick. She would *know* if he died. The closer she came to him physically, the stronger their mental link.

A rubble-strewn plaza separated her from the tower where he had been hiding. She and Berni were crouching behind several upturned consoles a safe distance from the action. She didn't know how Harrick could have moved so fast from the tower to the ground, but she had no doubt he had fired both the laser and the orange beam. Yet even after Coalson's people had fooled him into shooting that monolith, they couldn't locate him.

Rhose wanted to shout at them to stop, but they would just send her away. At least they were targeting the wrong place; Harrick had outsmarted their sensors and gone in the other direction. They had meant it about wanting him alive; otherwise, they could have leveled this entire area with beams from one of their ships. But she could tell they thought he had gone insane. Sooner or later they would get him, even if they had to kill him.

"He's injured," Rhose said. "Not crazy."

"Tell the people he kills," Berni muttered.

Rhose pretended to shuddered. "I don't think I can watch this."

Berni gave her a look of sympathy. "Perhaps it's best if you don't, Rhosie girl."

"Will you let me know what happened?"

"Yes. Certainly." He patted her arm. "I'll come by your house later this evening."

"Thanks, Berni."

Rhose eased back into the clutter of melted consoles and scorched furniture. When she was out of Berni's sight, she slipped through the ruins, quietly, so she wouldn't alert Coalson, who had asked Berni to keep an eye on her. Finally she crouched behind a mess of casecrete blocks directly across the plaza from the wall where she thought Harrick was hiding. She couldn't be certain; she was depending on a nebulous impression of his mind that matched what she had felt last night.

She saw no way to reach him without going into the open. Taking a deep breath, she steeled herself. Then she stood and walked into the plaza.

The wind rustled her hair around her cheeks. She sensed Harrick watching her, and she went slowly, keeping her hands by her sides so he could see she had no weapons. A shout came from behind her, Berni, it sounded like. A bead of sweat ran down her neck. Harrick hadn't killed her. Yet.

"Rhose Canterhaven." The amplified voice rumbled. "Leave the plaza immediately."

She kept going. She knew so little about Harrick's condition. She had to trust her instincts that he wouldn't shoot.

Footsteps sounded behind her in the plaza. Rhose turned to see Kames striding after her.

"No!" Rhose said. "Let me do this."

A beam of orange sparks cut through the air and hit the plaza in front of Kames. As she jumped back, the ground vanished in a flash of light, leaving a ragged crater.

Kames watched her from across the crater. "Rhose, come back."

Rhose shook her head. "You have to go. He won't let you any closer."

"You've no guarantee he won't shoot you, either."

"I know."

"And you still want to do this?"

Rose's gaze never wavered. "Yes. Please don't try to stop me."

Kames pushed her hand through her cap of dark hair. Then she nodded reluctantly. "Good luck."

"Thanks." Rhose resumed her walk toward a broken wall as high as her waist. As she drew nearer, a rustle came from behind it and the clink of rubble.

Then Harrick stood up behind the wall.

Her pulse lurched. He had a carbine gripped in one hand and the black bulk of his Jumbler in the other. This wasn't the man who had kissed her last night, held her in his arms, teased her with his rare smile.

He showed no emotion. This stranger was a machine.

She stopped a few steps away. "Harrick?"

"You are with my enemies." His voice was a monotone.

"I don't know them." Softly she added, "You came into town."

He stood motionless, a living statue.

"Did you come to see me?" She wanted to believe it was true.

No answer.

She walked to the wall and looked up at him. "Come back." Her voice caught. "Be the Harrick I knew last night."

His expression seemed to crumple. Then he gave a half-strangled groan. Still holding both guns, he reached across the wall for her, and Rhose went into his arms, embracing him, her cheek against his chest. He hugged her so tight, she could barely breathe. Blood had soaked his body-shirt, and he flinched when her arm scraped his side. But he never let her go. A blurred sense of his memories washed through her mind as he released his heightened combat sense and let himself remember his squadron.

"Gods," he whispered. The stock of his carbine was pressed along her back, aimed at the sky, and his other arm was tight around her shoulders. "I-I can't—"

"It's all right," she soothed. "You'll be all right."

His voice cracked. "Don't go away again."

"I won't." She drew back enough to look up at him. "But you must let these people help you."

He stared at her, his eyes dark. With a shaking hand, holding his Jumbler, he pushed back the hair that curled around her face. His gun brushed her skin, cold and hard. Then he looked over her head. Turning in his arms, Rhose saw Coalson and Kames a few paces away.

"Primary Harrick?" Coalson asked. "Will you come with us?"

Harrick breathed out, long and slow. After an endless moment, he let go of Rhose and carefully dropped his guns. Moving stiffly, with great care, he climbed over the wall.

Rhose offered him her hand. He hesitated, then reached out and folded his large hand around her small one. Then he walked with her toward Coalson.

"I pray he'll be all right," Rhose said. She was waiting outside the infirmary that ISC had set up in the community center. Coalson was standing with her in the hallway.

"His physical wounds will heal." Although Coalson spoke in a clipped style, his compassion came through. "The mental injuries will take more time."

"Will he stand trial?"

The colonel shook his head. "Our legal panel looked over the evidence for Blaster's death and the attack on my people. The download from Harrick's node matches the witness accounts. Could he have escaped without killing Blaster? Possibly. But how would he decide? He's designed to go into combat mode when attacked. If his mind hadn't been injured, he could have distinguished between the threat he faced here and a combat situation. But he *was* injured. Even then, the only time he shot anyone was when he was directly attacked." He spoke quietly. "They ruled his actions self-defense. But they also took him off active duty, until, or if, he recovers."

Rhose thought of the man she had held in her arms. "He hasn't been able to shut off being a soldier. He needs to relearn how to be a man instead of a weapon."

"Aye," Coalson said. "I think so."

The door slid open and a woman in the white jumpsuit of an ISC doctor looked out. "Rhose Canterhaven?"

"Yes?" Rhose asked.

The doctor had a shuttered gaze, giving away nothing. "Primary Harrick wishes to see you."

Rhose swallowed and nodded, suddenly nervous. As she entered the room, the doctor stepped outside and closed the door. Rhose stopped just inside. Harrick was lying on the bed, his eyes closed, his chest rising and falling in an even rhythm. Someone had cut his hair and given him a shave. The clean, chiseled lines of his features, his high cheekbones, his full lips and straight nose—he was a stunning man, truly fine to see, even more so than she had realized.

After a moment, he opened his eyes and gazed at the ceiling. Then he rolled his head to the side.

"Rhose!" He pushed up on one elbow. "How long have you been there?"

"Just a few moments." She went to the bed. "How do you feel?"

His grin flashed. "Better now."

A blush heated her cheeks. "A smile that gorgeous ought to be licensed. You could do damage with it."

Harrick laughed softly, the first time since they had met. She heard its undercurrents, his relief, as if he hadn't been sure he could ever laugh again. As he sat up, his hospital shift started to slip off one shoulder until the intelligent cloth contracted to keep itself in place.

"Come sit with me," he said.

As Rhose settled on the edge of the bed, he pulled her into his arms and laid his head on hers. She relaxed in his embrace and felt as if she had come home.

It was a while before he lifted his head. He cleared his throat. "Rhose, I would like to ask . . ."

She waited. "Yes?"

"If you would stay with me." He lifted her hand and kissed her knuckles. "I know I have no right to ask for permanence yet. But empaths are so rare. Compatibility like ours is even rarer. I—well, I hope we can let that grow."

She spoke quietly. "I also, Jason."

His face gentled. "I like it when you say my name like that." He pulled her close and spoke softly near her ear. "Will you let me court you, Rhose Canterhaven?" Almost inaudibly, he added, "Will you let me love you?"

"Always," she murmured. "If you do the same for me."

His voice caught. "Yes."

Holding him, she thought of the first time she had seen him in the ruins, his hand half covering his lamp. He had hidden even from its dim light, but now he was willing to let his inner light chase away his shadows, even in those dark places where his loss and pain dwelled. Rhose felt certain they could mend, all of them: Harrick, her family, Daretown, her people.

For the first time since the attack, she looked forward to the future.

"Another Man's Shoes"
by
Candice Kohl

British Colony of Georgia, 1779

Nicholas Sutcliffe sucked in a breath, opened his eyes, and squinted at the sky. The autumn day had dawned clear, but now it looked as though rain was moving in. It wasn't—musket and cannon fire had left a low, acrid cloud of smoke to color the air gray.

The gunfire had ceased. The battle cries had faded from blood-curdling shouts to soft moans. Horses no longer snorted, and the earth had ceased to rumble beneath their thundering hooves. Nearly a month's siege had ended abruptly, with little more than an hour's battle.

Wincing, Nicholas released the hilt of his saber and grabbed his throbbing shoulder, pushing himself up. Blood from a sword wound oozed between his splayed fingers as blood rushed behind his eyes from a pounding ache in his skull. Stopping before he gained his feet, he sat still and attempted to ignore his pain.

This place—Spring Hill, they called it—looked nothing like it had when he'd first laid eyes on it. Bodies lay everywhere, hundreds of them sprawled in grotesque and unnatural positions, all sleeping the eternal sleep of the dead. Though others walked, limped, and shuffled among the corpses, it seemed to him that far too many men would fail to leave the battlefield on their own legs.

There was no doubt who'd won the conflict. Yet he felt no joy in the triumph. No one could feel proud when the cost of victory had proved so dear.

"Annie," someone nearby muttered. "Oh, Annie."

Nicholas scuttled toward the fallen militia man, who was lying mere feet away. The Colonial's chest barely moved, and his ruined homespun shirt was wet with blood that glistened a more vivid hue than Nicholas' own crimson coat.

"Hold on," he urged, using his good arm to raise the man's head. "Help will be come soon. Your family—"

"I-I've no family here. Not . . . in Savannah."

It made no difference to Nicholas that a short while ago they'd been enemies. This Liberty Boy—hardly older than he himself—was suddenly at the end of his life. He deserved whatever comfort Nicholas could provide.

"I'll see you're sent home when your wound is tended," he promised, knowing, sadly, that he never would. The Colonial's belly wound would kill him long before any surgeon even could look at it.

The fellow grimaced and coughed blood that trickled in a thin line through the whiskers on his chin. "Thank . . . thank you," he whispered. "Annie needs . . . me. I vowed . . . I'd never leave her."

Nicholas strained to hear the words, and as he did, he thought perhaps it would have better served God's world if he were the one lying in the dirt, his life's blood seeping from a mortal wound. He'd yet to find love, let alone a wife. He had no children, either. Had he died helping to put down this insurrection in the king's name, precious few would mourn his passing.

The Colonial fingered a pouch at his waist; Nicholas quickly loosened its string. But before he could retrieve the contents, the man made a small noise and rolled toward him, burrowing a dirty but bloodless face against his chest.

A powerful wind snatched a scrap of coarse, yellow paper from the leather bag. Yet it also cleared a swatch through the stagnant haze hanging over the battlefield. Filtered sunshine lighted the smoke that still swirled about, so that, for some moments, Nicholas and his unlikely companion appeared to be haloed by a heavenly illumination.

Then the wind gusted again, violently. Bowing his head and holding the Continental close to protect him from the sand and grit pelting them, Nicholas found it difficult to breathe. Though he turned his face away from the wind, he could not inhale. He began to feel light-headed, almost weightless.

He gasped when it seemed someone gave him a sharp blow to the belly. And in that instant, the wind died as though it had been merely passing through on its way to another place.

Feeling heavy and anchored again, he dragged in a deep breath and righted himself to find that self-same scrap of paper he thought had blown away clinging to the front of his coat. Plucking it off the dirty, stained wool, he read the words written in a fine hand:

Nicholas Gnann
Ebenezer, State of Georgia

"I have your identity paper, Gnann," he told the fellow, nudging his shoulder. "We have our Christian names in common."

He glanced at Gnann, who now lay face up, in the crook of his arm. The Colonial's closed eyes would never open, never see his beloved Annie, again.

* * *

"I've no need to be in a bloody hospital," Nicholas growled. "My wound will heal well enough on its own."

Gritting his teeth, he fell back against his pallet, no longer straining against the hands attempting to hold him down. As the surgeon sewed the hole closed in his left shoulder, he bore the pain stoically.

"Consider it a reprieve, Sutcliffe. That's your name, soldier, is it not? Aye, you've earned a holiday from warring. So few of our own were killed in the battle, we've the luxury of treating the wounded. And you've the blessing of time to allow yourself to heal properly. 'Til the next battle comes 'round, that is," the surgeon added with a slow shake of his head.

Nicholas winced when the man splashed his wound with brandy before covering it with a bandage. "I'd prefer to drink the stuff, rather than be bathed in it."

"Here. One swig," the physician offered.

As he raised himself on his good arm to accept the flask, his head swam. He managed to take a long swallow, and as he did, he peered at his surroundings. "Is that an altar?" he asked, motioning with his chin.

"Aye, lad, it is. You're in a church we commandeered to house our wounded."

"But . . . I was aboard a vessel . . ."

"Lie down, man," the surgeon ordered gently, relieving him of the flask. "You took a wound to your shoulder, but you took a blow to your head, as well. Get some sleep, now. You'll feel far better once you've rested."

Nicholas did lie down again, this time touching his brow with his fingertips. He felt a bandage wrapped around his head and tried to determine when he'd been injured there. He couldn't. But an image flashed in his mind of being hit by shrapnel in his gut. Immediately, he looked down at his belly, surprised but relieved to see no bloody bandage.

The altar stood before him. And the pulpit, which sat high, with a pair of curved stairs leading up to it. The entire sanctuary seemed oddly familiar. But Nicholas told himself the church was much the same as any other.

* * *

"Nicholas."

The sound of his name on a woman's lips dragged him from his doze. Opening his eyes, he turned his head slightly.

He knew her immediately. Though two women stood near his pallet, he focused on the one he felt quite sure had said his name. She was *petite,* as the French would say, yet the low, square neckline of her simple dress revealed the curves of a nicely rounded bosom. Tendrils of light brown hair, which had escaped the mass she'd pinned up and crowned with a lacey cap, skimmed her oval face. That face proved the perfect canvas for her finely arched brows, her pert nose, and eyes he knew without question were blue. As blue as a summer sky.

But he couldn't see her eyes at the moment. She'd turned her head away from him as she spoke with the other lady.

"I've still had no word," she said, her voice taut with strain. "Oh, Ruth, all that I know is so many of our own died in the battle at Savannah. A thousand, they say. Perhaps more! Nicholas Henry Gnann could well be among the dead."

"You do not know that," the woman, Ruth, said firmly. "Thus, you should not fear the worst. It could take him a long time to make his way home or even to get word to you."

"Nicholas will not come home with the British here. I may not know for months if he survived. And what if he did, only to be killed in a future battle?"

She was Annie, Nicholas realized slowly. Annie Gnann, the dead Continental's wife. How was it possible that he'd come to her, that he'd been delivered to the town of Ebenezer, where the Gnanns lived, without any scheming on his own part?

Yet he was here, and all he had to do was speak up and confirm her worst fear. But he was unable to do it. Not knowing her husband's fate would leave the woman distraught; learning he'd been killed would prove a crushing blow that Nicholas had no desire to deliver. Given time, she'd be better prepared to hear the sad news. God willing, someone else would tell her.

"Stay busy, dear," Ruth urged. "The men here need a bit of washing, and there are bandages to be cut and rolled."

"I thoroughly dislike tending them," Annie admitted, dropping her voice, though she ground out her words. "Who are these British officers to order us about as though we are their lackeys? I'm a free woman, with crops to harvest and livestock to tend, and no husband to do either. Yet I do have two young sons who require a watchful eye. Instead, I'm neglecting them to nurse men who have slaughtered fine Patriots in the name of King George."

"Christopher and Paul are not mischief-makers, Annie. They are not likely to get themselves into any trouble. Give them enough chores to keep them busy. They can help you with the farm until Nicholas returns."

Nodding her bowed head, Annie turned away. Ruth put a hand on her shoulder and accompanied her through the maze of pallets until Nicholas could no longer see them without changing his position.

Yet he saw her with his mind's eye. And in that vision, Annie Gnann's hair was neither pinned up nor covered. Gone, too, was her serviceable brown dress. Instead her hair was long and loose, and she was wearing a nightgown of fine, snowy cambric, edged in lace at the neck and the sleeves.

His pulse quickened, and he felt ashamed. Was he lusting after that poor Colonial's widow? Though he couldn't deny she aroused in him primitive urges, he realized she ignited other feelings, too. Feelings he'd never felt before. Feelings he refused to consider.

Purposely, he closed his eyes tightly and erased all thought. In time, sleep covered him again.

* * *

"Can you eat?"

It was her voice, Annie's voice. At first, Nicholas thought he'd begun to dream of her. But when he opened his eyes, he found her standing above him, a bowl in her hands. Too quickly, he sat up, and a pain shot through his skull. Ignoring it, he said, "Yes, madam, of course, I can eat."

"I'm sure you are hungry. I was asking if you needed assistance."

"Fortunately, it was my left arm that was injured, not the one I eat with."

He reached to take the bowl from her. She hesitated a moment, her eyes moving from his bandaged shoulder to the center of his chest. Nicholas knew she was thinking it would be better if he'd been stabbed closer to his heart and killed.

But she handed him the bowl, which he saw was filled with stew. From her apron pocket, she retrieved a spoon, which she also held out to him.

"Mrs. Gnann."

Her brows came together in a frown. "You know me?"

He did, but he lied, "I overheard someone say your name."

One of her fine eyebrows arched suspiciously. "Oh. What is it you need?"

"I was wondering about this place."

"Many of your wounded were removed here, to New Ebenezer. The town is some miles upriver from Savannah."

"That's not what I was referring to."

"Did the blow to your head affect your memory? You do know you're presently in the colony of Georgia."

"Presently?" he repeated, peering at her curiously. "Have you heard something? Are any of us to move on to another colony? South Carolina, perhaps?"

She made a small, contemptuous sound. "Your officers do not include me in their plans for war. It is my opinion, and many others', too, that your forces shan't always remain victorious. When the Continental Army prevails, this place will be the state, not the colony, of Georgia. My husband—"

She broke off, apparently surprised with herself for having mentioned him. And having done so, her fears for his safety seemed to rush to the fore, knocking her off balance.

Nicholas quelled an urge to stand, to take her in his arms and comfort her. Gnann had been a fool to leave his loving wife to fight a war the Continentals couldn't win. The revolutionaries would never defeat Britain's strong, organized, well-equipped army. The rebels were a rag-tag lot with little training and insufficient ammunition for their guns and artillery. And they were only some of the colonists, for many remained loyal to England.

He set the bowl aside and looked at her again. "What I wished to know was the name of this church. The sanctuary"—he gestured with his good arm—"looks familiar. Yet I know I've not been here before. It is Anglican, is it not?"

"No. It is a Lutheran Church."

"Oh?" He was surprised.

"We're of Austrian stock here, in Ebenezer. None of us English, none of us Anglican."

None of us loyal to King George. Well, he'd certainly known that.

Almost guiltily, Nicholas tore his gaze from Annie and glanced about again. The brick floor remained littered with bedding, bodies, and a disarray of accoutrements required by the ill and injured. Yet he suddenly envisioned the room filled with people standing patiently, all of them wearing smiles and their best clothes. None of the men wore military uniforms, and beside them stood women and children. In that momentary flash, at the candle-lit altar, he could clearly see a vicar presiding over a marriage ceremony. The couple joining in wedlock were Annie and a dark-haired man, the fellow who'd died in his arms, Nicholas Gnann.

When he blinked, the vision vanished. Impulsively, he touched his own hair, free of its tie at the moment and badly in need of a wash. Still, it was fair, as pale as corn silk, not dark. Yet despite knowing that he'd only imagined the Gnanns' wedding day, it felt oddly like a memory.

"Are you well?" Annie asked.

Again, he looked at her. "As well as I could hope for, with a nagging ache in my head and a throbbing wound in my shoulder."

"You should thank God you're alive to feel the pain."

Her words were sharp, but he saw her lower lip tremble before she lifted her hems and hurried away, slipping around the sanctuary to flee through a small door behind it.

She knew. Without having been told, she knew her husband was dead. She simply would not accept it until she heard it said. Nicholas couldn't blame her, since it seemed clear she'd loved her husband as well as he'd loved her.

How difficult it had to be for Annie Gnann to nurse the very men she must believe had taken her husband's life. Nicholas understood that she felt little compassion for him or his fellow soldiers, who'd invaded her town, violated her church. Still, he sensed that she was angry with *him*. And he very much disliked it.

* * *

He left the red brick church carrying a fresh shirt and a chunk of soap. A number of injured soldiers loitered in the grassy yard beneath the live oak trees that dripped with Spanish moss. He spoke with a few of them before walking on.

Ebenezer seemed to be a thriving town of somewhere between one and two thousand inhabitants, including a small number of African slaves. Many neat, little houses and a few shops lined the streets. Not far from the church, he noticed a cemetery. But he turned away from it, heading toward the Savannah River. At the end of the road, he made his way down a steep, sandy slope to the river's edge. Avoiding the area where several boats were moored, he found a bit of privacy along the bank, removed the bandage from his head, stripped off his clothes, and waded into the water.

It was no small delight to be clean. Before pulling his clothes on over his damp skin, Nicholas removed the sodden bandage from his shoulder. Then he raked a comb through his wet hair and tied the length of it in a queue at the nape of his neck.

He found climbing up the slope more difficult, as his bad arm hung limply at his side. Slowly, he managed to scale the bluff and return to the road that led him back to the center of New Ebenezer.

Abruptly, he halted, his attention focused on a building near the heart of town. It wasn't a shop or a meeting hall. It wasn't a school or an inn. *The filature house.* He blinked, startled, for he had never heard the term. Yet he knew it, as he knew the structure was built to house silk worms; it was a place where the cocoons the worms spun were unraveled into reels of silken thread.

Furtively, Nicholas glanced around. There was no one at all near the building, so he hurried to the door and entered it.

The interior was dark and dusty, cobweb curtains hanging over the small windows. No one toiled within, nor had they for some time. Yet stacks of shelving remained where the worms had lain on beds of mulberry leaves, which they ate till they spun their cocoons. Vats for boiling the cocoons sat nearby. And reels for winding silken thread.

He stormed back outside, the wooden door shuddering as he slapped it open with the flat of his hands. The bright sunshine forced him to cover his eyes, and he felt his head begin to ache again.

Hurrying away from the filature house, he passed the church and the parsonage and headed beyond the town's precise streets. On a well-worn track, rutted by carts and packed hard by boots and hooves, he discovered land cleared for cultivation, where animals grazed in grassy pastures.

Breathing hard and sweating under a hot sun the likes of which England never suffered even at the height of summer, Nicholas leaned against a split rail fence to wipe his brow with his shirtsleeve.

"Get down!" he heard a young boy order. "Mam will be angry if we don't move the cows into the other pasture."

"I'm coming," another boy replied.

Nicholas turned, searching for the children. He saw one of them looking upward, into a tree that stood like a solitary sentry in the middle of the field. And he heard the distinctive *crack* of a breaking bough just before he heard the unseen child shriek.

Swinging a leg over the top rail, he streaked toward the boys. Halting directly beneath the breaking bough and the child perched on it, he raised both arms. "Let go!" he ordered. Though he braced himself, the small child hit him like a runaway carriage. Nicholas clutched him to his chest and fell backward, cushioning the boy's landing. Fortunately, he'd managed to dodge the falling bough, which landed an arm's length away.

"Thank you, sir," the boy said, scrambling off him. Then his blue eyes widened. "You're bleeding, and it's my fault. I—"

"You did not harm me, lad," Nicholas insisted, pushing himself to his feet and brushing off his backside. Glancing at the blood staining his one clean shirt, he said, "I took this wound in battle several days ago. It wasn't you who hurt me."

Both children looked up at him solemnly. The older boy said, "Our father went to fight in Savannah. Did you fight there, as well?"

"Did you fight with our father?" the younger one asked.

"You are the Gnann lads, Christopher and Paul?" he asked, somehow knowing that they were. When the brothers nodded, Nicholas did, too. "Aye. I fought with Nicholas Gnann."

The children spoke over each other. "Did he come home with you?" "Where is he? Mam's been waiting on his return."

He evaded their questions as they accompanied him back into town. Yet Nicholas knew he'd not be returning to the infirmary at the church. His heart wanted to soar at the prospect of seeing Annie again, but it couldn't take flight tied down as it was by the knot of dread in his stomach.

* * *

"Mam!" Christopher shouted as he pushed open the door to a small wooden house that sat well away from the center of town.

Annie was bent over the fire in the hearth, stirring a kettle. "Did you put the cows in the north pasture?"

"Mam," Paul said, "we've brought home a guest, Mr. Sutcliffe. He fought with Father in Savannah."

She straightened and whirled, her eyes huge when she spied him standing in the doorway between her two sons. Her face darkened as she recognized him, and though Nicholas felt sure she wanted to say something to him, she merely took a deep breath and told the boys, "Go wash, now, for supper."

"Mam, he's hurt," Paul explained. "Will you help him?"

"I've already done all—" Annie cut herself off, hesitated a moment, then nodded. "Go, do as I say. Supper will be on the table shortly."

The boys raced out of the house again, slamming the door in their wake.

Nicholas faced her squarely. He felt an urge to apologize, to put himself back in her favor. But he had yet to be in her favor.

"What are you doing with my sons?"

He didn't know. He couldn't say.

"Why are you here?"

"I was invited."

"Because you lied to them. You told them you fought beside my husband, Nicholas."

The door burst open again. Christopher looked at the table, set only with empty plates. "Mam, you said supper was ready."

"I thought you'd tend Mr. Sutcliffe's shoulder," Paul added. "It's why we brought him home."

"And so he might tell us of Father." Turning from his mother, Christopher said, "You did see him on the battlefield."

Nicholas glanced at Annie before replying. "Aye."

She spun away, lifting the pot hanging from the spider above the flames. "Sit, boys. Supper is ready."

"I'll get a plate for our guest," Christopher volunteered. "He can sit in Father's chair."

Annie closed her eyes tightly. When she opened them again, she moved about briskly, filling all four plates.

Reluctantly, Nicholas sat in her husband's chair. Paul said grace, and everyone began eating.

Annie toyed with her food. Nor did Nicholas have any intention of taking more than a polite bite. But he found the fare tasty and, hungrier than he had realized, he cleaned his plate.

"The meal was lovely, Mrs. Gnann. Better than anything I've had since . . . since I left home."

"It's Father's favorite," Christopher explained. "Ham hocks and collards."

Nicholas suppressed the urge to say it was his favorite, too. It was not. Yet it troubled him to realize it easily could become so.

"You haven't told us about our father," Paul reminded him. "When did you last see him? When is he coming home?"

"Likely, he shan't be coming home soon," Annie explained. "Not with the English Army residing among us."

"Bloody bastards," the eldest boy muttered.

"Christopher Gnann, would you like your mouth washed out with soap?"

"I'm sorry, Mam." Nicholas felt the boy's glance slide his way. "You are not from Ebenezer. Did our father send you with a message for us?"

Nicholas couldn't think what to say, so he looked to Annie.

"If he has," she said, "I am sure Mr. Sutcliffe wishes to give it first to me." She glanced toward a window. "There's still a bit of light left. Will you two bring some wood from the pile out back and stack it near the door?"

Their chairs scraped against the wooden floor. Seconds later the children were gone.

"Your shoulder's still bleeding," Annie said. "I'd best tend it, or Paul will wonder why I've neglected your wound, with you being a Patriot like their father."

"Forgive me—"

"For seeking out my children and lying to them?" she snapped as she rummaged in a box of fabric scraps.

"I didn't seek them out," Nicholas replied. "How could I have known who they were or where they might be? I happened upon them, and Paul had himself stuck in a tree. . . ."

She was at his side, opening his shirt. Her fingertips grazed his chest, and a shock shuddered through him, a delightful shock. He had to quell an impulse to grab her hand, kiss her wrist, and pull her down into his lap.

He raised his gaze to hers. She looked nearly as shocked as he felt.

She recovered her composure quickly, pulling his shirt away from his wound. "What happened to your bandage?"

"I removed it when I bathed."

"You should have replaced it." Efficiently, she did the task herself. "I appreciate your helping my son down from the tree, but not for telling my boys that you fought beside my husband."

Nicholas stood. "I said only that I fought with him."

She scowled angrily, turning away. "A play on words, a clever contrivance. You never knew my husband."

"But I did."

She turned back sharply. And the moment he'd hoped to avoid inevitably arrived. His stomach clenched as before a battle.

"Your husband and I found ourselves together on Spring Hill," he admitted.

"To— Together? Oh, God, you didn't kill him, did you?"

"No! No, I was wounded, as was he. We fell on the field side by side."

Her eyes welled with tears. "He's dead, then."

Nicholas nodded, and her knees buckled. He gathered her up in his arms and sat again in her husband's chair, this time holding her in his lap.

"I knew," she muttered.

"Yes. You would."

"How . . . How did you know him? Did you speak before he died?"

"Aye." Nicholas nodded his head against her cheek, which was wet, now, with tears. "The first word he said was your name. He told me he'd promised never to leave you."

"He did! On the day we married, at Jerusalem Church."

"There was a scrap of paper on him, bearing his name."

"Then you . . . you came here to find me and . . . tell me?"

"I had no chance to consider it. I fell unconscious where I was, and by the time I'd regained my wits, I was being transported." *Here. As though he'd sent me.*

The door banged open as the children returned. Annie flew from his lap, wiping her face with her hands.

Nicholas stood, too. "I shall be going, now. You'll wish to speak to your children alone."

He paused, looking down at the boys. He wished he could gather them into his arms and assure them that everything would be all right. But he didn't know that it would be.

* * *

"Gentlemen," Colonel Campbell said, addressing Nicholas and his fellow, wounded soldiers. "I called you here to inform you that you shall not be returning to your regiments. You will remain here to assist in fortifying the town against attack. As you are all well-recovered, you shall be quartered among the locals. The church will be used to stable our horses."

Nicholas felt a surge of resentment. Using the church to tend the wounded was one matter; to defile it with beasts of burden seemed unconscionable.

"My aide, here, will tell you with whom you are to board."

Nicholas knew his name would fall near the bottom of the alphabetized list. At last, he heard it:

"Sutcliffe, Nicholas, Private."

He sucked in a quick breath.

"Johann and Martha Zeigler."

He exhaled, surprised yet relieved.

"Wait," the aide continued. "That is not correct. Private, you will quarter with the widow Gnann and her children."

He'd known it would be so. Relief fled, yet he was not unhappy.

When he was dismissed, Nicholas grabbed his kit from the church and went to Annie's house. Finding no one home, he left his gear beside the door and began walking toward her farm outside of town.

He passed the cows grazing near the solitary tree Paul had fallen from; goats and sheep now shared the pasture, as well. Farther on, he spied a barn. Nearby, he saw pigs routing in the mud inside their pen and chickens pecking at feed strewn atop the sandy soil. He paused, taking in the other outbuildings and the cultivated fields of cotton. The vista looked endless and lush. He experienced a surge of good feeling, rather like pride, as though all this were his.

A horse inside the barn whinnied, and he heard Annie swear, "Damn you, Nicholas! Where are you when I need you?"

"I am here." He stepped into the doorway, letting his eyes adjust to the dim shadows inside the barn.

Squatting behind a fat mare that was down on her side, Annie pivoted toward him, her eyes alight. When she recognized him, she frowned. "*You* are Nicholas?"

"Aye."

She looked quickly away. "The mare's foaling. And having a hard time of it."

Nicholas shrugged off his coat, tossed it aside, and walked over to hunker down beside the mare. He felt the animal's flank, checked her eyes.

"My Nicholas always attended the births."

"I have assisted in a few four-legged births in my time," he said. "I will stay, if you'd like."

"Do you have a farm in England?"

"My father raises sheep. I see that you have a few."

"Ours is not the best climate for them. Pigs fare far better. There are many wild ones in the forest."

A minute passed, silently. Then Nicholas ventured, "Are you . . . managing . . . quite well?"

She met his gaze. "Since you told me that my Nicholas is dead? Yes, well enough. The boys, though, have taken it hard."

"Mam! Mam!"

As though her mention had conjured them, Christopher and Paul careened into the barn.

"Those bloody Red Coats stole our sow, Mam!" Christopher announced. "They have no right to—" He broke off, noticing that his mother was not alone. Turning his outrage on Nicholas, he commanded, "Get out! You killed my father and lied to us about it. Get out of our barn!"

Nicholas rose quickly to his feet. "No," he countered softly, "I did not kill your father, though we fought on opposite sides that frightful day in Savannah. We were both wounded, and we lay together on the ground. As he was worse wounded than I, I did my best for him, Christopher. I promise, I did. In those final minutes, we became friends."

"You lie, sir. You lie!" The boy launched himself toward him.

He was joined instantly by his brother, and together, they landed a few hurtful blows. But Nicholas stood still, allowing them to vent their grief and anger. When their small fists opened and their arms went slack, he leaned down and hugged them to his chest.

Christopher was the first to realize he'd sought solace in the arms of his enemy. He jumped away, and Paul quickly followed.

Annie came to her feet then, but before she could speak, three British soldiers appeared in the barn doorway.

"Why are you here?" Nicholas asked them.

"To take what we need," one of them replied. Striding down the aisle and peering into the stalls, he stopped before one containing the Gnanns' stallion. "Perhaps this fine animal will do."

"No!" Annie cried.

Nicholas put himself between the soldier and the beast. "He isn't yours, nor is he for sale."

The man laughed, and the others joined him. "We're the king's army, here to protect you fool Colonials from the rebels amongst you. We do not pay for the provisions we need."

"You took our sow!" Paul shouted.

One of the other two soldiers stepped toward him. "Only one? We'd best relieve you of the rest, then."

"Wouldn't want the old girl to be longing for her piglets, now, would we?" the third fellow added with a chuckle.

"Get out," Nicholas demanded, advancing.

"You wouldn't be a *patriot*, would you?" the nearest soldier sneered, cocking an eyebrow.

"Nay, I would not." He took two long strides and snatched his red coat from the pile of hay where he'd tossed it. "But I am quartered here, and I shan't let you steal from this family."

The soldier's gaze slid toward Annie, then back to him. His lip curled as he said, "I see the way of things, old boy. Nice piece o'—"

Nicholas' fist connected with the man's chin. The soldier quickly assumed a fighting stance, but his friends grabbed his arms.

Reluctantly, he sidled toward the door. "No matter how good this thing is you've got going, mate, remember you're the king's army, too. We're not here to protect rebels. We're here to put them down."

"I hardly think a woman and her two young sons might be rebels," Nicholas said dryly.

"I—" Christopher began.

Nicholas clamped a hand over the boy's mouth, keeping it there until the three men were gone.

Immediately, the lad announced, "I *am* a patriot."

"So you are, and I respect you for it. But there's no need to antagonize the soldiers occupying the town. You don't wish to make life more difficult for your mother, do you, lad?"

Christopher scowled, but he didn't argue.

Annie asked, "Have they really quartered you here?"

"Aye." Nicholas looked at her. "It was not at my request, I assure you. I've no wish to inconvenience your family. I can sleep in the barn."

The mare groaned and thrashed her hind legs.

Annie sighed. "I fear I'm the one who shall sleep in the barn to-night."

"I'll join you, then." Seeing her eyes widen, he quickly added, "'Til the mare has foaled."

* * *

Nicholas normally slept on a rough pallet stuffed with Spanish moss, near the hearth in Annie's house. She slept in her small bedroom, and the boys in the loft.

As autumn progressed, though, Nicholas found little rest as he lay on his lonely pallet night after night. His mind danced with images of her—how she turned her head just so, how she'd smiled at something he said, how the lips that formed that pretty smile tasted. Not that he'd tasted her lips. But in his daydreams, he imagined the pressure of them against his and felt their texture on his tongue. Yet it was more than imagination. He knew those lips. And he wanted badly to taste them again.

* * *

"Mam, are we done?" Paul whined. He was sitting cross-legged on the floor near the fireplace, his lap full of cotton bolls he'd been cleaning of seeds.

"For tonight," she told him. "But all the cotton must be cleaned, so I can spin it. You need new clothes, you've grown so."

"Why can't we plant something besides cotton?" Christopher complained. "Or get us some nigras to pick and clean."

Seated in her rocker, Annie looked at her eldest. "Your father didn't hold with owning slaves. It's why we don't have a large plantation, like some of our neighbors."

"But we could grow a lot more if we had coloreds to do the work. Why did Father not hold with owning slaves?"

"Because it isn't right for one people to own another," Nicholas explained.

"You wouldn't know what my father thought."

"Christopher Gnann, apologize," Annie ordered.

"But he cannot know."

"He does know," Paul countered, coming to his feet and walking over to Nicholas, sitting in his caned chair, and put a hand on his knee. "Father was with him when he died," he told his brother.

Nicholas put a hand over Paul's. The younger boy didn't blame him for the part he'd played in that fateful battle, and he was eternally grateful for the lad's generous heart.

"They were together for only minutes," Christopher pointed out, his gaze flickering toward Nicholas' uniform, hanging on a wall peg. "Father had no time to tell him his every thought."

"Be that as it may, Mr. Sutcliffe is correct," Annie announced. "Your father did not think it right to own slaves. Now, go up to bed. And do not forget to say your prayers."

"Yes, Mam."

Nicholas returned the smile Paul gave him. Then the lad kissed his mother's cheek and scampered up the ladder to the loft. But Christopher gave him only a quick glance and his mother a nod before following his brother.

Nicholas pulled his chair closer to Annie's. "Perhaps there is some sense in your son's suggestion," he said. "Why do you grow cotton?"

"My husband continued what his parents began, and they did as the colony's founder, General Oglethorpe, bade. We are too high, here on the bluff, to grow rice. Besides, we always produced silk in addition to the crops we planted. But the filature house has gone unused since the war began."

He recalled most vividly the day he'd first noticed the building.

"Can you manage as you are?" he inquired.

"We could, if the British— If you—" she stammered. Pausing to take a breath, she tried again. "If people stopped taking from me what I need to care for myself and my own, I could manage."

Nicholas wanted to justify the army's confiscations but could not. Nor could he justify Parliament's position on the colonies. Those who taxed the colonists had never even visited America. Like England itself, its government existed half a world away and shared nothing in common with this country that it sought to control.

"How did you come to join the army?" Annie asked him.

He shrugged. "I wanted to do more than raise sheep. I wanted to be off the farm. Signing on seemed a good means to see a bit of the world."

"And are you now eager to leave this part of the world?"

"No. I'm glad that I came here."

His gaze met hers, and she didn't blink. His heart quickened, for he'd imagined her looking at him just so. Impulsively he leaned toward her . . .

And she jerked her head back. Standing, she set aside the pile of cotton bolls she'd been cradling in her apron. "I think I shall make a quick run to the hen house and grab a bird to stew on the morrow."

"But it's dark," he said, frowning.

"The moon is full," she countered. "I can see easily."

Before he could argue further, she disappeared out the door. Alone, Nicholas called himself ten times a fool for trying to kiss a grieving widow. Yet he still thought it unwise for her to venture outside, without escort, at this hour. Wild animals prowled the forest and drunken soldiers, the town streets.

He didn't take his coat when he left to follow her. The late November temperatures remained mild, the evenings only pleasantly cool. And Annie had been right—the full moon thoroughly brightened his surroundings, lighting his way. He was nearly to the hen house when he heard her shout.

Nicholas' heart slammed against his ribs like a quick right jab. Breaking into a run, he bolted for the barn, slowing when he saw her, bathed in starlight, weeping into her hands.

"Annie, what is it? What's happened?" he demanded.

"Look!" she cried, dropping her hands to gesture. "The chickens are gone, along with the laying hens and the cock. The pigs, too."

Surveying the empty barnyard, he knew the animals hadn't escaped on their own. He felt as furious as she clearly was.

"I shall get them back," he vowed.

"You cannot." She shook her head and wiped at her damp cheeks with the heel of her hands. "The chickens will already be in someone's pot—or stomach. And it may not be your soldiers who stole them. It may be someone from town who has lost most all he owned to your army. Good God, Nicholas!" She shook her fisted hands. "The Red Coats have been in Ebenezer less than a year. They say they're protecting us, but if the occupation continues much longer, we shan't have anything left. Most everyone will leave. *I* shall have to leave." Her voice choking on tears, she whispered, "But I have nowhere to go."

He embraced her, noting only vaguely that she hadn't included him with the other occupying soldiers. And he felt sure she had called him by his Christian name. He was sharply aware, though, that he finally had the woman in his arms he had been longing to hold. He kissed her eyelids, her earlobes, her cheeks, and her neck. When her arms went around him, he kissed her lips.

He felt as though, at last, he had found his way home.

"If you must leave, Annie," he breathed between kisses, "I shall go with you."

"Oh, Nicholas," she muttered softly, still clinging to him.

He slipped his hands beneath her knees, lifted her, and carried her into the barn. He didn't pause to light a lantern, but the open doors allowed the moonlight to follow them inside. There, in an empty stall filled with fresh bedding straw, he tumbled with her.

He should have gone more slowly, taking time to memorize her body. But he felt too eager, and she seemed the same, deftly unfastening his buttons as he undid her ties. When he exposed her shoulder, he kissed it right where he knew she'd been marked at birth with a small, pink blossom. Catching her long hair in his fingers, he nuzzled the nape of her neck and heard her respond with a moan that sizzled his senses.

"Oh, Nicholas, yes," she whispered when he slid himself into her. "I have missed . . ." She allowed her words to trail off as she wrapped her legs about his waist and met him thrust for thrust.

He had missed her also, making his way to her over long miles and long years without realizing she was his destination. He felt no awkward newness between them. Rather, he sensed they'd spent a thousand nights together. And when they both found fulfillment, gasping each other's names in the moonlight, he knew it had always been so.

Afterward, reluctantly, he rolled off her, keeping her close in the crook of his arm so that his scarred shoulder pillowed her head. He thought they might slumber. It felt natural that they would sleep tucked together, skin against skin, heat against heat.

But Annie didn't doze. She sat up, dragging the bodice of her dress up over her bosom. "Forgive me," she begged. "This should not have happened."

Panic seized him, but he fought it, holding still and watching her face. She seemed distraught, though he couldn't fathom why. How could she not understand that they were meant to be together? He knew. In his soul, he knew.

"I am barely a widow," she said, "and I loved my husband well. I do not know what caused me to betray his memory, but—" She peered at him, searching his eyes. "You are like *my* Nicholas. Too like him. Still, I am to blame, not you. I was weak, and I was wrong. I should never have turned to you, not even in despair."

Standing, she righted her clothes and brushed the straw off her sleeves. "We shan't speak of this evening again, I hope."

Nicholas sighed, his heart breaking. "I will try not to speak of it," he said. "But I shall always treasure the memory."

* * *

The mild autumn was chased away by a furiously bitter winter as the year turned from 1779 to 1780. Nicholas toiled at his duties during the day, and, upon returning home, he did the chores Gnann would have done. During the final hours of evening, while Annie did her weaving on a large loom, he often helped Paul with his reading. Christopher refused his help and kept to himself.

Nicholas missed Annie, her kisses and her body. But he contented himself with their friendship and the comfort of her family. He could pretend that he was part of it—for a while, at least.

Late one afternoon, he returned to the house to find the children away and Annie in her room. When a knock sounded at the door, he opened it. A man, hat in hand, stood on the stoop.

"Excuse me," the gentleman said in a tone that bespoke his distaste at having to converse with a British soldier. "I have come to collect Mrs. Gnann."

"Collect her?"

"Aye. She's to be my guest at a party, at my plantation, River's Edge. Please tell her Robert Meyer is here."

Nicholas remained silent for several seconds. Meyer was a good deal older than he, but not bad looking. And he wore expensive, fashionable clothes.

"I fear I cannot do that," he said. "Mrs. Gnann is unwell. She shan't be going anywhere this evening."

"I spoke with her only yesterday. She seemed in fine health." Meyer put his foot on the threshold.

"That was yesterday, sir. Today she is suffering from fever." Nicholas began to push the door closed. "It's best you do not come in. You wouldn't wish to succumb to the same illness that's taken hold of An— of Mrs. Gnann."

"But—"

He closed the door. Meyer knocked again, loudly, but only once. Nicholas surmised he wasn't the type who would wish to be seen pounding on a lady's door or heard shouting her name.

"Was there someone at the door?"

He turned as Annie emerged from her bedroom. Though her frock was a somber, dark blue suitable for a widow, it was set off with a bit of white lace. She looked so fetching, he wanted to take it off her.

"No."

"Are you quite sure? I am expecting a Mr. Meyer to call."

"Are you? Would that be . . . proper?"

Her cheeks flushed pink, and she raised her chin. "You weren't concerned about propriety last November, that night in the barn."

It was first the time she'd mentioned their love-making, and Nicholas knew he should have felt suitably chastised. He did not. Ignoring her remark, he said, "I hardly realized you were accepting gentlemen callers these days."

"Gentleman. One man. A good friend. Nicholas, this isn't London or Paris, or even a quaint country village like one you'd find on the Continent. This land is little more than a savage wilderness. Life here is hard and ofttimes dangerous. Those who are widowed do not have the luxury of a full year to mourn."

"What are you saying?" He stepped toward her. "That you need a new husband to survive?"

She looked away. She might as well have nodded.

"Did I not help harvest your fields? Have I not chopped enough firewood to keep the house warm and hunted enough game to put meat on your table? You do not need a husband to do for you what I can do."

"But you will not remain with us," she said calmly. "I must consider my sons and their future."

"Annie, wait!" he pleaded as she grabbed her woolen cape and rushed to the door.

"No." She whirled about to face him. "You are a soldier quartered in my home. You have no say in my business. If I wish to attend a gathering with my friends, I shall certainly do so."

She opened the door but lingered long enough to tell him, "Paul and Christopher are having supper with the Seckingers. When they return, they're to go straight to bed."

"Am I their nanny, then?" he demanded, striding toward her. "While you are escorted to a party, I'm to stay here, waiting to tuck the children in at bedtime?"

"Of course not. Christopher is ten. The boys are fully capable of getting themselves to bed. You— You can stay or go, whatever you wish. Same as I," she added before closing the door behind her.

Nicholas went nowhere. He made himself some supper but barely touched it as he sat before the hearth, tending the fire. When the children returned, he urged them up to the loft, but he did not leave his post.

He peered out the window occasionally, looking for Annie. When the sky grew overcast, though, he doubted she would return before daybreak. With no moon to light their way, the party guests would have to remain at their host's home. Annie would be spending the night with Robert Meyer.

Though tired from a hard day's work, Nicholas could not numb his mind sufficiently to sleep. Knowing it would prove pointless to lie on his pallet, he remained in his chair, dozing occasionally. Just before dawn, he rose to stir the fire and put water on to boil. It was Sunday, and he had no official duties, so he again returned to his chair.

He realized he'd fallen into a light sleep when the rasp of the door latch brought his eyes open and he saw it was full light. Annie hurried inside, closing the door against the crisp, morning cold.

"Are the boys home and well?" she asked softly.

Without rising, he nodded.

"And . . . you?" She removed her cloak and gloves.

He shrugged. "Did you enjoy the party?"

"I . . . did." She walked to the fireplace, rubbing her hands briskly in the heat of its flames. "The water in the kettle has nearly boiled away. Did you fall asleep after setting it on?"

"Perhaps. I did not sleep very well last night. Did you?"

Taking a deep breath, she turned toward him. "Nicholas," she said, "I am going to tell you something straight out, so that you do not hear the news elsewhere. Mr. Meyer has asked me to marry him, and I've said yes."

He felt as he had when he'd been wounded in battle, except that the pain and shock struck him not in the shoulder but the gut. "Why?"

"Because he, too, is widowed, and he needs a wife."

"And, because he's a rich man, you will not have to struggle with the farm." Nicholas surged to his feet. "That is why you agreed, isn't it, not because you love him?"

She sighed. "No, I do not love him. I loved my husband, but he's gone. I shan't ever love any man as I loved him, so it is reasonable that I make a match for more practical reasons. In that regard, Robert Meyer is quite suitable."

"What of me?" Nicholas demanded, crossing to her in couple of strides. "That time we were together was the most tender and joyous time of my life. And we are even better friends, now, Annie. We know each other well. And I feel as though your sons are my own."

"They are not yours." She stepped away. "And we are not true friends. I was forced to give you temporary shelter. But you will move on, no doubt to kill more Patriots."

"No." He shook his head vehemently. But before he could say more, Paul popped his head over the edge of the loft and looked down at them.

"Why are you fighting, Mam?" he asked. "And where is Christopher?"

"What do you mean?" Annie's gaze shot from her son to Nicholas. "Did he go out already?"

"I did not see him," Nicholas replied, "but perhaps he slipped by me."

She grabbed her cloak again as he shrugged on his red coat. Outdoors, they called the boy but heard no answer. They split up to search, and while he was searching the barn for the second time, Annie came in, breathless.

"The Seckingers," she said. "I'll go speak to Ruth. Perhaps she knows something."

He nodded, falling in step with her as she hurried toward town. As they reached the town limits, Paul came running to join them. Together, they hurried to the Seckingers' house, where they discovered Ruth and her husband, Earnest, as distraught as they were.

"Our Harold's gone, too!" Ruth cried.

"They must have gone off together," Annie said. "Have you any idea where?"

"I think I might know," Paul announced. "Last night, after supper, they were speaking about joining the Continentals."

Annie gasped.

"Dear God!" Ruth exclaimed, pressing a fist over her heart.

"They are too young," her husband insisted. "They will be sent home."

"Not too young to be drummer boys," Paul said.

Nicholas thought Ruth looked as though she might faint. But Annie, made of stronger stuff, rushed into the street, declaring, "I'll find them. I'll bring them home."

"No!" Nicholas ran to stop her. "You stay with Paul. I'll find them."

"I'll go with you," Earnest announced, having followed them outside.

Realizing how upset the man was, Nicholas didn't point out that it might be unwise for a colonist to accompany a British soldier in search of two boys intent on joining the Continental Army.

As the two of them began walking together, Earnest said, "They would not go to Savannah. They know it remains under English control."

"So they'd likely cross the river into South Carolina," Nicholas concluded.

"Aye. Let's secure a boat."

Christopher and Harold were walking the narrow road that led to Charleston when Nicholas and Earnest spied them. The runaways were sauntering along, their kit tied in bundles, chatting as though they were going fishing, not to war.

After sharing a look of relief, the men sprinted forward and grabbed the boys' shoulders. Christopher and Harold spun around, their faces blanching nearly white.

"If the likes of us has frightened you, lads," Nicholas said, "you cannot begin to fathom what terror you'd feel on a battlefield."

Harold was speechless and hurried to keep up as his father marched him back, toward the river's edge.

Christopher, however, gave Nicholas a defiant look and spat in the dirt between their feet. "You cannot make me go home," he insisted. "You're one of the bloody British bastards I intend to kill, the way you Red Coats killed my father!"

Nicholas understood the boy's feelings, but it still cut him to the quick that the child despised him.

"No, lad," he argued softly. "You shan't be killing anyone, not for long years yet. I sincerely hope you will never kill at all."

He held the boy by the shirt collar as they followed the Seckingers down the narrow road. Halfway to the river, he said, "Remember when you were just a mite, you thought it would be grand to wear a vicar's robes? Boys called by God to the Church shouldn't wish to kill people."

Christopher halted and stared up at him. "Did Mam tell you that?"

Had she? Nicholas wanted to believe it, but he knew Annie had told him no such thing. It had been Gnann, Nicholas Gnann, in that long minute on the battlefield, when the wind had swirled and the smoke had cleared, and the Patriot had died in his arms.

Taking a deep breath, Nicholas felt a tremor run through him as the truth came to rest in his soul.

"No," he said. "It was your father."

The boy studied him, and Nicholas could see he was debating whether to believe or argue.

Then Christopher shrugged. "Well, I've no interest in being a vicar anymore."

"I know why not. They never curse."

The boy quirked his mouth to one side, trying desperately to retain his tight-lipped scowl. That he couldn't manage it gave Nicholas hope.

"Your mother and I want you to live long enough to make a decision about what you shall do with your life," he said as they resumed walking. "So there'll be no drumming for you, lad. Not while I am around."

"But you'll be leaving. Everyone knows that, come spring, the British are marching on Charleston."

Nicholas did know that. At least, he knew those were Colonel Campbell's plans. But he had his own plans, now.

Annie was relieved and happy to have Christopher safely home. But she punished the boy just the same, setting him to work with a host of chores and informing him that he would have nothing but tea and a biscuit for his supper.

Paul was sent to collect kindling.

Alone with Annie, Nicholas stood for a moment by the hearth, watching her as she sat at the table, peeling apples for a cobbler. He considered waiting for a time when she wasn't still recovering from the fear of nearly losing her son. But he'd waited months already, and if he restrained himself any longer, it might be too late.

Stepping up behind her chair, he leaned down and kissed the back of her neck.

She sucked in a breath but, to his relief, she did not pull away. Instead, she canted her head, allowing him better access. Then, slipping off the chair, she faced him, raised her arms, and clung to him.

They fitted together perfectly.

"Thank you for finding my son," she whispered. "He's a foolish, headstrong boy, more like me than his father."

"He learnt he was wrong, I hope. Can you?"

"What do you mean?" She leaned back a bit to peer up at him.

"I mean, marrying Meyer is not the best you can do. You would be better off marrying me."

"Oh, Nicholas," she said softly, stepping away, shaking her head. "Nothing's changed. You're a British soldier, and you'll be marching on to fight again. You are here to fight against all I hold dear, what my husband died fighting *for.*"

He shook his head slowly. "No more. In the time I've been here, I've come to see that the rebels are right. This land can no more be part of the Empire than China could be. I could not fathom raising a weapon against a Patriot ever again."

A frown flickered across her brow. "What are you saying?"

"If you'll have me, I shan't leave you," he replied, his steady gaze holding hers. "I love you, Annie, and I wish to remain in the colonies as your husband. And as a father to Paul and Christopher."

A shimmer of tears veiled her bright eyes. "But . . . it's not possible," she argued softly. "You're English, Nicholas, and a soldier. You will be ordered away to fight again."

"Not if I am not here to take orders."

"What—"

"Am I saying?" he completed her question with a smile. "I'm saying that I choose you over King George, America over England. But, though I could not fight the Colonials again, I've no wish to draw arms against the British, either. So, Annie, if you choose me, we must leave, take ourselves far away from the fighting. Will you do that? Will you bring the children and face the unknown with me?"

She hesitated only a moment. Then she pitched herself into his arms. "Aye, Nicholas Sutcliffe. I shall go with you, because your heart is not unknown to me. I love you truly, as though I always have, and my place now is at your side."

It was. It always had been. And it would ever be.

"The Stargazer's Familiar"
by
Mary Jo Putney

Dear Reader,

In New Orleans, they use the word "lagniappe." It means a little something extra, a bit of a bonus, like tossing an extra beignet in the bag. In a collection that examines the cost of war on warriors, "The Stargazer's Familiar" is a lagniappe. Originally published in the collection A Constellation of Cats (ed. Denise Little, DAW 2001), it's a light counterbalance to the more serious stories.

Yet oddly enough, "The Stargazer's Familiar" also fits well into The Journey Home because it's the tale of someone with a warrior soul who must fight to protect those he loves, and who pays a price for doing his duty. Courage is admirable, no matter what form it comes in.

I hope you enjoy Leo's story.
Mary Jo Putney

* * * * *

On a fantasy world far, far away . . .

It was a dark and stormy night. I didn't mind the wind, because building the celestial observation tower on the highest hill in the kingdom meant there was always wind, but rain was quite another matter. When the first gust struck, I dived inside through the window set in the angled roof.

Quite apart from a dislike of getting soaked, I knew from experience that the slate observatory roof was dangerously slippery when wet, even for someone as agile as I. A fall from this height would rob me of another of my nine lives, and already I was down to six. (Five if one counts that incident involving the wolfhound, but I'm sure my escape was entirely my own doing.)

The Stargazer glanced up when I leaped from the telescope to the floor. He was young for a royal astrologer, but he'd been raised in the

234 Mary Jo Putney

trade by his father—as I had been raised to be an astrologer's guardian by mine. "I see from your fur that the rain has started, Leo. Remind me to close the window as soon as I finish this calculation."

I ignored him, since it is not my job to remind an absentminded astrologer to use common sense. Settling into my spot on the hearth, I carefully licked away the raindrops. The Stargazer might not mind untidiness, but I have higher standards. There isn't another coat of fur in the kingdom as sleek and black as mine.

Grooming done, I settled down to doze and contemplate the pleasures of the evening ahead. Life had been exceptionally comfortable since The Stargazer brought The Lady home. Soft and sweet, she knew the very best way to stroke a throat or scratch behind an ear. She adored me, of course. What human female wouldn't? It was The Lady who'd thought to place a bed of fur beside my favorite fireplaces. So much nicer than cold stone. She saw that both The Stargazer and I were fed properly, as well. Just this morning, before seeing us off to work, she'd whispered a promise to find me a special bit of fish when she went to the market.

Best of all, she'd brought Melisande with her. Exquisite Melisande of the silky silver fur and insouciant tail. The mere thought of her made me purr.

Yes, life was good. . . .

My slumber was disturbed when the door opened with such force it banged against the wall. I came awake instantly, my fur prickling with warning. The man who entered wore the rich court dress of a nobleman, but jewels could not disguise the miasma of evil that clung to him. I backed into the shadows, tail lashing.

Though he lacked my perception, The Stargazer appeared wary when he greeted the intruder. "Lord Klothe. What an honor. What brings you to my humble observatory on such an unpleasant night?"

Klothe closed the door behind him, then strolled across the circular room, his velvet mantle shedding water. "I've a commission for you."

"I'm honored, my lord, but I'm very busy at the moment with work for the king. If your need is urgent, you'd best take it to Sorvinus, who is one of the finest astrologers in the kingdom." Though The Stargazer's words were perfectly polite, I knew his real desire was to see Klothe leave, but even famous astrologers don't say that to lords.

"Sorvinus is an amateur compared to you, and I need the best. This won't take long. 'Tis said the heavens are about to align in a pattern that will generate enough power to change the fate of nations." Klothe's black eyes gleamed. "I need an electional chart that will enable me to harness that power to achieve my ends."

The Stargazer's expression became so blank that I knew his concern equaled mine. "A Grand Conjunction exceeding any other in our lifetimes is imminent, but I could not cast a proper electional chart for a great enterprise without also doing an accurate natal chart for you. There is simply not enough time for me to calculate that before the Grand Conjunction occurs tomorrow morning."

"I have my chart here." Klothe drew a scroll from inside his mantle. "Your father himself cast it on the day I was born, so you cannot doubt its accuracy."

Reluctantly, The Stargazer accepted the scroll and unrolled it, scanning to get a sense of his guest's natal potentials. Blood drained from his face. "You wish to assassinate King Rolande!"

"Your skill is equal to your reputation." Klothe's smile was colder than ice on a winter tree. "A soothsayer once prophesied that in this year I would reach the highest place in the kingdom. The time has come to make my move. Determine the moment when the powers of heaven will grant me success, and you will find your new king to be a grateful patron."

"No." Hand shaking, The Stargazer hurled the scroll toward the fire. It bounced off the mantel and almost struck me. His aim had always been atrocious. "King Rolande is a strong, just man who has brought peace and prosperity to the whole kingdom. I would die before I would help a usurper murder my sovereign."

A hiss of steel against leather, and suddenly the tip of a blade was pressed above The Stargazer's heart. "That can be arranged. The choice is yours."

"How will killing me help you achieve your ends?" The Stargazer spoke back, beyond fear. "You're right, Sorvinus is an amateur. Only I can give you the information you seek, and if you slay me, you will fail in your enterprise."

Stalemate. Klothe was evil, but no fool. Seeing the man's uncertainty, The Stargazer said persuasively, "Put aside your ambition, and I swear your words will not go beyond this room. In return, I shall cast your chart and tell you how to use your strength and will to the best advantage. The best *legal* advantage."

Klothe lowered the sword a few inches, and I thought The Stargazer had won. Then my keen ears detected soft footsteps starting up the winding tower stairs. The Lady was coming to learn when her husband would be down for dinner, and her presence would change the balance of power.

Klothe must be disarmed. I growled menacingly. The Stargazer heard and looked in my direction. Praying he'd have the brains to take advantage of my intervention, I charged from the shadows, screaming the threats of my kind, and hurled myself at Klothe. With one mighty leap, I landed on the shoulder of his sword arm. The weapon clanged to the floor as my razor claws drew blood and my fangs ripped into his tender ear.

Yet Klothe was a trained warrior and fast, almost as fast as I. He fell back with an oath, wrenching at me. Through pure luck, he managed to tear me lose from my hold on his shoulder. As I fell toward the floor, he kicked. His booted foot sent me sailing across the room to crash into the wall.

"You shouldn't have sent your foul familiar!" he snarled. "Now I have reason to slay you even if no purpose is served."

"You've killed Leo!" The Stargazer ran to my side, tears in his eyes. "He's no familiar, and I am no sorcerer. He is simply a cat. The best of cats."

If I'd had the strength, I'd have slashed him with my claws. *Simply* a cat? How dare he! But the breath had been knocked from my body and pain seared through me. Worse than the pain was the knowledge that I had failed, because The Stargazer was too much of a dolt to seize Klothe's moment of distraction.

Now it was too late. The door opened and The Lady entered, a smile on her face. "Will you be down for dinner soon, dearest? The bread is just from the oven and smells delicious." Seeing Klothe, she halted, saying shyly, "I'm sorry. I didn't realize you had company."

To my shock, I saw Melisande trotting beside her. Both of the females were in kit, their bellies rounded with new life. The balance of power had shifted to disaster.

As clever as he was wicked, Klothe seized The Lady and yanked her against his chest, whipping out a dagger and laying the blade against her throat. "You might be willing to die for your king, but will you sacrifice your wife and unborn child?"

Horrified, The Stargazer gasped, "Dear God, don't hurt Serena! I'll do anything you wish."

"Then we have an agreement. Calculate the hour of my triumph, and you shall become my valued advisor. Defy me, and you all die. Try to fool me by offering the wrong time . . ." his smile was wicked beyond imagining. "Your little wife will leave with me today. If my attempt to kill the king fails, my servants will slay her even if I can't."

"You mean to kill King Rolande?" Aghast, The Lady struggled against her captor, but in vain. "You monster!"

Loyally Melisande sank her claws into Klothe's calf. He kicked out wildly. "Another damned cat! Why can't you have hounds, like a normal man?"

Since he was encumbered by his grip on The Lady, his kick went awry. Hissing curses I didn't know she'd ever heard, Melisande darted away to hide amidst piles of stacked books. When she saw where I lay unmoving, she gave a wrenching cry of grief. I reached out to her with my mind. *Have faith, beloved. While I live, there is hope.* She stilled, and her faith gave me strength.

"I shall calculate the best time," The Stargazer said dully, "but I cannot swear you will achieve the success you crave. Only God can guarantee that."

"The soothsayer has already promised success. You need only provide the time for me to act. Now do it!"

"This won't take long. I've already calculated a chart for the most powerful moment of the Grand Junction. King Rolande planned to use the time to send peace envoys to our neighbors." His voice became sardonic. "I need only find a time that will suit such a different purpose, and to incorporate your natal potentials."

He set to work, consulting his texts and jotting down calculations. Keeping a wary eye on him, Klothe tied The Lady to a wooden chair so he needn't continue to hold her. And I watched, as pain slowly ebbed and my strength returned.

Something about the calculations puzzled The Stargazer, for he frowned at his charts. "This is an extremely dangerous time for you, Lord Klothe. The Mars aspects are most threatening. For your own sake, I advise you to drop this endeavor."

"It's always dangerous to kill a king," Klothe said impatiently. "I care nothing for that, since I know I will achieve the highest place in the kingdom."

The Stargazer shrugged. "I've done my best to warn you. Your moment falls tomorrow morning, at—"

Klothe cut him off again. "Write down the time so I won't forget it."

"As you wish." The Stargazer dipped his quill into the ink and jotted down the time on a piece of parchment, then folded it into quarters. "Here is the time, calculated for an assault to take place at the castle."

"Excellent." Coolly Klothe raised his dagger and struck The Stargazer on the back of his head with the hilt, causing him to collapse on the floor as the parchment fluttered down beside him.

"You villain! God rot your wicked soul!" The Lady cried.

Unaffected by her outrage, Klothe tied The Stargazer's wrists together. "Don't worry, I only hit your husband hard enough to put him to sleep for several hours. I didn't want him to have foolish ideas of heroism."

It was now or never. With a prayer to Bast, goddess of my kind, I leaped to my feet, forcing myself to ignore the pain as I crossed the room with lightning swiftness.

This time I did not assault Klothe. Instead, I snatched up the fallen parchment, then leaped through the angled window onto the roof, giving thanks that The Stargazer hadn't bothered to close it.

Klothe bellowed with outrage. "You damnable beast! I'll rip your limbs off one by one and throw them into the fire."

Furiously he clambered up along the telescope, then through the opening to the ledge of roof that ran below the window. It was easily done, for the first stargazer who built this tower had designed it so that he and his descendants could see the stars with their own eyes, instead of the telescope, when they wished.

The rain had ceased, but the roof slates were still lethally slippery. Growling, all my hair on end, I backed away from Klothe, careful to stay just out of his reach.

The lord assessed the seemingly flat roof slates, then stepped out carefully, thinking he could corner me against the chimney that ran up the side of the observatory. But the roof was not flat. A slight downward incline caused Klothe to start slipping toward the edge.

Swearing, he dropped to his knees. When he'd regained his balance, he lunged toward me with one hand while the other held tight to the edge of the roof.

I dropped the folded parchment, and sank my fangs into the fleshy part of his hand. He screamed and jerked backward, dark blood spurting from his puncture wounds. The shock of assault made him release his grip on the roof edge.

He went from aggressor to panicky prey in an instant as he clawed like a trapped rodent in a vain effort to find a new grip. Shrieking, he pitched over the edge.

It was a long way down, and he made a most satisfactory splat when he hit.

The soothsayer had said Lord Klothe would reach the highest place in the kingdom, and this observation tower was it. She hadn't said how long he'd stay there. Limping and thanking Bast for Her help, I crossed the slates and jumped back through the window, landing more clumsily than was my custom.

Mrrrrping with joy, Melisande darted from her hiding place and ran to me. With one sleek paw, she pinned me to the floor and began frantically licking my ears and ruff, all the time scolding me for taking such a risk. I gave a sigh of pleasure, content to surrender to her gentle female punishment.

Having managed to loosen her bonds, The Lady stood, swaying a little after the terrors she'd seen. For a moment she knelt by me, her touch as light as Melisande's. "Dearest Leo, you saved us all. You are the hero of heroes."

Naturally, I accepted the tribute as my due.

The Lady crossed to her husband, who was already coming awake. Apparently Klothe wasn't a good judge of how hard to hit, or perhaps it was just that The Stargazer has an exceptionally hard head. Cradling him in her lap, The Lady explained what had happened, finishing with, "I had no idea Leo was such a fierce warrior."

The Stargazer and I shared a glance, for we both knew the answer to that.

My name is Leo.

But my sun and soul are *Scorpio*.

CPSIA information can be obtained at www.ICGtesting.com
Printed in the USA
LVOW090930191211

260099LV00001B/55/A

5

A sheep is big
and a lamb is little.

Big and little

A horse is big
and a foal is little.

A cow is big

and a calf is little.

A dog is big

and a puppy is little.

A cat is big

and a kitten is little.

A duck is big

and ducklings are little.

A hen is big

and chicks are little.

Mom is big and I am little.